JEAN CRAIGHEAD GEORGE

JULIE OF THE WOLVES TREASURY

JULIE OF THE WOLVES
JULIE
JULIE'S WOLF PACK

BARNES & NOBLE BOOKS
NEW YORK

For information address HarperCollins Children's Books, a division of HarperCollins Publishers, 1350 Avenue of the Americas, New York, NY 10019. ISBN 0-06-000239-5 www.harperchildrens.com

ALSO BY JEAN CRAIGHEAD GEORGE

Acorn Pancakes, Dandelion Salad
and 38 Other Wild Recipes

Animals Who Have Won Our Hearts

The Case of the Missing Cutthroats
An Ecological Mystery

The Cry of the Crow

Dear Rebecca, Winter Is Here

Everglades

The Fire Bug Connection
An Ecological Mystery

Going to the Sun

The Grizzly Bear with the Golden Ears

Julie

Julie's Wolf Pack

Look to the North: A Wolf Pup Diary

The Missing 'Gator of Gumbo Limbo
An Ecological Mystery

The Moon of the Alligators

The Moon of the Bears

The Moon of the Chickarees

The Moon of the Deer

The Moon of the Fox Pups

The Moon of the Gray Wolves

The Moon of the Moles

The Moon of the Monarch Butterflies

The Moon of the Mountain Lions

The Moon of the Owls

The Moon of the Salamanders

The Moon of the Wild Pigs

The Moon of the Winter Bird

One Day in the Alpine Tundra

One Day in the Desert

One Day in the Prairie

One Day in the Tropical Rain Forest

One Day in the Woods

Shark Beneath the Reef

The Summer of the Falcon

The Talking Earth

The Tarantula in My Purse

There's an Owl in the Shower

Water Sky

Who Really Killed Cock Robin?
An Ecological Mystery

The Wounded Wolf

JULIE OF THE WOLVES

JEAN CRAIGHEAD GEORGE

ILLUSTRATED BY JOHN SCHOENHERR

HarperCollins*Publishers*

JULIE OF THE WOLVES

 Printed in the United States of America. For information address HarperCollins Children's Books, a division of HarperCollins Publishers, 10 East 53rd Street, New York, NY 10022.

Library of Congress Catalog Card Number: 72-76509
ISBN 0-06-021943-2

Visit us on the World Wide Web!
www.harperchildrens.com

To Luke George who loves wolves
and the Eskimos of Alaska

CONTENTS

PART I
AMAROQ, THE WOLF
1

PART II
MIYAX, THE GIRL
71

PART III
KAPUGEN, THE HUNTER
105

PART I

AMAROQ, THE WOLF

MIYAX PUSHED BACK THE HOOD of her sealskin parka and looked at the Arctic sun. It was a yellow disc in a lime-green sky, the colors of six o'clock in the evening and the time when the wolves awoke. Quietly she put down her cooking pot and crept to the top of a dome-shaped frost heave, one of the many earth buckles that rise and fall in the crackling cold of the Arctic winter. Lying on her stomach, she looked across a vast lawn of grass and moss and focused her attention on the wolves she had come upon two sleeps ago. They were wagging their tails as they awoke and saw each other.

Her hands trembled and her heartbeat quickened, for she was frightened, not so much of the wolves, who were shy and many harpoon-shots away, but because of her desperate predicament. Miyax was lost. She had been lost without food for many sleeps on the North Slope of Alaska. The barren slope stretches for two hundred miles from the Brooks Range to the Arctic Ocean, and for more than eight hundred miles from Canada to the Chukchi Sea. No roads cross it; ponds and lakes freckle its immensity. Winds scream across it, and the view in every direction is exactly the same. Somewhere in this cosmos was Miyax; and the very life in her body, its spark and warmth, depended upon these wolves for survival. And she was not so sure they would help.

Miyax stared hard at the regal black wolf, hoping to catch his eye. She must somehow tell him that she was starving and ask him for food. This could be done she knew, for her father, an Eskimo hunter, had done so. One year he had camped near a wolf den while on a hunt. When a month had passed and her father had seen no game, he told the leader of the wolves that he was hungry and needed food. The next night the wolf called him from far away and her father went to him and found a freshly killed caribou. Unfortunately, Miyax's father never explained to her how he had told the wolf of his needs. And not long afterward he paddled his kayak into the Bering Sea to hunt for seal, and he never returned.

She had been watching the wolves for two days, trying to discern which of their sounds and movements expressed goodwill and friendship. Most animals had such signals. The little Arctic ground squirrels flicked their tails sideways to notify others of their kind that they were friendly. By imitating this signal with her forefinger, Miyax had lured many a squirrel to her hand. If she could discover such a gesture for the wolves she would be able to make friends with them and share their food, like a bird or a fox.

Propped on her elbows with her chin in her fists, she stared at the black wolf, trying to catch his eye. She had chosen him because he was much larger than the others, and because he walked like her father, Kapugen, with his head high and his chest out. The black wolf also possessed wisdom, she had observed. The pack looked to him when the wind carried strange scents or the birds cried nervously. If he was alarmed, they were alarmed. If he was calm, they were calm.

Long minutes passed, and the black wolf did not look at her. He had ignored her since she first came upon them, two sleeps ago. True, she moved slowly and quietly, so as not to alarm him; yet she did wish he would see the kindness in her eyes. Many animals could tell the difference between hostile hunters and friendly people by merely looking at them. But the big black wolf would not even glance her way.

A bird stretched in the grass. The wolf looked at it.

A flower twisted in the wind. He glanced at that. Then the breeze rippled the wolverine ruff on Miyax's parka and it glistened in the light. He did not look at that. She waited. Patience with the ways of nature had been instilled in her by her father. And so she knew better than to move or shout. Yet she must get food or die. Her hands shook slightly and she swallowed hard to keep calm.

Miyax was a classic Eskimo beauty, small of bone and delicately wired with strong muscles. Her face was pearl-round and her nose was flat. Her black eyes, which slanted gracefully, were moist and sparkling. Like the beautifully formed polar bears and foxes of the north, she was slightly short-limbed. The frigid environment of the Arctic has sculptured life into compact shapes. Unlike the long-limbed, long-bodied animals of the south that are cooled by dispensing heat on extended surfaces, all live things in the Arctic tend toward compactness, to conserve heat.

The length of her limbs and the beauty of her face were of no use to Miyax as she lay on the lichen-speckled frost heave in the midst of the bleak tundra. Her stomach ached and the royal black wolf was carefully ignoring her.

"*Amaroq, ilaya,* wolf, my friend," she finally called. "Look at me. Look at me."

She spoke half in Eskimo and half in English, as if

the instincts of her father and the science of the *gussaks,* the white-faced, might evoke some magical combination that would help her get her message through to the wolf.

Amaroq glanced at his paw and slowly turned his head her way without lifting his eyes. He licked his shoulder. A few matted hairs sprang apart and twinkled individually. Then his eyes sped to each of the three adult wolves that made up his pack and finally to the five pups who were sleeping in a fuzzy mass near the den entrance. The great wolf's eyes softened at the sight of the little wolves, then quickly hardened into brittle yellow jewels as he scanned the flat tundra.

Not a tree grew anywhere to break the monotony of the gold-green plain, for the soils of the tundra are permanently frozen. Only moss, grass, lichens, and a few hardy flowers take root in the thin upper layer that thaws briefly in summer. Nor do many species of animals live in this rigorous land, but those creatures that do dwell here exist in bountiful numbers. Amaroq watched a large cloud of Lapland longspurs wheel up into the sky, then alight in the grasses. Swarms of crane flies, one of the few insects that can survive the cold, darkened the tips of the mosses. Birds wheeled, turned, and called. Thousands sprang up from the ground like leaves in a wind.

The wolf's ears cupped forward and tuned in on

some distant message from the tundra. Miyax tensed and listened, too. Did he hear some brewing storm, some approaching enemy? Apparently not. His ears relaxed and he rolled to his side. She sighed, glanced at the vaulting sky, and was painfully aware of her predicament.

Here she was, watching wolves—she, Miyax, daughter of Kapugen, adopted child of Martha, citizen of the United States, pupil at the Bureau of Indian Affairs School in Barrow, Alaska, and thirteen-year-old wife of the boy Daniel. She shivered at the thought of Daniel, for it was he who had driven her to this fate. She had run away from him exactly seven sleeps ago, and because of this she had one more title by gussak standards—the child divorcée.

The wolf rolled to his belly.

"Amaroq," she whispered. "I am lost and the sun will not set for a month. There is no North Star to guide me."

Amaroq did not stir.

"And there are no berry bushes here to bend under the polar wind and point to the south. Nor are there any birds I can follow." She looked up. "Here the birds are buntings and longspurs. They do not fly to the sea twice a day like the puffins and sandpipers that my father followed."

The wolf groomed his chest with his tongue.

"I never dreamed I could get lost, Amaroq," she went on, talking out loud to ease her fear. "At home on Nunivak Island where I was born, the plants and birds pointed the way for wanderers. I thought they did so everywhere . . . and so, great black Amaroq, I'm without a compass."

It had been a frightening moment when two days ago she realized that the tundra was an ocean of grass on which she was circling around and around. Now as that fear overcame her again she closed her eyes. When she opened them her heart skipped excitedly. Amaroq was looking at her!

"*Ee-lie,*" she called and scrambled to her feet. The wolf arched his neck and narrowed his eyes. He pressed his ears forward. She waved. He drew back his lips and showed his teeth. Frightened by what seemed a snarl, she lay down again. When she was flat on her stomach, Amaroq flattened his ears and wagged his tail once. Then he tossed his head and looked away.

Discouraged, she wriggled backward down the frost heave and arrived at her camp feet first. The heave was between herself and the wolf pack and so she relaxed, stood up, and took stock of her home. It was a simple affair, for she had not been able to carry much when she ran away; she took just those things she would need for the journey—a backpack, food for a week or so, needles to mend clothes, matches, her sleeping skin, and ground cloth to go under it, two knives, and a pot.

She had intended to walk to Point Hope. There

she would meet the *North Star,* the ship that brings supplies from the States to the towns on the Arctic Ocean in August when the ice pack breaks up. The ship could always use dishwashers or laundresses, she had heard, and so she would work her way to San Francisco where Amy, her pen pal, lived. At the end of every letter Amy always wrote: "When are you coming to San Francisco?" Seven days ago she had been on her way—on her way to the glittering, white, postcard city that sat on a hill among trees, those enormous plants she had never seen. She had been on her way to see the television and carpeting in Amy's school, the glass buildings, traffic lights, and stores full of fruits; on her way to the harbor that never froze and the Golden Gate Bridge. But primarily she was on her way to be rid of Daniel, her terrifying husband.

She kicked the sod at the thought of her marriage; then shaking her head to forget, she surveyed her camp. It was nice. Upon discovering the wolves, she had settled down to live near them in the hope of sharing their food, until the sun set and the stars came out to guide her. She had built a house of sod, like the summer homes of the old Eskimos. Each brick had been cut with her *ulo,* the half-moon shaped woman's knife, so versatile it can trim a baby's hair, slice a tough bear, or chip an iceberg.

Her house was not well built for she had never

made one before, but it was cozy inside. She had windproofed it by sealing the sod bricks with mud from the pond at her door, and she had made it beautiful by spreading her caribou ground cloth on the floor. On this she had placed her sleeping skin, a moosehide bag lined with soft white rabbit skins. Next to her bed she had built a low table of sod on which to put her clothes when she slept. To decorate the house she had made three flowers of bird feathers and stuck them in the top of the table. Then she had built a fireplace outdoors and placed her pot beside it. The pot was empty, for she had not found even a lemming to eat.

Last winter, when she had walked to school in Barrow, these mice-like rodents were so numerous they ran out from under her feet wherever she stepped. There were thousands and thousands of them until December, when they suddenly vanished. Her teacher said that the lemmings had a chemical similar to antifreeze in their blood, that kept them active all winter when other little mammals were hibernating. "They eat grass and multiply all winter," Mrs. Franklin had said in her singsong voice. "When there are too many, they grow nervous at the sight of each other. Somehow this shoots too much antifreeze into their bloodstreams and it begins to poison them. They become restless, then crazy. They run in a frenzy until they die."

Of this phenomenon Miyax's father had simply said, "The hour of the lemming is over for four years."

Unfortunately for Miyax, the hour of the animals that prey on the lemmings was also over. The white fox, the snowy owl, the weasel, the jaeger, and the siskin had virtually disappeared. They had no food to eat and bore few or no young. Those that lived preyed on each other. With the passing of the lemmings, however, the grasses had grown high again and the hour of the caribou was upon the land. Healthy fat caribou cows gave birth to many calves. The caribou population increased, and this in turn increased the number of wolves who prey on the caribou. The abundance of the big deer of the north did Miyax no good, for she had not brought a gun on her trip. It had never occurred to her that she would not reach Point Hope before her food ran out.

A dull pain seized her stomach. She pulled blades of grass from their sheaths and ate the sweet ends. They were not very satisfying, so she picked a handful of caribou moss, a lichen. If the deer could survive in winter on this food, why not she? She munched, decided the plant might taste better if cooked, and went to the pond for water.

As she dipped her pot in, she thought about Amaroq. Why had he bared his teeth at her? Because she was young and he knew she couldn't hurt him?

No, she said to herself, it was because he was speaking to her! He had told her to lie down. She had even understood and obeyed him. He had talked to her not with his voice, but with his ears, eyes, and lips; and he had even commended her with a wag of his tail.

She dropped her pot, scrambled up the frost heave, and stretched out on her stomach.

"Amaroq," she called softly, "I understand what you said. Can you understand me? I'm hungry—very, very hungry. Please bring me some meat."

The great wolf did not look her way and she began to doubt her reasoning. After all, flattened ears and a tail-wag were scarcely a conversation. She dropped her forehead against the lichens and rethought what had gone between them.

"Then why did I lie down?" she asked, lifting her head and looking at Amaroq. "Why did I?" she called to the yawning wolves. Not one turned her way.

Amaroq got to his feet, and as he slowly arose he seemed to fill the sky and blot out the sun. He was enormous. He could swallow her without even chewing.

"But he won't," she reminded herself. "Wolves do not eat people. That's gussak talk. Kapugen said wolves are gentle brothers."

The black puppy was looking at her and wagging his tail. Hopefully, Miyax held out a pleading hand to him. His tail wagged harder. The mother rushed to him and stood above him sternly. When he licked her cheek apologetically, she pulled back her lips from her fine white teeth. They flashed as she smiled and forgave her cub.

"But don't let it happen again," said Miyax sarcastically, mimicking her own elders. The mother walked toward Amaroq.

"I should call you Martha after my stepmother,"

Miyax whispered. "But you're much too beautiful. I shall call you Silver instead."

Silver moved in a halo of light, for the sun sparkled on the guard hairs that grew out over the dense underfur and she seemed to glow.

The reprimanded pup snapped at a crane fly and shook himself. Bits of lichen and grass spun off his fur. He reeled unsteadily, took a wider stance, and looked down at his sleeping sister. With a yap he jumped on her and rolled her to her feet. She whined. He barked and picked up a bone. When he was sure she was watching, he ran down the slope with it. The sister tagged after him. He stopped and she grabbed the bone, too. She pulled; he pulled; then he pulled and she yanked.

Miyax could not help laughing. The puppies played with bones like Eskimo children played with leather ropes.

"I understand *that,*" she said to the pups. "That's tug-o-war. Now how do you say, 'I'm hungry'?"

Amaroq was pacing restlessly along the crest of the frost heave as if something were about to happen. His eyes shot to Silver, then to the gray wolf Miyax had named Nails. These glances seemed to be a summons, for Silver and Nails glided to him, spanked the ground with their forepaws, and bit him gently under the chin. He wagged his tail furiously and took Silver's slender nose in his mouth. She crouched before him, licked his cheek, and lovingly bit his lower jaw. Amaroq's tail flashed high as her mouthing charged him with vitality. He nosed her affectionately. Unlike the fox who met his mate only in the breeding season, Amaroq lived with his mate all year.

Next, Nails took Amaroq's jaw in his mouth and the leader bit the top of his nose. A third adult, a small male, came slinking up. He got down on his belly before Amaroq, rolled trembling to his back, and wriggled.

"Hello, Jello," Miyax whispered, for he reminded her of the quivering gussak dessert her mother-in-law made.

She had seen the wolves mouth Amaroq's chin twice before and so she concluded that it was a ceremony, a sort of "Hail to the Chief." He must indeed be their leader for he was clearly the wealthy wolf; that is, wealthy as she had known the meaning of the word on Nunivak Island. There the old Eskimo hunters she had known in her childhood thought the riches of life were intelligence, fearlessness, and love. A man with these gifts was rich and was a great spirit who was admired in the same way that the gussaks admired a man with money and goods.

The three adults paid tribute to Amaroq until he was almost smothered with love; then he bayed a wild note that sounded like the wind on the frozen sea. With that the others sat around him, the puppies scattered between them. Jello hunched forward and Silver shot a fierce glance at him. Intimidated, Jello pulled his ears together and back. He drew himself down until he looked smaller than ever.

Amaroq wailed again, stretching his neck until

his head was high above the others. They gazed at him affectionately and it was plain to see that he was their great spirit, a royal leader who held his group together with love and wisdom.

Any fear Miyax had of the wolves was dispelled by their affection for each other. They were friendly animals and so devoted to Amaroq that she needed only to be accepted by him to be accepted by all. She even knew how to achieve this—bite him under the chin. But how was she going to do that?

She studied the pups hoping they had a simpler way of expressing their love for him. The black puppy approached the leader, sat, then lay down and wagged his tail vigorously. He gazed up at Amaroq in pure adoration, and the royal eyes softened.

Well, that's what I'm doing! Miyax thought. She called to Amaroq. "I'm lying down gazing at you, too, but you don't look at *me* that way!"

When all the puppies were wagging his praises, Amaroq yipped, hit a high note, and crooned. As his voice rose and fell, the other adults sang out and the puppies yipped and bounced.

The song ended abruptly. Amaroq arose and trotted swiftly down the slope. Nails followed, and behind him ran Silver, then Jello. But Jello did not run far. Silver turned and looked him straight in the eye. She pressed her ears forward aggressively and lifted her tail. With that, Jello went back to the puppies and the three sped away like dark birds.

Miyax hunched forward on her elbows, the better to see and learn. She now knew how to be a good puppy, pay tribute to the leader, and even to be a leader by biting others on the top of the nose. She also knew how to tell Jello to baby-sit. If only she had big ears and a tail, she could lecture and talk to them all.

Flapping her hands on her head for ears, she flattened her fingers to make friends, pulled them together and back to express fear, and shot them forward to display her aggression and dominance. Then she folded her arms and studied the puppies again.

The black one greeted Jello by tackling his feet. Another jumped on his tail, and before he could discipline either, all five were upon him. He rolled and tumbled with them for almost an hour; then he ran down the slope, turned, and stopped. The pursuing pups plowed into him, tumbled, fell, and lay still. During a minute of surprised recovery there was no action. Then the black pup flashed his tail like a semaphore signal and they all jumped on Jello again.

Miyax rolled over and laughed aloud. "That's funny. They're really like kids."

When she looked back, Jello's tongue was hanging from his mouth and his sides were heaving. Four of the puppies had collapsed at his feet and were asleep. Jello flopped down, too, but the black pup still looked around. He was not the least bit tired. Miyax watched him, for there was something special about him.

He ran to the top of the den and barked. The smallest pup, whom Miyax called Sister, lifted her head, saw her favorite brother in action and, struggling to her feet, followed him devotedly. While they romped, Jello took the opportunity to rest behind a clump of sedge, a moisture-loving plant of the tundra. But hardly was he settled before a pup tracked him to his hideout and pounced on him. Jello narrowed his eyes, pressed his ears forward, and showed his teeth.

"I know what you're saying," she called to him. "You're saying, 'lie down.' " The puppy lay down, and Miyax got on all fours and looked for the nearest pup to speak to. It was Sister.

"Ummmm," she whined, and when Sister turned around Julie narrowed her eyes and showed her white teeth. Obediently, Sister lay down.

"I'm talking wolf! I'm talking wolf!" Miyax clapped, and tossing her head like a pup, crawled in a happy circle. As she was coming back she saw all five puppies sitting in a row watching her, their heads cocked in curiosity. Boldly the black pup came toward her, his fat backside swinging as he trotted to the bottom of her frost heave, and barked.

"You are *very* fearless and *very* smart," she said. "Now I know why you are special. You are wealthy and the leader of the puppies. There is no doubt what you'll grow up to be. So I shall name you after my father Kapugen, and I shall call you Kapu for short."

Kapu wrinkled his brow and turned an ear to tune in more acutely on her voice.

"You don't understand, do you?"

Hardly had she spoken than his tail went up, his mouth opened slightly, and he fairly grinned.

"Ee-lie!" she gasped. "You do understand. And that scares me." She perched on her heels. Jello whined an undulating note and Kapu turned back to the den.

Miyax imitated the call to come home. Kapu looked back over his shoulder in surprise. She giggled. He wagged his tail and jumped on Jello.

She clapped her hands and settled down to watch this language of jumps and tumbles, elated that she was at last breaking the wolf code. After a long time she decided they were not talking but roughhousing, and so she started home. Later she changed her mind. Roughhousing was very important to wolves. It occupied almost the entire night for the pups.

"Ee-lie, okay," she said. "I'll learn to roughhouse. Maybe then you'll accept me and feed me." She pranced, jumped, and whimpered; she growled, snarled, and rolled. But nobody came to roughhouse.

Sliding back to her camp, she heard the grass

swish and looked up to see Amaroq and his hunters sweep around her frost heave and stop about five feet away. She could smell the sweet scent of their fur.

The hairs on her neck rose and her eyes widened. Amaroq's ears went forward aggressively and she remembered that wide eyes meant fear to him. It was not good to show him she was afraid. Animals attacked the fearful. She tried to narrow them, but remembered that was not right either. Narrowed eyes were mean. In desperation she recalled that Kapu had moved forward when challenged. She pranced right up to Amaroq. Her heart beat furiously as she grunt-whined the sound of the puppy begging adoringly for attention. Then she got down on her belly and gazed at him with fondness.

The great wolf backed up and avoided her eyes. She had said something wrong! Perhaps even offended him. Some slight gesture that meant nothing to her had apparently meant something to the wolf. His ears shot forward angrily and it seemed all was lost. She wanted to get up and run, but she gathered her courage and pranced closer to him. Swiftly she patted him under the chin.

The signal went off. It sped through his body and triggered emotions of love. Amaroq's ears flattened and his tail wagged in friendship. He could not react in any other way to the chin pat, for the roots of this signal lay deep in wolf history. It was inherited from generations and generations of leaders before him. As his eyes softened, the sweet odor of ambrosia arose from the gland on the top of his tail and she was drenched lightly in wolf scent. Miyax was one of the pack.

ALL THROUGH THE SUNNY NIGHT she waited for Amaroq to come home with food for her and the pups. When at last she saw him on the horizon she got down on all fours and crawled to her lookout. He carried no food.

"*Ayi*," she cried. "The pups must be nursing—that's why there's no meat." Slumping back on her heels, she thought about this. Then she thought again.

"You can't be nursing," she said to Kapu, and plunked her hands on her hips. "Silver growls when you suckle, and drives you away." Kapu twisted his ears at the sound of her voice.

"Okay," she called to him. "Where are you getting the food that makes you so fat?" He ignored her, concentrating on Silver and Nails, who were coming slowly home from the hunt.

Miyax went back to her pot and stuffed on the cold raw moss until her stomach felt full if not satisfied. Then she crawled into her cozy home in the hope that sleep would soothe her hunger.

She smoothed the silver hairs of her beautiful wedding parka, then carefully took it off and rolled it up. Placing it and her fur pants in a bag made of whale bladder, she tied it securely so that no moisture would dampen her clothes while she slept. This she had learned in childhood, and it was one of the old Eskimo ways that she liked, perhaps the only one. She had never violated it, even in the warm, gas-heated house in Barrow, for damp clothes could mean death in the Arctic.

When her outer garments were put away she took off the bright-red tights her mother-in-law had bought for her at the American store in Barrow. Walking to the pond, she rinsed them and laid them in the sun. The cool air struck her naked body. She shivered and was glad that she had done one thing right—she had worn her winter clothes, not her light summer *kuspuck,* the woman's dress.

The wind gusted; Miyax scrambled through the low door and slid into her sleeping skin. The silken softness of the rabbit fur embraced her and she pulled the hood around her face so that only her nose was exposed. The fur captured her warm breath, held it against her face, and she became her own radiant stove. In this cozy micro-world she forgot her hunger and recalled what she already knew about wolves so that she could put it together with what she had observed.

Wolves are shy, Kapugen had said, and they desert their dens if discovered by man; yet this pack had not. Did Amaroq not know she was human? Perhaps not; she had never walked in his presence, the two-legged signal of "man" to wild animals. On the other hand, he must know. Kapugen had said that with one sniff a wolf knew if you were male or female, adult or child, if you were hunting or not hunting—even if you were happy or sad. She concluded that Amaroq tolerated her because she was young, had no gun, and was sad—a lost child.

She next considered Nails. Who was he? Amaroq's dependable friend, that was true, yet she suspected he was even more than that—a spiritual father of the pups. Nails took orders from Amaroq, but stayed close to Silver and the little wolves. He was father when their real father was busy. He was Amaroq's serious partner. But Jello? Who was he? Where had he come from? Was he a pup of a previous year? Or had he joined the pack just as she had, by soliciting Amaroq for membership in his tribe? There was much to learn about her family.

Miyax did not know how long she slept, for midnight was almost as bright as noon and it was difficult to judge the passing of time. It did not matter, however; time in the Arctic was the rhythm of life. The wolf pups were barking their excited *yipoo* that rang out the hour of the end of the hunt. The pack was coming home. With visions of caribou stew in her head, she got out of her sleeping skin and reached for her clothes.

The puppies may not have been eating, but certainly Amaroq would have to bring Jello some food. He had been home all night. Stepping into the sunlight, she put on her tights, danced a moment, and then pulled on her furs. Leaning over the pond, she saw in the glassy water the hollows of her cheeks. She was pleased, for she looked almost like the gussak girls in the magazines and movies—thin and gaunt, not moon-faced like an Eskimo. Her hair! She leaned closer to the tundra looking glass. Her hair was a mess. Pressing it into place with her hands, she wished she had taken Daniel's wedding brush and comb with her. They lay unused in the corner of a table drawer in the house at Barrow.

Quickly she climbed the frost heave, lay down, and looked at the wolves. There was no meat to be seen. The three hunters were stretched out on their sides, their bellies extended with food. Jello was gone. Of course, she said to herself, he had been relieved of his duties and had backtracked the hunters to the kill. She winced, for she had been so certain that today she would eat. So I won't, she said to herself, and that's that.

Miyax knew when to stop dreaming and be practical. She slid down the heave, brushed off her parka, and faced the tundra. The plants around the pond had edible seeds, as did all of the many grasses. There were thousands of crane fly and mosquito larvae in the water, and the wildflowers were filling if not very nourishing. But they were all small and took time to gather. She looked around for something bigger.

Her black eyes were alert as several Lapland longspurs darted overhead. They might still have young in their nests. Staying on one side of the heave, so the wolves would not see her two-leggedness, she skipped into the grass. The birds vanished. Their dark pointed wings were erased from the sky as if they had sensed her deadly purpose. Miyax crouched down. Kapugen had taught her how to hunt birds by sitting still and being patient. She crossed her feet and blended into the plants, still as a stone.

Presently a grass blade trembled and Miyax saw a young bird fluttering its wings as it begged to be fed. A brown lark-like parent winged down and stuffed its open beak. Another youngster begged and the parent flew to it. Unfortunately, the second little bird was so far from the first that Miyax knew they were out of the nest and impossible to catch. She shifted her attention to the snow buntings.

A movement in the sky above the horizon caught her attention, and she recognized the pointed tail and black head of a jaeger. She knew this bird well, for it hunted the shore and tundra of Nunivak Island. A bold sea bird, it resembled its close relative the gull, but was not a fisher. The jaeger preyed upon lemmings, small birds, and occasionally carrion. Miyax wondered what prey it was hunting. Three more jaegers joined the first, circled close together as if over a target, then dropped out of sight below the horizon.

"The wolf kill!" she fairly shouted. "They're sharing the wolf kill."

Jumping to her feet, she lined up the spot where they had disappeared with a patch of brown lichens in the distance, and ran with joy along the invisible line. When she had gone a quarter of a mile, she stopped and looked back. The endless tundra rolled around her and she could not tell which frost heave was which.

"Oh, no!" she cried. She turned around and laboriously searched out the plants crushed by her feet. Near a pool she lost all sight of her steps and then with relief recognized an empty lemming nest, a round ball of grass that she had kicked open. She pounced on it, saw a flower she had trampled, and ran up the heave to it. From the top she looked across the distance to her own precious house.

She reminded herself not to be so careless again. "One can get lost out here," she said aloud.

Miyax flopped down in the grass to rest. Her hand touched a patch of Arctic peas. They were tiny but numerous; she took off her boot and then her sock, and filled its toe with the vegetables. When all were harvested, she swung the sock over her shoulder and, striding joyously, rounded her pond and plunked the peas in her pot. She rolled them around with her fingers and they rattled musically. She rolled them again and made up words to fit their rhythm:

Peas that go tink, *peas that go* tot,
Peas that will never grow outside my pot.

The puppies yapped and Silver ran out across the tundra. She leaped with grace, her fur gleaming like metal; then she swept into a dip in the landscape and vanished. Up from the horizon rose the jaegers, announcing that Silver had gone to the kill. Clutching the cooking pot to her breast, Miyax excitedly waited to see her bring back meat for the pups.

The jaegers circled, the longspurs tumbled on their wings, and at last Silver came home. Her mouth was empty.

"I just don't understand," she said to the pups. "What is keeping you alive?" Putting down her pot, she went to her lookout to try to solve the riddle.

Silver came up the long slope, gave the grunt-whine that summoned the pups, and Kapu ran to meet her. She pulled back her lips in a smile and nosed him affectionately. Then Kapu stuck his nose in the corner of her mouth. Silver arched her back, her neck rippled, and she choked up a big mound of meat. Kapu set upon it with a snarl.

"So that's it!" said Miyax. "The meat's in the belly-basket. Now what do I do?"

Kapu let Sister share the meal with him, but not Zing, Zat, and Zit—as Miyax had dubbed the three tawny pups who had little personality as yet. Zing rushed over to the resting Silver and cuddled up against her. He rammed his nose against her teats and taking one in his mouth, ravenously nursed. Silver tolerated this for a moment, then growled. He did not let go and she snapped at him. He pulled away, but when she stretched out he dove back into her belly fur again. With a loud bark she rolled onto her stomach and cut off her milk from him. Zing got up, walked over to Amaroq, and stuck his nose in the corner of his mouth. Amaroq regurgitated food.

The secret of the fat pups was out. They were being weaned from mother's milk to well-chewed and partially digested food.

They might eat food from the belly-basket for weeks before they were brought chunks of meat that Miyax could share, and so she went out into the grasses again to look for buntings. Soon Silver and Nails trotted off in the direction of the kill. Having fed the puppies, they were now feeding themselves. Miyax cautiously peered around the heave. Jello had not gone with them. Yet he had been to the kill. He would have food in his belly-basket.

When the jaegers arose into the air she picked up the pot and climbed once again to the top of her frost heave. Getting to her hands and knees, she gave the grunt-whine call. "Look at me. I'm nice," it said.

Jello strode toward her. So pushed around was he by Silver, so respectful of Amaroq and even Nails, that he was excited by a voice more humble than his own. He even lifted his tail and head higher than Miyax had ever seen him do, and, acting like the boss wolf, loped up her frost heave. Curious Kapu trotted behind.

As Miyax scurried to meet Jello, he hesitated, growled softly, and urinated. "Don't be scared," she said and whimpered. He circled closer. Quickly rising to her knees, grunting the note of friendship, she slipped her hand over his head and clasped the top of his nose firmly in her fingers.

"I'm boss," she said as his tail and head went down in deference to the symbol of leadership. She started to slip her hand into the corner of his mouth, but he jerked away. Then Kapu, as if he understood what Miyax wanted, swept up to Jello and nuzzled his mouth. Jello heaved, opened his jaws, and deposited food on the ground.

"I'll live! I'll live!" Miyax cried jubilantly as Jello turned, put his tail between his legs, and raced back to the other pups. Kapu sat down and watched with wrinkled forehead as she scooped the meat into the pot. When she had retrieved every morsel, she gently closed her lips on the bridge of his nose. His tail wagged respectfully and he gazed softly into her eyes.

"Kapu," she whispered. "We Eskimos have joking partners—people to have fun with—and serious partners—people to work and think with. You and I are both. We are joking-serious partners." He wagged his tail excitedly and blinked. "And that's the best of all." She reached out to hug him, for his eyes were mellow and his fuzz irresistible. But he was like water and slipped through her hands.

On two knees and one hand, holding the pot with the other, Miyax hobbled toward her camp. Kapu bit her heel softly and she glanced over her shoulder. His head was cocked and his tail swished slowly.

"What are you saying now?" she asked. He gave the grunt-whine for attention.

Of course, she was his big sister and he wanted to play. Reaching into her pocket she pulled out a mitten and before she could flash it in front of his nose, he had leaped, caught it, and was pulling and shaking her whole arm and torso with incredible strength.

Miyax let go lest she spill her meat, and Kapu rolled head over heels into the lichens. Taking a firm grip on the mitten, he flattened his ears in spirited fellowship, dashed down the slope and up to his den. There he turned to see if she was following.

"Bring back my mitten," she called. "I need it." He flashed the wolf smile of apology, shook the mitten, and romped into the midst of his other brothers.

Kapu scratched a wide swath on the ground with his hind feet. The three tawny pups sniffed the mark and Zit sat down before it. Bold Kapu had written his signature and it was deep and impressive. Miyax wondered if the mitten victory was responsible. It was quite a trophy to win.

Placing her pot by her fireplace, she walked out on the tundra and gathered dry grass and lichens in her sock, for there was, of course, no wood to burn. Although caribou droppings were a better fuel, she was too fearful of getting lost to hunt them. Piling the grass and lichens in the center of the stones, she went into her house, took a small cookie tin from her pack, and removed one precious match. Then she lit the tinder.

The grass burst into flame and the lichens smoldered slowly, giving her time to dig the peat that the dead grasses had laid down for thousands and thousands of years. Gradually the peat glowed, the water boiled, and an hour later Miyax had a pot of caribou stew.

"At last!" she said. On it floated great chunks of golden grease, more delicious than the butter from the gussak store. She put a savory bite in her mouth, sucked the juices, then chewed a long time before she swallowed. She must not eat too fast or too much. Kapugen had said that an old lady, rescued from the snow after weeks of starvation, so stuffed herself that she died the next day.

Munching another bite, she went out to the grass clump to check on buntings, and a long time later returned to eat two more chunks of caribou. The rest, though she longed for it, she stored inside her house. Then she patted her stomach and told it to wait.

For the first time in days she could think of something other than food. Her mind turned to the problem of which direction was north and in which direction lay the town of Point Hope. The dips and heaves of the tundra spread out all around her and still looked the same in every direction.

"Oh, ho!" she said aloud. "More lichens grow on one side of the frost heaves than on the other." She pondered this, as well as the oblong shape of her pond, which was caused by the flow of the ice as it moved with the wind. But did the wind come down from the north or out of the west on the North Slope of Alaska? She did not know. Next, she noted that the grasses grew in different spots than the mosses, and the more she studied, the more the face of the tundra emerged; a face that could tell her which way was north, if she had listened more carefully to Kapugen.

Her legs began to buckle and her body swayed. She crumpled to her knees, for the food was making her both dizzy and sleepy. She staggered into her fur-carpeted house and lay down.

MIYAX'S EYELIDS FLUTTERED; the black lashes parted, then framed her wide eyes like ferns around a pool. She had eaten, slept for many hours; and the dull, tired feeling of starvation was gone. She felt bright and very much alive.

Rolling to her stomach, she propped herself on her elbows, and reached into her pot to eat. She ate a lot. The food in the pot lowered drastically. When but two meals remained, she made up her mind to tell Amaroq she wanted a whole shank of caribou. Wolves did bring food to their dens. Kapugen had seen them walk long miles in spring, with legs and ribs for the mothers who stayed in the ground with their pups for almost ten days after birth.

Well, she had no puppies to induce Amaroq to feed her, so she pondered again. Kapugen had once told her of a wolf who was wounded by the hoofs of a caribou. He limped to a rock cave and lay down to recover. Every night his leader trotted over the snow, bringing him meat until he was well and could rejoin the pack.

Miyax did not want to suffer a wound, but it

seemed to her that in order to be fed by wolves one had to be helpless.

"If that's the case," she said to herself, "I should be buried in food. I'm helpless enough. I cannot fell a caribou or catch a bird. And I'm lost, besides." She thrust her head out the door.

"Amaroq, I'm helpless," she cried. The chilly air tingled her nose and she noticed that the cotton grasses by the pond were seeding out into white puffs. This was worrisome, for they marked the coming of autumn, the snows, and the white-outs. White-outs could be dangerous. When the cotton grass heads were gone, the winds would lift the snow from the ground to the air and she would not be able to see her feet. She would be imprisoned wherever she stood . . . maybe for days . . . maybe till death.

Amaroq howled the long note to assemble. Silver and Nails barked a brief "Coming," and it was the beginning of a new day for Miyax and the wolves. Although the clocks in Barrow would say it was time to get ready for bed, she was getting up, for she was on wolf time. Since there was no darkness to hamper her vision, night was as good a time to work as day, and much better if you were a wolf girl. Rehearsing whimpers and groveling positions as she climbed to her lookout, she got ready to tell Amaroq how helpless she was in his own language.

He was awake, lying on his side, watching Sister's

paw twitch as she slept. He got up and licked the restless sleeper as if to say "All's well." The paw relaxed.

Miyax whimpered and twisted her head appealingly. Amaroq shot her a glance and wagged his tail as if she had said "Hello," not "I'm helpless."

Suddenly his head lifted, his ears went up, and Amaroq sniffed the wind. Miyax sniffed the wind and smelled nothing, although Amaroq was on his feet now, electric with the airborne message. He snapped his hunters to attention and led them down the slope and off across the tundra. Jello stayed home with the pups.

The pack moved in single file almost to the horizon, then swerved and came back. Shading her eyes, Miyax finally saw what the wind had told Amaroq. A herd of caribou was passing through. She held her breath as the hunters sped toward a large buck. The animal opened his stride and gracefully gained ground. He could so easily outrun the wolves that Amaroq let him go and trotted toward another. This one, too, outdistanced the pack and Amaroq swerved and tested another. Just as Miyax was wondering how the wolves ever caught anything, Amaroq put on full speed and bore down on a third.

This animal could not outrun him, and when Amaroq attacked he turned and struck with his powerful hoofs. Like a bouncing ball the leader sprang away. Nails and Silver fanned out to either side of the beast, then veered and closed in. The caribou bellowed, pressed back his ears, zigzagged over a frost heave, and disappeared from sight.

"They're chasing the weakest," Miyax said in astonishment. "It's just like Kapugen said—wolves take the old and sick."

She looked from the empty tundra to the busy den site. Kapu was staring at her, his eyes narrowed, his ears thrown forward aggressively.

"Now why are you so hostile?" she asked, then looked at her feet and legs. "Ee-lie, Ee-lie." She dropped to all fours and smiled apologetically.

"*Ayi*, Kapu. You've never seen a man in all your life. What is it that tells you to beware? Some spirit of your ancestors that still dwells in your body?"

She gave the grunt-whine and Kapu pressed down his ears, snatched up a bone, and brought it over to her. She grabbed it, he tugged, she pulled, he growled, she giggled, and Jello called Kapu home. He cocked an ear, rolled his eyes, and ignored the babysitter.

"You're naughty," she said and covered a grin with her hand. "Martha would scold me for that."

Kapu dropped the bone. She leaned down, picked it up in her teeth, and tried to run on all fours. She had barely begun to move away when Kapu leaped on her back and took her bare neck in his teeth. She started to scream, checked herself and, closing her eyes, waited for the teeth to pierce her skin. They did not even bruise, so controlled was this grip that said "Drop the bone." She let it go, and in one swish Kapu leaped to the ground and snatched it.

As she started after him something struck her boot and she looked around to see Zit, Zat, and Sister at her heels. Zing charged up the knoll, hit her arm with great force, and knocked her to the ground. She growled, flashed her teeth, and narrowed her eyes. Kapu dropped the bone and lay down. Zing backed up, and for a moment not a puppy moved.

"Phew." She smiled. "That did it."

Too late she remembered that such a smile was an apology, a sort of "I didn't mean it," and before she could growl all five little wolves jumped on her again.

"Stop!" She was angry. They sensed it and backed away. "Shoo! Go!" She waved her arm above her head and the threatening pose spoke louder than all her words. Drooping their tails, glancing warily at her, they trotted away—all but Kapu. He licked her cheek.

"Dear Kapu." She was about to stroke his head, when he picked up the bone and carried it back to the den. But he was not done with play. He never was. Kapu was tireless. Diving into a tunnel, he came out on the other side and landed on Jello's tail.

When Miyax saw this she sat back on her heels.

Open-ended tunnels reminded her of something. In the spring, wolf packs stay at a nursery den where the pups are born deep in the earth at the end of long tunnels. When the pups are about six weeks old and big enough to walk and run, the leaders move the entire group to a summer den. These are mere shelters for the pups and are open at two ends. For a few weeks the packs stay at this den; then they leave and take up the nomadic winter life of the wolf.

The cold chill of fear ran up Miyax's spine—the wolves would soon depart! Then what would she do? She could not follow them; they often ran fifty miles in a night and slept in different spots each day.

Her hands trembled and she pressed them together to make them stop, for Kapugen had taught her that fear can so cripple a person that he cannot think or act. Already she was too scared to crawl.

"Change your ways when fear seizes," he had said, "for it usually means you are doing something wrong."

She knew what it was—she should not depend upon the wolves for survival. She must go on her own. Instantly she felt relieved, her legs moved, her hands stopped shaking, and she remembered that when Kapugen was a boy, he had told her, he made snares of rawhide and caught little birds.

"Buntings, beware!" she shouted and slid down to her camp. Stepping out of her pants, she slipped off her tights and cut a swath of cloth from the hip with her ulo. She tore the cloth into small strips, then ate some stew, and started off to hunt birds. Every so often she tied a bit of red cloth to a clump of grass or around a conspicuous stone. If she was going to hunt in this confusing land, she must leave a trail to lead her home. She could not smell her way back as the wolves did.

As she tied the first piece of cloth to a bent sedge, she looked down on a small pile of droppings. "Ee-lie," she said. "A bird roost. Someone sleeps here every night." Quickly she took the thongs from her boots, made a noose, and placed it under the sedge. Holding the pull-rope, she moved back as far as she could and lay down to await the return of the bird.

The sun slid slowly down the sky, hung still for a moment, then started up again. It was midnight. A flock of swift-flying Arctic terns darted overhead, and one by one dropped into the grasses. Ruddy turnstones called sleepily from their scattered roosts, and sandpipers whistled. The creatures of the tundra were going to sleep, as they did also at noon in the constant daylight. Each called from his roost—all but the little bird of the sedge. It had not come back.

A bird chirped three feet from her face, and Miyax rolled her eyes to the left. A bunting on a grass blade tucked its bill into the feathers on its back, fluffed, and went to sleep. Where, she asked, was the bird of the sedge? Had it been killed by a fox or a weasel?

She was about to get to her feet and hunt elsewhere, but she remembered that Kapugen never gave up. Sometimes he would stand motionless for five hours at a seal breathing hole in the ice waiting for a seal to come up for a breath. She must wait, too.

The sun moved on around the sky and, when it was directly behind her, the sleeping bunting lifted its head and chirped. It hopped to a higher blade of grass, preened, and sang its morning song. The sleep was over. Her bird had not come back.

Suddenly a shadow passed. A snowy owl, white wings folded in a plummeting dive, threw out his feathered feet and struck the little gray bunting. The owl bounced up, and came down almost on Miyax's outstretched hand, the bird caught in his foot. Her first instinct was to pounce on the owl, but she instantly thought better of that. Even if she could catch him, she would have his powerful claws and beak to contend with, and she knew what damage they could do. Besides, she had a better idea—to lie still and watch where he flew. Perhaps he had owlets in the nest, for these little birds took almost six weeks to get on their wings. If there were owlets, there would also be food, lots of it, for the male owls are constantly bringing food to the young. Once, she had counted eighty lemmings piled at the nest of a snowy owl.

So close was the *ukpik,* the white owl of the north, that she could see the clove markings on his wings and the dense white feathers that covered his legs and feet. His large yellow eyes were pixieish, and he looked like a funny little Eskimo in white parka and maklaks. The wind stirred the wolverine trim on Miyax's hood and the owl turned his gleaming eyes upon her. She tried not to blink and belie the life in her stone-still body, but he was suspicious. He turned his head almost upside down to get a more acute focus on her; then unwinding swiftly, he lifted his body and sped off. His wings arched deeply as he steered into a wind and shot like a bullet toward the sun. As Miyax rolled to a sitting position, the owl scooped his wings up, braked, and dropped onto an exceptionally large frost heave. He left the bird and flew out over the tundra, screaming the demonic call of the hunting ukpik.

Miyax tied another red patch on the sedge, rounded a boggy pond, and climbed the heave where the owl lived. There lay an almost dead owlet, its big beak resting on the edge of the stone-lined nest. It lifted its head, laboriously hissed, and collapsed. The owlet was starving, for there was only the bunting, when there should have been dozens of lemmings. It would not live, in this time of no lemmings.

She picked up the bunting and owlet, regretting that she had found a provider only to lose him again.

The male owl would not bring food to an empty nest.

Collecting her red markers as she walked home, she kicked open old lemming nests in the hope of finding baby weasels. These small relatives of the mink, with their valuable fur that turns white in winter, enter lemming nests and kill and eat the young. Then they move into the round grassy structures to give birth to their own young. Although Miyax kicked seven nests, there were no weasels—for there were no lemmings to eat.

When in sight of her house she took a shortcut and came upon a pile of old caribou droppings—fuel for her fire! Gleefully, she stuffed her pockets, tied a marker at the site for later use, and skipped home dreaming of owlet stew.

She plucked the birds, laid them on the ground, and skillfully cut them open with her ulo. Lifting out the warm viscera, she tipped back her head and popped them into her mouth. They were delicious—the nuts and candy of the Arctic. She had forgotten how good they tasted. They were rich in vitamins and minerals and her starving body welcomed them.

Treats over, she sliced her birds into delicate strips and simmered them slowly and not too long.

"Chicken of the North," Miyax gave a toast to the birds. Then she drank the rich juices and popped the tender meat in her mouth. Had she been a boy this day would be one to celebrate. When a boy caught his first bird in Nunivak, he was supposed to fast for a day, then celebrate the Feast of the Bird. When he killed his first seal his mother took off her rings, for he was a man, and this was her way of bragging without saying a word.

Silly, she said to herself. but nevertheless she sang Kapugen's song of the Bird Feast.

> Tornait, tornait,
> *Spirit of the bird,*
> *Fly into my body*
> *And bring me*
> *The power of the sun.*

Kapu yapped to say that the hunters were coming home, and Miyax washed out her pot and went to her lookout to tell them goodnight. Amaroq and Jello were facing each other, ruffs up, ready to fight. Before Jello could attack, Amaroq lifted his head and Jello bowed before him. The dispute was over. No blood was shed. The difference had been settled with the pose of leadership.

Miyax wondered what had happened to put them at odds with each other. Whatever the problem, Jello had surrendered. He was on his back flashing the white fur on his belly that signaled "I give up!"—and no one, not even the pups, could strike him.

"The white flag of surrender," she murmured. "Jello lost." Amaroq walked gracefully away.

He was not done with what he had to say, however. With a dash, he picked up her mitten and tore it to shreds, then rolled in its many pieces and stood up. Nails, Silver, and the pups sniffed him and wagged their tails in great excitement. Then Amaroq narrowed his eyes and glanced her way. With a chill she realized he was going to attack. She flattened herself like an obedient pup as he glided down his slope and up hers. Her breathing quickened, her heart raced.

When Amaroq was but five feet away and she could see each hair on his long fine nose, he gave the grunt-whine. He was calling her! Cautiously she crawled toward him. He wagged his tail and led her down the hill, through the sedges, and up the long slope to the wolf den. Patiently adjusting his stride to her clumsy crawl he brought her home to the pack, perhaps against Jello's will—she would never know.

At the den site he promptly ignored her and went to his bed, a dish-like scoop in the soil on the highest point. Circling three or four times, scratching the earth to prepare it for sleep, he lay down.

Miyax glanced out of the corner of her eyes to see Nails preparing his bed also with scratches and turns. Silver was already in her scoop, snapping at the nursing Zing. Jello was off by himself.

Now it was Miyax's turn to say she was home. Patting the ground, circling first to the left and then to the right, she lay down and pulled her knees up to her chin. She closed her eyes, but not completely.

Through her lashes she peeked at Amaroq for reassurance, just as she had seen the other wolves do. The wind played across his black ruff and his ears twitched from time to time as he listened to the birds and winds in his sleep. All was well with the world, and apparently with her, for Amaroq rested in peace.

But Miyax could not sleep. The sun reached its apogee and started down the blue sky of early afternoon. The elegant Arctic terns cut swirls in the sky, a spider crept under a stone, and the snow buntings flitted and called. From some distant spot a loon cried. Then the pale green of evening was upon the land and Miyax closed her eyes.

She awoke with a start a short time later and looked about in puzzlement. The sky vaulted above her. A grass blade tickled her face, and she remembered where she was—up on the frost heave with the wolf pack! Breathing deeply to quell a sense of uneasiness, she finally relaxed, unrolled, and sat up. Kapu was curled against her leg. His feet were flipping and he yipped as if challenging some wolf badman in his dreams. Softly she stroked his fur.

"All's well," she whispered and his paws stopped moving. He sighed and dreamed on peacefully.

She glanced around. All of the wolves were asleep, although they usually went hunting when the sky was lime-green. Perhaps they knew something she didn't know. Sniffing and turning her head, she saw nothing different from any other evening. Then in the distance a thick wall of fog arose. It blotted out the horizon, the far dips and heaves, the grasses, the pond, and finally her own frost heave. The fog streamed up the wolf slope and enveloped the members of the pack one by one until only Kapu was visible. Fogs were part of the Arctic summer, rolling in from the sea for only an hour or for many days, but Miyax had never given them much thought. Now she remembered that when the fog rolled over Barrow, airplanes were grounded, ships and boats had to be anchored, and even the two jeeps in town sat where they had stopped in the fog. She also remembered that people were prisoners of the fog, too. They could not see to hunt.

Now, if the wolves did not bring her some meat, she might not eat for days. She could resort to the belly-basket again, but Jello was jumpy and she doubted if she had enough courage to put her hands in the mouths of the others. Perhaps Kapu would share his meals with her.

"Kapu?" He sighed and pushed tighter against her. The whiskers that protected his sensitive nose and warned him of objects nearby, twitched as her breath touched them. His lips curled up. Whatever he was dreaming about now must be funny, she thought.

She hoped so, for her wide-awake dream was hardly amusing—it was desperate.

She was looking at Silver stretched not far away in a thin spot of fog. Zing, the incorrigible Zing, was nursing again. Silver growled. The pup rolled to his back, paws outstretched like an upside-down chair. Then Sister moved out of the fog. She snuggled up to her mother, suckled two or three times, more for comfort than food, and fell back to sleep.

This brief sucking of the pups had started Silver's milk flowing. Miyax stared at this unexpected source of food.

She inched forward on her stomach and elbows until she was close to the mother. Miyax had drunk the milk of other wild mammals on Nunivak and each time had found it sweet and good. True, the walrus and musk oxen had been milked by her father, but if he had done it, why couldn't she? Slipping her hand beneath a nipple she caught several drops, keeping her eyes on Silver to discern her mood. Slowly Miyax brought the milk to her mouth, lapped, and found it as rich as butter. She reached out again, but as she did so, Silver closed her jaws on Miyax's shoulder and held her immobile. She stifled a scream.

Suddenly Amaroq appeared and lifted his head. Silver let go. Miyax rubbed her shoulder and crept back to Kapu. He was awake, peering up at her, his head on his paws. When their eyes met, he flipped one ear humorously and Miyax sensed he had been through this, too.

"Guess I'm weaned," she said. He wagged his tail.

The fog thickened and, like an eraser on a blackboard, wiped out Amaroq and Silver and the tip of Kapu's tail. She cuddled closer to Kapu, wondering if Amaroq would hunt tonight. After a long time she decided he would not—his family was content and well fed. Not she, however; two drops of milk were scarcely life-sustaining. She patted Kapu, crawled off in the fog, and stood up when she thought she was safely out of sight. Amaroq snarled. She dropped to her knees. His tail beat the ground and she gasped.

"I know you can't see me," she called, "so how do you know what I'm doing? Can you hear me stand up?" His tail beat again and she scrambled to her house, awed by the sensitivity of Amaroq. He knew about fogs and the sneaky ways of human beings.

The sedges around her pond were visible if she crawled, and so on hands and knees she rounded the bank, picking seeds, digging up the nut-like roots of the sedges, and snatching crane fly larvae from the water. As she crept she ate. After what seemed like hours of constant foraging she was still hungry—but not starving.

She came back to her house in a fog so thick she could almost hold it in her hands. For long hours she was suspended between sleep and wakefulness. She listened to the birds call to keep in touch with each other in the fog. Like herself they could not smell their food; they needed to see. As time dragged on, she sang to pass the hours. At first she invented rhymes about the tundra and sang them to tunes she had learned at school. When she tired of these melodies she improvised on the songs of her childhood. They were better suited to improvisation, for they had been invented for just this purpose—to pass the hours in creative fun when the weather closed in.

She sang about the wolves, her house, and the little feather flower on her table; and when she had no more to say, she crawled to her door and looked out. The fog was somewhat lighter. She could see the empty pot by her fireplace and, low overhead, a few birds in the sky.

Then an airplane droned in the distance, grew louder, then fainter, then louder again. The pilot was circling, waiting to see if the weather might suddenly clear so he could land. The same thing had happened to her when she was flown from Nunivak to Barrow. As their plane came over the town, a dense fog rolled in and the pilot had circled for almost an hour.

"If we cannot land on this turn," he had finally announced over the intercom, "we will head straight back to Fairbanks." But suddenly the fog had cleared, and they had landed in Barrow.

The sound of the plane grew louder. Through the thinning fog, she saw the commercial plane that flew from Fairbanks to Barrow and back. Her heart pounded. If the pilot could see her he might send help. She ran out to wave, but the fog had swirled in again and she could barely see her hand. The engines accelerated, and the plane sped off in what must be the direction of Fairbanks. She listened to its sound and, bending down, drew a line in the soil in the direction it had gone.

"That way should be Fairbanks," she said. "At least I know that much."

Picking up pebbles, she pounded them into the line to make it more permanent, and stood up. "That way," she said, pointing in the opposite direction, "is the coast and Point Hope."

Amaroq howled. Nails barked. Then Amaroq slid into a musical crescendo that Silver joined in. Their voices undulated as each harmonized with the other. Jello's windy voice barked out and, like the beat of drums, the five pups whooped and yipped. Miyax rubbed her chin; something was different about this hunt song. It was eerie and restless. It spoke of things she did not understand and she was frightened.

The fog cleared again and she saw Amaroq, his hunters, and the pups running across the tundra. Even Jello was with them. Were they leaving her? Was this their day to take up the wandering life of the wolves? Was she now on her own? Picking up her red markers, she crawled around her frost heave and frantically gathered the leafy plants that the caribou eat. She stuffed mushroom-like fungi in her pockets, and bits of reindeer moss. She could no longer afford to pass up anything that might be edible.

As she worked on her hands and knees, she felt a rhythmical beat, like the rumble of Eskimo drums. Pressing her ear to the ground she heard the vibration of many feet—a herd of caribou was not far away.

The fog thinned more and Kapu came into view. As alert as an eagle, he was sniffing the wind and wagging his tail as if reading some amusing wolf story. She sniffed too, but for her the pages were blank.

The vibrations in the earth grew stronger; Miyax drew back, as out of the fog came a huge caribou, running her way. His head was out straight and his eyes rolled wildly. At his neck, leaping with the power of an ocean wave, was Amaroq. Nails was diving in and out under his legs, and at his flank dashed Silver. Miyax held her breath, wondering whether to run or dodge.

Then Amaroq jumped, floated in the air for an instant, and sank his teeth into the shoulder of the beast. He hung on while Silver attacked from the side. Then he dropped to the ground as the bull bellowed. The fog closed in briefly, and when it thinned the caribou was poised above Amaroq, his cleaver-like hoofs aimed at his head. There was a low grunt, a flash of hoofs, and the huge feet cut uselessly into the sod; for Amaroq had vaulted into the air again and had sunk his teeth in the animal's back. Snarling, using the weight of his body as a tool, he rode the circling and stumbling beast. Silver leaped in front of the bull trying to trip him or slow him down. Nails had a grip on one hind leg. The caribou

bucked, writhed, then dropped to his knees. His antlers pierced the ground; he bellowed and fell.

He was dying, his eyes glazed with the pain-killing

drug of shock; yet his muscles still flexed. His hoofs flailed at the three who were ending the hunt with slashes and blood-letting bites.

After what seemed to Miyax an eternity, the bull lay still. Amaroq tore open his side as if it were a loaf of bread and, without ceremony, fell to the feast.

Kapu and the little wolves came cautiously up to the huge animal and sniffed. They did not know what to do with this beast. It was the first one they had seen and so they wandered curiously around the kill, watching their elders. Amaroq snarled with pleasure as he ate, then licked his lips and looked at Kapu. Kapu pounced on a piece of meat and snarled, too; then he looked at Amaroq again. The leader growled and ate. Kapu growled and ate.

Miyax could not believe her good fortune—an entire caribou felled practically at her door. This was enough food to last her for months, perhaps a year. She would smoke it to make it lighter to carry, pack it, and walk on to the coast. She would make it to Point Hope.

Plans racing in her head, she squatted to watch the wolves eat, measuring, as time passed, the enormous amounts they were consuming—pounds at each bite. As she saw her life-food vanishing, she decided she had better get her share while she could, and went into her house for her knife.

As she crept up toward the bull she wondered if she should come so close to wolves that were eating.

Dogs would bite people under similar conditions. But dogs would refuse to share their food with others of their kind, as the wolves were doing now, growling pleasantly and feasting in friendship.

She was inching forward, when Kapu splintered a bone with his mere baby teeth. She thought better of taking her share; instead she waited patiently for the wolves to finish.

Amaroq left the kill first, glanced her way, and disappeared in the fog. Silver and Nails departed soon after and the pups followed at their mother's heels.

"Ee-lie!" Miyax shouted and ran to the food. Suddenly Jello came out of the fog and leaped upon a leg of the kill. She drew back. Why had he not eaten with the others? she asked herself. He had not been baby-sitting. He must be in some kind of wolf disgrace, for he walked with his tail between his legs and he was not allowed to eat with the pack.

When he too had feasted and left, she walked over to the caribou and admired the mountain of food. Impulsively, she paid tribute to the spirit of the caribou by lifting her arms to the sun. Then, scoffing at herself for being such an old-fashioned Eskimo, she sharpened her man's knife on a stone and set to work.

The skin was tough and she marveled that the wolves tore it so easily. Even as she peeled it away from the flesh with her knife, she was surprised how difficult it was to cut and handle, but she worked diligently, for the pelt was almost as valuable as the meat. Hours and hours later, the last bit of hide came free and she flopped on her back to rest.

"Such hard work!" she gasped aloud. "No wonder this job is given to Eskimo men and boys." With a sigh she got to her feet, dragged the skin to her house, and laid it out to dry. Scraping and cleaning the skin was something she knew more about, for that was a woman's job, but she was too busy to do that now. It was time to carve and eat! She cut open the belly and lifted out the warm liver, the "candy" of her people. With a deft twist of the ulo, she cut off a slice and savored each bite of this, the most nourishing part of the animal. So rich is the liver that most of it is presented to the women and girls, an ancient custom with wisdom at its core—since women give birth to babies, they need the iron and blood of the liver.

All during the wolf sleep Miyax stayed up, cutting off strips of caribou and hanging them over the fire. As she worked, a song came to mind.

Amaroq, wolf, my friend,
You are my adopted father.
My feet shall run because of you.
My heart shall beat because of you.
And I shall love because of you.

She stood up, peeked around the heave, and added,

"But not Daniel. I'm a wolf now, and wolves love leaders."

The umbrella of fog had lifted and Miyax ran up the side of her frost heave to see how her family was. They were sleeping peacefully—all but Amaroq. He shot her a glance, lifted his lips, and spoke with his teeth.

"Oh, all right. Ee-lie, Ee-lie." Miyax got down on all fours. "But how am I going to follow you if you won't let me walk? I am me, your two-legged pup." She stood up. Amaroq lifted his eyebrows, but did not reprimand her. He seemed to understand she could not change. His tail banged once and he went back to sleep.

HUNTS CAME AND WENT. The smoke curled up from Miyax's fire, and caribou strips shrank and dried. One night she watched the dipping sun, trying to guess the date. It must be the second week of August, for the sun sat almost on the rim of the earth.

The wolves had no doubt about the date; they were using a calendar set by the pups, and today was the second day of exploration. Yesterday, Silver had taken them out on the tundra to chase caribou and now they were bouncing around her, ready to go again. Kapu dashed off a few steps, came back, and spun in a circle. Silver finally gave the signal to go, and led him and the others down the hill and out behind the pond.

Miyax watched them trot off to learn about the scent of caribou and the joy of chasing foxes. She wished she could learn such things, too. Shouldering her pack, she wandered through the grasses in search of fuel, a much less exciting assignment. About an hour later she saw Silver and the pups and paused to watch them chase a lively young buck. Kapu ran with a skill that almost matched his mother's. Miyax waved to them and started home.

As she rounded the pond she squinted at the sun again, for it had not climbed up the sky but was still sitting on the horizon. This worried her; it was later than she thought. Autumn was almost here. A glance across the barrens reaffirmed this. The flowers were gone; the birds flocked in great clouds, and among them were eider and old squaw ducks that kept to the rivers and beaches except when they migrated south. Finally, she saw, like hundreds of huge black fingers, the antlers of the caribou beyond the turn of the horizon. They were moving to their wintering ground ahead of the deep freeze and the snow.

She wondered why they passed so close to their enemies the wolves, then recalled how swiftly they could run. The young and the healthy ones did not fear the wolves, and the sick and the old were doomed in winter. Her caribou had been so infested with the larvae of nose flies it had not been able to eat. A weakling, it had become food to give strength both to her and to the wolves.

After storing her fuel she returned to the kill to cut off more strips to smoke. As she approached she saw Jello there and she felt uneasy, for the wolves had not touched the caribou since the night they had felled it. She liked to think they had given it to her.

Jello snarled. "That's not nice," she said. "Go away!" He growled fiercely and she realized she had not seen him with the rest of the pack for several sleeps. He was not even baby-sitting now, for the pups went out with their mother at night. She shouted again, for she needed every bite of that meat. Hearing anger in her voice he stood up, the hairs on his back rising menacingly. She backed away.

Hurrying to camp, she got out her man's knife and began to dig. Every Eskimo family had a deep cellar in the permafrost into which they put game. So cold is the ground that huge whales and caribou freeze overnight, preserved for the months to come. Miyax dug to the frost line, then whacked at the ice until, many hours later, she had chopped three feet into it. This was not the eighteen-foot-deep cellar of her mother-in-law, but perhaps it would keep the rest of her food from Jello. Cautiously she went back to the kill. Jello was gone. Working swiftly, she chopped off the best pieces and dragged them to her refrigerator.

Then she covered the hole with a large slab of sod.

She was heating a pot of stew when Kapu came around the hill with a bone in his mouth. Miyax laughed at the sight, for although he ran like an adult on the tundra, he was still a puppy with games on his mind. She lifted a chunk of cooked meat from the pot and held it out to her brother.

"It's good," she said. "Try some Eskimo food." Kapu sniffed the meat, gulped, licked his jaws, and whined for more. She gave him a second bite; then Silver called and he trotted obediently home. A few minutes later he was back for another bite.

"Maybe you'll learn to like it so much, you'll travel with me," she said, and threw him another chunk of meat. "That would be nice, for I will be lonely without you." Kapu suddenly looked at her and pressed back his ears. She understood his problem instantly and danced lightly from one foot to the other.

"It's all right, Kapu," she said. "Amaroq has agreed that I can go on two feet. I am, after all, a person."

Unnumbered evenings later, when most of the meat was smoked, Miyax decided she had time to make herself a new mitten. She cut off a piece of the new caribou hide and was scraping it clean of fur when a snowstorm of cotton-grass seeds blew past her face. "Autumn," she whispered and scraped faster. She saw several birds on the sedges. They were twisting and turning and pointing their beaks toward the sun as they took their readings and plotted their courses south.

With a start, Miyax noticed the sun. It was halfway below the horizon. Shading her eyes, she watched it disappear completely. The sky turned navy blue, the clouds turned bright yellow, and twilight was upon the land. The sun had set. In a few weeks the land would be white with snow and in three months the long Arctic night that lasted for sixty-six days would darken the top of the world. She tore a fiber from the skin, threaded her needle, and began to stitch the mitten.

About an hour later, the sun arose and marked the date for Miyax. It was August twenty-fourth, the day the *North Star* reached Barrow. Of this she was sure, for on that day the sun lingered below the horizon for about one hour. After that, the nights lengthened rapidly until November twenty-first, when the sun disappeared for the winter.

In bed that evening, Miyax's spirit was stirred by the seeding grass and the restless birds and she could not sleep. She got up, stored some of the smoked meat in her pack, spread the rest in the sun to pack later, and hurried out to the caribou hide. She scraped all the fat from it and stuffed it in the bladder she had saved. The fat was excellent fuel, and gave light when burned. Finally she crept to her cellar for the rest of the meat and found Jello digging through the lid of sod.

"No!" she screamed. He snarled and came toward her. There was nothing to do but assert her authority. She rose to her feet and tapped the top of his nose with her man's knife. With that, he stuck his tail between his legs and slunk swiftly away, while Miyax stood still, surprised by the power she felt. The knife made her a predator, and a dangerous one.

Clutching her food, she ran home, banked the fire, and put the last of the meat on the coals. She was about to go to bed when Kapu bounced down her heave, leaped over her house, and landed silently by her side.

"Oh, wow!" she said. "I'm so glad to see you. Jello scares me to death these days." She reached into her pot for a piece of cooked meat for him and this time he ate from her fingers. Then he spanked the ground to play. Picking up a scrap from the mitten, she swung it around her head. Kapu leaped and snatched it so easily that she was startled. He was quick and powerful, an adult not a pup. She hesitated to chase him, and he bounded up the heave and dashed away.

The next morning when she went out to soften the hide by pounding and chewing it, she saw two bright eyes peering at her from behind the antlers, about all that was left of her caribou. The eyes belonged to an Arctic fox and she walked toward him upright to scare him away. He continued to gnaw the bones.

"Things are tough, eh, little fox?" she whispered. "I cannot drive you away from the food." At the sound of her voice, however, his ears twisted, his tail drooped, and he departed like a leaf on the wind. The fox's brown fur of summer was splotched with white patches, reminding Miyax again that winter was coming, for the fur of the fox changes each season to match the color of the land. He would soon be white, like the snow.

Before sundown the temperature dropped and Miyax crawled into her sleeping skin early. Hardly had she snuggled down in her furs than a wolf howled to the south.

"I am here!" Amaroq answered with a bark, and the distant wolf said something else—she did not know what. Then each pack counted off and when the totals were in, Miyax's wolves yipped among themselves as if discussing the tundra news—a pack of twelve wolves to the north. So wild had their voices been that Miyax crept to her door to call Kapu to come and ease her fears. She started with surprise. There by her pond was Amaroq. The wind was blowing his fur and his tribe was gathered around him, biting his chin, kissing his cheeks. With a sudden sprint he sped into the green shadows of sunrise and one by one his family fell in behind, according to their status in the pack. Nails ran second, then Silver, Kapu, Sister, Zit, Zat, Zing, and finally, far behind came Jello.

Miyax at last was sure of what had happened to Jello. He was low man on the totem pole, the bottom of the ladder. She recalled the day Amaroq had put him down and forced him to surrender, the many times Silver had made him go back and sit with the pups, and the times that Kapu had ignored his calls to come home to the den. He was indeed a lowly wolf—a poor spirit, with fears and without friends.

Scrambling to her feet she watched the pack run along the horizon, a flowing line of magnificent beasts, all cooperating for the sake of each other, all wholly content—except Jello. He ran head down, low to the ground—in the manner of the lone wolf.

"That is not good," she said aloud.

An Arctic tern skimmed low and she jumped to her feet, for it was flying with a determination that she had not seen in the birds all summer. Its white wings cut a flashing V against the indigo sky as it moved due south across the tundra. There was no doubt in her mind what that steady flight meant—the migration was on.

"Good-bye!" she called sadly. "Good-bye."

Another tern passed overhead, then another, and another. Miyax walked to the fireplace and threw on more fuel.

Amaroq howled in the distance, his royal voice ringing out in a firm command. Somehow, she felt, he was calling her. But she could not go on this hunt. She must finish smoking every morsel of meat. Hurriedly she picked up her markers and started off for more fuel.

Several hours later, her tights bulging with caribou chips, she saw the wolves again. Amaroq, Nails, and Silver were testing the herd and Kapu was pouncing and bouncing. She knew what that meant; the hour of the lemmings was returning. Of this she was sure; she had often seen the dogs, foxes, and children hop and jump after lemmings in this same laughable way.

"I'm glad to know that," she called to her friend, and hurried back to the fire.

As the chips glowed red, Miyax saw another Arctic tern flying the same route as the others. Quickly she drew its course across the mark on the ground to Fairbanks; then, peeling off a strip of sinew, she stood in the center of the X and held the ends of the thread in both hands. When one arm was pointing to the coast and the other was pointing in the direction the bird was taking, she cut off the remainder of the strip.

"There," she said, "I have a compass. I can't take the stones with me, but every time a tern flies over, I can line up one arm with him, stretch the sinew out, and my other hand will point to the coast and Point Barrow."

That night she unzipped a small pocket in her

pack and took out a battered letter from Amy.

. . . And when you get to San Francisco, we will buy you summer dresses, and because you like curls, we'll curl your hair. Then we'll ride the trolley to the theater and sit on velvet seats.

Mom says you can have the pink bedroom that looks over the garden and down on the bay and the Golden Gate Bridge.

When are you coming to San Francisco?

Your pen pal,
Amy

"The theater," she whispered, "and the Golden Gate Bridge." That night she slept with the letter under her cheek.

In the evening of the following day Miyax hastily put on her clothes and crawled up the frost heave. Like a good puppy she got down on her stomach.

"Amaroq," she called. "I'm ready to go when you are!"

The wind blew across the wolf den, shattering the heads of the cotton grass and shooting their seedlets south with the birds. No one answered. The wolves were gone.

PART II

MIYAX,

THE GIRL

THE WIND, THE EMPTY SKY, the deserted earth—Miyax had felt the bleakness of being left behind once before.

She could not remember her mother very well, for Miyax was scarcely four when she died, but she did remember the day of her death. The wind was screaming wild high notes and hurling ice-filled waves against the beach. Kapugen was holding her hand and they were walking. When she stumbled he put her on his shoulders, and high above the beach she saw thousands of birds diving toward the sea. The jaegers screamed and the sandpipers cried. The feathered horns of the comical puffins drooped low, and Kapugen told her they seemed to be grieving with him.

She saw this, but she was not sad. She was divinely happy going somewhere alone with Kapugen. Occasionally he climbed the cliffs and brought her eggs to eat; occasionally he took her in his arms and leaned against a rock. She slept at times in the warmth of his big sealskin parka. Then they walked on. She did not know how far.

Later, Kapugen's Aunt Martha told her that he had lost his mind the day her mother died. He had grabbed Miyax up and walked out of his fine house in Mekoryuk. He had left his important job as manager of the reindeer herd, and he had left all his possessions.

"He walked you all the way to seal camp," Martha told her. "And he never did anything good after that."

To Miyax the years at seal camp were infinitely good. The scenes and events were beautiful color spots in her memory. There was Kapugen's little house of driftwood, not far from the beach. It was rosy-gray on the outside. Inside, it was gold-brown. Walrus tusks gleamed and drums, harpoons, and man's knives decorated the walls. The sealskin kayak beside the door glowed as if the moon had been stretched across it and its graceful ribs shone black. Dark gold and soft brown were the old men who sat around Kapugen's camp stove and talked to him by day and night.

The ocean was green and white, and was rimmed

by fur, for she saw it through Kapugen's hood as she rode to sea with him on his back inside the parka. Through this frame she saw the soft eyes of the seals on the ice. Kapugen's back would grow taut as he lifted his arms and fired his gun. Then the ice would turn red.

The celebration of the Bladder Feast was many colors—black, blue, purple, fire-red; but Kapugen's hand around hers was rose-colored and that was the color of her memory of the Feast. A shaman, an old priestess whom everyone called "the bent woman," danced. Her face was streaked with black soot. When she finally bowed, a fiery spirit came out of the dark wearing a huge mask that jingled and terrified Miyax. Once, in sheer bravery, she peeked up under a mask and saw that the dancer was not a spirit at all but Naka, Kapugen's serious partner. She whispered his name and he laughed, took off his mask, and sat down beside Kapugen. They talked and the old men joined them. Later that day Kapugen blew up seal bladders and he and the old men carried them out on the ice. There they dropped them into the sea, while Miyax watched and listened to their songs. When she came back to camp the bent woman told her that the men had returned the bladders to the seals.

"Bladders hold the spirits of the animals," she said. "Now the spirits can enter the bodies of the newborn seals and keep them safe until we harvest them again." That night the bent woman seemed all violet-colored as she tied a piece of seal fur and blubber to Miyax's belt. "It's an *i'noGo tied,*" she said. "It's a nice little spirit for you."

Another memory was flickering-yellow—it was of the old men beating their drums around Kapugen's stove. She saw them through a scarf of tiny crystals that was her breath on the cold night air inside the house.

Naka and Kapugen were on their hands and knees, prancing lightly, moving swiftly. When Naka tapped Kapugen's chin with his head, Kapugen rose to his knees. He threw back his head, then rocked back on his heels. Naka sat up and together they sang the song of the wolves. When the dance was over the old men cheered and beat their paddle-like drums.

"You are wolves, you are real wolves," they had cried.

After that Kapugen told her about the wolves he had known on the mainland when he went to high school in Nome. He and his joking partner would hunt the wilderness for months, calling to the wolves, speaking their language to ask where the game was. When they were successful, they returned to Nome with sled-loads of caribou.

"Wolves are brotherly," he said. "They love each other, and if you learn to speak to them, they will love you too."

He told her that the birds and animals all had languages and if you listened and watched them you could learn about their enemies, where their food lay, and when big storms were coming.

A silver memory was the day when the sun came over the horizon for the first time in winter. She was at the beach, close to Kapugen, helping him haul in a huge gleaming net. In it was a beautiful white whale. Out of sight on the other side of the whale, she could hear the old men as they cheered this gift from the sea.

The whale was a mountain so high she could not see the cliffs beyond, only the sunlit clouds. Kapugen's huge, black, frostbitten hand seemed small as it touched the great body of the whale.

Not far away the bent woman was dancing and gathering invisible things from the air. Miyax was frightened but Kapugen explained that she was putting the spirit of the whale in her i'noGo tied.

"She will return it to the sea and the whales," he said.

Walking the tundra with Kapugen was all laughter and fun. He would hail the blue sky and shout out his praise for the grasses and bushes. On these trips they ate salmon berries, then lay in the sun watching the birds. Sometimes Kapugen would whistle sandpiper songs and the birds would dip down to see which of their members had gotten lost in the grass. When they saw him and darted away, Kapugen would laugh.

Fishing with Kapugen was murky-tan in her memory, for they would wade out into the river mouth where the stone weirs were built and drive the fish into nets between the walls. Kapugen would spear them or grab them in his hand and throw them to the men in the wooden boats. Occasionally he skimmed after the biggest cod and halibut in his kayak and he would whoop with joy when he caught one and would hold it above his head. It gleamed as it twisted in the sun.

Summers at seal camp were not as beautiful to Miyax as the autumns and winters, for during this season many families from Mekoryuk came to Nash Harbor to hunt and fish and Kapugen was busy. Sometimes he helped people set nets; sometimes he scouted the ocean in his kayak as he searched for seal colonies.

During these hours Miyax was left with the other children on the beach. She played tag and grass ball with them and she pried prickly sea urchins off the rocks, to eat the sweet meat inside. Often she dug for clams and when Kapugen returned he would crack them open and smack his lips as he swallowed them whole.

The Eskimos from Mekoryuk spoke English almost all the time. They called her father Charlie Edwards and Miyax was Julie, for they all had two names, Eskimo and English. Her mother had also called her Julie, so she did not mind her summer name until one day when Kapugen called her that. She stomped her foot and told him her name was Miyax. "I am Eskimo, not a gussak!" she had said, and he had tossed her into the air and hugged her to him.

"Yes, you are Eskimo," he had said. "And never forget it. We live as no other people can, for we truly understand the earth."

But winters always returned. Blizzards came and the temperatures dropped to thirty and forty below zero, and those who stayed at hunting camp spoke only in Eskimo and did only Eskimo things. They scraped hides, mended boots, made boats, and carved walrus tusks. In the evenings Kapugen sang and danced with the old men, and all of their songs and dances were about the sea and the land and the creatures that dwelled there.

One year, probably in September, for the canvas tents were down and the campground almost empty, Kapugen came into the house with a sealskin. It was a harbor seal, but had so few spots that it was a rare prize.

"We must make you a new coat," he had said. "You are getting big. Since your mother is not here to help us, I will do her work. Now watch and learn."

The skin was metallic silver-gold and so beautiful that even the velveteen parkas of the children from Mekoryuk paled by comparison. Miyax stroked it lovingly as Kapugen lay her old coat upon it and began to cut a larger one. As he worked he hummed, and she made up words about the seal who wanted to be a coat. Presently they became aware of the distant throb of a motorboat. The sound grew louder, then shut off at the beach. Footsteps crunched, the cold air rushed in the door, and there was Martha, Kapugen's aunt. She was thin and her face was pinched. Miyax disliked her immediately, but was spared the necessity of speaking nicely to her, for Martha had words only for Kapugen.

She talked swiftly in English, which Miyax barely understood, and she was angry and upset. Martha shook her finger at Kapugen and glanced at Miyax from time to time. The two were arguing very loudly when Martha pulled a sheet of paper from her pocket and showed it to Kapugen.

"No!" he shouted.

"We'll see!" Martha screamed, turned around, and went toward the boat where a white man waited. Kapugen followed her and stood by the boat, talking to the man for a long time.

The next morning Miyax was awakened as Kapugen lifted her up in his arms and held her close. Gently he pushed the hair out of her eyes and, speaking softly in Eskimo, told her she was going to live with Aunt Martha.

"There's a law that says you must go to school . . .

and I guess you should. You are nine years old. And I must go to war. The government is fighting somewhere."

Miyax grabbed him around the neck, but did not protest. It never occurred to her that anything that Kapugen decided was not absolutely perfect. She whimpered however.

"Listen closely," he said. "If anything happens to me, and if you are unhappy, when you are thirteen you can leave Aunt Martha by marrying Daniel, Naka's son. Naka is going to Barrow on the Arctic Ocean. I shall make arrangements with him. He is like me, an old-time Eskimo who likes our traditions. He will agree."

Miyax listened carefully, then he put her down and hastily packed her bladder-bag, wrapped her in an oilskin against the wild spray of the sea, and carried her to the boat. She sat down beside Martha and stared bravely at Kapugen. The motor started and Kapugen looked at her until the boat moved, then he turned his back and walked quickly away. The launch sped up a huge wave, slammed down into a foaming trough, and Kapugen was no longer visible.

With that Miyax became Julie. She was given a cot near the door in Martha's little house and was soon walking to school in the darkness. She liked to learn the printed English words in books, and so a month passed rather happily.

One morning when the air was cold and the puddles around the house were solid ice, an old man from seal camp arrived at the door. He spoke softly to Martha, then pulled his hood tightly around his face and went away. Martha came to Miyax's bed.

"Your father," she said, "went seal hunting in that ridiculous kayak. He has been gone a month this day. He will not be back. Bits of his kayak washed up on the shore." Martha stumped to the fire and turned her back.

Julie ran out of the house into the dark morning. She darted past the store, the reindeer-packing house, the church. She did not stop until she came to the beach. There she crouched among the oil drums and looked out on the sea.

The wind blew across the water, shattering the tips of the waves and shooting ice-sparklets north with the storm. "Kapugen!" she called. No one answered. Kapugen was gone. The earth was empty and bleak.

GRADUALLY JULIE PUSHED KAPUGEN out of her heart and accepted the people of Mekoryuk. The many years in seal camp alone with Kapugen had been dear and wonderful, but she realized now that she had lived a strange life. The girls her age could speak and write English and they knew the names of presidents, astronauts, and radio and movie personalities who lived below the top of the world. Maybe the Europeans once thought the earth was flat, but the Eskimos always knew it was round. One only needed to look at the earth's relatives, the sun and the moon, to know that.

One day as she walked home across the snowy town she caught up with her schoolmates, Judith and Rose. Their boots squeaked in the cold and their voices sounded far away, for the temperature was far below zero. Judith invited her into her house and the three of them huddled close to the oil stove. Judith and Rose chatted, but Julie's eyes wandered around the room and she saw for the first time a gas cooking stove, a couch, framed pictures on the wall, and curtains of cotton print. Then Judith took her into her own room and she beheld a bed with a headboard, a table, and a reading lamp. On the table lay a little chain on which hung a dog, a hat, and a boat. This she was glad to see—something familiar.

"What a lovely i'noGo tied!" Julie said politely.

"A what?" asked Judith. Julie repeated the Eskimo word for the house of the spirits.

Judith snickered. "That's a charm bracelet," she said. Rose giggled and both laughed derisively. Julie felt the blood rush to her face as she met, for the first but not the last time, the new attitudes of the Americanized Eskimos. She had much to learn besides reading. That night she threw her i'noGo tied away.

English and math came easily to her, and by the end of the year Julie was reading and writing. That summer she worked at the mission beside the church sweeping the floor and greeting the visitors from the lower states who came to see real Eskimos. She read the encyclopedia when there was nothing else to do.

The next year Julie worked at the hospital on weekends. After school she cut out dresses in the domestic science room and sewed them on the electric machines. She bobbed her hair and put it in rollers to make the ends curl.

One Sunday, as she was coming home from the hospital, a jeep pulled up beside her and a gussak hailed her. He leaned on the steering wheel, a warm smile on his face.

"I'm Mr. Pollock. I own stock in the Reindeer Corporation here on the island," he said. "And I have a daughter your age. The last thing she asked me before I left San Francisco was to find a girl in the town of Mekoryuk on Nunivak Island and ask if she would like to exchange letters. How about being her pen pal?"

Julie needed no explanation for that term. Many letters came into the mission from children in the States who wanted to write letters. She had never done so before, but now she was ready.

"I would like that," she answered.

"My daughter's name is Amy," he said, taking a

letter from his inside pocket. "She told me to give this to the nicest girl I could find—and that's you, with your twinkling eyes and rosy cheeks."

Julie smiled and slowly took the extended letter, then skipped off to open it in the privacy of the mission library. She was enchanted by what she read:

Hello, my new friend,

I am Amy Pollock and I have blue eyes and brown hair. Next month I will be twelve years old, and I hope I'll be five feet tall by then. I have a quarter of an inch to go. I wear a size nine dress and a size six shoe, which my mother finds embarrassingly big. Frankly, I like my big feet. They get me up and down the steep hills of San Francisco and shoot me through the water like a frog when I swim. I am in the eighth grade and am studying French. I hate it, but would like to learn Eskimo. My father goes to Alaska often and he has taught me a few words. They are pretty words that sound like bells, but I can't spell them. Can you? How do you spell the word for "daylight?" Quaq?

I take dancing lessons, which l love, and I also like to play baseball with the kids that live on our hill. When I grow up I think I'll be a dancer, but it is an awful lot of work. One of the dancers at the San Francisco Opera House said so, so maybe I'll be a schoolteacher like my aunt and have the whole summer off.

Last month at school we saw your island on a television show. It was so beautiful, with the birds flying over it and the flowers blooming on its hills, that I wanted to write to someone who lives there, a girl like me.

Here is a picture of my house. That is me standing on one foot on the patio wall. Please write soon.

Your new friend,

Amy

P.S. When are you coming to live with us in San Francisco?

Julie folded the letter and whispered to herself: "Daylight is spelled A-M-Y."

The wonders of Mekoryuk dimmed as weekly letters from Amy arrived. Julie learned about television, sports cars, blue jeans, bikinis, hero sandwiches, and wall-to-wall carpeting in the high school Amy would soon be attending. Mekoryuk had no high school. The Eskimo children of the more prosperous families were sent to the mainland for further schooling, something which Aunt Martha could not afford. But, she thought, if she married Daniel, perhaps Naka could send her to school.

As the winter passed, Martha became irritated with her. She nagged Julie for wearing her hair short, and complained about Judith. "She's disrespectful of her parents," she snapped. "And she's bad." That's all she would say except, "The old ways are best."

After that Martha gave her chores to do on weekends and refused to let her attend the movies with her friends. The winter nights in the dark little house became nightmares. Julie waited for letters from Amy and the call from Naka.

The call came suddenly. One morning in June as Julie was dressing to go to the store, the head of the Indian Affairs in Mekoryuk appeared at the door. He explained that Naka had written, requesting Julie to come to Barrow and marry his son.

"You are now thirteen," the man said, "and I have in my files an agreement for this arrangement signed by Kapugen and Naka." Martha sputtered and whispered in her ear that she could say no if she wanted to.

"The old ways are best," Julie said, and Martha could not protest.

The next day transportation was arranged for her by the Bureau of Indian Affairs and Julie packed her few possessions in a moosehide bag and walked to the airport with Martha. The old lady dragged behind, taking slow steps, and by the time they reached the airport she was limping.

"What shall I do when I'm too crippled to get out of bed?" she said angrily. Julie was about to remind her how strong her legs had been a few hours ago, but had time to say no more than good-bye. The pilot himself escorted her up the steps into the gleaming cabin and showed her how to fasten her seat belt.

Cautiously she looked at the upholstery, the overhead lights, the open door to the pilot's cabin—then she closed her eyes. She was afraid the plane could not really fly. The engines roared, the ship moved, and minutes later she opened her eyes to see the houses of Nunivak shrink to specks and the island grow smaller and smaller. When it was but a jewel in the sea, she touched her seat and her armrest and stared down at herself.

"I'm sitting in the sky!" she said to the man beside her. He winked and she pressed her head against the window. She was an eagle seeking out new pinnacles. After a long time she relaxed and her wonder at the miraculous airship changed to curiosity.

"What makes us stay up here?" she asked the man.

"That's not a good question," he said, and she lapsed into silence. The plane landed in Anchorage, then Fairbanks. Here she was put on another plane, a smaller one—the only one that flew to remote Barrow.

Rugged mountain passes and valleys passed below her; the trees became smaller and more scarce, then disappeared entirely as the craft shot out over the North Slope and the pilot announced that they were crossing the Arctic Circle. The gussaks cheered and opened bottles to toast the mythical line, but hardly had they taken sips than the windows became white and the plane was bumping along through a summer fog.

They made wide circles over Barrow for an hour and a half before the pilot announced they would try once more to find an opening in the fog, then head back to Fairbanks. Julie had her nose pressed tightly to the window, for she could see the long threads that spoke of a clearing. Suddenly Barrow appeared below, its houses huddled against the ice-piled shore like a cluster of lonely birds.

As the plane began its descent into Barrow, Julie could see in the distance the towers of the Distant Early Warning System that marked the presence of the military in Barrow, and a narrow road along the coast that led to a group of buildings. The pilot announced that they belonged to the Navy and the University of Alaska. "The Arctic Research Laboratory," he said, "where scientists study the Arctic. People from all over the world come here to investigate the top of the world. We now know a lot about living in the cold."

The wheels struck the runway and the plane pulled up by a small wooden house on the tundra, the terminal building. For a moment Julie had misgivings about her fate; then the stewardess brought her coat and escorted her to the door. She looked down at two people she knew must be Naka and his wife, Nusan. Daniel was hiding behind them. Slowly Julie walked down the steps, crossed the stretch of macadam and took Naka's hand. He was dressed in a Navy Arctic field jacket and his eyes were dark and smiling. She remembered those eyes from her color wheel of memories and she felt better.

Nusan was dressed in a kuspuck trimmed with Japanese lace flowers and she was smiling at Julie. They had not met before. Nusan had never gone to seal camp.

Then Julie saw Daniel. She knew from his grin and dull eyes that something was wrong with him. Nusan must have seen the disappointment that flashed over her face, for she put her arm around Julie.

"Daniel has a few problems," she said quickly. "But he's a very good boy, and he's a good worker. He cleans the animal cages at the research lab. He will be like a brother to you."

With those words Julie relaxed, and pushed him out of her mind. He would just be a brother. That was fine. She looked at the little houses surrounded by boats, oil drums, tires, buckets, broken cars, and rags and bags, and happily followed her new parents home.

The very next day, however, to Julie's surprise, there was a wedding. The minister came to Naka's house with two strangers and Nusan took Julie into the kitchen and gave her a beautiful sealskin suit. She helped her to dress. Daniel put on a dark blue shirt and gussak pants. They were told to stand in the doorway between the living room and kitchen, and the minister began to read. Daniel grasped her hand. His was as clammy with anxiety as hers. She stared at the floor wondering if Kapugen had known that Daniel was dull. She would not believe he did.

When the reading was over Daniel escaped to the kitchen and sat on his bed. He began to tinker with a radio and mumble to himself. Naka walked outside with the minister and the two strangers, and Nusan sat down at her sewing machine.

"I've got to finish these boots for a tourist," she said. "Make yourself at home." The sewing machine hummed and the radio droned on. Julie stepped outside and sat down on an oil drum. The streets were hushed for it was the rest hour. She did not know how long she sat in quiet terror, but it was a long time. Presently a little girl came around a rusted ship's engine, pulling a smaller girl by the hand.

"Come on," she ordered the reluctant child. "It's time for the blanket toss." As they hurried along, other children gathered from all directions and clustered in front of the community house. Several men unfolded a huge skin. Eskimos and tourists took hold of it. A child got in the center, bounced, and then was flipped twenty feet up in the air, like a toy rocket. Giggling, the child kicked her feet as if she were running, and came gracefully down.

Julie looked away. Snow buntings whirled around

the house, an Arctic tern darted over the ocean, and the waves lapped the ice that was piled high on the shore. She was desperately homesick for Mekoryuk. She dropped her head on her knees.

"Julie?" a tall girl tapped her arm. "I'm Pearl Norton, Pani NalaGan." She began speaking in Iñupiat. Julie shook her head. She spoke Yupik.

"We'd better use English," she said. Pearl nodded and laughed.

"I said, 'Let's go to the quonset.'" Julie jumped to her feet and followed Pearl around a broken box, over a battered auto door, and into an alley. In silence they passed the wooden hotel, where a tourist was huddled on the porch out of the wind; then they stepped onto the main street, where the stores stood. Crossing the street they entered an enormous quonset hut. When Julie's eyes had adjusted to the dim light she could see a dozen or more young men and girls, some in blue jeans and field jackets, some in kuspucks and parkas. They were seated at tables or leaning against pinball machines as they listened to rock and roll music. Pearl bought a Coke, got two straws, and they sat down at a table near the door.

"I know how you feel, Julie. I was married last year," Pearl began. "Don't pay any attention to it. No one does. All you have to do is leave the house or run away and everything's forgotten. Most of these arrangements are for convenience. I'm sure you are here to help Nusan make parkas and mittens for the tourists." Pearl leaned back. "Even in the old days they didn't make kids stick with these marriages if they didn't like each other. They just drifted apart."

Julie listened, her head swimming in confusion . . . Daniel, marriage, parkas, tourists, jukeboxes, pinball machines . . . divorce.

"I must go," Julie said. "Can I talk to you again?"

"I'll meet you here tomorrow. All the kids come here to have fun."

Daniel was gone when Julie stepped into the kitchen and nervously glanced around.

"Do you know how to sew?" Nusan yelled from the floor where she was cutting a short length of rabbit fur.

"A little," Julie answered as she unzipped her coat and folded it carefully.

"You shall know a lot when I'm through with you," Nusan replied and pointed to a large box in the corner. "Yard goods and rickrack. We have to make thirty parkas for the airlines by the end of the month. They lend them to the tourists who come here. None of them know how to dress. They'd freeze without parkas." Nusan threaded a needle and whipped the rabbit fur onto the top of a mukluk. She glanced up at Julie.

"You'll do nicely," she said. "You're smart and you're pretty."

Julie saw little of Daniel that summer and even less of him after school started. And so, by October she was beginning to enjoy her new home. She cooked and sewed for Nusan, studied at night, and had a few

hours in the afternoon when she met Pearl at the quonset.

As the months passed, the letters from Amy became the most important thing in Julie's life and the house in San Francisco grew more real than the house in Barrow. She knew each flower on the hill where Amy's house stood, each brick in the wall

around the garden, and each tall blowing tree. She also knew the curls in the wrought-iron gate, and how many steps led up to the big front door; she could almost see the black-and-white tile on the floor of the foyer. If she closed her eyes she could imagine the arched doorway, the Persian rug on the living-room floor, the yellow chairs and the huge window that looked over the bay. Radios, lamps, coffee tables—all these she could see. And if she shut her eyes tight, she could feel Amy's hand in her hand and hear Amy's big feet tap the sidewalk.

The second floor was always fun to dream about. At the top of the winding stairs four doors opened upon rooms lit with sunshine. And one was the pink room, the one that would be hers when she got to San Francisco.

DURING THE WINTER Julie came to understand Naka. At first she thought he had a very important job, for he would be gone for days, often weeks, and be very tired and angry when he came home. He slept sometimes for two days. But when the subzero weather set in, Naka stayed home, and Julie realized that he did not work at all. He drank. The more he drank the angrier he became. Sometimes he struck Nusan; more often he picked a fight with his neighbor. Finally, numbness would overcome him and he would drop on the bed like a huge limp seal and sleep for days.

When he awoke he would be pleasant again, sitting in the fur- and scrap-filled room, making moosehide masks for the summer tourist trade. He would sing the old songs of seal camp, and tell Julie about the animals that he and Kapugen had known. On those occasions, she would understand why Kapugen had loved him.

One night he struck Nusan over and over again. When she screamed and hit back, Julie ran to the quonset to look for Pearl. She was not there, but in a corner sat Russell, the young man who had been campaigning around the village, begging the Eskimos to vote "No" on requests for liquor licenses by the local restaurants.

Julie sat down. "Naka is evil again," she said. "His spirit has fled."

Russell nodded. "He, like many others, cannot tolerate alcohol. There's a man from San Francisco who does lots of business in Alaska. He has been able to help people like Naka. He helped my father. And me," Russell added. "Now we all join together and help each other not to drink. But Naka must agree to see him. If he does I'll try to get in touch with—"

Julie leaned forward, knowing exactly what Russell was going to say. "Mr. Pollock," she whispered.

"Ee-lie. How did you know?"

The pink room in San Francisco had a new dimension.

January twenty-third was a day of celebration. Beginning about the twenty-first, the top of the world began to glow like an eclipse as the sun circled just below the horizon. The Americans began to smile and the Eskimos put away their winter games of yo-yo and darts. Excitement mounted higher and higher each day.

The morning of the twenty-third Julie and Pearl ran all the way to school, for this was the most beautiful day of the year, the day of the sunrise.

Just before noon Julie and her classmates put on their parkas and mittens and skipped out the school door in awesome silence. The gussak principal was already outside watching the southeastern sky anxiously. His face seemed to say he really did not believe the miracle would happen.

"There it is!" a little boy shouted, as a brilliant light, first green then red, exploded on the horizon. Slowly the life-giving star arose until it was round and burning red in the sky. The Eskimos lifted their arms and turned their palms to the source of all life. Slowly, without any self-consciousness, every gussak raised his arms, too. Not one person snickered at the old Eskimo tradition.

For an hour and a half the sun moved above the

horizon, reminding the Eskimos that the birds and mammals would come back, that the snow would melt, and that the great ice pack that pressed against the shore would begin to retreat and set them free to hunt and fish.

Even on Nunivak there was no such wonderful day, for the sun appeared for a little while every day of the year.

"Bright sun, I missed you so," Julie whispered, and her palms felt vibrant with life.

The little house in Barrow became home as Julie fitted into Nusan's routine, and summer was upon the land before she knew it. Tourists arrived at the hotel every day; the research lab buzzed with activity. Julie stitched, sewed, and occasionally visited Pearl and her family.

Late one evening Nusan came back from the store. "Naka's in jail," she said angrily. "I've got to go get him. Finish these maklaks." She pointed. "A man wants them tomorrow." She hurried out the door and Julie picked up the boots. She was cutting a tiny black square to sew into the intricate band at the top when the door opened and Daniel came in.

She did not look up, for she knew his routine. He would fix himself a TV dinner, open a Coke, and sit on his cot listening to the radio.

"You!" he shouted. She looked up in surprise.

"You. You're my wife."

"Daniel, what's wrong?"

"They're laughing at me. That's what's wrong. They say, 'Ha, ha. Dumb Daniel. He's got a wife and he can't mate her. Ha.'"

He pulled her to her feet and pressed his lips against her mouth. She pulled away.

"We don't have to," she cried.

"They're laughin'," he repeated, and tore her dress from her shoulder. She clutched it and pulled away. Daniel grew angry. He tripped her and followed her to the floor. His lips curled back and his tongue touched her mouth. Crushing her with his body, he twisted her down onto the floor. He was as frightened as she.

The room spun, and grew blurry. Daniel cursed, kicked violently, and lay still. Suddenly he got to his feet and ran out of the house. "Tomorrow, tomorrow I can, I can, can, can, ha ha," he bleated piteously.

Julie rolled to her stomach and vomited. Slowly she got to her feet. "When fear seizes," she whispered, "change what you are doing. You are doing something wrong."

She got her red tights from a box on the shelf, slipped into a warm shirt, and put on her wedding parka and pants. Next she opened a box under the bed and picked out a pair of warm woolen socks. Shoving her feet into her boots she laced and knotted them. Daniel's old pack was under his cot. She got that, then opened a cardboard box by the stove and took out her man's knife and ulo which she had brought from Nunivak. Then she grabbed handfuls of wooden matches and dropped them into a moisture-proof cookie can.

She opened the door and walked calmly through the midnight light to Pearl's house. Stealing quietly past her sleeping brothers and parents, she crept into Pearl's room.

"Pearl, I'm leaving," Julie whispered.

Almost instantly Pearl was awake. "Daniel?"

Julie nodded. "He is dumb. Everyone's teasing him."

Pearl slipped out of bed and together they crept to the kitchen. When the door was closed Pearl sat down.

"Where are you going?"

"I won't tell you. Then they won't bother you. I need food."

Pearl glanced at the shelves above the stove and pushed a box under them; she took down bread, cheeses, dried fruits, meats, and a bag of oats and sugar.

"That's fine," Julie said. "I only need enough for a week or so. But I need to borrow a sleeping skin and ground cloth. I'll mail them back when I get where I'm going."

Pearl slipped out to the shed and came back with the sleeping skin and hide.

"They're a wedding present." She smiled. "You can keep them. No one uses these old-timers."

"Some needles, please," Julie said, "and that'll be all." Stuffing the sleeping skin into her pack, she tied the caribou hide to the bottom and shouldered her load.

"Are you sure you'll be all right?" Pearl asked.

"My father was a great hunter. He taught me much. If Nusan asks where I am, tell her you saw me walking out on the ice. She won't look for me long after that."

With a sob Julie threw her arms around Pearl, then stepped out the door and closed it quietly behind her. She walked to the beach, climbed onto the ice, and looked back. No one was on the street but a single tourist who was photographing the sun in the sky. His back was to her. Julie ducked below the ice rim and made her way along it on hands and feet until she was beyond the village and out of sight of the rooftops of Barrow. Then she stood up and looked at the ocean.

"Julie is gone," she said. "I am Miyax now."

She leaped lightly up the bank and onto the tundra. Her stride opened wider and wider, for she was on her way to San Francisco.

PART III

KAPUGEN,

THE HUNTER

THE MEMORIES VANISHED. The wind screamed *ooooooooeeeeeeeeee.* Miyax touched the lichens on the top of her frost heave.

"Amaroq," she called again, then ran down the slope and climbed to the wolf den. The site was silent and eerie and the puppies' playground was speckled with bleached bones like tombstones in a graveyard.

She picked one up and saw that it was jagged with the marks of little teeth. With some carving, it could be made into the comb she had been wanting. Glancing around, she saw the club-like base of an antler. "A weapon," she said. "I may need it."

A snowy owl floated past, turning his head as he peered down at her curiously.

"I'll see you in San Francisco," she called. He set

his eyes on some distant goal, bowed his wings, and flew southward as silently as the shadow he cast.

The wind twisted a strand of her hair, and as she stood on the wolf hill she felt the presence of the great animals she had lived with: Amaroq, Nails, Silver, Kapu. She wondered if she would ever see them again. The wind gusted; she turned and walked slowly back home, trailing her fingers on the tips of the sedges and thinking about her departure. At the top of her frost heave, she froze in her tracks. Her house was crushed in and her sleeping skins were torn and strewn over the grass. The meat she had laid out on the grass was gone. Her icebox was opened and empty.

"Ayi!" she cried. "My food! My life! I'm dead!"

Running from broken house to dumped cooking pot to icebox, she felt needles of fear move up her spine, spread into her arms, and pierce her whole body. Who had done this? What bestial creature had taken her food? She looked desperately around and saw, crouched in the reeds almost beside her, the angry Jello. His tail was swishing slowly, his ears were forward. She understood his message and stepped back. Then she knew that was wrong; she must not give in. Hand tightening on the antler club, brandishing it, growling, she flung herself upon him and bit the top of his nose. His eyes widened, his ears and body drooped, and his tail went between his legs.

He groveled on his belly and came up to her smiling, head lowered humbly.

Desperate, furious, she lunged at him. Jello rolled to his back and flashed the white hair of surrender. She did not strike; she could not strike a coward.

"Jello!" she cried. "Why? Why did you do it?"

Holding him in abeyance with the antler, she glanced around the ruins of her home and took stock of the damage. All the food in the cellar and on the ground was gone, and her pack was not in sight. Brandishing her weapon, growling at Jello, she backed toward the sod house, kicked back the ruins, and saw the pack under the crushed roof. It was intact. Jello had not found the meat in it. Her mind raced. She had a little food and Kapu had told her that the lemmings were coming back. She could yet make it.

"Gnarlllllllllll," she snapped at Jello and lowered her club. He rolled over, stood up and, tail between his legs, fled into the twilight.

When he was gone she stood for a long time. Finally she picked up her sleeping skin and tore a fiber from the new hide. She got out her needle and, sitting with her legs out straight in the manner of Eskimo women, began to sew.

A lemming ran across a lichen patch. She stopped working and watched the little animal add a mouthful of grass to its round nest. A movement caught her eye and she glanced up to see a least weasel washing his belly on the other side of the knoll. New white fur was splotched across his gold back. He finished his toilet, and when he sat down he disappeared under the reindeer moss. "You are tiny," she said and smiled. Another cycle was beginning. The animals who preyed on the lemmings were also coming back.

Miyax put her needle away, rolled her ground skin into a tight bundle, and tied it to the bottom of

the pack. Then she got her pot and sleeping skin, her ulo and man's knife, the bones and her flowers. She packed them, tied a thong to the new caribou skin so she could drag it behind her, and lined up her pointer stones with a distant frost heave.

"It's time to go," she said and walked away, not looking back.

Many hours later she opened her pack, spread her skins, and took out a strand of smoked meat. A snowshoe hare screamed and, recognizing the cry of death, Miyax picked up her club and ran off to take the rabbit from its killer. Rounding a clump of grass she came upon an enormous wolverine, the king of the Arctic weasel family. Slowly he lifted his head.

The wolverine was built low to the ground, and his powerful front feet were almost as big as a man's hand. Utterly fearless, he looked her in the face.

"Shoooo," she said and jumped at him. He left the rabbit and came toward her. She jumped back and raised her club. He leapt lightly to the side, snarled, and sauntered away. Gingerly she snatched the hare, turned, and fled back to camp. The wolverine's fearlessness sent goose bumps up her spine. Hastily throwing the hare on the caribou skin she was dragging for just such a purpose, she walked on.

A tern floated past. She took out her sinew, held her arm under the bird, and singing aloud strode toward Point Hope.

At sunset the clouds were dark and soft-edged, like bears. They could dump a foot of snow or a sprinkle of snow. She dug a niche in the side of a heave with her man's knife, folded her ground skin into an envelope, and pushed it into the cave. With deft hands she pressed her sleeping skin into the envelope, then undressed. The fur nestled her, and when each toe and finger was warm she peered solemnly out of her den. The sky darkened, the clouds lowered, and the wind blew like a charging buck. In less than a minute she could see no more than the fur around her face. The snow had come.

Buried in her skins like an animal in its lair, Miyax wondered about Amaroq and Kapu. Would they be curled in furry balls, or would they be running joyously through the first storm of the winter, following their noses to game?

When she awoke the sun was out, the sky was clear, and only a feathering of snow covered the tundra—just enough to make it winter. Before she had dressed, however, the crystals had melted—all but a few on the north sides of the slopes, that spoke of things to come.

Miyax pulled a snarl out of her hair with her fingers, then looked around. Someone was watching her. Running to the top of a low hill, she scanned the flatness. A dozen stout caribou, their white necks gleaming in the sunlight, browsed in the distance; but there was nothing else. She laughed at herself, went back to her camp, and ate a piece of smoked meat. Rolling her skins and shouldering her pack, she walked to her caribou skin to pick up the leads. It was empty. Someone had taken her rabbit in the night. A wolverine, she thought; but there was not a footstep to tell which way the thief had gone.

She spun around. Again she felt as if someone were watching her. Again there was no one; there was only a large flock of terns in the sky. Taking a bearing on them with her sinew and adjusting her pack, she gave the skin-drag a yank and walked on.

All day the birds moved overhead. She walked a straight line to the ocean, for the pools had frozen and she could follow her compass without deviating.

When the eerie feeling of being watched persisted, Miyax began to wonder if the vast nothingness was driving her mad, as it did many gussaks. To occupy her mind she sang as she gathered caribou droppings and put them on her drag:

Amaroq, wolf, my friend,
You are my adopted father.
My feet shall run because of you.
My heart shall beat because of you.
And I shall love because of you.

That evening she stopped early, built a bright fire and cooked a stew, adding to it a sweet-leather lichen from the tundra. While the pot simmered and the steam hung above it like a gray spirit, she took out a needle and thread and mended a hole in her old mitten.

The earth trembled. She glanced up to see two of the largest caribou she had ever beheld. She could tell by the massiveness of their antlers that they were males, for those of the females are more slender and shorter. As the two ran side by side, the gleam of their headpieces told her it was the breeding season of the caribou. When the last fuzzy antler-coating of summer is rubbed off and the horns glow and shimmer, the mating season begins—a season of bellowing and short tempers.

Suddenly the lead bull circled and came toward the other. Both lowered their heads and clashed antlers with a clanging crack that sounded like a shot. Neither was hurt. They shook their heads and stepped back, tossed their antlers, and bellowed. Colliding again, they pawed the ground and then peacefully trotted away. Miyax wondered who they were fighting over, for not a female was to be seen. All the bravado and glamour seemed lost on the grass and the sky.

Nevertheless, when she had eaten she picked up her pack, tugged on her cumbersome drag, and moved on; for the thundering animals told her she was along the migration path and she did not want to camp in the middle of a caribou love nest.

Far from the herd, she stopped by a pond and made her bed. She was not sleepy, so she took out the wolf-puppy bone and, holding the ulo between her knees, carved a tooth in the comb.

Orange and purple shadows crept over the land as

the sun went down that night, and Miyax crawled into her sleeping skin noting that the days were growing shorter. She felt restless like the birds and mammals, and in the middle of the night she awakened and peered out at the sky. A star twinkled in the half-lit dome—the first of the year! She smiled, sat up, and hugged her knees.

The guidepost of her ancestors, the North Star, would soon be visible and would point her way when the birds had all gone South.

Softly across the distance a wolf barked, then another. The first bark was one of inquiry, a sort of "Where are you and what are you doing?" The answer was a casual "I am here." The next call, however, was disquieting. The wolf seemed to be saying there was danger in the air. Miyax looked around to see what it might be. Then the wolf changed the subject and shifted to a joyous howl. As the others joined in she recognized the hunt song of her pack. Amaroq's rich tones rose and fell like a violin; then came the flute-like voice of Silver. Nails's voice arose, less strong than Amaroq's, bringing variation to the theme. Cupping her hands behind her ears, she listened intently. Yes, the pups were singing too, sounding very mature and grown up—until Kapu added his laugh-bark.

She listened for Jello to sound forth. He did not. The concert ended abruptly and she heard other sounds in the dimness. A lemming screamed in death, and a flock of migrating eider ducks called out their positions to each other.

Suddenly something moved. She bolted out of bed and grabbed her club. The grass crackled behind her and she spun around. Sedges bobbed to say it was only the wind.

"Ayi!" She was disgusted by her fears. She kicked a stone to change something, since she could not change what she was doing, as Kapugen advised. Feeling better, she slid back in her sleeping skin. "I guess," she said to herself, "that the sun's been up so long I've forgotten the sounds of the night." As she waited for sleep she listened to the polar wind whistle, and the dry grasses whined like the voice of the old bent lady.

"Jello!" she screamed, sitting bolt upright. He was almost beside her, his teeth bared as he growled. Then he picked up her pack and ran. She jumped out of bed and started after him, for her very life was in that pack—food, needles, knives, even her boots. The wind chilled her naked body and she stopped to collect her wits. She must act with wisdom. She must think! Her clothes, where were her clothes? They, too, were gone. No, she remembered they were safe in the bladder bag under the caribou skin.

Quickly she pulled them out and clutched them to her chest, but they were of little comfort. She could go nowhere without boots; nor could she make new ones. Her needles and ulo, the tools of survival, were all in the pack. Shivering, she slid into bed and cried. A tear fell on the grass and froze solid.

"My tombstone."

She lay very still wondering how long it would take for life to leave her.

When she opened her eyes it was daylight and the warm yellow of the land gave her hope. She could eat her caribou skin if she had to. Rolling to her stomach, she smelled something sweet and recognized the scent of wolf urine. It had been dropped at the edge of her bag and was frozen but fresh. Someone had greeted her during the night. It could not have been Jello for the scent did not have the bitter odor of an angry and desolate wolf. Furthermore, it was sparsely given, not the dousing given to hostile objects. It must have been Amaroq. She sniffed again but her nose was not sensitive enough to read the other messages in the urine that meant "all is well." Yet its light and loving scent gave her a sense of security and she smiled at the sun, dressed, and put her mind to inventing boots.

Wrapping the drag around one foot and her sleeping skin around the other, she clomped awkwardly through the grass in a wider and wider circle hoping that Jello, having eaten her meat, would have abandoned the pack. She did not care about the food anymore. Her ulo and needles and matches were more important to find. With them she could make shoes, hunt, and cook. She marveled at how valuable these simple things were, how beautiful and precious. With them she could make a home, a larder, a sled, and clothes. And the cold air was equally precious. With it she could, like her father, freeze leather and sinew into sleds, spears, and harpoons. She would not die here if she could find her ulo and needles.

As she carefully searched the ground she began to think about seal camp. The old Eskimos were scientists too. By using the plants, animals, and temperature, they had changed the harsh Arctic into a home, a feat as incredible as sending rockets to the moon. She smiled. The people at seal camp had not been as outdated and old-fashioned as she had been led to believe. No, on the contrary, they had been wise. They had adjusted to nature instead of to man-made gadgets.

"Ayi!" she gasped. On the side of a ground swell lay Jello, his body torn in bloody shreds, his face contorted. Beside him lay her backpack!

Instantly she knew what had happened; Amaroq had turned on him. Once Kapugen had told her that some wolves had tolerated a lone wolf until the day he stole meat from the pups. With that, the leader gave a signal and his pack turned, struck, and tore the lone wolf to pieces. "There is no room in the wolf society for an animal who cannot contribute," he had said.

Jello had been so cowed he was useless. And now he was dead.

Slowly she opened her pack. The food was gone but her needles, ulo, and boots were tucked in the pockets where she had put them. They were now more wonderful to Miyax than airplanes, ocean liners, and great wide bridges. As she put on her shoes she checked for her man's knife and matches. They were there, too. Life was hers again! Slinging her pack to her shoulders, she placed a stone at Jello's head and turned away.

"You've got to be a super-wolf to live," she said. "Poor Jello was not." She left him to the jaegers and foxes.

"Amaroq, wolf, my friend," she sang as she walked along. "Amaroq, my adopted father."

Reaching Point Hope seemed less important, now that she had come to truly understand the value of her ulo and needles. If she missed the boat she could live well until another year. Her voice rang out happily as she sang and followed the birds and her compass.

ONE EVENING AS SHE LOOKED FOR A CAMPSITE, she felt lonely. To amuse herself she thought of the hill where the white house stood in San Francisco. When it seemed almost real enough to touch, and very beautiful, it vanished abruptly; for the tundra was even more beautiful—a glistening gold, and its shadows were purple and blue. Lemon-yellow clouds sailed a green sky and every wind-tossed sedge was a silver thread.

"Oh," she whispered in awe, and stopped where she was to view the painted earth. As she dropped her pack it clanged out a frozen note, reminding her again that autumn was over. The season had been brief; the flash of bird wings, the thunder of migrating herds. That was all. Now it was winter, and the top of the soil was solid. No blue sea would be lapping the shores of Barrow; instead the Arctic Ocean would be a roaring white cauldron forming ice that would join the land with the polar cap.

She was not afraid. Singing her Amaroq song, she gathered grass and rolled it into cylinders. With deft strokes she chopped a hole in the icebound lake, soaked the grass sticks, and laid them out in the air to freeze. Hours later they had snapped and crackled into ice poles. She cut the drag in two pieces and, pushing the poles under one piece, she erected a tent.

Inside her shelter she cut a long thread of hide and twisted it into a snare. A snowshoe rabbit trail ran along the lake and she set off to find the resting place of the one who had made it. The air was cold and she blew her breath into the wolverine trim of her parka hood. There it hung and warmed her face.

Amaroq called and she called back, not to tell him she needed food as she had once done, but to tell him where she was.

A lemming burst out of the grass near her foot and she spun around to look for its nest and young. Not finding them, she turned back in time to see a fox ripple like a ribbon as he pounced and sped off with the lemming. She grinned, made a mental note to be quicker, and walked carefully along the rabbit trail. Finally she came upon a concave dish in the ground—the roost. In it the rabbit would hide from enemies or rest when not eating. She spread her snare, elevated it with an ice stick, and paid out enough hideline to be out of the sight of the hare.

Flat on her stomach she watched the roost. Minutes turned into hours and the pinks and greens of sunset colored the frozen prairie. Suddenly down the trail, ears back, feet flying, came the rabbit. It made a sharp turn and plopped to a halt in its roost. Miyax yanked and caught its left hind foot. She killed it quickly, and ran back to camp.

The grass rustled and she turned around. "Kapu!"

He was trotting down the rabbit trail with a leg of caribou in his mouth. His head bucked as he fought the awkward weight of the meat.

"Kapu!" she repeated. He wagged his tail, took a

better grip on his burden, and trotted up to her. He dropped it at her feet. With a skip and a leap she told him in wolf language how glad she was to see him. He replied by dashing around in a small circle, then in three big circles. Finally he stopped and wagged his tail.

"Is this for me?" she asked pointing to the leg. He spanked the ground with his front paw, leaped to the side, and spanked the ground again. With a grin she reached in her pocket, found a strip of caribou hide, and thrust it at him. Kapu snatched it, and with one pull not only wrested it from her, but sent her sprawling on her back. Tail held straight out, he streaked like a rocket across the lichens, turned, and came back with the hide. He shook it in front of her, daring her to take it away.

"You're much much too strong for me now, Kapu," she said and slowly got to her feet. "I can't play with you anymore." Shaking the hide, he danced, barked, and then ran over the tundra until he was but a speck in the distance.

Miyax laughed, and dragged the caribou leg back to her tent. She cut it up and built a small fire. She skinned the rabbit, saving the fur to line her new mitten.

As the stew cooked, the crackling cold inspired her to dance. She stepped forward on the vast stage at the top of the world and bowed to her immense audience.

Curving her arms out, bending her knees, she hopped on one foot and beat time with the other. Then she glided and shifted her weight, gracefully executing a combination of steps which the bent woman had danced long ago at seal camp. When she came to the refrain, however, she did not do the dance about evil spirits, but improvised—as Eskimos do at this point. She told the story of a young wolf who had brought the lost girl a shank of meat, and ended the performance with a Kapu-like caper. She spun laughing to a stop. She was warm. Her blood tingled.

"Ee-lie," she thought. "The old Eskimo customs are not so foolish—they have purpose. I'm as warm as the center of a lemming's nest."

As the sky darkened, Kapu came back. He barked softly.

"I know what you want," she called, holding out a large piece of cooked meat. Kapu took it so gently from her fingers that she could not even feel his teeth. As she watched him run off into the night, her eyes lifted to the sky. There, twinkling in the distance, was the North Star, the permanent light that had guided the Eskimos for thousands of years. She sang:

Bright star, still star,
Lead me to the sea . . .

Hastily, she cut the remaining half of her caribou skin into four strips and a circle. Cracking open the ice on the lake, she weighted the pieces with stones and sent them to the bottom.

Around midnight she awoke to hear her wolves in the distance talking softly among themselves—probably paying tribute to Amaroq as they moved along the trail, she thought. Peering out of her tent she saw that the star was gone. A cold flake struck her nose, melted, fell into her fur, and froze. The wind blared, the wolves called joyously, and Miyax snuggled deep in her furs. Let it snow. Kapu had known it was coming and had brought food for her.

She slept until daybreak, saw that it was still snowing, and dozed, off and on, through the white, wild day as the weasels and foxes did. That night the sky cleared, and at dawn she crawled out of her skins. The tundra was white with the snow that would lock up the Arctic till June. The cold had deepened.

After breakfast she cracked open the lake ice again, pulled out the water-soaked circle and laid it out on the ground. Using her man's knife, she turned up the edges, tied them in place, and let the cup freeze in the air. As it hardened she stepped into the bottom, tramped it into a bowl, and then cut two holes in one side. Through these she ran leather thongs and tied them together.

Next she took two strips of skin from the water

and held them in place while they froze to the bottom of the bowl, in the shape of flat rockers. Then she stood up. Her sled was done.

Working quickly, for she had only a few hours of daylight, she formed tear-shaped hoops out of the last two strips. These she laid out to freeze. When they were solid she webbed them with hide, made loops for her toes, and put on her snowshoes. They crackled and snapped, but kept her up on the drifts. Now she could travel the top of the snow.

She cut the rest of the caribou leg into bite-size chunks and stored them in her sled. Then, adjusting her mittens in the darkness, she took a bearing on the North Star and started off.

Her icy sled jingled over the wind-swept lakes and she sang as she traveled. The stars grew brighter as the hours passed and the tundra began to glow, for the snow reflected each twinkle a billion times over, turning the night to silver. By this light she could see the footsteps of the wolves. She followed them, for they were going her way.

Just before sunrise the wolf prints grew closer together. They were slowing down for the sleep. She felt their presence everywhere, but could not see them. Running out on a lake, she called. Shadows flickered on the top of a frost heave. There they were! She quickened her stride. She would camp with them and do the dance of the wolf-pup-feeding-the-lost-girl for Kapu. He would surely run in circles when he saw it.

The shadows flattened as she walked, and by the time she reached the other shore they had turned into sky and vanished. There were no footsteps in the snow to say her pack had been there and she knew the Arctic dawn had tricked her eyes. "Frost spirits," she said, as she pitched her tent by the lake and crawled into bed.

By the yellow-green light of the low noon sun Miyax could see that she had camped on the edge of the wintering grounds of the caribou. Their many gleaming antlers formed a forest on the horizon. Such a herd would certainly attract her pack. She crawled out of bed and saw that she had pitched her tent in a tiny forest about three inches high. Her heart pounded excitedly, for she had not seen one of these willow groves since Nunivak. She was making progress, for they grew, not near Barrow, but in slightly warmer and wetter lands near the coast. She smelled the air in the hopes that it bore the salty odor of the ocean, but it smelled only of the cold.

The dawn cracked and hummed and the snow was so fine that it floated above the ground when a breeze stirred. Not a bird passed overhead. The buntings, longspurs, and terns were gone from the top of the world.

A willow ptarmigan, the chicken of the tundra, clucked behind her and whistled softly as it hunted seeds. The Arctic Circle had been returned to its permanent bird resident, the hardy ptarmigan. The millions of voices of summer had died down to one plaintive note.

Aha, ahahahahahaha! Miyax sat up, wondering what that was. Creeping halfway out of her bag, she peered into the sky to see a great brown bird maneuver its wings and speed west.

"A skua!" She was closer to the ocean than she thought, for the skua is a bird of the coastal waters of the Arctic. As her eyes followed it, they came to rest on an oil drum, the signpost of American civilization in the North. How excited she would have been to see this a month ago; now she was not so sure. She had her ulo and needles, her sled and her tent, and the world of her ancestors. And she liked the simplicity of that world. It was easy to understand. Out here she understood how she fitted into the scheme of the moon and stars and the constant rise and fall of life on the earth. Even the snow was part of her, she melted it and drank it.

Amaroq barked. He sounded as if he was no more than a quarter of a mile away.

"*Ow, ooo,*" she called. Nails answered, and then the whole pack howled briefly.

"I'm over here!" she shouted joyously, jumping up

and down. "Here by the lake." She paused. "You know that. You know everything about me all the time."

The wind began to rise as the sun started back to the horizon. The lake responded with a boom that sounded like a pistol shot. The freeze was deepening. Miyax lit a fire and put on her pot. A warm stew would taste good and the smoke and flames would make the tundra home.

Presently Amaroq barked forcefully, and the pack answered. Then the royal voice sounded from another position, and Silver checked in from across the lake. Nails gave a warning snarl and the pups whispered in "woofs." Miyax shaded her eyes; her wolves were barking from points around a huge circle and she was in the middle. This was strange—they almost always stayed together. Suddenly Amaroq barked ferociously, his voice angry and authoritative. Silver yelped, then Nails and Kapu. They had something at bay.

She stepped onto the lake and skipped toward them. Halfway across she saw a dark head rise above the hill, and a beast with a head as large as the moon rose to its hind feet, massive paws swinging.

"Grizzly!" she gasped and stopped stone-still, as the huge animal rushed onto the ice. Amaroq and Nails leapt at its face and sprang away before the bear could strike. They were heading it off, trying to prevent it from crossing. The bear snarled, lunged forward, and galloped toward Miyax.

She ran toward her tent. The wind was in her face and she realized she was upwind of the bear, her scent blowing right to him. She darted off in another direction, for bears have poor eyesight and cannot track if they cannot smell. Slipping and sliding, she reached the south bank as the grizzly staggered forward, then crumpled to its knees and sat down. She wondered why he was not in hibernation. The wolves had been sleeping all day—they could not have wakened the bear. She sniffed the air to try to smell the cause, but only odorless ice crystals stung her nose.

The pack kept harassing the sleepy beast, barking and snarling, but with no intention of killing it. They were simply trying to drive it away—away from her, she realized.

Slowly the bear got to its feet and permitted itself to be herded up the lake bank and back to where it had come from. Reluctantly, blindly, it staggered before the wolves. Occasionally it stood up like a giant, but mostly it roared in the agony of sleepiness.

Yapping, barking, darting, the wolves drove the grizzly far out on the tundra. Finally they veered away and, breaking into a joyous gallop, dashed over the snow and out of sight. Their duty done, they were running—not to hunt, not to kill—but simply for fun.

Miyax was trembling. She had not realized the size and ferocity of the dark bear of the North, who is called "grizzly" inland, and "brown bear" along the coasts—*Ursus arctos.* Large ones, like the grizzly her wolves had driven away, weighed over a thousand pounds and stood nine feet tall when they reared. Miyax wiped a bead of perspiration from her forehead. Had he come upon her tent, with one curious sweep of his paw he would have snuffed out her life while she slept.

"Amaroq, Nails, Kapu," she called. "I thank you. I thank you."

As she packed to travel on, she thought about her escorts. Wolves did not like civilization. Where they had once dwelled all over North America they now lived in remote parts of Canada, in only two of the lower forty-eight states, and in the wilderness of Alaska. Even the roadless North Slope had fewer wolves than it did before the gussaks erected their military bases and brought airplanes, snowmobiles, electricity, and jeeps to the Arctic.

As she thought about the gussaks she suddenly knew why the brown bear was awake. The Americans' hunting season had begun! Her wolves were in danger! The gussaks were paid to shoot them. A man who brought in the left ear of a wolf to the warden was rewarded with a bounty of fifty dollars. The bounty was evil to the old men at seal camp, for it encouraged killing for money, rather than need.

Kapugen considered the bounty the gussaks' way of deciding that the amaroqs could not live on this earth anymore. "And no men have that right," he would say. "When the wolves are gone there will be too many caribou grazing the grass and the lemmings will starve. Without the lemmings the foxes and birds and weasels will die. Their passing will end smaller lives upon which even man depends, whether he knows it or not, and the top of the world will pass into silence."

Miyax was worried. The oil drum she had seen when the skua flew over marked the beginning of civilization and the end of the wilderness. She must warn her pack of the danger ahead. She had learned to say many things to them; but now, the most important of all, the ear-twist or bark that would turn them back, she did not know.

How, she thought, do I shout "Go away! Go far, far away!" She sang:

Go away, royal wolf,
Go away, do not follow.
I'm a gun at your head,
When I pass the oil drum.

Threads of clouds spun up from the earth and trailed across the tundra. They marked the beginning of a white-out. Miyax changed her plans to travel that night, crept into her shelter, and watched the air turn white as the snow arose from the ground and hung all around her. She closed her tent flap and took out her pot. In it she put a piece of fat from the bladder-bag and a scrap of sinew. She lit the sinew and a flame illuminated her tiny home. She took out the comb.

As she carved she saw that it was not a comb at all, but Amaroq. The teeth were his legs, the handle his head. He was waiting to be released from the bone. Surprised to see him, she carved carefully for hours and finally she let him out. His neck was arched, his head and tail were lifted. Even his ears had a message. "I love you," they said.

A bird called faintly in the darkness. Miyax wondered what kind it was and what it was doing so far north at this date. Too sleepy to think, she unlaced her boots, undressed, and folded her clothes. The bird called from the edge of her sleeping skin. Holding her candle above her head, she crept toward the door and peered into the bright eyes of a golden plover. He was young, for he wore the splotched plumage of the juvenile and still had a trace of baby-yellow around his beak. He slumped against her skins.

Gently she slipped her hand under his feet, picked him up, and brought him close to her. His black and gold feathers gleamed in the sputtering light. She had never beheld a plover so closely and now understood why Kapugen had called them "the spirit of the birds." The plover's golden eye and red noseband made it look like one of the dancers in the Bladder Feast.

"You are lost," she said. "You should be far from here. Perhaps in Labrador. Perhaps even in your winter home on the plains of Argentina. And so you are dying. You need insects and meat. But I'm so glad you're here." Then she added, "I shall call you Tornait, the bird spirit."

She eased the bird inside her warm sleeping skin, cut off a small piece of caribou meat, and held it out. Tornait ate ravenously, then rested. She fed him once more, and then he tucked his head in his back feathers and went to sleep.

The following night the white-out was still so dense she could not see the ground when she crept out for snow to melt and drink.

"I won't go on tonight," she said to Tornait when she came inside. "But I do not care. I have food, light, furs, fire, and a pretty companion." That evening she polished her carving of Amaroq and talked to Tornait. The plover was incredibly tame, perhaps because he lived in the most barren parts of the world where there were no people, perhaps because he was lonely. Tornait ran over her skins, flitted to her head and shoulders, and sang when she sang.

On the next afternoon the white-out was but a frosty mist. Miyax was cooking dinner when Tornait drew his feathers to his body and stood up in alarm. She listened for a long time before she heard the snow scream as footsteps pressed it. Scrambling to the door, she saw Kapu in the mist, frost on his whiskers.

"Hi!" she called. He did not turn around for he was looking at something in the distance. Presently Amaroq swept into view and stopped beside him.

"Amaroq!" she shouted. "Amaroq, how are you?" Tossing her head in wolf happiness, she crawled out of her tent on all fours and nudged him under the chin. He arched his neck grandly. Then, with a glance at Kapu, he ran out on the lake. The young wolf followed, and, laughing joyously, Miyax crawled after them both. She had not gone far before Amaroq stopped and glared at her. She stayed where she was. The regal pair leaped away, snow billowing up from their strides like smoke.

Getting to her knees she looked for Silver, Nails, and the other pups, but they did not follow the pair. Miyax rocked back on her heels. Could it be that the leader of the pack was teaching the leader of the pups? She nodded slowly as she comprehended. Of course. To be a leader required not only fearlessness and intelligence, but experience and schooling. The head of a wolf pack needed to be trained, and who better to do this than Amaroq?

"And I know what you'll teach," she called out. "You'll teach him which animal to harvest. You'll teach him to make all decisions. You'll teach him how to close in on a caribou, and where to bed the wolf pack down; and you'll teach him to love and protect."

The white-out vanished, the stars blazed out, and San Francisco called to Miyax. It was time to move on. Kapu was now in school.

"But how shall I tell them not to follow me anymore?" she asked Tornait as she crawled back into her tent.

"Of course!" she gasped. She had been told by Amaroq himself how to say "stay back" when he had wanted Kapu alone. He had walked forward, turned around, and glared into her eyes. She had stopped in her tracks and gone home. Eagerly she practiced. She ran forward, looked over her shoulder, and glared.

"Stay, Amaroq. Stay where you are!"

Humming to herself she took down her tent, rolled it into a bundle, and threw it on the new sled. Then she stuffed her pack and tucked Tornait in the hood of her parka. Sticking her toes in her snowshoes, she took a bearing on the constant star. The snow squeaked under her feet, and for the first time she felt the dry bite of the cold right through her parka and boots. To her this meant the temperature was zero, the point every year when she began to feel chilly. Dancing and swinging her arms to get warm, she picked up the thongs of her sled and walked toward the sea. The sled glided lightly behind her.

She did not hear the airplane; she saw it. The low sun of noon struck its aluminum body and it sparkled like a star in the sky. It was a small plane, the type bush pilots use to carry people over the roadless tundra and across the rugged mountains of Alaska where cars cannot go. Presently its sound reached her ears and the throb of the engines reminded her that this was the beginning of the season when bush pilots took the gussaks out to hunt. The craft tipped its wings and zigzagged across the sky. When it continued to zag she realized the pilot was following a meandering river where game wintered. A river, she thought; rivers led to the sea. I am nearing the end of my journey; Point Hope might be but one sleep away. She quickened her pace.

The airplane banked, turned, and came toward her. It seemed as big as an eagle as it skimmed low over the ground. Bright flashes of fire burst from its side.

"They *are* hunting," she said to Tornait. "Let's get in the oil drum. I look like a bear in these clothes."

Just before she reached the drum she crossed the footsteps of Amaroq and Kapu. They had passed this way only moments ago, for the snow crystals their warm feet had melted were not yet frozen again. The plane continued to come toward her. Apparently she had been seen. She kicked snow over her sled and pack and crawled to the front of the barrel. It was sealed. She could not get inside. Scurrying to the other end she found that it, too, was closed. Desperately she threw herself under the curve of the drum and lay still. Much of her was still exposed. Flailing her hands and feet, she stirred up the light snow. It arose like a cloud and settled upon her as the plane soared above.

Shots rang out. The plane roared away and Miyax opened her eyes. She was still alive and the air hunters were over the river. The plane banked and flew back, this time very low. Tornait struggled.

"Be still," she said. The gunfire snapped again and, eyes wide open, she saw that it was not aimed at her.

"Amaroq!" Horrified, she watched him leap into the air as a splatter of shots burst beside him. Digging in his claws, he veered to the right and left as Kapu ran to join him. Teeth bared, angrily growling, Amaroq told him to go. Kapu sped off. The plane hesitated, then pursued Amaroq.

Shots hit the snow in front of him. He reared and turned.

"Amaroq!" she screamed. "Here! Come here!"

The plane swerved, dove, and skimmed about thirty feet above the ground. Its guns blasted. Amaroq stumbled, pressed back his ears, and galloped across the tundra like a shooting star. Then he reared, and dropped on the snow.

He was dead.

"For a bounty," she screamed. "For money, the magnificent Amaroq is dead!" Her throat constricted with grief, and sobs choked her.

The plane banked and came back. Kapu was running to Amaroq. His ears were pressed to his head and his legs moved so swiftly they were a blur. Bullets showered the snow around him. He leaped, dodged, and headed for the oil drum. His wide eyes and open mouth told Miyax he was afraid for the first time in his life. Blindly he ran, and as he came by she reached out and tripped him. He sprawled across the snow and lay still. While the plane coasted off to make another turn, she covered Kapu with flakes.

The snow turned red with blood from his shoulder. Miyax rolled under the barrel.

The air exploded and she stared up into the belly of the plane. Bolts, doors, wheels, red, white, silver, and black, the plane flashed before her eyes. In that instant she saw great cities, bridges, radios, school books. She saw the pink room, long highways, TV sets, telephones, and electric lights. Black exhaust enveloped her, and civilization became this monster that snarled across the sky.

The plane shrank before her eyes, then turned and grew big again. Tornait flew to the top of the barrel, screaming his alarm cry and beating his wings.

Kapu tried to get up.

"Don't move," Miyax whispered. "They're coming for Amaroq." Knowing Kapu did not understand, she reached out and softly stroked him, singing: "Lie still. Lie still." She watched him slump back in the snow without a sound.

The plane returned at so low a level she could see the men in the cockpit, their coat collars pulled up around their necks, their crash helmets and goggles gleaming. They were laughing and watching the ground. Desperately Miyax thought about Silver, Nails, and the pups. Where were they? They must be clear targets on the white snow. Maybe not—they were light in color, not black.

Suddenly the engine accelerated, the wing flaps pressed down, and the craft climbed, banked, and sailed down the river like a migrating bird. It did not turn around.

Miyax buried her fingers in Kapu's fur. "They did not even stop to get him!" she cried. "They did not even kill him for money. I don't understand. I don't understand. *Ta vun ga vun ga,*" she cried. *"Pisupa gasu punga."* She spoke of her sadness in Eskimo, for she could not recall any English.

Kapu's blood spread like fish ripples on the snow. She wriggled to him and clamped her thumb on the vein that was gushing. She held the pressure—a minute, an hour—she did not know how long. Then Tornait called hungrily. Cautiously she lifted her hand. The bleeding had stopped.

"Ta gasu," she said to Kapu. She brushed the snow off her sled and took out her poles. She set up her tent beside the barrel, banked the snow around the bottom to seal out the wind, and spread her ground cloth

under it. When she tried to push Kapu into the shelter she found him too heavy. He lifted his head, then dropped it wearily. Miyax decided to build the tent around him. She took everything down and started all over again.

This time she eased the ground skin under him inch by inch until he lay on the fur. Then she kicked the oil drum to free it from the ice, rolled it close to him, and erected her tent against it. She sealed the gaps with snow.

The drum was old, for it had different markings than those around Barrow, but like them, it was barely rusted. The frigid winters and the dry desert-like conditions of the tundra prevent metals, papers, garbage, and refuse from deteriorating as it does in warmer zones. In the Arctic, all artifacts are preserved for ages. Even throwing them into the oceans does not work a change, for the water freezes around them, and in the ice floes they come back on the shores. The summer sun unveils them again.

Miyax melted snow, cut off meat for Tornait, and fed him. He flew down from the barrel and ran into the tent. Hopping onto her furry sleeping skin, he puffed his feathers, stood on one foot, and went to sleep.

With the stew bubbling, Kapu resting, and Tornait asleep, Miyax dared to think of Amaroq. She would go and bid him good-bye. She tried to get up, but she could not move. Grief held her in a vise-like clamp.

About an hour later Kapu lifted his head, rolled his eyes around the cozy interior of the tent, and accepted chunks of stew. Miyax petted his head and told him in Eskimo to lie still while she looked at his wound. It was long and deep and she knew it must be sewn together.

Taking a piece of sinew from the ground skin, she threaded it into her needle and pierced the soft flesh. Kapu growled.

"Xo lur pajau, sexo," she sang soothingly. *"Lupir*

pajau se suri vanga pangmane majo riva pangmane." Monotonously repeating over and over the healing song of the old bent lady, she hypnotized Kapu as she closed the wound. The perspiration was running down her cheeks when she was done, but she was

able to tell him that he would get well and return to lead their pack.

The sun set in a navy blue sky, and the stars sparkled on and off as they spoke of their vast distances from the earth. About midnight the inside of the tent began to glow green and Kapu's eyes shone like emeralds. Miyax peered out the flap door. Fountains of green fire rose from the earth and shot to the top of the black velvet sky. Red and white lights sprayed out of the green. The northern lights were dancing. The lakes boomed, and Nails howled mournfully beyond the tent.

Miyax howled back to tell him where she was. Then Silver barked and the pups called, too. Each voice sounded closer than the last; the pack was coming toward the oil drum as they searched for Amaroq and Kapu.

Miyax stepped into the light of the aurora. It was time to bid Amaroq farewell. She tried to go forward but her feet would not move. Grief still held them useless. Clutching her left knee in both hands, she lifted her foot and put it down; then she lifted the other and put it down, slowly making her way across the turquoise snow.

Amaroq lay where he had fallen, his fur shining in the strange magnetic light.

"Amaroq . . ." She took her carving from her pocket, and got down on her knees. Singing softly in Eskimo, she told him she had no bladder for his spirit to dwell in, but that she had his totem. She asked him to enter the totem and be with her forever.

For a long time she held the carving over his body. Presently, the pain in her breast grew lighter and she knew the wolf was with her.

The stars had slipped down the sky when at last she stood up and walked swiftly back to Kapu.

All night Miyax sat beside him and listened to Silver, Nails, and the pups.

"*Ow ow ow ow owwwwwww,*" they cried in a tone she had never heard before, and she knew they were crying for Amaroq.

THE SUN WENT DOWN ON NOVEMBER TENTH not to arise again for sixty-six days. In the darkness Kapu got up to exercise by walking out on the tundra and back. Tornait was not so comfortable in the continuous night. He slept in Miyax's furs most of the time, waiting for the dawn. When it did not come, hunger awoke him; he ran from his roost to Miyax, pecked on her boot, and fluttered his wings for food. Then the darkness would say to him "sleep," and he would run back to his roost, pull his foot into his breast feathers, and close his eyes.

For her part, Miyax found the clear nights quite

manageable. She could hunt caribou chips by star and moonlight, cook outside, and even sew. When the sky was overcast, however, the tundra was black and she would stay inside, light her candle, and talk to Kapu and Tornait.

At these times she began to shape the antler-weapon into a more elaborate design. As she worked she saw five puppies in it. Carefully she carved out their ears and toes until they were running in single file, Kapu in the lead. She grew tired, took out Amaroq's totem, and thought about his life and brave spirit.

"The pink room is red with your blood," she said. "I cannot go there. But where can I go? Not back to Barrow and Daniel. Not back to Nunivak and Martha . . . and you cannot take care of me anymore."

Snowstorms came and went; the wind blew constantly. One starry night Miyax heard a whimper and opened the tent flap to see Silver at the door. She had a large hare in her mouth, and although Miyax was glad for food, she was distressed to realize that her pack was not eating well. Disorganized without Amaroq, they were forced to hunt rabbits and small game. These would not sustain them. Miyax reached out, petted Silver on the shoulder, and felt her bony back. Without a leader the pack would not live through the winter.

Silver nudged her hand, Miyax opened the flap wider, and the beautiful wolf came in. She dropped the rabbit and walked over to Kapu. He got to his feet, and arching his neck, lifted his head above hers. She greeted him, wagging her tail excitedly. Then she tried to bite the top of his nose to tell him she was the leader, but Kapu drew up tall. Gently he took her nose in his mouth. She bit him under the chin, hailing the new chief.

Kapu pushed past her and slipped out of the tent. Silver followed the prince of the wolves.

In the darkness he sang of his leadership, but, too weak to run, turned wearily back to the tent.

A new grandeur attended his movements as he came through the door and Miyax squeezed his chin. He lay down and watched her skin the rabbit.

She gave him the flesh and went out to hunt lemmings for herself. Since the end of summer the little rodents had doubled, tripled, even quadrupled their numbers. By following their runways she found seven nests and caught eighty furred young. She skinned and cooked them, and found them delicious. The next night Silver brought her a part of a moose. She had not killed it, for it was old and frozen. Miyax knew she had been down to the river. No moose wandered the tundra.

Several sleeps later Kapu ran over the snow without stumbling and Miyax decided it was time to move to the river. Game would be more abundant in the dwarf willows that bordered the waterways. There rabbits and ptarmigan gathered to eat seeds out of the wind, and moose wintered on the twigs of the willows. Perhaps Silver and Nails would find a sick yearling and with help from the pups be able to kill it. Life would be kinder there.

She packed, put Tornait in her parka hood and, picking up her sled ropes, set off once more. Kapu limped as he walked beside her, but less and less as they plodded along. The exercise seemed to help him and by the end of the night he was running fifty steps to her one. Often he took her hand and mouthed it affectionately.

The river would not be hard to find, for she had marked its position by the faithful North Star and so, hours later, as the constellation of the hunter moved to the other side of her, she reached the brushy bank. In the distance loomed the massive wall of the Brooks Range, the massive mountains that rimmed the North Slope on the south. Her journey was coming to an end. The rivers that flow out of the Brooks Range are close to the sea.

After making camp Miyax and Kapu went out to snare ptarmigan and rabbits. Silver called from a short distance away and they answered her.

Hours later when Miyax crawled into her sleeping skin the wolves were so near that she could hear the pups scratching the snow as they made their beds.

As she had anticipated, the hunting was excellent, and upon checking her snares the next day she found three rabbits and two ptarmigan. For several days she was busy skinning and cooking.

One night while Miyax sewed a new boot, Kapu licked her ear and trotted off. When he did not come back by the time the moon had swung all the way around her tent and was back again, a whole day, she went out to look for him. The snow glowed blue and green and the constellations glittered, not only in the sky, but on the ice in the river and on the snow on the bushes and trees. There was, however, no sign of Kapu. She was about to go to bed when the horizon quivered and she saw her pack running the bank. Kapu was in the lead. She crawled into her tent and awakened Tornait.

"Kapu's leading the hunt. All's well," she said. "And now we must leave them."

At dawn she hastily took down her tent, hoisted her pack to her back, and stepped onto the frozen river where walking was easier. Many miles along her way she came upon wolverine tracks and followed them up to a den. There, as she suspected, lay several rabbits and ptarmigan. She loaded them on her sled and returned to the river, listening to Tornait peep soft plover songs in the warmth of her parka hood.

She kissed his beak gently. They were helping each other. She kept him warm and fed him and he radiated heat in her hood. But more important, his whisperings kept her from being totally and hopelessly lonely without Kapu and her wolf pack.

With every mile she traveled now, the oil drums became more and more numerous and the tracks of the wolverine more and more scarce. Like the wolf, the wolverine is an animal of the wilderness, and when Miyax saw no more tracks she knew she was approaching man. One night she counted fifty drums on a spit in the river, and there she made camp. She must stop and think about what she wanted to do.

When she thought of San Francisco, she thought about the airplane and the fire and blood and the flashes and death. When she took out her needle and sewed, she thought about peace and Amaroq.

She knew what she had to do. Live like an Eskimo—hunt and carve and be with Tornait.

The next day she took out her man's knife and cut blocks of snow. These she stacked and shaped into a house that was generously large. If she was going to live as the Eskimos once lived, she needed a home, not just a camp.

When her ice house was completed and her skins were spread over the floor, she sat down and took out the totem of Amaroq. Her fingers had rubbed him to a soft glow in her pocket and he looked rich and regal. Placing him over her door, she blew him a kiss, and as she did so, happiness welled up in her. She knew he was taking care of her spirit.

Time passed, fountains of the magnetic northern lights came and went, and the moon waxed and waned many times. Miyax found her life very satisfying. She became an expert at catching small game and she took great pleasure in carving. When she had finished the carving of the puppies, she found a stone by the river and began chipping it into an owl. Always she listened for her pack, but they did not call. She was both glad and miserable.

Miyax was not without things to do. When she was not hunting, or carving, she danced, sewed, chopped wood or made candles. Sometimes she tried to spell Eskimo words with the English alphabet. Such beautiful words must be preserved forever.

One night she began a tiny coat of ptarmigan feathers for Tornait. He had been shivering lately, even in her parka hood, and she was concerned about him. She stitched the plumes to a paper-thin rabbit hide and fashioned a bird-like coat.

On the moonrise when the coat was finished and she was trying to slip it on Tornait, she heard in the distance the crackle of feet on the ice. The sound grew louder and she poked her head into the night to see a man on the river running beside his sled and team of dogs. Her heart leaped—an Eskimo hunter, one of her own pack, truly. Rushing onto the river ice she waited until the sled drew close.

"Ayi!" she called.

"Ayi!" a voice answered, and within minutes the hunter pulled the sled up beside her and greeted her warmly. Nestled in the furs was the man's woman and child. Their eyes glistened softly in the moonlight.

Miyax's voice was hoarse from disuse, but she managed to greet them happily in Eskimo and invite them into her house for a sleep. The woman was glad to stop, she told Miyax in the Yupik dialect, as she climbed from the sled. They had not rested since they had left Kangik, a town on Kuk Bay at the mouth of the Avalik River, the river they were on.

At last Miyax knew where she was. Kangik was inland from Wainwright and still many sleeps from Point Barrow. But she no longer cared.

"I'm Roland," the man said in English as he unloaded his sleeping skins on the floor of the igloo and spread them out. "Are you alone?"

Miyax smiled at him as if she did not understand and put a twisted spruce log on the fire. When it blazed and man and woman were warming their backs, Roland asked her again, but this time in Yupik, her own beautiful tongue. She answered that she was.

"I'm Alice," the pretty mother said. Miyax gestured hopelessly. "Uma," the woman said, pointing to herself. "Atik," she said, pointing to the man and, lifting the baby above her head, called him Sorqaq. Miyax found the names so nice that, as she took her cooking pot from the fire to offer her guests hot ptarmigan, she hummed and sang. Then she went to her sleeping skin, picked up Tornait, and held him before Sorqaq, who was now on his mother's back in her kuspuck. He peeked over her shoulder, laughed at the bird, kicked, and disappeared. In his excitement he had lost his knee grip and had dropped to his mother's belt. Miyax laughed aloud. Uma giggled and gave him a boost; his round face reappeared and he reached for the bird.

Miyax suddenly wanted to talk. Speaking rapidly in Yupik, she told her guests about the river, the game, the fuel, and the stars—but not about the wolves or her past. They listened and smiled.

When dinner was over Atik talked slowly and softly, and Miyax learned that Kangik was an Eskimo village with an airport and a mission school. A generator had been built, and electricity lighted the houses in winter. A few men even owned snowmobiles there. Atik was proud of his town.

Before going to bed he went out to feed the dogs. Then Uma talked. She said they were headed for the mountains to hunt caribou. When Atik returned, Miyax told him he did not need to go to the mountains—that a large herd was yarded not far up the river. She drew a map on the floor and showed him where the wintering grounds of the caribou lay. He was happy to learn this, he said, for the Brooks Range was treacherous in winter; whole mountainsides avalanched, and storms brewed up in mere minutes.

Uma nursed the baby, tucked him into their furs, and softly sang him to sleep as the fire began to die down. Presently her head nodded, and she slipped into bed, where Atik joined her.

Miyax alone was awake, visions of Kangik filling her head. She would go there and be useful. Perhaps she would teach children how to snare rabbits, make parkas, and carve; or she might live with some family that needed her help. She might even work in the store. In Kangik she would live as her ancestors had, in rhythm with the animals and the climate. She would stay far away from San Francisco where men were taught to kill without reason. She did not fall asleep for hours.

Tornait awoke first and called softly. Miyax dressed, cut off a piece of meat, and held it out to him. He snatched the food and swallowed it noisily. That awoke the baby and the baby awoke Uma, who reached out, took him to her breast, and rocked him as she lay in the furry warmth of her skins. It was almost zero in the house and she did not hurry to get up.

Atik awoke, yawned, and roared, "I'm hungry." Uma laughed and Miyax put the pot on the fire. Atik dressed, went out to his sled, and brought back bacon, bread, beans, and butter. Miyax had forgotten there were such good things and her mouth fairly watered as she smelled them cooking. At first she refused the food when Uma offered it, but seeing how disappointed she was she accepted the bacon and sucked on it quietly, remembering with pain the tastes of Barrow.

After breakfast Atik went out to harness the dogs, Miyax cleaned up, and Uma played with her baby. As she tossed him she chatted happily about her love for Atik and how excited she had been when he decided to take her on the hunt. Most Eskimo wives were left home these days; with the advent of gussak frozen foods, cooks were no longer needed for the hunt. And the women never tanned hides anymore; all skins for the tourist trade must go to Seattle to be tanned correctly for the temperate climates where most were shipped.

Uma rambled on. Atik had been raised in Anchorage and knew very little about hunting, for his father had been a mechanic. But he had died, and Atik was sent to live with his grandfather in Kangik. He had become enamored of hunting and fishing and became so skilled that when his grandfather died he was adopted by the greatest of all living Eskimo hunters.

"Kapugen taught Atik where the seals live and how to smell a caribou trail."

Miyax stopped cleaning her pot. Her blood raced hot, then cold. Turning slowly around she stared at Uma.

"Where was this Kapugen born?" she asked in Eskimo.

"He has never said. He paddled up the river one day, beached his kayak, and built a house where he landed. All I know is that he came out of the Bering Sea. But he was wealthy in the Eskimo sense—intelligent, fearless, full of love—and he soon became a leader of Kangik."

Miyax did not take her eyes off Uma's lips as they formed soft words of Kapugen. "*U i ya* Kangik?" she asked.

"Yes, but not in the center of town where the rich men live. Although Kapugen is also rich, he lives in a simple green house on the river bank. It is upstream, beside the wilderness, where the people he loves feel free to visit."

Trembling with eagerness, Miyax asked Uma to tell her more about Kapugen, and Uma, spilling over with enthusiasm, told how the town and its people had grown poor and hungry several years ago. The walrus had all but vanished from the coast; the gray whales were rare, and the seals were few and far between. The Bureau of Indian Affairs put most everyone on pensions, and so they drank and forgot all they knew. Then Kapugen arrived. He was full of pride and held his head high. He went out into the wilderness and came back with musk-oxen. These he bred and raised. The men helped him; the women made the fur into thread and then into mittens and beautiful sweaters and scarves. These were sold to the gussaks who paid high prices for them, and within a few years the people of Kangik became independent and prosperous.

"But there is still a need for caribou and wolverine furs for clothing and trim," she said, "so Kapugen and Atik go hunting every winter to supply the town."

"Kapugen did not come this year," she went on. "He let me come instead." She smiled, slipped her baby into her kuspuck, tightened her belt, and stood up. "Kapugen is wise and strong."

Miyax turned her back to Uma. She must not see the quivering of her body at every mention of her father's name. He had been dead to her, for so long that she was almost frightened by the knowledge that he lived. Yet she loved each cold chill that told her it was true.

Outside the dogs began fighting over their rations, and Atik's whip cracked like a gunshot. Miyax shivered at the sound. She thought of Amaroq and tears welled in her eyes but did not fall, for she was also thinking about Kapugen. She must find him. He would save the wolves just as he had saved the people of Kangik.

"Amaroq, Amaroq," she sang as she fluffed up her furs. Uma turned to her in surprise.

"You are happy after all," she said in Eskimo. "I thought perhaps this was the beginning of your periods and that your family had sent you to a hut to be alone. The old grandmother who raised me did that, and I was miserable and so unhappy, because no one does that anymore."

Miyax shook her head. "I am not yet a woman."

Uma did not inquire further, but hugged her. Then she put her baby in her kuspuck and crept out the door to join Atik in the starlit darkness. It was day and the constellations of the Southern Hemisphere were shining overhead. The dogs were biting their harnesses and fighting each other, and Atik was trying to make them hold still. Suddenly they lunged in all directions and the sled was moving. Atik picked up Uma and the baby, put them on the sled and, calling his grateful thanks to Miyax, took off.

She waved until they were lost in the darkness, then rushed into her house, rolled up her sleeping skins, and loaded her sled. She hoisted her pack to her back and picked up Tornait. Carefully she slipped the feather coat around his breast and, leaving his wings free, tied the little coat on his back. He looked silly. She laughed, rubbed her nose against his beak, and tucked him into the hood of her parka.

"Amna a-ya, a-ya-amna," she sang as she slid to the river, put on her snowshoes, and strode down the snapping ice bed.

She had gone about a mile when she heard Kapu bark. She knew it was he. His voice was unmistakable. Terrified, she turned around.

"Stay! Stay!" she screamed. The wind picked up her words and blew them down the river. Kapu ran up to her, followed by Nails and the pups. All were yipping authoritatively as they told her to join them.

"I cannot," she cried. "My own Amaroq lives. I must go to him!"

She walked forward a few steps, and turned and glared as the wolf leader had done. For a moment they hesitated, as if not believing her message. Then they dashed away and ran up the river. They called from the bank, and then they were gone.

Miyax had spoken her last words to her wolves.

She thought of Kapugen and hurried on. What would she say to him? Would they rub noses when they met? Surely he would hug his favorite child and let her enter his house, tan his hides, sew his clothes, cook his food. There was so much she could do for this great hunter now; prepare caribou, catch rabbits, pluck birds, and even make tools with water and the freezing air. She would be very useful to him and they would live as they were meant to live—with the cold and the birds and the beasts.

She tried to recall Kapugen's face—his dark eyes and the brows that drooped kindly. Would his cheeks still be strong and creased by laughter? Would he still have long hair and stand tall?

A green fountain of magnetic light shot up into the sky, its edges rimmed with sparks. The air crackled, the river groaned, and Miyax pointed her boots toward Kapugen.

SHE COULD SEE THE VILLAGE OF KANGIK long before she got to it. Its lights twinkled in the winter night on the first bench of the river near the sea. When she could make out windows and the dark outlines of houses, she pulled her sled to the second bench above the river and stopped. She needed to think before meeting Kapugen.

She pitched her tent and spread out her sleeping skins. Lying on her stomach, she peered down on the town. It consisted of about fifty wooden houses. A few were large, but all had the same rectangular design

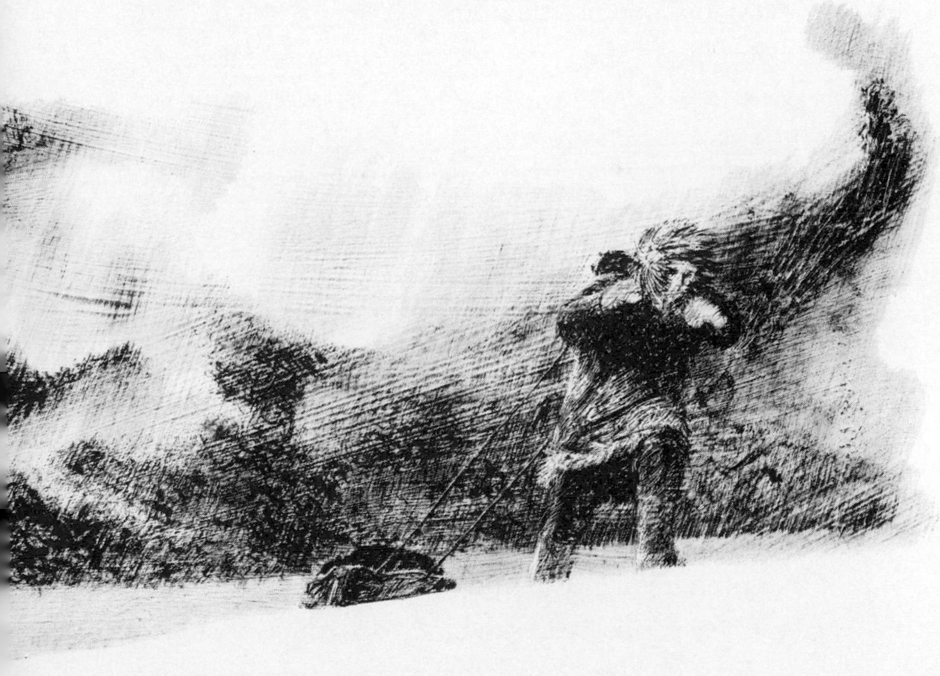

with peaked roof. Kangik was so snowy she could not see if there was trash in the streets, but even if there had been she would not have cared. Kapugen's home had to be beautiful.

The village had one crossroad, where the church and mission stood. On either side of them were the stores, which Miyax recognized by the many people who wandered in and out. She listened. Dog teams barked from both ends of town, and although she knew there were snowmobiles, the village was essentially a sled-dog town—an old-fashioned Eskimo settlement. That pleased her.

Her eyes roamed the street. A few children were out romping in the snow and she guessed that it was about ten o'clock in the morning—the time Eskimo children were sent out to play. By that hour their mothers had completed their morning chores, and had time to dress the little ones and send them outside, cold as it was.

Below the town, she could see the musk-oxen Uma had spoken about. They were circled together near the gate of their enclosure, heads facing out to protect themselves from wolves and bears. Her heart thrilled to see these wondrous oxen of the north. She could help Kapugen take care of the herd.

Two children burst out of a house, put a board across a barrel like a seesaw, and took their positions standing on either end of the board. They began jumping, sending each other higher and higher, and coming down on the board with incredible accuracy. Miyax had seen this game in Barrow, and she watched the flying figures with fascination. Then she slowly lifted her eyes and concentrated on the houses.

There were two green houses near the wilderness. She was debating which one was Kapugen's when the door opened in the smaller one and three children tumbled out. She decided he must live in the other one—with the windows, the annex, and two wooden boats in the yard.

A woman came out of Kapugen's house and hurried across the snow.

"Of course," Miyax thought. "He has married. He has someone to sew and cook for him. But I can still help him with the oxen."

The woman passed the church and stopped at the mission door. She was engulfed in light for an instant, then the door closed behind her. Miyax arose. It was time to seek out her father. He would be alone.

Her feet skimmed the snow as she ran down the hill and across the road, where the children were hitching a dog to a sled. They giggled, and Tornait answered their high bird-like voices from inside her hood.

As Miyax neared the green house she took Tornait in her hand and ran right up to the door. She knocked.

Footsteps sounded from a far corner of the house. The door opened and there stood Kapugen. He was just as she remembered him—rugged, but with dark gentle eyes. Not a word came to her mind. Not even his name or a greeting. She was too moved by the sight of him to speak. Then Tornait peeped. She held him out.

"I have a present for you," she said at last in Eskimo. The feather coat rustled and Tornait's amber head pulled into the covering like a turtle.

"What is it?" Kapugen's voice was resonant and warm and seemed to come from the seashore at Nunivak where the birds sang and the sea was framed with the fur of his parka. "Come in. I've never seen such a bird." He spoke English and she smiled and shook her head. He repeated his invitation in Yupik. Miyax stepped across the threshold and into his home.

The big room was warm and smelled of skins and fat. Harpoons hung on the wall, and under the window was a long couch of furs. The kayak hung from the ceiling, and a little stove glowed in the center of the room. Kapugen's house in Kangik looked just like Kapugen's house in seal camp. She was home!

Tornait hopped to the floor, his feather coat blooming behind him like a courting ptarmigan. He ran under a fur.

"He wears a coat!" Kapugen laughed and got down on his knees to peer at the bird.

"Yes," Miyax said. "He is the spirit of the birds. He is a golden plover."

"A golden plover, the spirit of the birds? Where did you hear that?" Kapugen arose and pushed back her parka hood.

"Who are you?"

"Julie Edwards Miyax Kapugen."

The great frost-blackened hands ran softly over her face.

"Ee-lie," he whispered. "Yes, you are she. You are beautiful like your mother." He opened his arms. She ran into them and for a long time he held her tightly.

"When they sent you to school," he said softly, "Nunivak was too much to bear. I left and began a new life. Last year when at last I was rich I went back to get you. You were gone." His fingers touched her hair and he hugged her once more.

The door opened and the woman came in. "Who have we here?" she asked in English.

Miyax saw that her face was pale and her hair was reddish gold. A chill spread over her. What had Kapugen done? What had happened to him that he would marry a gussak? What was his new life?

Kapugen and his woman talked—she loudly, Kapugen quietly. Miyax's eyes went around the room again. This time she saw not just the furs and the kayak, but electric lamps, a radio-phonograph, cotton curtains and, through the door to the annex, the edge of an electric stove, a coffee pot, and china dishes.

There were bookshelves and a framed picture on the wall of some American country garden. Then she saw a helmet and goggles on a chair. Miyax stared at them until Kapugen noticed her.

"Aw, that," he said. "I now own an airplane, Miyax. It's the only way to hunt today. The seals are scarce and the whales are almost gone; but sportsmen can still hunt from planes."

Miyax heard no more. It could not be, it could not be. She would not let it be. She instantly buried what she was thinking in the shadows of her mind.

"Miyax," the wife said in bad Yupik, "I teach in the school here. We shall enroll you tomorrow. You can learn to read and write English. It's very difficult to live even in this Eskimo town without knowing English."

Miyax looked at Kapugen. "I am on my way to San Francisco," she said softly in Yupik. "The gussaks in Wainwright have arranged transportation for me. I shall go tomorrow."

A telephone rang. Kapugen answered it and jotted down a note.

"I'll be right back," he said to Miyax. "I'll be right back. Then we'll talk." He hugged her. Miyax stiffened and looked at the helmet.

"Ellen, fix her some food," he called as he put on his coat, a long American-made Arctic field jacket. He zipped it with a flourish and went out the door.

Ellen went into the kitchen and Miyax was alone.

Slowly she picked up Tornait, put on her sealskin parka, and placed the little bird in her hood. Then she snapped on the radio, and as it crackled, whined, and picked up music, she opened the door and softly closed it behind her. Kapugen, after all, was dead to her.

On the second bench of the river above town she found her tent and pack, threw them onto her sled and, bending forward, hauled on it. She walked on up the river toward her house. She was an Eskimo, and as an Eskimo she must live. The hour of the lemming was upon the land, cycling slowly toward the hour of Miyax. She would build snowhouses in winter, a sod house in summer. She would carve and sew and trap. And someday there would be a boy like herself. They would raise children, who would live with the rhythm of the beasts and the land.

"The seals are scarce and the whales are almost gone," she heard Kapugen say. "When are you coming to live with us in San Francisco?" called Amy.

Miyax walked backward, watching the river valley. When the last light of Kangik disappeared, the stars lit the snow and the cold deepened far below zero. The ice thundered and boomed, roaring like drumbeats across the Arctic.

Tornait peeped. Miyax turned her head, touched

him with her chin, and felt his limpness. She stopped walking and lifted him into the cold.

"Tornait. What is wrong with you? Are you sick?" Swiftly opening her pack, she took out some meat, chewed it to thaw it, and gave it to the bird. He refused to eat. She put him inside her parka and pitched her tent out of the wind. When she had banked it with snow, she lit a small fire. The tent glowed, then warmed. Tornait lay in her hands, his head on her fingers; he peeped softly and closed his eyes.

Many hours later she buried him in the snow. The totem of Amaroq was in her pocket. Her fingers ran over it but she did not take it out. She sang to the spirit of Amaroq in her best English:

The seals are scarce and the whales are almost gone.
The spirits of the animals are passing away.
Amaroq, Amaroq, you are my adopted father.
My feet dance because of you.
My eyes see because of you.
My mind thinks because of you. And it thinks, on
this thundering night,
That the hour of the wolf and the Eskimo is over.

Julie pointed her boots toward Kapugen.

JEAN CRAIGHEAD GEORGE is one of the best-loved nature writers for children today. She is the author of more than sixty books for children and the recipient of three awards recognizing the body of her work.

Mrs. George spent a summer studying wolves and the tundra at the Arctic Research Laboratory at Barrow. That summer, she observed a magnificent alpha wolf, leader of a pack at Denali National Park. She was also moved by a glimpse of a young girl walking the vast tundra all alone. In that moment, the seed was planted for this children's classic, JULIE OF THE WOLVES.

JOHN SCHOENHERR has illustrated numerous books for children, including Jane Yolen's OWL MOON (Philomel), winner of the 1988 Caldecott Medal for illustrations.

JULIE

ALSO BY JEAN CRAIGHEAD GEORGE

Animals Who Have Won Our Hearts

The Cry of the Crow

Dear Rebecca, Winter Is Here

The Fire Bug Connection
An Ecological Mystery

Going to the Sun

The Grizzly Bear with the Golden Ears

Julie of the Wolves

The Missing 'Gator of Gumbo Limbo
An Ecological Mystery

The Moon of the Alligators

The Moon of the Bears

The Moon of the Chickarees

The Moon of the Deer

The Moon of the Fox Pups

The Moon of the Gray Wolves

The Moon of the Moles

The Moon of the Monarch Butterflies

The Moon of the Mountain Lions

The Moon of the Owls

The Moon of the Salamanders

The Moon of the Wild Pigs

The Moon of the Winter Bird

One Day in the Alpine Tundra

One Day in the Desert

One Day in the Prairie

One Day in the Tropical Rain Forest

One Day in the Woods

Shark Beneath the Reef

The Summer of the Falcon

The Talking Earth

Water Sky

Who Really Killed Cock Robin?
An Ecological Mystery

The Wounded Wolf

JEAN CRAIGHEAD GEORGE

ILLUSTRATED BY WENDELL MINOR

JULIE

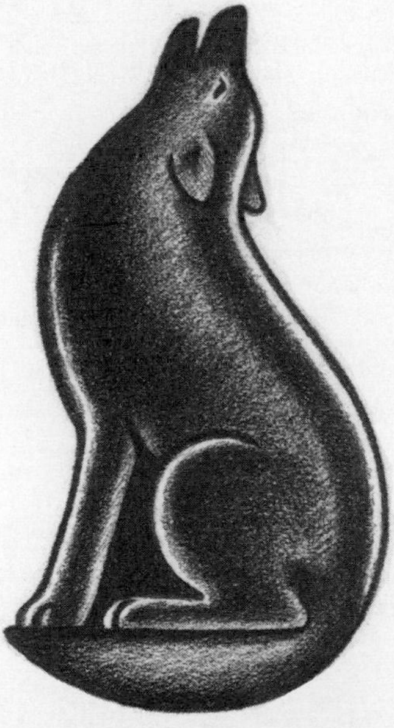

HarperCollins*Publishers*

Grateful acknowledgment is made to Carol Preston for the use of the lyrics to "The Far Northland" and to Boosey and Hawkes for their assistance.

 Printed in the United States of America. For information address HarperCollins Children's Books, a division of HarperCollins Publishers, 10 East 53rd Street, New York, NY 10022.

Library of Congress Cataloging-in-Publication Data
George, Jean Craighead, date
Julie / Jean Craighead George ; illustrated by Wendell Minor.
p. cm.
Sequel to: Julie of the wolves. 1972.
Summary: When Julie returns to her father's Eskimo village, she struggles to find a way to save her beloved wolves in a changing Arctic world and she falls in love with a young Siberian man.
ISBN 0-06-023528-4. — ISBN 0-06-023529-2 (lib. bdg.)
1. Eskimos—Juvenile fiction. [1. Eskimos—Fiction. 2. Indians of North America—Alaska—Fiction. 3. Wolves—Fiction.] I. Minor, Wendell, ill. II. Title.
PZ7.G2933Ju 1994 93-27738
[Fic]—dc20 CIP
AC

Typography by Wendell Minor and Al Cetta
10
❖

To Cyd,
who loves the wind and snow
of the Arctic

CONTENTS

PART I
KAPUGEN, THE HUNTER 1

PART II
AMY, THE WOLF PUP 95

PART III
MIYAX, THE YOUNG WOMAN 161

PART I

KAPUGEN, THE HUNTER

A wolf howled. He began on a note lower than a bear's growl, then climbed the scale to the highest pitch of the wind and held it there.

The cry traveled across the snowy tundra and was heard by a young girl standing at the door of a small green house. The wooden structure sat on the edge of an Eskimo village on the bank of the frozen Avalik River in Alaska. She pushed back the halo of fur that framed her lovely face and listened. The wolf was telling her to come with him. She did not answer.

Julie Edwards Miyax Kapugen knew the wolf well. He had shared food with her when she had been lost on the endless tundra. He had run and played with her. He had rested in her tent while she had nursed him back to health from his bullet wounds. Now he was trying to locate her. He must not find her. He must go away, far away. After many years of separation, Julie was going home to her father,

Kapugen, and he, she knew, would kill the wolf.

"That is how it is," she whispered to the howler. "If you come near Kapugen, he will shoot you. He is like all Eskimo hunters. He will say, 'The wolf gave himself to me.'"

The howl rose and fell.

Julie squinted toward the distant caller. "Stay away, beloved Kapu. I am going home."

She waited. The wolf she had named Kapu after her father, the great hunter and leader, did not call again. Quickly she opened and closed the first door that led into Kapugen's house. She walked into the qanitchaq, an entry room designed to keep out the cold. Its walls were hung with parkas and boots, and on the floor stood paddles, guns, and gasoline cans. She put down her pack, took off her sealskin parka and maklaks, or boots, and hung them on pegs. She stepped to the second door, which opened into the living room, and hesitated.

She thought of her childhood on the Eskimo island of Nunivak in the Bering Sea, and of her maidenhood in Barrow on the Arctic Ocean. Then she thought of the day she had left that town desperate to end an arranged marriage. She had gone out on the tundra planning to walk to Point Hope and take a boat to San Francisco to meet her pen pal, Amy.

On the tundra wilderness she had become hopelessly lost.

She tried not to think about the lovable wolf pack that had felled a caribou and saved her life. She must put them in the past. She had found her beloved father and was going home to him.

Yesterday he had welcomed her in this very house. Her heart had lightened and her burden of loneliness had fallen away. Her head had danced with joyful thoughts.

Her happiness had not lasted long. Within a short time she had realized Kapugen was not the same father who had taken her hunting and fishing with the seasons on Nunivak.

He was not the father who had lived in grace with the sea and land. Kapugen had changed. He had a white-American wife, a gussak. He had radios, a telephone, and a modern stove. Julie could have accepted these things had not her eyes fallen on Kapugen's airplane pilot helmet and goggles. She had seen them on the man in the airplane window who had shot Amaroq, the magnificent leader of her wolf pack. This she could not reconcile. When Kapugen had left the house, she had put on her pack and returned to her camp along the barren river.

There, alone in the crackling Arctic night with

the hoarfrost spangling her tent with ice ferns, she knew she must return. No matter what he had done, Kapugen was her father, and she loved him.

"We do not judge our people," she heard the Eskimo elders say, and Julie pointed her boots toward Kapugen.

Now, only a wooden door stood between them.

She opened it and stepped inside. Kapugen was home. He was seated on a caribou skin on the floor sharpening his man's knife. He was alone.

He did not look up, although Julie knew he had heard her enter. She tiptoed to the iglek, a pile of furs stacked into a couch almost as tall as she. She climbed up on it, sat, and folded her hands in her lap.

Kapugen sighted along his knife to see if it was satisfactorily sharp. Julie picked a thread from her woolen sock. Kapugen selected a section of bearded-seal hide and cut a slender thong from it. He tied the thong around his boot. Julie sat quietly.

Presently Kapugen looked out the window at the marine-blue sky of the sunless winter day.

"The wind has died down," he said. "That is good."

"The stars are bright," Julie added.

"That is good," said Kapugen.

A silence followed. Kapugen tightened the boot

thong and at last looked at her.

"Did you hear the wolf?" he asked, looking into her eyes.

"I heard the wolf," she answered.

Another silence ensued. Kapugen did not take his eyes from her eyes. Julie knew he was speaking to her in the manner of the Eskimo hunter who communicates without sound. His eyes were saying that a wolf did not give that call of friendship very often.

Julie did not answer. She studied her father.

Kapugen was a stocky man with a broad back and powerful arms. His face was burned brown from the Arctic wind and sun, and his hands were blackened by frostbite. His hair was shorter than she remembered, but his chin was still smooth and plucked hairless. A faint mustache darkened his upper lip. He sat with his legs straight out before him.

"The wolf knows you." He spoke slowly and thoughtfully.

"He does," Julie answered.

Kapugen picked up the seal hide and cut another thong. Julie waited for him to speak again. He did not. He gave his knife one last hone and put it in the sheath on his belt. In one movement he rose to his feet and opened his arms. She jumped down from the iglek and ran to him.

After a long, comforting embrace, Kapugen lifted Julie's chin and touched the smooth olive skin of her cheek.

"I'm glad you came back," he said. "I was afraid I had lost you for a second time. I love you with the fullness of the white moon."

"That's a lot," she said shyly. He crossed his feet and lowered himself to the caribou skin, then patted it and invited Julie to sit. Julie saw the question on his face. She answered it.

"I broke the marriage arrangement with the son of your serious partner." Her voice was very soft.

"If a man and a woman," Kapugen said in a low, even voice, "do not love, they part company. That is the right way."

They sat quietly.

Kapugen, Julie saw, wanted to know more about her past, but, respecting her privacy, he did not ask. She must tell him no matter how painful her memories were.

"Do you not know," she asked in her gentle voice, "where I've been since that day Aunt Martha took me away from you to attend school?"

"I only know you went to Barrow when you were thirteen and old enough to marry," he answered, pacing his words slowly. "I happened to meet Nusan, your mother-in-law, in that town. She said you had run off and died."

"That was a terribly sad thing for her to say when she didn't really know," Julie said. "I am sorry. I will try to tell you what happened—perhaps not all—some things are still too sad."

Julie told him about her unhappy life in Mekoryok, the town on Nunivak, her days in Barrow, her marriage, and how deeply she feared Daniel, her angry husband. She recounted her days on the tundra with the gentle wolf pack and its kind leader, Amaroq, but she could not bring herself to say that Kapugen had killed him. The words would not form.

When she was done, Kapugen lowered his eyes for a moment, then looked up at her. His eyes said how much he loved her and how grateful he was that she was alive.

Julie buried her head on his shoulder, and he hugged her against his strong chest. This time as he held her, she felt forgiveness run up her spine and into her heart and mind. Kapugen, after all, was a provider for his family and village. Eskimo providers hunted.

"I am very tired," she finally said, her shoulders slumping. Kapugen brushed a strand of hair from her forehead. He lifted her in his arms, carried her to the iglek, and placed her upon it. She sank down into the sweet, soft furs and pulled a grizzly-bear skin over herself.

"I am glad you came home, Miyax," he said, and kissed her. She smiled to hear him call her by her Eskimo name. Like most Eskimos, Julie had two names, English and Eskimo—Julie Edwards and Miyax Kapugen. Hearing her father call her Miyax made her feel closer to him, and she decided she would let only him call her that. The name bound the two of them to her mother, who had given it to her, and to each other. To the rest of the people she would be Julie.

She closed her eyes and slept deeply.

"Good morning, Kapugen. Good morning."

Julie sat straight up in her furry bed and looked around. The man's voice was loud and crackly, but there was no one in the room. Kapugen came out of the bedroom.

"Good morning." He spoke to the glittering CB radio on the bookshelf. "Good morning, Atik. Good morning." Julie recognized the name of the hunter she had met with his wife, Uma, and baby on the frozen Avalik River. Astounded to hear him in the room, she slid off the iglek and sat on Kapugen's caribou skin, watching the radio and listening intently.

"Good morning, Malek," said a woman's voice. "Good morning."

"Good morning, Marie. Good morning."

For almost an hour the villagers of Kangik awoke and greeted each other on their CBs. Their voices filled the darkness of the sunless morning with cheer.

Ellen, Kapugen's wife, came out of the bedroom and, seeing that Julie was awake, greeted her.

"Good morning, Miyax," she said.

"Julie," she said softly but firmly.

"As you wish," said Ellen, and turned her back to dip up tea water from a thirty-gallon plastic container. There was no running water in frozen Kangik.

Julie studied Ellen. Her bright-red hair with its strange curls was an oddity to her, as were her pale eyes and eyelashes. Julie found herself staring and wondering about her father's new wife. When breakfast was over, she climbed up on the iglek and watched Ellen at her desk. She wrote in a book, glancing up at Julie now and then as if to ask if she was all right. Julie said nothing.

Next Ellen read a book. When lunchtime came around she even cooked by looking at a book. In the early afternoon Ellen phoned her mother in Minnesota.

"Hello, Mom," she said. "I have a daughter." She

smiled and glanced at Julie.

"Yes, she's pretty," Ellen said. "Beautiful smooth skin and big almond eyes. Her hair is as black and shiny as polished ebony." Embarrassed, Julie slid back under the grizzly fur and peered at her father's wife over the ruff. She wondered how this woman had gotten so far from home and why she did not go back.

"Want to say hello to my mom, Julie?" Ellen asked.

She did not answer. Julie knew English perfectly. Briefly she had forgotten it after Amaroq had been killed, but now she understood every word being said. She just did not feel like talking to Ellen.

Julie had been terribly disappointed to discover her father had taken a wife from the outside. To the Eskimos there are two peoples—the people within the circle of ice and the people outside it. Ellen was not from within. She moved and talked too swiftly. Her voice was harsh, and she laughed loudly like the jaeger seabirds.

Julie slowly adapted to her new life. She washed dishes and cooked fish and caribou meat for Ellen. She scraped skins and prepared them for the market, and she chopped ice in the river and put it in the container to melt.

She read Ellen's books when Ellen was out. Her English schooling in Nunivak had been excellent. She read the books avidly, eager to learn about the outside world. From time to time when no one was around, she would walk along the river and listen for her wolves. Once she heard Kapu, and looking around to see if Kapugen was outside, she cupped her hands and howl-barked a warning. Kapu replied with silence. He had gotten the message.

One day while Julie was scraping a bearded-seal skin to make boots, a new voice came in over the CB.

"Good morning, Kapugen. Good morning."

"Good morning, Peter Sugluk," said Kapugen. "You are back, are you?"

"I am back, all right," he said. "And I am picking up two qivit sweaters Marie asked me to bring to you." Julie recalled Uma telling her that the women of Kangik knitted sweaters and scarves from the warm, featherweight underfur of the musk ox. Kapugen, she had said, sold these incredibly warm clothes to merchants in Anchorage and Fairbanks for enormous prices, many hundreds of dollars.

"Come on over," said Kapugen, and turned to Julie. "Peter Sugluk is my business partner's adopted son," he said.

"He speaks with a strange accent," said Julie.

"It should not be strange," said Kapugen. "He speaks Yupik like we do, not Iñupiat like the people of Barrow and Point Hope."

The Eskimo language has two branches. Yuk, or Yupik, is spoken in southwestern Alaska and Siberia. Inuk, or Iñupiat, is spoken across northern Alaska, Canada, and Greenland. Julie had learned Yupik in Nunivak and Iñupiat in Barrow. Although she understood Peter, who spoke Yupik, she could not place his accent. She wondered where he came from.

Presently there was a rap on the inner qanitchaq door.

"Come in," called Kapugen, and Peter Sugluk stepped into the warm room.

"Good morning, Kapugen," he said, and glanced at Julie. "You must be Julie. Good morning." His smile was beguiling and friendly.

Julie looked up at a bronze-faced young Eskimo. He was tall. His nose was straight, his cheekbones high, and his eyes were bright half-moons under dark brows. He wore a tunic of reindeer over close-fitting leather trousers. His maklaks were of polar bear, trimmed with sled dogs in black-and-white calfskin. Ermine tails with black tips danced along the trim of his sleeves and boots when he moved. He looked old to Julie, perhaps eighteen or nineteen as compared to her fourteen, going on fifteen, years. She looked down at her sealskin and went back to her scraping.

"What they say is right," she heard Peter say. "You are beautiful."

Julie went on working. She did not want to be known for her beauty, but for her wisdom and fortitude, Eskimo virtues. She did not look up until he opened the door and was gone, but she thought she had seen him tap a toe and raise his palms in the dance symbol of celebration.

Two weeks passed. The days became turquoise blue as the earth tilted into the sun. By the time the bloody red ball came over the horizon on January twenty-second, Julie felt comfortable in her new home and village.

One day when Ellen was teaching at the school and Kapugen was at the desk poring over papers, she put down her work and stood before him.

"Aapa," she said softly, "I have been gone a long time on the tundra and I have been deep in a dream world with the wolves. Now I am awake. What can I do to help you?"

"That is good, all right," he said, looking up at her. Noticing that she was studying the papers he was working on, he spoke.

"These papers are the records of our musk oxen. Malek, Peter, and I keep track of them for the bank in Fairbanks. The bank finances our industry."

"Industry?"

"All Eskimo villages are corporations now," Kapugen said rising to his feet. "Unlike the American Indians, who live on reservations under government supervision, we run ourselves like a business. Our people own stock in the village corporation and share the profits." This did not make sense to Julie, but Kapugen seemed to think it was important, so she listened. "The Kangik Iñupiat Corporation is pretty big, all right," he said, pointing to numerals in the book. "We have a musk-ox business, a construction company, a store, and an electrical-generator company. We also get money from the oil taken from our land." She still did not comment, so Kapugen stood up and took her hands.

"Miyax, you must learn to hunt."

"I can hunt," she answered. "I can trap ptarmigan and snowshoe hares."

"You must learn to shoot a gun," he said. "We need you. Kangik is almost a deserted village. Many of the houses are empty, all right. The caribou have not circled back to us for two years, and the people are hungry. Many have moved to Wainwright and Barrow."

"That is too bad," Julie said.

"We are suffering," he said. "That is how it is." Kapugen went into his bedroom. He returned with a .22 rifle and cracked open the barrel.

"Is there really so much hardship in Kangik?" Julie asked. "I met your friends Uma and Atik up the river. Uma said that the people of Kangik make lots of money knitting musk-ox qivit into mittens and sweaters. She said you are raising musk oxen to help your village; and that you are a great leader."

"Uma is cheerful," Kapugen said, and smiled. "She was raised to admire a leader no matter what he does."

"I understand that," Julie said softly.

"You do, all right," he said, and looked at his helmet and goggles. "You do, all right," he repeated. Kapugen's face told Julie that her father now knew that the wolf he had shot from his plane was her friend. He looked very unhappy.

"Food is scarce in Kangik," he said, hastily changing the subject.

"Can't you fly your airplane and get gussak food for the village?"

"When the caribou fail to return, no white man's food can keep us healthy."

"The fish?" she asked.

"We also need flesh and fat to survive in the

cold," he answered. "And nothing tastes so good as the caribou and the whale."

Julie smiled. "That is true."

Kapugen slipped several bullets into the .22 and put on the safety so the gun could not be fired. He handed it to her. They went into the qanitchaq and put on their warmest clothing. Kapugen picked up his bear rifle. He put the carrying strap around his neck and rested the gun on his back. When Julie was dressed, he opened the door. The cold air sucked the breath from their mouths and swirled snow in their faces.

The sun was just rising, although it was ten o'clock. The rosy light illuminated a dip in the landscape that was the frozen Avalik River, and beyond it the huge platter that was Kuk Inlet. But for the village, a cluster of little wooden houses on pilings that kept them from melting the permafrost, all else was barren tundra.

Julie glanced at Kangik and held her breath. The village, which had seemed so vibrant on that first night she had laid eyes on it, was plain and dreary. Several of the houses were packing boxes in which snowplows and trucks had been shipped to the villages along the Arctic coast. Many were boarded up and deserted.

A dull murmur caught her attention.

"What is that?" Julie asked. "I hear it often at night."

"The electric generator," Kapugen said. "It runs on gasoline and makes electricity for our radios and stoves and lights."

The humming generator, sounding like a sleeping bear, gave a strange kind of life to the still, cold village. Julie listened for another sound. A dog barked once, a door squealed as it swung on its hinges, and a voice called out. The sounds were swallowed by the subzero cold. She listened more intently. There was no sound from Kapu.

Kapugen signaled her to follow him, and they walked east on the river ice in the somber polar light. After a short distance they both stopped and watched the sun light up the treeless, blue-green snow.

"You will like Ellen, I think, all right," Kapugen said after a while. Julie did not answer.

They went on up the river. Their footfalls smashed the ice into snow. It squeaked like glass, swirled up, and fell softly, making a trail of powder behind them. The sun had rolled along the horizon for almost an hour, and now it was setting. Kapugen turned to Julie.

"We will hunt foxes," he said. "Some live near the

musk-ox corral. Watch what I do. I learned to hunt in my father's boot steps. It is the best way."

Julie stepped in his boot tracks and followed him off the river ice onto the tundra. The ice fog that had arrived with the dawn began to thicken.

After a short hike Kapugen opened a gate, and he and Julie entered a large corral. Dark boulderlike forms loomed in the blue fog. Eleven musk oxen stared at them. Small clouds of frozen breath hung above their heads.

A wolf howled. Julie looked at Kapugen in alarm.

"The hunt is over," he said. "The foxes hide when the wolf howls."

"Ee-lie, Kapu," Julie whispered to the wolf, "stay away, stay far, far away."

Kapugen and Julie walked home.

Ice fog erased the landscape, and it was many days before Julie and Kapugen returned to the corral to hunt foxes again. They walked through a galaxy of sparkling ice crystals that floated over the quiet tundra. Kapugen led, and Julie stepped in his tracks.

After a long walk Kapugen stopped. He fixed his eyes on a distant spot, and Julie followed his gaze. A figure appeared and disappeared and reappeared like starlight on water.

"Lift your gun," Kapugen whispered. "When the fox stops moving, put the bead of the front sight into the notch in the rear sight. Click off the safety and pull the trigger slowly."

Julie fired and missed. Kapugen walked on, turning his head from right to left as he scanned the snowscape. His gun was slung across his back parallel to the ground; his hands were grasped behind him. He was alert to the most subtle movements and faintest sounds. Kapugen hunted like a wolf, and like a wolf he knew when there was no game. He stopped in the corral to check the uminmaks.

As he turned to go home, he kicked back the snow. It was not very deep, the wind having stripped the flat tundra of snow and exposed the grasses and sedges. For this reason the Arctic tundra was a perfect home for the grass-eating, well-garbed musk oxen. The tip of Kapugen's maklak touched an ancient ground birch that was only a seven inches high. He leaned down. Around it grew bilberry, Labrador tea plants, and a few dwarf willows.

"The uminmak's favorite foods," he said to Julie, then looked at the plants more carefully. "They have been eaten too close to the roots. The oxen are running out of wild food."

"The grasses are taller outside the fence," Julie

said. "Why don't you let them roam free?"

"So we can gather the qivit easily," Kapugen answered. "And," he added with bluntness, "so the wolves will not kill the oxen."

Julie felt a flush of blood run through her. She closed her eyes and swallowed hard.

"Soon," Kapugen said, "I must fly to Barrow to buy alfalfa pellets for the uminmaks. They need more food." He walked on. Julie placed her feet in his boot tracks.

"A white fox hide," Kapugen said turning to her, "brings fifty dollars in Fairbanks."

"Fifty dollars," Julie repeated to herself, and looked back toward the village. For the past seven months she had thought about no one but herself and her wolves. For seven long months she had directed all her thoughts inward toward staying alive. Now, as she walked behind her father, she knew it was time to become an Eskimo again, a person who helps the family and the village community.

She would not miss the next fox.

Julie not only followed Kapugen, she looked where he looked, she sniffed the winds he sniffed. When he stopped and listened, she stopped and listened.

A ptarmigan burst out of the snow and vanished

behind the ice cloud it had created.

"How much do they give for a ptarmigan?" she asked.

"Ten dollars," said Kapugen. She thought of the huge polar bear she had seen in Barrow. His great white hide must be so valuable, it could feed all of Kangik.

"How much do they give for nanuq?" she called above the wind.

"Nothing," replied Kapugen. "Only the Eskimos can harvest nanuq, the great white bear, and we cannot sell him. He gives himself to us. We give him to our people. That has always been so." Julie nodded.

They arrived at a three-sided shelter in the musk-ox corral. Snow was drifted high around the sturdy structure of heavy plywood. It was roofed with corrugated steel.

"This is where we put the hay and pellets for the uminmaks," Kapugen said. "It keeps the food from being buried under the drifts."

He looked up and smiled. Julie looked up too. A solitary bull was running toward them. She glanced at her father. Kapugen did not seem alarmed, and sure enough, when the bull was only a few yards away, he stopped. He ogled them. Shreds of qivit trailed from his shoulders.

The bull was massive but not very tall. He barely came up to Kapugen's chest. His huge neck muscles formed a hump on his back that was higher than his head. His tail was remarkably short, his hair so long it swept the ground like a skirt. His feet were enormous ice choppers. A bold boss of horn, curved tips pointed forward, met in the middle of his forehead like a helmet. The chunky rocklike animal bore a strong resemblance to the wooly mammoths of the past. He snorted.

"One of the last old-time animals," Kapugen said. "White men say he is a goat-antelope. To the Eskimo he is uminmak, the animal born to the ice and the wind and the snow." Kapugen held out a bilberry stalk to him. "Once," he went on, "there were millions of uminmaks in northern Alaska. When the Eskimo got guns, they shot them all. Every one.

"The U.S. government tried to bring them back. They got thirty-three calves from Greenland and set them free on Nunivak in 1930. When that herd was large, they brought some calves to Fairbanks and later set them free. We have a few wild ones on the North Slope now.

"The government helped me bring bull and cow calves to Kangik to start a qivit industry."

The bull snorted and pawed the ground, then

rubbed his head against his foreleg.

"Is he angry?" Julie asked.

"He is rubbing a gland near his eye on his leg. The scent from the gland warns the herd. It is not musk, as the white man calls it. It smells fresh and clean, like snow."

"What is he afraid of?" Julie asked.

"He is prey," Kapugen said. "He is concerned about all things; you, me, our guns, and the odors on the wind." Kapugen sniffed and squinted into the glaring snow. "He is saying the grizzly bear is awake."

"The grizzly bear?" Julie asked.

"Aklaq awakened last week in a warm spell," he said. "She has two yearling cubs and they are hungry. She has been staying close to the musk oxen, all right," he said. "That is not good. Like the wolf, the grizzly can kill an uminmak. Uminmak is smaller than a bear and not very bright."

Kapugen cupped his hands behind his ears.

"The herd is coming," he said, and smiled proudly. Out of a bright spot of ice glare the other musk oxen appeared, rolling along as if on wheels and seemingly pushed by the wind. They were a sturdy, well-knit group. The beasts slowed down, hesitated, then, circling like a whirlpool, forced the yearlings and calves into the center of their group for protection.

"They are alarmed," said Kapugen, looking around.

"The bear?" Julie asked, afraid that he was going to say wolf.

"I do not know," he answered.

The herd was quite close, and Julie could see the difference between the males and the females. The females were smaller, and their horns did not meet on their brows, as did those of the males. Both sexes had large eyes that protruded from their heads several inches. With these eyes they could see to the sides, the front, and the rear, and they could see in the dark as well as in the painful light of ice glare. The uminmaks are creatures honed by darkness, sun, and intense cold.

Kapugen moo-grunted.

A female left the group and came toward him. She hesitated when she saw Julie. Kapugen walked slowly up to her making soft sounds. When she was close, he reached out and scratched her head.

"This is Siku, Miyax," he said. "I found her on the tundra. Her mother had just been killed by a wolf pack. Siku was moving inside her. I opened the belly and lifted this little musk ox onto the ice—the siku; then I wrapped her in a caribou skin and took her home.

"I fed her on a bottle, and she lived and gave me the idea to raise musk oxen."

"Is it hard to raise them?" Julie asked.

"Not too hard," Kapugen replied. "Once, not too long ago, when the caribou were scarce, the people of Kangik, Wainwright, and Barrow raised reindeer. Malek was a herder. I met him and told him of my dream. He came to Kangik to join me. The state of Alaska gave us several more oxen to go with Siku. In time we had a herd and gathered qivit." Julie reached slowly out and touched Siku. The large eyes rolled her way, but the cow did not move.

"Siku," he said, laughing and rubbing her head roughly. "You started it all." She snorted and went back to the herd. The uminmaks had broken their fortress circle and were cropping grass.

"How many musk oxen do you have, Aapa?" Julie asked.

"Four bulls and seven females and yearlings. Not many, but the herd is growing. There will be four little calves in May or June if the wolves do not get them." He looked directly into her eyes.

Julie did not speak. She was thinking of that day on the tundra when an airplane came out of the mist and, with the burst of gunfire, killed Amaroq, the intelligent and kindly leader of her wolf pack.

She turned away from Kapugen's gaze. He was telling her he had killed the wolf to protect these musk oxen. He was thinking of his people, his eyes said, and they added that he would do it again if he had to.

Julie was terrified for Kapu and his pack. Wherever the caribou were, she fervently hoped her wolves were with them.

The sun, which had been up for two hours, was now sinking behind a horizon of ice mist. It glowed sparkling red, then disappeared. The long polar twilight entombed the top of the world as Julie and Kapugen turned homeward. In the short time it took to walk back to the village, the temperature dropped ten degrees. The wind gathered force. Kapugen pulled a bit of underfur from his parka ruff, wetted it, and held it up in the gale. It bent and froze in a hook.

"The wind is from the west," he said. "Tomorrow ought to be still and clear."

He pushed back his dark glasses and looked at the sky. "If the wind doesn't change in the night, tomorrow I will fly to Barrow."

"To get food for the uminmaks?"

"If I have time. Tomorrow I must take my wife to the doctor. "

"Is Ellen sick?" she asked tentatively.

"She is pregnant," Kapugen answered, and smiled so broadly his teeth shone white even in the dark twilight.

Pregnant, Julie thought. A child would be born. She was both pleased and not pleased. The very thought of a baby stirred warm feelings within her, but she also knew she had found her father only to lose him again. She walked along in silence. Distant barks sounded in the purple dusk.

"The dogs," said Julie. "I often hear them bark. Are they yours?"

"I have a team," he said.

"But you have snowmobiles," Julie said. "You don't need a team."

"I have snowmobiles," he answered. "But I love the dogs."

"I love the dogs, too," she said, thinking of the wonderful animals who were descendants of the wolves.

North of the town they came to a large Quonset hut. It faced a flat windswept plain that was covered with a long sheet of steel chain.

"Airplane iglu," Kapugen said, pointing to the hangar. Here her father's airplane resided. "Airplane runway," he added, gesturing to the metal-mesh landing strip. "I must check out the plane for tomorrow. Do you want to see it?"

She really didn't. She did not want to see that airplane from which the fatal shots had come—ever. She still felt the pain of Amaroq's death. Inside that iglu were the wings of a father she did not know.

She took off her mitten and reached into her pocket. There she kept the totem of Amaroq she had carved to hold his spirit after his death. She clutched the totem and felt better.

"Coming in?" Kapugen asked.

"I'll keep hunting," she said. "A ptarmigan will bring ten dollars, and you can buy food for Siku."

"I have a treasure for you in there," he said, pointing to the Quonset with a broad smile. Julie drew back. She did not want to see that airplane.

"I have ermine," he said, reaching out for her hand. "Beautiful glistening white ermine. They are for you to make something regal for yourself." His eyes told of his love for her. "Come see them. They are in a box by the door. I was going to sell them to the furrier in Fairbanks, but when you came back to me, I wanted to wrap them around you. They are yours."

Kapugen opened a small door in the big door of the Quonset and held it for Julie.

"I must learn to hunt," she said, drawing away. "I will bring you a fox or a ptarmigan. Later I will come see my treasure." She smiled and backed around the corner of the Quonset. Kapugen went inside and closed the door.

A wolf howled.

Julie shut her eyes and wished that tomorrow would be clear and windless so the metal bird would take Kapugen and Ellen to Barrow. A day alone would give her an opportunity to call to her wolves and tell them to go far away from the hunter who would protect his oxen at all costs.

An hour before Kapugen was to depart for Barrow, the wind shifted.

Clouds darkened the skies over Kangik, and Kapugen changed his plans.

"Today we will stay home," he said, looking out the window as a gust of whirling, blowing snow whitened the town.

Julie's plans were also changed. She could not warn Kapu. She nestled down on the iglek and thought about her wolves. They would be curled in snow scoops, their noses in their tails, their feet tucked under them. Soon they would be as white as the storm itself. She smiled. They would not come after the musk oxen today.

Julie picked up the parka she was making to replace her old one and began to stitch a seam. She would line it with caribou fur, the best insulation known. When it was done, she could go out in temperatures of fifty degrees below zero and be almost as snug as her wolves.

Ellen, who had dressed for the trip to Barrow, changed back into her qaliguuraq, the long Eskimo dress that is flanked with a deep ruffle. Then she turned on the CB.

"Children of Kangik," she said in her harsh American voice. "There will be school today. Do you hear me, Roy, Ernie, Edna, Benjamin, Larry? There *will* be school today. Over." She opened the receiver switch.

"Morning, Teacher Ellen, morning," a child's voice said. "I hear you loud and clear. School today. Out." He sounded quite happy.

Ellen picked up her lesson bag and opened the door to the qanitchaq. As she passed the iglek, Julie noticed her figure for the first time. Her stomach was rounding out under her qaliguuraq. Julie wondered if the baby would have red hair.

At the door Ellen hesitated and turned to Kapugen.

"Kapugen," she said, looking at Julie, "would you ask Julie if she would like to come to the school with me today? She doesn't understand English. Please tell her I would enjoy her company."

"Miyax," he said softly, "minuaqtugvik?"

Julie shook her head to say no.

Ellen's pale eyes flashed. She asked Kapugen to insist. He smiled and tenderly kissed her cheek, but did not tell Julie to obey.

Ellen shrugged. When she opened the outer door, the wind rushed in, rattling the inner door; then Ellen was gone. Julie and Kapugen sat in silence. Kapugen picked up the book in which he recorded the items the villagers had given him to sell in Fairbanks. He opened it and then slowly closed it.

"Let's go fishing, Miyax," he said. "We can fish in the storm. We need more fish for the dogs and the villagers."

Julie slid down to the floor. "I would like that," she said.

"When we have many iqaluk," said Kapugen, "we'll store them in my game cellar." Julie nodded. The deep cellars in the icy permafrost kept fish and game frozen solid winter and summer.

"When we are done," he went on, "would you take the dog team out to duck camp for a good run? They need exercise."

"I would like to do that," said Julie, trying not to sound too eager. This was the opportunity to go out on the tundra and howl-bark to warn her wolves to stay away.

"I will fish with you until noon," Kapugen said as he worked. "Then I must come back. I am expecting a noon call from the chairman of the board of directors of the Kangik Iñupiat Corporation."

"How do I find duck camp?" Julie asked. She ignored the high-sounding title of the authority that could bring her father home from fishing.

"The dogs know the way," he said. "The black-and-white dog with the white eyebrows is CB, the lead dog. He will take you there and back with good spirit."

"That is good," Julie said, and put on her warm parka and boots.

In the quiet of falling snow Kapugen and Julie carried a fish net and ice choppers out onto the river ice. With his man's knife, Kapugen cut snow blocks and stacked them into a wall to break the wind. Then he reopened several holes in the thick ice—they had frozen over since their last use. He secured an end of the gill net above the ice, then dropped the net into one of the holes. He went to the next hole, reached into it with a long hooked pole, hooked the net, and brought it up. He secured a side of it with a stake and dropped the net again. Humming to himself, he went from hole to hole. In a short time he reached the last one and secured the end of the net to another stake. Then he went back along the line and pulled out all the stakes but the first and last. The net hung taut under the ice.

"My grandfather taught me how to drop a net." he said. "And his father taught him. Pass it along to your children, Miyax. It is a good method, all right."

"I will, Aapa," she said. "I will."

Kapugen spread his caribou skin and they sat down in the snow-block shelter to watch the clouds, the white river, and the land.

After a long wait Kapugen jiggled the net and felt fish. Together he and Julie pulled them out through the first hole, which was larger than the rest. About sixty silvery fish flopped on the ice. Kapugen took them from the net with his bare hands and put them in a twine bag. Julie dragged it to the ice cellar and dropped it in. Together they reset the net and sat on the caribou skin. With sticks they had brought from home, Kapugen made a small fire. The white walls reflected back the heat of the flame, and they were soon quite warm. Julie brought out some caribou jerky and a piece of frozen whale maktak. They ate quietly, watching the snow fall around them.

They chatted as they waited to bring more fish from the dark water beneath the ice. An aura of the father she remembered settled over Julie, and she felt completely content. Kapugen made them each a cup of tea, and the long years of separation seemed to have never been.

The snowfall became lighter and lighter until only tiny sparklets of ice floated in the air. Just before noon Kapugen returned to the house to wait for his phone call. Julie pulled up several more catches and then went out to harness the dogs.

She found Kapugen's six Alaskan malamutes behind the Quonset. They greeted her warmly, then burst into joyful barking when she took a harness off its peg on the back of the hangar. They knew they were going for a run. Each dog had its name on its harness and collar. She learned them before pulling the sled into the open and attaching the line. She stretched the line out on the snow, found CB's harness, and snapped him to it. Next she set the brake on the sled. Each dog she harnessed leaped, pranced, and pulled until she stopped talking to them in Yupik and spoke to them in wolf talk. She mouthed their muzzles to tell them she was in charge. They looked at her curiously and stood still. She had to yell at a dog named Minnesota, who she presumed was Ellen's dog. When that did not work, she growled at her and showed her teeth. Minnesota slunk away and stopped snapping at CB.

Julie hugged one of the gentle wheel dogs, Snowbird, then fastened his neck line to the lead. He whimpered his friendship. When they were all harnessed, but before she stepped on the runners at the back of the sled, CB lunged forward with such force, he pulled the brake out of the snow. The team was off.

Julie ran, grabbed the sled, and hopping aboard, threw all her weight on the brake, driving the long wooden prong deep into the snow. The team came to a stop. She walked up to CB, arms out to make herself look big and threatening. She put her mouth over his muzzle, then looked directly in his eyes.

"I'm boss," she said. CB lowered his tail and ears in submission, then licked her face. She laughed, rubbed his ears, and walked slowly to the rear of the sled, ready to growl if CB moved. As she passed by, the team members wagged their tails and whimpered to her.

"I love you, too," Julie said, happy to be speaking to these cousins of the wolves.

When she reached the end of the line, she slowly stepped up on the runners again. CB and his team waited respectfully for orders. Julie pulled the brake out of the snow but did not give a command to go. The dogs looked back at her to see what was the matter. She stood tall, her head high in the regal pose of Amaroq, who had led his pack with this silent language of authority. The dogs saw and wagged their tails. She grinned.

"Hut," she called, and the team took off.

She halted them at Kapugen's green boat to make sure she was in control. CB made a sudden lunge forward. Julie growled. He looked back at her, smiled with his mouth open, and wagged his tail once. He was saying he was sorry he had teased her.

Kapugen, who had been watching through the window, saw Julie and the dogs conversing. He grinned with pleasure. The spirit of the wild things lived in his daughter.

"Hut," Julie called, and CB and his team took off at a run. They soon left Kangik behind.

Through the snow sparklets Julie scanned the horizon for her wolves. She stopped at the corral gate to see if they had been there. The snow had covered the deep hoofprints of the oxen. The shallow tracks of wolves would be blanketed too.

"Hut!" she called, and the sled jerked forward. Minnesota pulled to the left and the sled tipped. Julie was about to be dumped when CB jerked to the right and the sled dropped back on both runners again. Bending his head to the task, he set a pace suitable for a long haul. As the sled slipped quietly out onto the flat tundra, Minnesota looked back at Julie with a wry eye.

"Ha," Julie shouted to her, "I'm still here. You did not knock me off." She laughed, Minnesota uncurled her tail to say she was disappointed, and CB led on, now listening attentively for Julie's commands. She did not have to give any. The sensitive dog followed the trail although it was buried under the snow.

Five miles on, CB pulled Julie and the sled into duck camp. He stopped before a cluster of little shacks that stood on a bend of the Avalik River. They were almost covered with drifted snow.

Julie untied the snowshoes on the sled, put them on, and tramped to one of the shacks looking for wolf sign.

"Grrf!" She froze. Aklaq, the grizzly, came around the corner and snorted a warning. Clumsy in her snowshoes, Julie ran the other way around the shed. The bear stopped and looked for her. Julie also stopped. She now had the shack between the bear

and the sled. Reaching into her pocket for some of the uneaten maktak, she hurled it over the shack and dashed for the sled.

The bear stopped to gobble the whale blubber.

"Hut!" Julie called, clutching the sled ropes. The dogs needed no second order. They smelled grizzly bear. They ran. Julie threw herself on the sled, unstrapped her snowshoes, and climbed over the back board to stand on the runners. She and the dogs were a quarter of a mile away from the bear when she stopped them and looked back. No longer interested in Julie, Aklaq was digging in the snow for more maktak. Satisfied, Julie ran the dogs on.

"Halt," Julie called before the dogs had gone another quarter of a mile. They obeyed, but CB looked back at her as if to say she was out of her mind to stop when the smell of grizzly bear saturated the wind.

Julie had spotted two yearling bear cubs. They were digging near a den in the bank of the Avalik River. Kapugen was right: The mother grizzly was up early in the season, probably because her cubs were hungry. This was not good. The huge Aklaq could easily knock down the corral fence and take a musk ox.

Julie started the team again, calling "Haw" (left)

as soon as they were moving.

CB did not heed. He ran straight ahead. He did not want to go back toward the bears.

"Haw," Julie called with great force. CB finally pulled to the left. The two front dogs pulled right. The sled wove and tipped.

"Haw," Julie growled. The team went left, but too far. The sled tipped.

"Gee," Julie called, and dogs, traces, and sled straightened out and moved smoothly. By this time they were far from the big cubs, and CB held the course Julie had told him to take, northward over the tundra.

They were going along nicely when Minnesota snarled at her partner, Snowbird, then lunged at her neck. Julie howled a wolf command. They stopped fighting.

CB led his team over the snowy landscape for almost an hour while Julie scanned hummock and rise for wolves. Kapu and his pack were nowhere to be seen, nor were any foxes or wolverines. It was plain to Julie that the only wolf food in the vast area were the musk oxen.

A raven flew overhead. Julie stopped the team to watch this messenger of the tundra. The dogs lay down panting, even though it was ten below zero.

They bit snow to quench their thirst.

Ravens, Julie knew, were the first to find wolf kills and share the banquet with them. Eskimo hunters knew this and would follow the large black birds to find wolves. Julie guessed this flying bird could see fifteen miles in all directions. Since he was circling and flapping, he must not have sighted a wolf kill; he would be flying in a straight line to the food. The raven was fluttering and diving, which meant he was hunting lemmings. Julie was discouraged. For at least fifteen miles in all directions there were no wolves. She turned back.

A roar reached her ears as over a rise in the land a snowmobile appeared. She waved.

The driver pulled his vehicle up beside Julie's sled, but it was not until the man pushed back his dark snow glasses that she recognized Atik.

"The weather has turned nice," she said. "Are you hunting?"

"I am scouting for caribou," he said. "The females should be coming to Kangik now. They come ahead of the bulls. They will calve on the tundra in May."

"Did you find any?" she asked eagerly.

"There are no caribou from Kangik to Anaktuvuk, more than two hundred miles away," he said. "I have just talked to David Bradford, the Alaska Fish and Game man. He told me that. He brought his helicopter down near me. He said he heard the beeping of one of the radio collars he puts on moose to learn where they go."

"Where was the moose?" asked Julie with some excitement.

"There was no moose," he answered. "The collar had fallen off. He found it on the ground. Sometimes that happens, he said."

Julie scanned the frosty horizon.

"Do you think the caribou will come to Kangik this year?" she asked.

"They will not come. It is too bad," said Atik. "Kangik will suffer."

"When I first met you on the river," she said hopefully, "I told you of a small herd I had seen. Did you find them?"

"I never did," he said. Julie was surprised.

"I saw their tracks," Atik said. "They disappeared in the drainage passes."

"Did you see any wolves today?" she asked.

"David Bradford saw a pack from his helicopter," Atik said.

Julie's heart beat furiously. "Where were they?"

"Not far from here. He said the leader was a big black fellow."

"Kapu," Julie said under her breath. "Did he say how many wolves were in the pack?"

"He said eight."

"Eight?"

"He saw the black wolf and a white one and three dark-gray and three light-gray wolves."

The white one was Silver, she said to herself. The three light-gray wolves would be Zit, Zat, and Zing, the now-grown-up pups. The dark-gray wolves would be Nails and Sister, but who was the third dark-gray wolf, Julie wondered. Had Kapu taken a mate? It was, after all, time for pups.

Atik saw that the sky was magenta and turning blue-black. The sun was below the horizon. The long twilight was over and night was upon them. He nodded to Julie and sped off.

CB watched him go and then looked at Julie.

"All right, CB," she said. "Hut!" She sent them straight out on the tundra again. She smiled at the eager dogs, who kept looking back at her wondering why she was not going home.

"We're circling the bears," she called. Then after a short while she shouted, "Haw," and brought them back to the riverbank. CB joyfully broke into a run. The only sound as the moon came up was the swish of the runners and the panting of the dogs.

Julie threw back her head and reveled in the cold beauty of the night. She was worried, though. Her wolves were nearby and the only food for them was musk ox.

The wolves did not call during February, March, and early April. Julie relaxed. She took their silence to mean they were hunting caribou in the Brooks Mountain Range, about eighty miles south. But just as Atik had predicted, this also meant that no caribou would come through Kangik again this year. That was not good news. The families that needed four or five caribou each year to sustain their lives were leaving Kangik and moving in with relatives in bigger towns. Others were wandering in search of food as they had before white men came to Alaska. Atik went to the coast and brought back a walrus for his family. Malek made plans to go whaling on the sea ice.

One morning Peter came to Kapugen's house and Julie answered the door.

"Kapugen is in Fairbanks," she said.

"That is too bad, all right." Peter's dark brows stitched together. "Malek and I have been invited to join a whaling crew in Wainwright. I had hoped I could leave the musk oxen in Kapugen's care for several weeks. I see I cannot. He is gone and Malek is leaving today." He turned to go.

"I will take care of the uminmaks," she said. He spun around quickly.

"Would you?" His even teeth shone white against his bronze skin as he smiled broadly. "The villagers are hungry for maktak, Miyax," he said. "They need that good whale skin and blubber to lift their spirits. They all will thank you if we are lucky."

"Go along," she said. "I like to be out with the oxen on the tundra, and I know what to do. Kapugen has taught me."

"Ee-lie," he said, and lifted his arms in celebration. He ran off as swiftly and lightly as a tundra bird.

When he was gone, she wondered why she had not corrected him when he had called her Miyax.

That very afternoon she took over the musk-ox chores. It was a pleasant day. She hitched the dogs to a sled load of hay and alfalfa pellets and rode out to the shelter. She counted the herd, as Kapugen always did, and noted that the grasses were thrusting up through the rotting snow. Then, according to Kapugen's routine, she drove the dog team around the corral to make sure none of these hardy beasts with their muscular bodies had damaged the fence. Finally, work done, she turned the dog team east and ran them along the riverbank. The air was so cold, the frozen breath of the dogs left a long white vapor trail behind them.

At duck camp she stopped and listened for Kapu and his wolves. She heard nothing.

"They are gone," she said happily, then added, "Stay away, dear Kapu, stay away."

As she mushed home free from worry, she felt like a wolf running great distances for the pure joy of it. The wind blew back her wolverine ruff, and she leaned forward and sang her qimmiq, or dog, song.

"Wise qimmiqs, brave qimmiqs,
Run with your tails up.
Run with your tails up.
When wind bites and cold numbs,
Run with your tails up.
Run, qimmiqs, run,
In life's stormy weather,
Run with your tails up.
Ee-lie, ee-lie, ee-lie, ee-lie. La, la, la la."

The dogs wagged their tails in rhythm to the song and now and then looked back at Julie and smiled.

Ellen closed the school in mid-April. The hunting season had begun. The parents who had not gone to the coast for whale and seal had taken their children inland to duck camp. The waterfowl were returning from the south in long black ribbons. Every half hour or so a band of thousands and thousands of eider ducks passed over Kangik, skimming low along the ground and over the houses as they migrated home. Julie would watch them, her head back, her eyes half closed, and she would wonder what magic brought them back each year.

On a sunny day in May, before the sun came up to stay for three months, Harry Ulugaq drove up to Kapugen's house on his three-wheeled motor bike. He brought a basket for Kapugen to sell in Fairbanks. It was made from fine strips Harry had cut from a piece of bowhead-whale baleen, the long, narrow filters in the whale's mouth.

"The museum would like this," Kapugen said after admiring the glow of the very black baleen and the symmetry of the work of art. "But I can probably get more from a collector—perhaps thirty-five hundred dollars." Harry nodded. He was one of the last baleen artists on the Arctic coast and knew well the value of his craft. But this day he had more exciting matters on his mind than money. After Kapugen listed the basket and its worth in his book, Harry went to the window and pointed toward Kuk Inlet.

"We have good luck," he said as Julie came up beside him. "A southerly storm has brought millions of smelt to the open water at the sea end of Kuk Inlet." His eyes twinkled. "Lots of fun."

"Lots of good eating," Kapugen said. "I have a fine market for smelt. Lots of Barrow families find it a treat."

When Kapugen had seen Harry Ulugaq to the door, he returned to Julie and Ellen.

"It's time for us all to go fishing," he said with a broad grin. "Smelt fishing is good fun, all right."

"Who will feed the musk oxen?" Julie asked.

"I fed them well today," said Kapugen. "We will not be long. The grasses are growing fast in the new sun, and they will find much to eat."

"Good," said Ellen, getting down the camping food box. "I'll pack enough food for a week. Kapugen, get the tent and sleeping skins."

Smelt camp was lively. Families slept in tents and mingled outdoors. Julie fell easily into the rhythm of community life. She and the older children helped lift the nets, clean and split the fish open, and put them on drying racks. Two or three days later, when the fish had dried in the sun and air, they helped pack them in boxes.

When the tide came in, Julie went to the shore to watch the glistening clouds of smelt swim in from the sea. When the tide turned, Julie and her friends would walk down the beach with the ebbing water to find the deep pools where thousands of fish were trapped. They would throw nets over them, and the men and women would hurry from camp to help pull the fish out of the water and up to the drying racks.

Between tides, the young people raced snowmobiles out on the tundra or drove them back to the Kangik store for gasoline and staples. Sometimes Julie rode with them, but she preferred to paddle the umiaq along the edge of the ice that filled the upper inlet and watch the snowstorm of birds nesting and defending territory. Julie also watched the side streams to see if the graylings, Kapugen's favorite fish, were spawning in the shallows yet.

At fish camp no one looked at watches. The sun was up almost twenty-four hours each day. Children napped and ate when they felt like it. The adults slept when the tide was in and fished when it went out. Between work and sleep adults and children played one-foot-high kick—a game played by kicking a fur ball on a thong hung one foot above their heads. They rolled kayaks and chased each other like wolf pups. Harry Ulugaq organized a baseball game, and then everyone danced away the rosy hours before the sun set briefly.

When the winds changed, the smelt did not return to the Kuk Inlet. Tents came down, and barrels of the dried fish were loaded onto snowmobiles and taken home to game cellars or to the Quonset to be flown to Fairbanks and Barrow.

That evening a radio message came from the Eskimos in Anaktuvuk Pass. They reported that the caribou of the western herd were moving northward on the easternmost border of the great circle they took from south to north to south. They would not come through Kangik. Hearing the final word, many families went out to the coast to hunt seal and beluga whales.

On May tenth, the sun did not set. The North Pole had tilted full into the sun for the next three months. The white fox turned gray-brown and the ptarmigan became splotched with white and blue-gray feathers to match the snow-and-grass-mottled tundra. The pretty white-and-black snow buntings returned from the south and hopped through the village streets. Feeding them bread crumbs made a good excuse for Julie to run outside and up the river shore to listen for her wolves. They did not call.

One clear day in late May Kapugen arranged to take the airplane to Fairbanks to attend a meeting of the corporation officers and the bankers. He carefully wrapped Harry's baleen basket, a lovely sweater, and the pelts of the four white foxes that had given themselves to Julie. She had skinned and prepared them for the market after making the meat into stew for her family. She asked Kapugen to buy musk-ox pellets with the money they brought.

"That will help the industry," she said, still somewhat unsure of what she was talking about.

Julie was fishing when Kapugen, the furs and artifacts in a pack on his back, came down to the river shore to speak to her. The constant sun had softened the ice, and it was too dangerous to stand on and fish. The breakup was imminent.

"Miyax," he said, "my plans have changed. Harry Ulugaq is very ill. I am taking him to the hospital in Barrow." He walked a few steps closer. "I am worried about Siku. I checked her this morning. She is bawling and her calf is not due for many weeks, I think. I cannot stay to help her."

"I will go to Siku," Julie said, and followed him into the house. Ellen, who was enjoying music on her cassette player, turned down the volume to listen to Kapugen tell her that Julie was going out to the corral to check on Siku. Then he turned to Julie, gave her pills to relax his favorite ox, and showed her how to make Siku swallow them.

"And Miyax," he said as he crossed the room, "you had better walk. It is almost forty degrees, too hot to run the dogs."

He hurried out the door, and Julie and Ellen were alone. Ellen watched Julie pack the medicine; her ulu, the woman's knife; needle and thread; and a change of clothes.

"I would like to go with you, Julie," she said in barely understandable Yupik. "I need the exercise." Julie listened to Ellen labor over the words, and although Julie could have easily told her in English to come along with her, she did not. She still did not have it in her heart to speak English to Ellen. She nodded instead.

Ellen dressed warmly in many sweaters, her parka, down pants, and fur-lined sealskin boots. It was still May, but the weather often played tricks.

Julie opened the house refrigerator and stowed cheese and bread in her pack. Since she did not know how long Siku might be in trouble, she also packed a large quantity of dried caribou from the jerky barrel. Then she rolled up a caribou skin to sit on and tied it to the bottom of her pack. Finally she took down

Kapugen's man's knife from the wall and slid it under her belt. She hung her gun across her shoulder.

"Itqanait" (I am ready), she said and hurried out of the house.

They watched Kapugen's plane take off and head into the sun, and then, side by side, they walked the riverbank. The river ice had cracked like a jigsaw puzzle and was beginning to move. It heaved and creaked.

"The breakup is late this year," said Ellen in English. She had to talk even if she thought Julie did not understand. "Kapugen said it will be vicious when it goes."

As they walked, Julie pointed to a king eider duck on the ice. He was a gorgeous bird, with his orange-yellow-and-green head and black-and-white back. "Qinalik," Julie said. Ellen repeated the word three or four times. A white-fronted goose was feeding in the slushy water in the reeds. "Niglivik," said Julie, and Ellen repeated that.

When they arrived at the corral, Siku was standing near the shelter. Her fur was rumpled and her large eyes were glazed. Julie ran to her and gently rubbed her head and back while speaking softly to her. The ox wobbled and stumbled forward. Her big knees buckled.

"She's ill," Ellen said. "She mustn't die. We need her so."

Julie glanced at her. Ellen had spoken with great feeling.

Quickly Julie took off a boot thong and, tying it around Siku's neck, led Kapugen's favorite animal into the shelter. Ellen spread hay for her. Siku went down on her knees, then rolled to her side with a moan. Her huge cloven feet plopped heavily to earth.

Julie spread the caribou skin and indicated to Ellen that she should sit down. Then she took one of the extra woolen socks from her bag and rolled it in the snow. She placed it inside her parka. The snow quickly turned to water, and she dripped it between Siku's parched lips. The animal drank and lay still. Julie opened Siku's mouth, placed the pill on the large tongue, and held her mouth closed as Kapugen had instructed. Siku swallowed the pill. Julie gave her more water.

Ellen put her hand on the ox's large belly. "She's in labor," she said, surprising Julie with her expertise. Siku lifted her head, rolled her eyes, and lay still.

For an hour Julie and Ellen watched her strain to give birth until she could strain no more. The calf would not be born.

Julie thought of Oliver Ahgeak, who, like Malek,

had been a reindeer herder in his youth. He was still in the village. He would know what to do.

"Oliver Ahgeak," Julie said, pointing to Siku, then gesturing to say she would go get him.

Ellen nodded and Julie turned to leave. She drew back. A dark, sinister cloud was rolling down upon them.

"Hilla, the weather spirit," Julie said in Yupik. "It has turned against us. This is a storm to be dreaded." Knowing Ellen did not understand, she pointed to the cloud. Ellen, who had seen many bad storms in her three years in Kangik, looked at this one and drew in her breath.

"You can't leave now," she said. "What do we do?"

Julie was on the move. She drew Kapugen's knife from her belt and tramped to the lee side of the shelter, where the last snow of the season was packed high and hard. With consummate skill she cut blocks. They were about three feet long and two wide. They were almost six inches deep. Working quickly, she stacked them to make a wall on the open side of the shelter. Ellen, seeing what Julie was doing, took the blocks from her as she came around the end of the shelter and stacked them. Swiftly, Julie used more snow as a plaster to keep the wind from blowing through the cracks. The wall went up. When there were but two more bricks to lay, the wind struck with such force the wall buckled, but held. The gust brought snow so dense that Julie could not see the shelter although she was right beside it. Feeling her way with one hand, she rounded the corner with a last brick and crawled inside. She sealed the wall with the block.

They huddled in the gloomy shelter. Even the constant sun could not penetrate the blackness of the storm.

"How long will this last?" Ellen murmured to herself and listened to the shrill wind. Julie patted more snow against the inner wall, then took from her pack a small jar of the whale blubber she used to grease her ulu and gun. She made a wick for the jar by cutting a slender bit of cloth off the bottom of her shirt and lit it with a match from her pack. The tiny light flickered, almost went out, then drew oil and brightened. The shelter glowed and warmed. Ellen smiled gratefully.

The wind thundered against the north end of the shelter and Julie looked anxiously at Ellen. Her face was amazingly calm.

Siku bawled weakly.

"We've got to deliver this calf," Ellen said.

"How do we do it?" Julie asked in perfect English.

Ellen stared at her. "You speak English."

"Yes."

Ellen frowned perplexedly, but Julie told Ellen with her eyes that she had come to like her. Then she looked down at the cow.

Water flowed from the birth canal and Siku groaned. Ellen got down on her knees; Julie knelt beside her.

"The calf is coming out rear feet first," Ellen said. "That's the wrong way. It'll never make it, and neither will Siku."

The wind shook the shelter. Fine bits of ice sifted in through the snow bricks despite Julie's caulking. They settled like flour dust on everything.

"I'll cut her open, like Kapugen did to her mother, and take the calf," said Julie.

Siku tried once more to deliver the calf. Her tongue rolled from her mouth, swollen and dark purple, and she gave up and lay still. Julie picked up her ulu.

"In Minnesota," Ellen said, "we reach into the womb and turn the calf around." She tore off her parka, rolled up her sleeves, and plunged her hand deep into the womb. Julie was astounded. Siku lifted her head, then relaxed her abdomen.

"Hobble her feet so she won't kick," Ellen said. Julie removed her boot thong from Siku's neck and tied her rear feet down. When Siku thrashed, Julie lay across her neck and whispered soothingly into her ear.

Perspiration poured from Ellen's face as she slowly but correctly turned the calf. Its forefeet appeared, then its head.

"Help me to get Siku up on her feet," Ellen said. Julie slid off the uminmak's body and, reaching under her shoulders, lifted the laboring Siku to her feet. As she arose, the calf slipped from her body onto the hay. Siku wobbled and sank back, exhausted.

"A girl," Ellen said. "Good. Unclog her nostrils of mucus."

Julie cleaned the calf's nose; Ellen blew into her mouth. The calf sucked in air and breathed. She was fully formed and fat. Apparently Kapugen had the delivery date wrong. Julie reached into her pack for her extra shirt and wiped the calf dry. It got to its feet and wobbled to its mother's side. She arose slowly and the calf nursed. Julie and Ellen looked at the newborn and relaxed.

"It's gotten awfully cold," Ellen said. "I hope the little thing makes it."

"She will," said Julie. "She's a musk ox. She was made by a storm."

Ellen smiled. Shivering, she pulled out a red bandana, wiped her hand and arm clean, and put on another sweater and parka.

The wind gusted, blasting more fine snow through the cracks. Julie picked up the whale-blubber lamp and held the flame near the block seams. The heat melted the snow, which quickly turned to ice and ceiled the inside of the wall.

In a short while Siku delivered the afterbirth.

"She will eat it," Ellen said. "It gives her protein and vitamins."

"That will take too long," Julie said. "There is a grizzly who travels this area. She would knock down the fence and our shelter for such food."

"In a storm like this?"

"It is nothing to her. She has two yearling cubs to feed," Julie replied.

"What do we do?"

"I will take the afterbirth outside the corral," Julie said, and put on her parka.

She wrapped the afterbirth in hay, pulled out the bottom snow block, and crawled out into the storm. The wind stung her face with snow darts. A powerful gust knocked her to her knees. When she struggled back to her feet, she could see nothing but snow—no ground, no sky, no up, no down. She was inside Hilla, the all-white weather spirit. She could not even see her knees. She would have to crawl. Crawling would make a deep trough that she could follow back to the shelter. She put the bundle in her parka, touched the totem of Amaroq, and moved out into the storm. Finally, she found the gate and threw the afterbirth as far as she could.

Then she turned and dropped to her knees to crawl back. The trough she had dug was not there. In one instant the wind and falling snow had leveled it. Julie shivered even in her caribou-lined coat. She had absolutely no idea which way to go.

"Ellen," she called.

No answer.

"Ellen!" The wind stopped her words before they could leave her mouth. She turned her back on it and let the wind carry her voice on its speeding journey.

"ELLEN! ELLEN!" No reply. Ellen, she realized, could not hear her over the shrieking gale. Knowing better than to move, she waited until there was a lull in the wind screams.

"ELLEN! ELLEN!"

"Julie, where are you?" The voice was so faint, she could not tell from which direction it had come.

"Shout, Ellen, sing! I can't find my way back."

"Julie. Julie. JULIE," Ellen shouted over and over, and Julie, hanging on to the sound as if it were a rope, crept forward. Her head hit the snow wall. She pulled back the block and crawled in.

"You look like ugruk, the seal," Ellen gasped, brushing snow from Julie's parka.

"I guess we are not going anywhere tonight," Julie said. "And maybe not tomorrow night, either," she added.

The hours crept by. Julie and Ellen stomped their feet to keep themselves warm, ate dried caribou, and huddled against Siku's warm body. The roar of the wind grew ever louder.

"Hilla will not go away," Julie said.

"What do Eskimos do now?" Ellen asked. She patted the calf, who was curled beside her mother.

"We sing and we eat and we wait," Julie said. "We do not move."

"I am shivering," Ellen said.

"Siku's skirt is long and very warm. Wrap your hands in it and blow on them." Ellen tucked her hands and feet in the incredibly light and warm fur, and she stopped shivering.

They sat quietly in the cold gloom. Finally Ellen spoke.

"You speak beautiful English, Julie," she said. "I did not know that."

"I lost my English voice on the tundra," Julie said, "when Amaroq, a noble black wolf who had befriended me, was shot. He saved my life."

"He saved your life?"

Ellen looked as if she would like to hear the story, but Julie could not bring herself to speak about it. Someday she would tell Ellen about Amaroq, someday when she could tell the story without crying.

"Anyway," Julie went on, "the truth is my knowledge of English came back to me when I saw Kapugen's house, but . . ." She looked at Ellen.

"I understand," she said. "I am glad you've decided I'm okay."

"You are. You are," Julie said, her eyes shining.

In silence they warmed their hands and feet on Siku and listened to the wild raging storm. The whale-blubber lamp glowed. They did not close their eyes.

Long hours later Ellen sat up.

"Do you know the words to 'The Far Northland,' Julie?" she asked.

"No," Julie answered, laughing at the title. "Please teach me. This is the perfect place to learn a song with that name."

Ellen cleared her throat.

"It's the far northland that's a-calling me away,
As take I with my knapsack to the road."

Julie's eyes twinkled and she clapped her hands to her mouth. "What's next?"

"It's the call on me of the forest in the north,
As step I with the sunlight for my load."

"Go on."

"By Lake Duncan and Clear Water
And the Bear Skin I will go,
Where you see the loon and hear its plaintive wail.
If you're thinking in your inner heart
There's swagger in my step,
You've never been along the border trail."

"Teach me, teach me," Julie cried.

By the time Julie had learned the chorus and all the verses to the song, Ellen was nodding and she herself was very sleepy. She checked Ellen to make sure her face was not freezing, then curled up against Siku and dozed.

The storm roared on and on. Julie and Ellen did not know how long they had been in the shelter or what day it was. They would open their eyes, listen to the wind, melt snow for tea, take a bite of cheese and bread, and close their eyes again. Ellen did not complain. The warm Siku and Julie's insulated wall were keeping them from freezing to death.

When Julie saw that Ellen had awakened during a furious blow and could not go back to sleep, she ventured to ask why she had come to the North Slope. Ellen rolled up to a sitting position, hugged her knees, and stared at the cheerful whale-blubber light.

"Like the song says," she began, "it was the far northland that was 'a-calling me away.' When I got my master's degree in education from the University of Minnesota, I saw a newspaper ad for a teacher in an Alaskan village. I could think of nothing more inspiring than that. I applied to the North Slope Borough, was interviewed, and got the job. I was sent to Kangik." She looked up at Julie. "Believe it or not, I liked it."

"Was my father here then?"

"He was here. We met the day after I arrived and soon fell in love. It was that simple. I called home and told my mother I was marrying an Eskimo."

"What did she say?"

" 'Is he kind?' "

"What did you say?"

"'That's why I love him.'" Her face softened and then she smiled. "When I married Kapugen, I had no idea I would face so many hardships, even though I grew up on my grandfather's farm in Minnesota."

"Minnesota has trees," said Julie.

"And all that goes with trees: flowers, warm sunshine, hot and cold running water, flush toilets, bathtubs . . ." She looked into the yellow flame. "Yet I do not want to go back, and particularly now that I am going to have an Eskimo child."

"Yes," said Julie confidently. "He will be happier here. We like Eskimo babies of all shades, and especially with red hair."

Ellen laughed heartily. "Maybe he'll have black hair and red eyelashes." That made them laugh even more.

"Did Kapugen have the corporation when you met him?" she asked.

"Kapugen was just starting the musk-ox business when we married. The corporation paid for his training as a pilot. The only way to do business on the North Slope is by plane. We lived in Fairbanks during his training. He returned several times to Nunivak to find you. No one except Aunt Martha knew where you had gone. And she was dead. No one knew what had happened to you. Kapugen came home depressed and discouraged from each trip. He would talk endlessly about you and how you and he would hunt and fish together after your mother died."

Julie listened to this story about a man and a little girl he could not find. It seemed like a folktale about people she did not know.

"On a trip to Barrow last fall," Ellen went on, "Kapugen happened to meet Nusan, the wife of Naka. She told him that Naka was dead. Then she said with bitterness that you had just run from your marriage to her son, Daniel, and gone inland. She said you had died on the tundra."

"He told me that," said Julie. "But what then?"

"When Kapugen came back from Barrow, he kayaked up the Avalik for almost a week to grieve alone. Then he came home. 'That is how it is,' he said. 'It cannot be helped.' And we decided it was time to have a baby." Julie bowed her head, overwhelmed by the knowledge that she had been sought and talked about all this time.

"You must know the joy he felt when you knocked at his door," Ellen said.

"And to think I almost did not come back," Julie said softly. "When I realized he had killed Amaroq, I could not bear to be with him."

"I didn't know he killed your friend."

"It is still very hard for me to understand Kapugen," Julie said, her eyes glistening. "He did not even use the valuable fur."

"Wolves kill oxen," said Ellen.

"Is that his reason?" Julie asked softly.

"I think it must have been," she said. "He was worried about wolves at that time."

"But the other man? Who was he?"

"A gussak who had paid him well to take them both wolf hunting. White hunters hate wolves. They kill the caribou and deer they want."

Julie sighed and leaned against Siku. Ellen turned over on her side. The wind shook the shelter, and snow sifted down upon them. The little calf was resting and the mother was breathing quietly. They all fell asleep.

After a long time had passed, Julie was awakened by a change in the wind song. It had lost its rage. She pulled back a snow block and looked outside. She could see.

Ten snowy musk oxen stood in a circle around the shelter, their soft brown eyes upon her.

"Friends," she called, taking down another block and carrying pellets to them, "you have a new clan member."

As she crawled through the opening, she observed the sky.

"Ellen," she said, "there's no light to be seen where the sun should be. I think we are here for a few more days." Ellen did not say a word. Julie scrambled back into the shelter, took out the cheese and bread, and melted tea water in a tin cup over the whale-blubber candle.

"Can you teach me more songs, Ellen?" she asked. Ellen had many more to teach her. They sang the hours away.

Many hours later the interior of the shelter grew lighter and lighter. The wind stopped shrieking. Julie stuck her head outside.

"Ellen," she called exuberantly, "the sun is shining. We can go home."

Siku and her calf, whom Julie had named Far Northland, watched Ellen and Julie tear down the snow wall and let in the sunshine. As Julie and Ellen ran toward the gate, Siku and Far Northland followed them. The herd rubbed their eye glands against their forelegs, and the mother and calf smelled this message of warning. Siku nudged her calf and turned back toward the herd. Her long fur swung around her feet as she walked slowly into the sun sparkle. The oxen gathered around her and looked long and steadily at the new baby.

Singing happily, Julie and Ellen opened the gate and started out across the hard, wind-pounded snow. It squeaked under their footsteps and boomed as if they were walking on a drum. In a short distance they came upon strewn hay and the claw marks where Aklaq had found the afterbirth. They looked at each other knowingly and plowed down the river trail.

Three wolves howled, first one at a time, then in unison. Julie's heart beat wildly. "Go away, go away," she cried inside herself. "Go away."

Ellen was singing and seemed not to have heard the voices. Julie touched her Amaroq totem and squeezed her eyes tightly shut.

Kapugen came home two days after the storm ended. He had stayed the extra days to give Harry Ulugaq time to recover from the appendicitis operation so he could bring him home.

He was hardly in the door before Julie began to tell the story of Ellen and how she had saved Siku and Far Northland. Kapugen stared at her, not hearing what she was saying.

"You are speaking English," he whispered hoarsely. "You have not spoken it since you came home." She nodded, and her already-rosy cheeks brightened with the excitement of it.

"Then I am forgiven," he said.

"Forgiven?" Julie wondered what made him say that.

"Forgiven for marrying a gussak," he said.

Julie smiled and ran to Ellen and took her hand.

"I love her," she said. "She is my aaka, my mother and my friend."

"I am glad, all right," he said. "I am glad."

"I am glad, all right, too," said Ellen. "I know I am strange to you, Julie, but thank you for those beautiful words."

"Minnesota has fine people," Julie said, and smiled.

"They are fine, all right," Kapugen said, touching Ellen's red curly hair. "Look at this—it is so fine it stands up and curls." Kapugen constantly found her curls a source of wonder. He was quiet as he wound one around his finger.

Julie sensed he had more to say. When Ellen had gone to the bedroom, he walked to the window and back several times. Finally he took Julie's hands in his.

"And am I also forgiven for killing the wolf who saved your life?" he asked.

"How did you know you killed my Amaroq?" she asked after a long pause. "I did not tell you."

"The wolves told me," he replied, and she knew that was true.

Julie blinked and looked at the floor. "It hurts my throat and lungs to speak of Amaroq." She looked up. "But I love you."

"Then I am forgiven?" he asked again. Julie looked into his face a long time as she reached back to the voices of her past. "We do not judge our people," she finally said. "I love you."

Kapugen placed his cold-toughened hands on each of Julie's flushed cheeks and tipped her face until their eyes met. She saw the sorrow he was feeling for her, but she also saw that he would do it again if he had to.

Over their thoughts they heard the spit and chime of running water. Snowmelt was the harmonics. It was tinkling off the roof, out from under the house, down the windows, and over the land to the river. The storm spirit had gone, and the unending sunlight was turning the snow and ice to water. The ocean, the tundra, the rivers were coming out of their frigid straitjackets. Yesterday the ice-stilled Avalik River had buckled with a boom and fractured into millions of pieces. Abetted by water flowing off the tundra, the river had flooded its banks and was hurtling ice and snowmelt seaward toward Kangik and the inlet. The breakup was here.

A moaning roar sounded close by, and above the noise a voice was heard.

"Kapugen! Your boat!"

"Your boat, Kapugen!"

Kapugen rushed out of the house. Julie and Ellen, who had heard and come running, found the ice-filled river almost at the door. It had picked up Kapugen's motor launch and would have carried it away, had not Peter been passing by. He had grabbed it by the bow and was pulling it landward. Kapugen leaped from the doorstep and pulled too, his boots ankle deep in flowing ice and water. Suddenly a house-sized chunk of ice rose like a whale from the river and rolled toward them.

Julie saw she was needed and splashed into the water. She grabbed the gunwale across from Kapugen and she, too, heaved. The boat was jerked landward. Then the huge ice block rose and fell. It created a wave almost as high as a man. Peter saw that it would carry off the boat and wrapped the rope around one of the posts that held Kapugen's house above the permafrost.

Julie saw the wave too, let go of the gunwale, and ran, but Kapugen did not. His back was to the wave. It lifted him off his feet, and, losing his grip, he was swirled into the water. Ellen ran to Julie and clung to her in horror as Kapugen was swept away.

Peter grabbed another rope from the boat and ran beside him, looking for a chance to throw it to him. Swimming crosswise to the current, Kapugen was pushed landward.

Ellen covered her eyes. "Dear, baby," she said. "Lie still. Lie still. It will be all right."

Another swell lifted Kapugen high and dumped him on an overturned fishing shed. He clung to it while the wave ran out and back into the river; then he leaped to the beach and ran.

"Nangaun!" he cried in praise, lifting his arms.

Julie did not begin trembling until Kapugen was almost back to them. She hugged Ellen, only to find she was shaking too.

Not Kapugen. He was laughing. His clothes were dripping and his wolverine ruff was wet but not soggy. His hair was plastered against his head. He slapped Peter on the back and said something, and Peter laughed, too.

"Why are they laughing?" Ellen asked in shock.

"You must have a sense of humor to live in the Arctic," Julie said. "Eskimos laugh. It's the best way."

"At prank jokes," Ellen said. "Not at death."

"At death," said Julie. "It's the best way."

Kapugen and Peter pulled the boat far up on shore; then Kapugen changed his clothes and put on his rubber breakup boots. He joined the villagers, who had come running when they heard the river had taken Kapugen and given him back.

Atik and Uma arrived. Uma's little son, Sorqaq, whose English name was Perry, peered over her shoulder. He was inside her amaunnaq, the woman's coat designed to carry babies and toddlers. A belt around Uma's coat at her waist kept Perry from slipping to the ground. He stood up on it and looked out. A wind hit his face, and he slid down against his mother's warm body.

Malek came running, and behind him came Marie, the storekeeper.

"Aaya," Marie said to Kapugen. "You must have offended the spirit of the river. She did not take you." The friends laughed.

Marie was joined by her husband, Ernest Adams, a famous walrus-tusk carver. His grandfather had been a Boston whaling captain who had settled in Wainwright and married AnugI, the best bootmaker on the Arctic coast. It was AnugI's father who had taught Ernest to carve ivory.

Julie studied Ernest Adams, for he was both Eskimo and gussak. His skin was lighter than Marie's and his face more elongated, but he had the dark eyes and broad, high cheekbones of the Eskimos. Ernest's appearance was not exceptional. Many Eskimos had white fathers or grandfathers, and recently some had been born to white mothers. More and more women from the lower forty-eight were coming to the Arctic to teach, practice medicine, and take a variety of jobs. Several, like Ellen, had married native men, stayed, and raised families. Julie looked from Ernest to Ellen's full figure. She was excited about the little child who would soon be among them.

Another woman joined the group, greeting Ellen. Her six-year-old son smiled shyly, and Ellen turned to Julie.

"This is Benjamin, my student," she said. "And Benjamin, this is my daughter, Julie." He smiled shyly at Julie and ran to Kapugen. "I am glad the river gave you back," he said to him.

"You bet," answered Kapugen. "I'm too nasty. It did not want me." Benjamin laughed, picked up a stone, and threw it at the water.

"Bad river," he said. "I punish the river." Kapugen laughed and, picking up the little boy, put him on his shoulders as Peter walked up.

"The water is rising close to your house," Peter

said. "Should we tie ropes to it and try to save it?"

Kapugen jounced Benjamin playfully. "The worst is past," he said, pointing upriver. "When I was flying home this morning, I saw that most of the tundra is snow bare and there are no dams of ice to break loose."

"Did you see the one that brought this flood?"

"I think I did, near duck camp, but I do not know. The one I saw did not look so big. The breakup plays pranks."

The river began to recede, and the villagers were told they were not needed to save Kapugen's house, but no one went home. It was sunny and warm, almost forty degrees. Everyone was happy to be outdoors. A snowbird trilled a cascade of sweet notes, and Julie turned to find him. The bird flew off with seeds in his beak.

"It's summer," exclaimed Julie. "The snowbirds are feeding their babies."

"It's summer," cried Benjamin, and slid down Kapugen's back.

"It's time to celebrate," said Kapugen. "I brought back a big sack of flour from Barrow. We'll make Eskimo doughnuts."

"I have whale meat and maktak," said Malek, who

had just returned from a successful whale hunt. A great cheer went up.

"Maktak," Benjamin shouted, and danced in a circle. "I love maktak better than candy."

"Kangik will have a whale festival, Nalukataq," Malek said. "It is time to share."

"How many whales did Wainwright take?" Atik asked.

"Five. That is their quota this year," Malek said. "It is not enough for everyone, but it cannot be helped. We cannot take more than the whaling commission permits us."

"Why?" shouted Benjamin. "I love lots and lots and lots of maktak."

"We want the whales to live," said Malek, "so that you, your children, and your grandchildren will have maktak."

"And Nalukataq, and blanket tosses," added Marie.

"Where is the blanket?" asked Atik.

"In the back of the store," Marie said. "Come help me get it—everyone come help."

"A blanket toss, a blanket toss," said Benjamin. He met his friend Roy, and together they jumped into one puddle after the other as they made their way down the pebbly street to the church. Other children were running and splashing in every puddle they could find on their way to Nalukataq. It was puddle time for the Arctic children and for Julie. She had on her breakup boots and was standing in a deep pool, kicking water and laughing. Puddles were a rare treat in the Arctic.

Nalukataq was held on the grounds in front of the church. The church was primarily a community center for the villagers, since the minister came to Kangik only a few times a year. Today it had become a community festival ground.

The river roar was a backdrop for the activity. Coleman stoves were set in a circle, and pots of water for cooking put on to boil. Malek pulled his sled of whale meat and blubber into the midst of the cooks and celebrants and cut the long slabs of meat into chunks for the pots. He carved the delicious skin into small bites with a strip of blubber on each—this was the maktak. Then he carved the fluke into thin slices. Taktuk, his wife, would distribute the fluke in a ceremony that some elders said was four thousand years old.

Only about fifty people remained in town, but in less than an hour every house was empty and the festival was in full swing. The sealskin blanket was spread on the ground. Marie served duck soup, and Uma and Taktuk passed out the raw maktak. Four drummers put up a band shell of caribou skins. They tuned up their round flat drums, which were on sticks like lollypops, and sat down on furs, their backs straight. Harry Ulugaq, who was still weak from his operation, was helped to the drum stand. He was determined to play and sing.

The first ponderous beat of the whale-liver-skin drum sounded. It gave a special sound for the opening of Nalukataq. Julie and Ellen hurried home to make the Eskimo doughnuts Kapugen had promised. Julie hung her wet mittens to dry on one of the wooden beams that held Kapugen's kayak near the ceiling.

"How do you make Eskimo doughnuts?" Ellen asked.

"I don't know," Julie said, laughing. "I'll go ask Marie—she should know." She ran off and returned a few moments later, grinning sheepishly.

"You put fifteen handfuls of flour into a bowl with some water and sugar and let it ferment for five days. Then you roll it, cut it, and cook it in deep whale oil."

"Really?" Ellen said, and winked. "Eskimo women have a big sense of humor, too. Let's do it the Minnesota way." She took out a large pot, opened her cookbook, and told Julie to read off the ingredients as she mixed.

Julie read and thumbed through the book between directions.

"What is apple pie?" she asked.

Ellen looked up with a start.

"I thought everyone knew," she said. "I'm always forgetting that I'm in the Arctic. Apple pie is to the lower forty-eight as maktak is to the North Slope. Gussaks love apple pie. They have to, because everyone says they do." She laughed and dumped the mix on the table, patted it, then flattened it out. "When Nalukataq is over, I will bake you an apple pie."

"What are apples?" Julie asked. Ellen threw up her sticky hands.

"I will never get used to no trees," she said. "I still think I can run out in the backyard and pick apples. It's a delicious fruit that grows on a tree." Ellen's eyes glistened, and Julie knew she must be homesick. She remembered how she had felt in Barrow when someone talked about Nunivak. Minnesota was even farther away.

The drums throbbed, and voices rose in rhythmic song. Ellen showed Julie how to cut the flattened dough into round circles with a drinking glass and put a hole in the center with the mouth of an empty pop bottle. After she tested the oil, they dropped in the doughnuts three at a time.

"When they are brown, lift them out with this strainer," Ellen said. She began opening cans and mixing an enormous bean salad.

Kapugen came in to get his Eskimo yo-yos, two fur-covered bags on two strings, for the yo-yo contest and picked up a doughnut cooling on the rack. He turned it curiously.

"Minnesota doughnut," said Julie. Kapugen took a big bite, said "Ummmm," and took another.

"This needs salmon to make it really good," he said.

"Salmon?" said Ellen, horrified, but Kapugen did not hear. He had hurried outside and opened his game cellar, a twelve-foot-deep square hole in the permafrost. He climbed down the ladder into the eighteen-degree atmosphere and came back into the house with three huge salmon.

"And now to celebrate the great whale," he said, putting the fish in a bag and slinging it over his shoulder. Julie carried the doughnuts in a large bucket, and Ellen brought the salad. The Kapugen family joined the celebrants to the beat of the tundra drums.

When the villagers had gathered, Taktuk stood on her family's sled.

"Anyone here have a husband and three children?" she called.

"Me," called Marie, and ran forward laughing.

"A precious piece of the flipper for Marie," Taktuk said, handing her a prized morsel. Everyone clapped as Marie ran back to her stove.

"Anyone here with a gold tooth?" Taktuk called.

"Henry, Henry Smith," everyone shouted, and pushed a nimble little man into the center of the circle. Taktuk called for many more people by spouses, numbers of children, color of parkas, sizes of breakup boots.

"One more piece," she finally called. "Anyone here who loves Kapugen's Julie?"

"I do," a young man called instantly.

"I do," Kapugen and Ellen called simultaneously, but too late. Peter Sugluk was dancing out into the circle to claim the prize.

The schoolboys leaped and laughed and the girls giggled. The adults smiled and told jokes. Julie stepped behind Kapugen and buried her face in his attigi, the summer parka, then peered around him.

Peter took his large slab of flipper and, holding it

high, walked over to Ellen and presented it to her. He was dressed in his traditional clothing, a reindeer parka with wolverine trim.

Peter bent his knees, took a wide stance, and stamped his toe. The drummers picked up his rhythm as he danced into the center of the circle.

Peter danced lightly and gracefully. He held his arms out as he beat a complicated rhythm with toes, arms, and body. He shot an imaginary spear into the sky. He skinned a mysterious animal, scraped it, and wrapped it around his shoulders. He moved so nimbly, he seemed more like a fox hunting in the snow than a person. Finally he stopped and bowed to the villagers.

"As you know," he said in Yupik, "I am grateful to my adopted parents, Malek and Taktuk. I now dance for them."

Peter danced like a reindeer coming across the tundra, like a flock of snow geese speeding over the sea ice, like a seal, like a whale, like a herd of caribou. His hands, feet, and body were as graceful as the ivory gull. No one had ever seen such dancing before, and they watched with rapt attention, Julie among them.

Then he beckoned to her. She hesitated. Kapugen urged her into the circle, and with a smile she began to dance. She held up her hands, wrists bent, thumbs tucked, and danced while Peter's feet kept time. She danced a woman's dance she had learned in Nunivak. When her dance was done, she bowed and Peter performed another man's dance, ending it with swift, complicated footwork. Then he walked over to Julie as if to claim her.

"Where did you learn the dance?" Julie asked shyly. "It's very wonderful."

"Siberia," he said. "That is my home."

"Siberia?" Julie at last knew why his accent was different. He came from far away. "How did you get here?" she asked. He took her arm and walked with her to the blanket for the blanket toss.

"With the Siberian Yupik Dancers," he said. "We have been dancing in Barrow and Kaktovik in Alaska and Kraulshavn in Greenland. I come from Provideniya, Siberia. We are all one people, you know, we who live around the North Pole. I speak Yupik. You speak Yupik. We hunt and fish. You hunt and fish. Nations make borders, cultures do not. I am here and we're dancing the same steps although we never met before." He leaned over and picked up a side of the blanket. Julie took a firm grip, as did the other villagers.

"Where are your dancing friends?" she asked

when everyone had a place around the sealskin blanket.

"They have gone home. Our visiting time was up. I liked it here. One day I met Malek. He told me Kangik had musk oxen and that he needed help with them.

"I told him I knew about them. We have musk oxen on our side of the Arctic Ocean, too. So that I could stay, Malek and Taktuk legally adopted me, and I have been very happy."

"Siberia," Julie repeated.

"We Eskimos were cut off from each other by the white man's politics for so long," Peter said gripping the blanket more tightly, "that we each forgot the other was there. Not our dances and languages. They remember six thousand years back. It is very exciting."

"Hup, hup," called Kapugen, and the villagers lowered the blanket to the ground so Benjamin could step onto the center of it. Carefully everyone lifted it up, then down, moving the blanket in a rhythm.

"Up!"

Benjamin flew fifteen feet in the air, pumping his feet and moving his arms to keep his balance. He hung in space a moment, a bright figure in a blue parka with white trim, then came pumping down. He hit the leather blanket and went flying up again. Three times he sped up into the blue sky and down. Then everyone rested.

After Benjamin, Edna Ulugak was tossed. She sped like a little bird and made graceful movements with her arms to much cheering. When she was tired, her big brother was tossed.

The blanket toss went on until everyone who wished had flown up and down like a bouncing ball, perfecting their poses and twists at the top of the ride. When there were no more volunteers, the blanket was put away for the night.

Julie gave Peter a Minnesota doughnut. He put it on his finger, danced a doughnut dance, and ate it. "Strange," he said. Marie gave them maktak on paper plates, and they sat down on the ground to eat.

"Yummm," Peter said. "Just like home."

"One thing you will find that is not like home," Julie said, "is that on this side of the Pole we don't say we love someone unless we do."

"We don't either." Peter said. "I love you." He looked at her. "In Siberia we know right away when we're in love. Over here it seems to take longer. Too much white-man influence. American white men wait until they go to school, get a job, have a house. When they are old men, they fall in love."

Chewing on her maktak, Julie thought of Daniel and her marriage to him at thirteen. She thought the white men were right.

The sun dipped low and then started up the sky. It was very late. Noticing that Ellen was packing up, Julie got up to help her. Peter arose.

"Julie," he said, taking her arm and walking her away from the crowd, "I also wanted to talk to you about your wolves."

She cried in terror, "You know about them?"

"I do."

"How? How?" she asked.

"The wolf," he said, as if she should know better than to ask, "speaks to you of friendship."

"Kapu is a wild wolf," she answered tartly. "That's all." She ran toward Ellen.

"Julie." Peter caught up with her and pulled her aside again. "Kapu and his pack killed a musk ox last night."

Julie spun around. "No," she cried. "No, he didn't. He is in Anaktuvuk Pass with the caribou."

"The grizzly knocked down the fence," Peter said softly and slowly. "I drove her far inland with rifle shots in the air. While I was gone, the wolves came in. They were leaving the carcass when I found them.

They ran off. I fixed the fence and waited to see if they would come back. They did not."

"No, Peter, no," Julie cried. "Kapugen will kill them." She ran off a few steps and came back.

"Please don't tell him," she said. "I must do it."

PART II

AMY, THE WOLF PUP

Julie felt as lost as she had been in the blinding snowstorm. She stood motionless thinking of what Kapu had done. The drummers were putting their drums away, leftover food was being toted home, and sleepy children were being carried off to bed. Kapugen and Ellen were teaching Benjamin, Roy, and little Edna Ulugak the foot and arm movements of the caribou dance, but Julie saw none of this. She could see only the terrible fate of her wolves.

She did not even see Peter, who was walking backward watching her. In the hazy sunlight of one o'clock in the morning he looked as if he had been cast in an orange bronze.

Julie walked to Kapugen's rescued boat and sat down. She stared at the raging river. The water had abated, but huge blocks of ice roiled up, boomed, sank, and reemerged far downstream. The roar of the

breakup was comforting. It was a sound wall that isolated her from the now-sleepy merriment of Kangik. She could concentrate on what to do about her wolves.

Kapu must have puppies now, she thought. He would not go far from them, and so she laid a plan.

Into her consciousness came the crackle of Kapugen's CB.

"White Fox Base," she heard. "This is Wainwright Rescue Base. Do you read me, Kapugen? Over."

Julie sat quietly thinking of Kapu. The call was repeated again before she shook her head and hurried into the house. She flipped on the CB.

"Wainwright Rescue Base, I read you. Kapugen is not here. Over."

"White Fox Base. This is Search and Rescue calling. Emergency. Emergency. Can you get him? Over."

"I will get him. Out." Kapugen was a member of the Search and Rescue Team of the North Slope. He was needed. Julie ran.

She found Kapugen, Ellen, and Uma dancing in the sunlight near the church. The children were gone, and Uma was showing Ellen how to move her feet to perform a special chorus of the woman's dance. Ellen was following her steps with great artistry. Julie ran up to Kapugen.

"Aapa," she said, "Search and Rescue wants you." Kapugen stopped dancing and, taking Ellen's hand, hurried home with her. Julie followed slowly, thinking up words to tell Kapugen about Kapu and the musk ox.

When she entered the house, Kapugen was getting into his flying jacket.

"Not good news," he said. "A lawyer and his wife from Barrow are lost in the sea. Before the storm they headed out in their boat for Kuk Inlet. No word from them since. I am flying out to see if I can find them." He stepped to his CB and flicked it on.

"Malek," he said into the speaker, "Kapugen speaking. Do you hear me?" A pause.

"I hear you, Kapugen, but not too good. I am sleepy. Over."

"Clear your head, my good co-pilot," he said, "and meet me at the Quonset. Two people are missing in the sea. Out."

He snapped off the radio, kissed Ellen, and patted Julie's cheek.

"I'll be back," he said.

"Aapa." Julie ran to the door with him. "I have something I must tell you."

"Later, later," he said, and rushed into the copper sunlight of the small hours of the day.

"He must find them," Ellen said to Julie's back. "This country has more than its share of tragedies."

"That is how it is," Julie said, and climbed up on the iglek. Ellen went into her bedroom and pulled the blinds so she could sleep. The dogs barked, Kapugen's airplane took off, and Kangik was quiet. Nalukataq was over.

Kapugen was gone two days. When he returned, he was somber and thoughtful. He stopped by the store to tell Marie and a few shoppers that he had located the boat upside down on a lonely beach. It was empty. The lawyer's log book said he had turned around when he saw the storm that had trapped Julie and Ellen. It overtook him. The shoppers shook their heads at the news. They knew what Hilla, the weather spirit, could do, and they were saddened.

For the next week Kapugen was in and out of the house and too busy to either talk to Julie or go to the corral. He and Malek flew back and forth to Barrow on legal matters for the lawyer's family and over the lonely beaches and capes searching for their bodies. Malek turned over the management of the herd to Peter.

Julie waited for a chance to speak to Kapugen. She read some new books she had found when she had helped Ellen clean the schoolroom for the summer. She fished, fed the dogs, and checked the corral fence. In the late afternoon she would go out on the tundra and note the tracks of the mammals and the activities of the birds. She was practicing for the plan she had devised.

The uminmaks were shedding great swatches of qivit as the season changed. Peter came by the house to ask Julie to help him gather it. She accepted, eager to fill in the time until she could speak to Kapugen. When they were done, she would go out on the tundra and listen for messages from her wolves.

Two calves were born one afternoon, and Julie ran all the way home, her black hair flying behind.

"Ellen," she said with great excitement, "Far Northland has two new friends."

"Two more oxen," Ellen said, smiling. "Very good. Very good. We will soon have a herd large enough to make this industry pay for itself." She opened the record book and wrote down the births. "Were they girls or boys?"

"They are both females," Julie replied.

"Good. That means more little ones."

"Let's celebrate," said Julie. "I will catch you a chum, the best salmon. They are beginning to come up the river from the sea."

"Splendid," said Ellen. "I'll cook it the Minnesota way."

It did not take Julie long to catch the fish. She filleted it with deft movements, then watched Ellen stuff it with herbs and dried fruit her mother had sent.

"Julie," Ellen said, straightening up after placing the fish in the oven, "I've been noticing the books you are reading. You are much too advanced to go to school in Kangik next winter."

"I am?" Julie said. "That's too bad. I would like to be a student here."

"You can be a student," Ellen said, "but not here. In a year or so the North Slope Borough will build a high school in Kangik, but until they do, the borough sends Kangik high school students to Barrow, Anchorage, or Fairbanks. You can then go on to the University of Alaska or even to the lower forty-eight to colleges and universities there."

Julie listened attentively.

"If you are interested," Ellen said, "I will get an application for you."

"I will think about it," Julie replied without enthusiasm.

"You would not be alone," Ellen urged. "There would be other young Eskimos your age. You would go to dances and basketball and volleyball games."

Julie was quiet. Ellen tried harder.

"One of my students graduated from the Anchorage high school last year. He will go to the University of Alaska in Fairbanks this fall. Wouldn't that be fun?"

"What do the students do after they are educated?" Julie asked.

"Most come back to the North Slope," Ellen replied. "One is now the Superintendent of Schools. Another is a banker. Another from Barrow is an expert on the Iñupiat language and she's even compiled an Iñupiat dictionary. There is a lot to be done with an education up here. The Eskimo want to keep their culture and at the same time learn more modern skills like using computers and libraries."

Julie sat as still as a hunted rabbit. A week and a half ago she would probably have asked Ellen to get her an application. Today she could not. She had a contract with her wolves. She must save them.

Ellen turned on her symphonic music. She served the salmon.

"Shall I apply for you?" she asked.

"I must think." Ellen, sensing Julie was up against some emotional wall, walked over to the calendar.

"Your little brother or sister will be with us on

the fifth of July, the doctor says. We'll talk about school after the baby comes." They ate quietly, listening to the wind rattling the windows accompanied by Ellen's music.

"Ellen," Julie finally said, "I am very selfish. I have not made a present for my little paipiuraq." She scraped the dishes and put them in a pan of dishwater.

"I sew well," she went on. "I once made beautiful parkas for Nusan, the wife of Kapugen's serious partner." Julie pulled on her rubber breakup boots. "I'll wash the dishes when I come back. I want to go to the Quonset. Kapugen gave me his white ermines. He said they were for me. He said he wanted me to make something beautiful for myself out of them. But I am going to make the baby a glistening white parka of ermine." She put on her attigi. "I am not so selfish anymore," she said.

"You have never been selfish," Ellen replied.

Julie smiled shyly and hurried outside into the cool sunshine. A soft wind was blowing from the distant ocean. The tiny sedges and reeds along the river were sheltering geese and ducks on their nests. Out on Kuk Inlet, now a deep blue-green, men and women in fishing boats were catching the first salmon and whitefish that were on their way inland to spawn and lay eggs. The whale, duck, and seal seasons were over; the fishing season had begun.

Splashing through the mud puddles, Julie designed the ermine parka in her head as she skipped and ran to the Quonset. She did not see Peter until she was almost upon him.

"Julie," he said, smiling. "I was coming to find you. I saw your wolves."

She stopped still. Her eyes did the speaking: *Where*? they asked.

"About forty miles up the Avalik," he answered. "They were carrying food."

"Good. That means they are feeding a mother. They are at a den."

"That's what I thought."

"How many adults did you see?"

"Three."

"Three," she said. "Do you think you saw them all? Atik saw eight in the winter."

"The winter has been hard on wolves. No food. Some have probably starved."

She bit her lip. "I must go to them. Forty miles is not far enough for a wolf. They will be back for another musk ox." She started to leave.

"Can you join me at the shelter?" he asked. "The fourth calf is about to be born, and the cow is acting strangely."

"I will join you later in the day," she said. "I am on my way to get ermine from Kapugen's fur pile in the Quonset. I am going to make Ellen's baby a beautiful coat."

Peter smiled and looked at her over the top of his dark glasses.

"I love you," he said. "Do you love me?"

"Peter Sugluk," she said. "I must finish high school and college and get a master's degree in Yupik and Iñupiat before I can think of being in love."

"Has Ellen been talking to you?"

"She has."

"Ellen has been talking to me also," Peter said. "I have applied to the University of Alaska."

"You are going to school?" Julie asked, and laughed. "You are full of surprises." She put her hands on her hips. "I don't know what to think about you."

"Yes, you do," he said, taking her around the waist and swinging her off her feet. He circled twice before he put her down facing the Quonset.

"Now go get the ermine for the baby present," he said. "I'll meet you at the shelter."

Julie caught her balance, then ran around the church and up the trail to the Quonset. Stepping inside, she peered back at Peter. His white attigi flapped as he ran. He was a gyrfalcon speeding to its roost.

I like him, Julie said to herself. *That's all.* But she did not take her eyes away from him until he was out of sight.

It was midnight. The plane engine droned off in the distance, grew louder and lower, and finally cut out. Julie listened from her iglek and waited. Kapugen and Ellen were returning from the doctor in Barrow. Julie had not slept since the midnight sun had colored the tundra orange, for this was the day she would tell Kapugen that Kapu had killed a musk ox. Almost a week had passed since the incident. She was frightened but determined.

Ellen came in the door first and passed the iglek on tiptoes, assuming Julie was asleep. She crossed the room in her stocking feet, winding her red hair on the top of her head. When it was all pulled up and tied, she dipped a pan of water from the thirty-gallon plastic container beside the refrigerator. Ellen took a long drink of cold, fresh river water. Since the breakup the people of Kangik could once again dip their water from the Avalik.

Ellen brushed her teeth over an enamel basin and threw the water down the kitchen sink. At last she went into the bedroom.

Julie listened to the water run down the sink pipe and splash on the ground under the house. She heard it trickle away. This was a sound of summer. The sink water was no longer freezing in a glass cone under the house.

Kapugen opened the doors and came in. Julie wiggled to the edge of the iglek.

"Aapa," she whispered, "I have something to tell you." She was almost eye to eye with him.

"Ee-lie, pretty Miyax," he said, and winked. "So you have a love?"

"Aapa," she said, ignoring him. "Please be serious."

"Ee-lie," he said, and kissed her cheek. "Is it that you want to get married?" He brushed back a strand of her hair.

"Aapa, Aapa." Julie slid off the iglek and stood before him. "I want you to listen to what I have to tell you with a soft heart."

Kapugen looked puzzled. "Don't I always?"

"The wolves killed an ox."

The cheerful twinkle left Kapugen's eyes. After a thoughtful silence he turned and went into the qanitchaq. He put on his flying jacket and picked up his wolf gun.

"Please don't," Julie begged. She followed him

into the two-A.M. sunlight.

"Please don't," she pled again.

"It cannot be helped," he answered, taking the path to the Quonset and his airplane. "We need the musk oxen."

"Please, Kapugen, my aapa." Julie ran beside him in her bare feet. "I will keep the wolves away from the oxen. Please do not shoot them. They saved my life." She stopped and reached out her arms to him.

"It cannot be helped," he repeated, but his pace did slow. Julie's eyes filled with tears. She hurried to catch up with him.

"Please, Aapa, it will never happen again. It will never happen again. I know what to do."

"Perhaps the killers are not the wolves who saved you," Kapugen said, wanting to believe this, although he knew there was only one pack between Wainwright and the mountains.

"They are. Don't shoot them," she answered. "Peter saw the pack. One was silver and one was gray. The leader was black."

"But I shot your black leader."

"The black one is his pup. You shot him, too, but not badly. I nursed him back to health." She hesitated. "I named him after you. His name is Kapu. He is a great leader."

"The musk oxen must live," said Kapugen. "We need money for the villagers."

"Atik has walrus, Malek has whale. Duck and goose eggs are everywhere in the river reeds. The whitefish and salmon are beginning their runs."

"We cannot hunt forever," said Kapugen. "The wild animals are passing off the earth. We must find a new way to live in the Arctic. Industry. The musk oxen are our industry."

Kapugen had slowed his pace to a hesitant walk. His face reflected such sadness that Julie could not bear to look at him.

"It cannot be helped," he said once more. "I must shoot the wolves that killed the ox."

"Let me go to them," she said. "I know what to do. You once talked to the wolves. Like you, I learned their language when I was with them on the tundra. I will tell them where the caribou are and send them off to find them. They will do that."

Kapugen ran his weather-darkened fingers over his brow, as if changing his mind. Then his resolve returned and he strode on toward the Quonset. Julie ran after him.

"Please, let me try," she begged. "If I don't succeed, then I will understand. Please, Aapa."

Kapugen let her catch up to him. "In Minnesota,"

he said, "the wolves are protected. No one can shoot them.

"They roam the forests taking deer and moose and an animal they call the beaver. But when a wolf comes onto a person's land and kills his cattle, then the government environmental officers come and shoot him. They shoot the ones that compete with humans. They think that is fair. That is how it is between humans and wolves in Minnesota."

"But not here," Julie said. "We are different. We know the wolf is from the earth and must live so we all can live."

"Not when we live as the white men do." Kapugen had stopped walking. "Eskimos," he said, his voice low as he paced his words carefully, "now live by the Minnesota rules."

"The old rules are best," said Julie.

"I taught you that, didn't I?"

"You taught me that, Aapa."

"I was wrong."

Slender clouds were forming over the bay as the sun began its endless circle around the top of the world again. Julie and her father noted them, as they noted all clouds.

"Sunshine," said Julie. "I can travel."

"Then you will go to them?" Kapugen said quietly.

"I will go to them."

"And what will you do?"

"I do not quite know until I talk to them."

"How will you travel? You cannot take the dogs."

"On foot, until I find them. Then I will travel as they travel." She dropped to her hands and feet and pranced lightly around Kapugen, whimpering and whining like a wolf.

"You did learn their language," he said, pulling her gently to her feet. "Go to them. I know your efforts will be wasted. Wolves do not know about people's property. They see their rightful prey and take it. Wolves have to be wolves."

"Wolves know about borders," Julie said. "They have hunting lands like we do. They mark and patrol them. It is too bad that our musk oxen are on Kapu's land. He thinks they are his."

Kapugen put the gun sling around his neck and let the rifle hang on his back.

"It is useless," he said.

"You will let me try?" she asked.

"I cannot refuse," he said, touching her shiny black hair with the gentleness of a wolf with a puppy. "I will let you try." He rose on his toes, then rocked back on his heels. "If they kill again, I must go by the Minnesota rules."

"All right," she said. "But you will not have to." She wiped her eyes with a knuckle and thanked him with a teary smile.

Kapugen slipped his arm around her shoulder and they walked back home, casting long purple shadows before them.

"Take your .22," he said as they approached the house. "I will give you ammunition."

"I do not want my .22." She remembered the gun blasts that had killed Amaroq and the fear her wolves harbored for guns.

"There are grizzly bears out there," Kapugen went on. "Shoot the gun in the air. It will scare them."

Julie nodded. "Maybe I will take it," she said, recalling the grizzly who had attacked her. Had it not been for Amaroq and his pack, she might not be here now.

Kapugen said no more until he put his hand on the qanitchaq doorknob.

"I will come for you," he said. "My old dog CB will pick up your trail and lead me to you. He's a good tracker, all right. He can smell a seal four miles away and go find it."

"Give me two weeks," she said. "Enough time to get through to them." Kapugen nodded once. He understood. One had to be patient with the Arctic.

Julie spent the next few hours provisioning herself for the trip. She took food, her ulu bag and whale oil, and a change of clothing. She hummed as she made her preparations. She was looking forward to walking in freedom on the open tundra again. This time she would walk without fear of starvation.

When she was packed, she went outside and tacked the white ermines to a board. Carefully she cut them into strips with her ulu. She sat down and stitched them into a single beautiful hide. All the glistening guard hairs lay in one direction. She held up the block of fur and drew in her breath. The ermine bunting was going to be breathtakingly beautiful. She wrapped it around her shoulders, then ran to Ellen's mirror above the kitchen sink. The ice-white fur made her soft olive skin glow and her black eyes more lustrous. She carried it to the iglek and tucked it under the grizzly skin. She would complete the bunting when the baby was born. That would bring the child good luck. She lay down on the iglek and slept.

Hours later, her pack on her back, she stepped outside. She had read the clouds correctly. The air was clear, the sky cloudless. The horizon shimmered.

At least this part of the three-month-long day was going to be beautiful. She walked to the river trail. There she took the totem of Amaroq out of her pocket and held it against her cheek. Then she started off on her journey.

As she approached the corral, she saw Peter and called to him. He waved and came running to greet her. His wide smile clearly said he was glad to see her.

"The calf is born," he called. "Another girl."

Julie smiled, but she did not comment. She had but one thought on her mind.

"Tell me again, Peter Sugluk," she said. "Where did you last see the wolves?"

Peter described an elbow bend in the river and a long beach of white stones. "I saw them walking there."

"Were there any pretty flowers around?" she asked.

"Ee-lie, come to think of it, there were. Why do you ask?"

"Silver likes flowers around her den. They might be denning somewhere near flowers. Were the banks high?"

"They were."

"They like to den high so they can look out over the land."

Peter folded his arms on his chest and tipped his head. His eyes twinkled appreciatively at her knowledge. Then his expression changed.

"What did Kapugen say?" he asked anxiously.

"That he would let me try to save them," she answered. "He will give me this chance. He must shoot them if they kill again."

"What is your plan?" Peter asked.

"I will take them to the caribou, wherever they are," she said.

"How will you do that?" he asked.

"With wolf reasoning," she answered.

Peter grinned and reached into his attigi pocket. "Take this," he said, handing her a small object that was carved out of walrus-tusk ivory. It hung on a thong.

"It's very nice," she said. "What is it?"

"A ground-squirrel whistle," he answered. "I made it. It will amuse you when you are discouraged." She turned it over in her hand, then put it around her neck.

"A ground-squirrel whistle," she said, ducking her chin and looking up at him with laughing eyes. "I will think of you when I blow it."

"That is what it is really for," he said. "To make you think of me." He folded his arms. "And you *will* think of me when you blow it," he reassured her, and chuckled.

"I am sure I will not be able to help it," she said. "It's a funny gift. A ground-squirrel whistle."

Peter laughed, and his white teeth shone brightly against his bronze skin. The ermine tails on his boots danced.

"I would go with you," he finally said, "but Malek needs me."

"I must go alone," she said. "The wolves are my friends."

Julie looked out across the tundra and pointed her boots toward the wolves.

She stepped lightly around small snow patches as she followed the Avalik River toward its source. Her heels barely touched the ground as she walked. She skipped around poppies and waved to the snow buntings that flew up from the flowers.

A day's walk beyond duck camp, Julie came upon a weasel standing on his hind feet, paws draped on his chest. He was no longer wearing his winter fur of white ermine, but a golden-brown coat that blended with the summer tundra. He was boldly blocking her way. Julie stamped her foot at him. He showed his sharp teeth and screamed but did not run.

Julie walked closer. When she was almost two feet from him, she stopped.

"I am a person," she said. "Why aren't you afraid of me? Is it because you have never seen a human before?" She lifted her arms and swayed from side to side.

"See how big I am?" The weasel twitched his whiskers and stood his ground. "Learn to be afraid of two-legged animals," she said. "They shoot little weasels in the winter and make them into glorious ermine coats." The bright-eyed, pointed-faced weasel stood firm, so she blew him a kiss and went on.

The next day Julie passed a snowy owl on her nest. Like the weasel, the large white bird with its huge golden eyes was not afraid of her. She let Julie come almost up to her fluffy babies before getting up on her feet.

Julie pondered about what she was seeing. The animals were talking to her. The owl and the weasel were saying they were not afraid of people because they rarely saw them. They were saying that Julie was in a wilderness where people did not come. In such country, she knew, the wolves of the Arctic raise their young.

A redpoll flew up from.a grassy spot with a piece of fur in her bill. Julie spun around. That was wolf fur. She looked down. The grass had been bent by soft, padded feet, not sharp hoofs. She followed the subtle trail and came upon the sleeping scoop of a wolf. The bits of fur within it were black. Kapu had been here. The trail she was following was his. Her spirits lightened.

Bending low, noting every trampled blade of grass, she traced Kapu's footsteps from his sleeping scoop to an elbow bend in the river. There before her was the white, stony beach Peter had mentioned. The footsteps became lost on the gravel. She went on upriver. Two wolf tracks appeared in the silt, then three, then many, as if wolves were playing. She rounded a bend, and there before her was a high, sandy bank. Scanning it carefully, she located a dark spot—a den. Just above it a garden of yellow poppies bobbed in the wind.

"That's it," she said. She put her pack on a gravel bar in the riverbed where she could clearly see the den and sat down. For several hours she remained absolutely still, not even turning her head.

Nothing moved at the den. But everywhere around it there was great activity. The little birds of the tundra were attending their nests. Longspurs and buntings, redpolls and sandpipers fluttered up and over the riverbank and swiftly back down. Julie continued sitting still. Her plan was going to work. This den was a whelping den, not like the summer nursery with its two exits where she had first met Amaroq and his family. Kapu's pups would still be young, and that was very good.

Carefully, slowly, Julie put up the tent she had made from the caribou Amaroq had felled for her many months ago. Then she spread out her ground skin and lay down to wait for her wolves.

After many hours she heard a wavering cry, then a plaintive whimper. It was Kapu. Her heart beat faster. He walked swiftly along the water's edge. His big feet and long legs were wet with river splash, and his dark body made a bold outline against the sandy bank. He did not see or smell her. He had one thing in mind—the den. He walked directly to it, head and tail held high, fur glistening in the sun, and a wolf smile on his face. He was a glorious animal.

His tail began wagging forty feet from the den entrance and did not stop until he reached it. There he whimpered coaxingly. The white wolf came out. She was not Silver, the mother of Kapu. Julie knew Silver as she knew Kapugen and Ellen. What had become of Silver? Had she succumbed to the food scarcity of the winter and spring?

Before she could think more about this, a fuzzy

pup thrust her nose out of the den and whimpered to her father, then ran up to him. She was black like Kapu. Her nose was short and blunt. She had big paws and a chubby body, and Julie wanted to run to her and pick her up and hug her.

The mother greeted Kapu by licking his cheek; then she pushed her cub back into the den. Julie named the white wolf Aaka, or mother. She named the puppy Amy in honor of her pen pal named Amy. She had been on her way to visit her pen pal when she had become lost and eventually had met Amaroq and his pack on the tundra. "Amy," she whispered to herself as she watched the perky pup. When she got home, she would write her friend and tell her there was a wolf puppy named for her. Amy now had an atiQ, a namesake. She would like that.

Kapu looked up and over the den. He barked the doglike hey-look-who's-coming bark of the wolf. Julie turned her head ever so slightly and saw a third adult wolf trotting home. She immediately recognized Zing, Kapu's brother. He was carrying a ground squirrel in his mouth. Zing leaped over the poppies and dropped it in front of the den, a toy for Amy. For the rest of the summer Amy would be developing her skills with such presents from the tundra.

Zing's presence told Julie a great deal about her old pack. Either Silver had died or Kapu had left her to find a mate and had taken along his good friend and strong brother, Zing. Wolves need partners. One wolf cannot fell big game. Somewhere on the barren tundra the brothers had met Aaka and invited her to join them. Julie imagined the battle for her. It would have been brief. Kapu was bigger and more intelligent than Zing. He would have snarled, showed his canines, even grabbed Zing's ruff. Zing would have dropped to the ground and flashed his white belly fur, the flag of surrender. He would have accepted his defeat, then gotten up and licked Kapu's face. They would have been friends again.

Aaka and Kapu would have mated, and the three would have formed a working pack and traveled their eighty-mile-square territory looking for food. Kapugen's musk ox was an easy take through the broken fence.

Just before the pups were due, all three adult wolves would have dug a den midway up the riverbank. It would be shallow, for it takes Arctic wolves years to dig a deep den in the stonelike permafrost.

Julie wondered about the number of puppies. When food is scarce, wolves give birth to fewer pups; sometimes none at all if they are starving. She did not think there could be many this year, and she was soon proven right. When Aaka came out of the den to stretch and take a swift, exhilarating run, Julie could see to the back and bottom of this first-year den. There was only one puppy. The winter had been hard on the wolves as well as the villagers of Kangik.

Zing approached Aaka but was turned back by Kapu. He stood over him, head up, one canine tooth bared, a friendly reminder to his brother that Aaka was his. "Keep your distance," he was saying, and Zing lowered his ears and tail and walked off.

The wind shifted and Kapu lifted his nose toward the riverbed. Cocking his head to one side, he sniffed. He sniffed again. With that his ears shot forward. He smelled Julie. She moved and he saw her. For a moment he stared; then, wagging his tail furiously, he pulled back his lips in a smile and spanked the ground with both front feet.

"Kapu," she called, "you remember me." With her mouth open she whimpered to show him how happy she was that he had not forgotten her.

Kapu romped toward her, then stopped. He threw back his head and howled a long melodious note that began with a bear's growl and rose to a wind scream. He was saying a pack member was here. Julie howled, harmonizing with him. Zing now saw her and lifted his black lip over one canine tooth and growled.

"Zing, it's me," Julie said, and whined her love for him. Zing wagged his tail. He ran to her and, looking straight in her eyes, said she was family and welcome.

Kapu became excited. He sped like a sea eagle down the beach and back to Julie. She threw him her mitten. He caught it, tossed it in the air, and caught it again. He ran in circles and dropped it. Julie laughed and picked it up. Kapu had not lost his sense of humor even though he was a father and the leader of his pack.

Zing circled Julie several times, then lay down near her. He turned his head and half closed his eyes, saying all was well with him. His strange sister was back. Kapu let himself down on his belly in front of her and crossed his paws. He stared at the mitten. Julie hid it. Kapu lifted his head and threw his ears up and forward. He wanted the mitten. He arose and stood above her, trying to pull rank. Julie laughed and threw it to him.

No more adult wolves joined the pack, nor did any more pups appear. There were only two adults to do the hunting, Kapu and Zing. Aaka must guard her pup. The story was there for Julie to read. The other members of the original group had either joined distant packs or started their own as Kapu had done. Or they were dead—the life of a wolf is dangerous.

The sun circled the top of the world twice, and with each swing Julie moved closer to the den. Kapu and Zing did not care, but Aaka did. She became nervous every time Julie inched her way forward. She growled and bared her teeth. Julie tossed her a mitten, but Aaka would not play. She was proving to be a problem—and she was the most important wolf in Julie's plan. She must get Aaka's confidence if she was going to help her wolves.

Julie was patient. She moved back a few yards and quietly went about a routine of eating and sleeping and waiting. On the fifth morning Kapu scooped a sleeping bed four feet from Julie's tent. He circled and circled, then lay down and went to sleep.

Aaka watched this from the den entrance. After a long time she came down the embankment and walked over to Kapu. She lay down beside him and rested her head on his back. She watched the river out of her cool yellow-brown eyes. Finally she twitched her ears and glanced at Julie. Julie looked at her. Aaka looked away. Julie looked away, but sneaked a glance out of the corner of her eyes. Slowly, thoughtfully, Aaka turned her head and looked right into Julie's eyes. She did not look away. Julie's heart ached with happiness. By looking in her eyes, Aaka was saying she had accepted Julie into the family. Everything was going to be all right.

From that moment on Aaka stopped growling at Julie, and after the next sleep Julie moved her tent almost up to the den door. Aaka made friends with her but would not let Amy come out and play. That was the next problem. Julie needed not only Aaka's friendship but Amy's.

During this time Kapu and Zing were gone long hours hunting for ground squirrels, snowshoe hare, foxes, ptarmigan—anything they could find. One hunt lasted so long, Julie feared Kapu and Zing had gone back to the corral for a musk ox. She was greatly relieved when they returned with a snowshoe hare for Aaka.

In the middle of the next sunny night Julie was awakened by the whimperings and woofs of the wolves. Kapu had dragged a calf carcass to the den, and they were discussing it in their mysterious way. The carcass was so old and battered that Julie was not sure what it was, but it looked to her like a caribou calf.

She was excited. If there was a little calf, the caribou herd could not be far away. Later in the sunny night, when the wolves had abandoned the carcass, Julie looked at it closely. The animal wore a radio collar around its neck like the one Atik had described.

She took it off and cleaned it in the river. A tag on it read: Return to Alaska Fish and Game Department, Fairbanks, AK. She put it in her pack. She would do that.

Another day passed and Julie still could not get close to Amy. The mother wolf was keeping her pup hidden even though she herself was comfortable with Julie. Julie wondered why, but then she remembered that wolves did not think like people. They thought with scents and sounds as well as vision. This left them either completely disconnected or, if they chose, so alert they could sense aggression. She decided that Aaka was being alert and had read her plan in her face or eyes—and did not like it.

Julie thought about how to get Amy to be her friend. It was absolutely essential to her next move that the little pup trust her. She was thinking about what to do when Aaka sat down beside her. Julie whimpered pleasantly to her. Aaka whimpered, then turned and looked back at the den. Amy was sitting out in the open under the poppies. Julie whimpered. The little pup got up and ran to her. She grabbed her boot thong and tugged, growling ferociously while wagging her tail. Then she looked at Julie and spanked the ground with her forepaws to say, "Let's play." She longed to pick up the adorable pup, but Aaka's eyes said she was not ready for that.

Amy woofed. Julie woofed back. She held out a bone from the caribou carcass. Amy grabbed it in her teeth and pulled. She growled joyfully, pulling harder, then let go. Julie fell backward. After another game of tug-of-war and one game of boneball, Aaka got up and led Amy back to the den. But a great barrier had been crossed. Julie closed her eyes and breathed with relief. Things were progressing.

The next day when Kapu and Zing went off to hunt, Aaka led Amy to Julie again. Julie picked up the bone and waggled it before Amy, who grabbed and shook it. They tugged and chased while Aaka walked off and stretched out in the sun. She closed her eyes to say she had complete confidence in Julie at last.

"Can I pet you?" Julie whispered to Amy. The pup twisted her head curiously and Julie gently reached out and buried her fingers in the soft fur. She scratched the little head and the pointed ears. Amy closed her eyes and Julie took her hand away. Amy nudged her hand for more scratches. Julie petted her again, then held out the bone. Amy grabbed it, pulled powerfully, and let go. Again Julie went over backward, and this time the pup pounced on her. Amy yipping, and Julie laughing, they tumbled on the gravelly beach. Aaka did not lift her head.

After a while Aaka got to her feet, shook, stretched, and yawned. Then, without looking back, she wagged her tail and ran off.

Aaka sped over the tundra like a bird released from a cage. She ran in circles, chased cotton-grass seeds, then disappeared around the bend in the river. Julie got to her feet, her heart pounding, her hopes high. She could see Aaka racing across the tundra tracking Kapu and Zing. Julie saw that she was going to win. Aaka trusted her to be the baby-sitter.

Amy played with a bone for a short while, then crawled into Julie's lap. She whimpered and Julie sang her songs until the little pup sighed and slumped into a deep sleep. Then Julie picked her up and carried her back to the den.

Her baby asleep, Julie got her .22 and walked into the grasses. She wandered for quite a while before she saw a ptarmigan and shot it. This, too, was part of her plan.

When she returned to the den, Amy was awake. She sniffed the bird, shook it, then dropped it and looked at Julie as if to ask what she should do with it.

Julie skinned it and offered her a tasty morsel. Amy licked it, then grabbed it in her sharp teeth and gulped. She came back for more. This time Amy took the bird, which she ate after smashing it, bones and all, with her small but powerful teeth and jaws.

The little wolf decided one wing was a toy. She shook it in Julie's face. When Julie grabbed it, Amy pulled it away and ran in circles. Julie tricked her by flashing the calf bone in one hand. Amy dropped the wing for the bone, and Julie got the wing. With that Amy sat down. She would not play anymore, even when Julie gave her the wing. For the remainder of the time the hunters were away, Amy ignored Julie.

"You didn't like that, did you Amy?" Julie said to her. "You don't like to be tricked. I am sorry." To make up for her error, Julie offered her a piece of dried caribou. Amy looked right through it as if it were not there. She did not even seem to see Julie. *Where does the mind of the wolf go at times like these?* Julie wondered. *Far out on the tundra? Over the river?* She did not know.

The next day Amy was playful again. Whatever had been in her wolf mind was not there today. She left the adult wolves and romped to Julie, chewed her boot thong, and asked to be scratched and petted. When they were as close as sisters, Julie gently, gently picked her up. The pup cuddled. Julie glanced at Aaka. She was lying on her side completely unconcerned. Julie was overjoyed. She carried Amy down to the river. Kapu and Zing awoke, stretched, yawned, and shook themselves. After a short howl they trotted off to hunt. Aaka went with them, leaving Amy in Julie's arms. Julie was part of the wolf pack.

When the wolves came home, their bellies were rounded with food and they slept for a long time. When they all finally awoke, Kapu inaugurated the leadership ceremony. He did this each wolf morning. He stood above Zing, who lowered his head and licked Kapu's cheeks. Then Kapu mouthed his muzzle and shook it gently. Aaka approached him, ears down, head down, and he lifted his head above hers. She licked him under the chin and along his neck to tell him he was a fine leader. Kapu, like all wolf leaders, needed lots of reassurance from his pack. Having gotten it, he trotted to the highest point on the embankment, poised himself, and howled. Zing and Aaka howled. Amy yipped. They sang their music for many minutes. During the concert, the noisy birds quieted down and the ground squirrels retired to their elaborate underground tunnels and dens. When they were done, Zing turned to Aaka and seized her muzzle to tell her he had more status than she did.

She quickly corrected that.

That evening when the hunters were gone, Julie put Amy in her backpack and carried her along the riverside to find another bird to eat. The wolf pup did not try to get out of the pack; rather, she peered around at the world, seemingly pleased with her high seat. Julie walked a long distance without finding anything and was starting back to the den when a ground squirrel dove into one of the many entrances into his underground city.

"Peter," she said, "I'm thinking of you." And she pulled the whistle out of her shirt and blew it.

Eeekk-chirp. Two ground squirrels poked their heads out of the burrow. She blew it again. Three more appeared. The more she blew, the more little squirrels appeared. Amy yipped and Julie put her down on the ground. She blew the whistle again; another head popped up. The little wolf pup pounced, and all the ground squirrels disappeared.

"What a special gift, Peter," she said, and laughed right out loud. "This will come in very handy."

When Kapu, Aaka, and Zing came home, this time with their stomachs empty, Julie walked to the ground-squirrel colony and blew the whistle. Up came the ground squirrels. The wolves saw, wagged their tails, and gobbled.

"Ee-lie, Kapu," she said when he had eaten his fill, "it is time to move on."

The clouds were sailing in a marine-blue sky. The birds were flying to nests of hungry babies. Julie packed her belongings.

She picked up Amy and put her in the pack. When Julie had reached the top of the embankment above the den, Aaka opened her eyes. Julie walked on. Aaka got to her feet. She sensed a new attitude in Julie. Kapu awoke. Zing stood up. They all watched Julie walk south with Amy in her pack. Aaka trotted right after them. Kapu followed, then Zing.

Their pup was going somewhere, and they were going with her.

Julie turned to her friends. "We are going on a long walk to the mountains," she said. "The caribou are there. You can eat your fill."

She walked faster. Kapu, Aaka, and Zing walked faster.

At first Julie thought the white blazes on the horizon were sunlit clouds, but as she walked on they became more solid and she realized she was looking at the splendorous Brooks Mountain Range. She stopped to rest and take in the spiritual force of the mountains; then she proceeded on south toward the Colville River.

All the while she walked she sang "The Far Northland" and "Peas That Go *Tink*, Peas That Go *Tot*," a song she had made up last year on the tundra. Amy and her somber line of relatives seemed to listen and smile at her music. Occasionally a tail wagged when she sang a sour note.

She looked for caribou droppings and their hoofprints. The prints would be half circles, split in the middle and about five inches long. Dewclaws on the front feet would leave two dots behind each track. She saw no caribou sign.

The wolf pack patiently followed their pup. They were not much concerned about why Amy was in the backpack. She was in view, and that was all that mattered. They trotted along looking at the scenery and sniffing the air.

Kapu occasionally made a wide circuit to search for game. He had been over this ground many times. He and his pack, like other wolves of the Arctic, knew every pond, grass clump, and large animal on their huge territories. Kapu could inspect a vast swatch of tundra with his nose, for he could smell game more than ten miles away.

Julie was glad for Kapu's all-seeing sense of smell. The herd had to be somewhere nearby. A calf does not wander far from its mother, and Kapu's nose could "see" them long before her eyes. She hurried along.

Amy rode quietly in the backpack. The pup was young enough to heed the voice of authority. A growl, a snarl, or a snappy bark from Julie, and Amy would stop chewing her way out of the pack and lie still.

The strange party covered almost thirty miles in one sun orbit before they stopped to sleep. The wolves were not tired, but Julie was. She sat down with a thump on a warm, grassy hummock and stretched out her legs. She chewed on caribou jerky and felt the permanence of the mountains that rose so high above her. Among the lines of dark-green trees dwelled the wild things. They lived out their lives there, had young, and lived on. She liked the nurturing mountains.

At her feet the little birds chirped, dipped, and flew around her, reminding her of a snowstorm. The mosquitoes hummed but did not bite. She was odorless to the big Arctic mosquito. A smaller one would plague her when she reached the Colville unless she covered herself with fish oil, which she had remembered to bring.

Julie had settled down, but the wolves were restless. They paced back and forth, sniffing and twisting their ears. After a while they lay down, ears up.

When they seemed to be settled, Julie took Amy out of the pack and gave her to Aaka to nurse. But Aaka could not provide much milk. She had not eaten well for months. After a few frustrating suckles, Amy gave up. She looked around for Kapu and poked her nose into the corner of his mouth to ask for food. The stomach basket was empty. He had nothing to give. Amy whimpered in pain, and Julie got to her feet, loaded her .22, and kicked through the grasses.

She came back with a snowshoe hare and gave it to Aaka, who tore it apart and shared it with Amy. Kapu and Zing slept to conserve energy.

Julie joined the sleep. She put down her caribou skin and was dreaming before she could take off her boots. Hours later she was awakened by the plaintive cry of a peregrine falcon. She sat up. Peregrines feed largely on ducks and geese. Ducks and geese live by water. The voice of the peregrine told her she and her wolves were near the Colville River—and caribou.

Suddenly the falcon folded its wings and plummeted earthward. A puff of feathers spiraled into the air, and Julie rolled to her knees. Kapu lifted his head, sniffed, and leaped to his feet. He raced toward the falcon's kill. The falcon beat her wings as Kapu approached and took off, leaving the goose. Kapu walked up to it and took it in his mouth. Then he dropped it and came jogging back to camp. He lay down and glanced at each member of his pack to say, "I didn't take it—don't you."

The peregrine circled back. She had seen Kapu walk away from her meal and lie down. When he was very still, she dropped like a meteor upon her kill. Taking it in her talons, she beat her strong wings and soared away.

"Why did you do that, Kapu?" Julie asked. "Why did you leave the goose? You've barely eaten anything for days, yet you gave the food to the falcon." Kapu's eyes softened. He looked at Julie, then stretched out on his side and watched the sky.

"Kapu," Julie whispered on, "do you know what the Eskimo knows? Did you let the peregrine falcon eat and live because the tundra community needs falcons? Is that why you did not take her food? I believe so. The elders say the wolf sacrifices not only for its family, but for the whole environment."

Julie got to her feet, put Amy in her pack, and went on. Aaka followed close behind the two. Kapu and Zing circled out and back as they moved along, always keeping that pup in sight, as if pups were the only thing wolves lived for. And at this time of year, Julie knew, it was true. Her plan was working.

A few hours later Julie came into the foothills of the Brooks Range. Above them the great snow-covered mountains filled half the sky. Julie had come to the rugged winter home of a western caribou herd. She climbed a knoll to look around. Below her snaked a line of green.

"The Colville River," she exclaimed aloud, and ran down the slope searching for caribou.

But there were no caribou hoofprints. No ladder-like horns clawed the sky.

She sat down to cry, but mostly to think. There seemed to be little point in going on. Yet she must. She had been abroad for eleven sleeps, but the Kangik musk oxen were only a running day away for the wolves. She must get the pack near Anaktuvuk Pass, where Atik had said a few caribou had been seen. The pass was almost two hundred miles away, but she must go. She let Amy out of the backpack to romp and play, shot a ptarmigan for the pup, and took a nap. Then she packed up and walked toward a bluff over the river.

The wolves followed their pup. Their feet moved so smoothly under them, they seemed to float on a sea of wind. Suddenly Kapu stopped. He put his scent on a clump of grass, sprayed a dwarf willow, and ran back to Julie. He scratched a deep blaze on the ground. She shrugged and walked on. The wolves did not follow. Julie whimpered impatiently. Kapu barked.

"Come on, come on," Julie urged. Kapu howled and ran the exact same path he had just run. Zing also ran the line and put his scent on the grass and willow.

Aaka ran the line, returned, and put her front feet on Julie's pack as she reached up to grasp Amy. Julie growled. Aaka cowered. Quickly Julie apologized and hugged the gentle mother wolf.

"We must go on," she said urgently, and started off again. Anatukvuk Pass was ten sleeps away, and Kapugen was probably already on his way to find her. He would locate her quickly with CB tracking her. She did not want that. She must get the wolves to a new food source before she met her father. Determined, she took Amy out of the backpack and carried her in her arms as she headed southeast.

She crossed the invisible line again.

Kapu wolf barked and stood where he was. He would not follow. Zing barked, Aaka whined. Julie walked on. They whimpered and called to Amy, but they would not cross the line. It was as if a huge wall of glass had been erected and they could not go through it. They ran north and south, but not toward the pass. When Amy tried to squirm out of Julie's arms, Aaka trotted over the invisible line to get her. Kapu bark-snarled, lifting his lips to expose not one but both canine teeth. Aaka came back. She did not make another move to get Amy, although Julie was running farther and farther away, determined to make them follow.

They would not. All three stood on the knoll looking at her. Then Kapu lifted his head and howled a deep, lugubrious note. Zing harmonized with him, and Aaka called out a sweet, pained cry. To the wolves their song was about losing loved ones. To Julie it spoke of heartbreak, and she turned back to them.

As she came over the invisible line, tails wagged and wolf tongues licked her hands. She sat down and wondered what to do. Then Kapu got down on his belly and put his head on his forepaws. He stared toward the river bottomlands.

With that Julie finally realized what the three wolves were saying. This invisible line, marked with urine and paw marks, was the end of the pack's territory. One step over and they were breaking a wolf taboo. She was heartsick. She could not reach caribou land with her wolves.

In distress she hugged little Amy, who licked her chin, then looked at her mother. Kapu trotted off a short distance and mouthed Zing's muzzle, then Aaka's. They wagged their tails and lowered their ears and tails as if agreeing with him. Aaka tossed her head and swiveled her ears. Gradually Julie realized an important message was being sent around the wolf pack, but she did not know what it was.

And then they told her. They ran out on the tundra and sped away like bird shadows.

"Humpf," she said aloud. "I'm the baby-sitter again." She hugged furry Amy.

After spreading her caribou skin, she romped in the grass with Amy before giving her a piece of caribou jerky. The pup growled and ate pleasurably. Julie stretched out on her belly.

Chin in her hands, she studied the river. The caribou country beyond was to have been the new home of her pack. Now that could not be. She could not get her wolves to move across the river. Their territory had ended. She had to leave them to their fate.

Julie blinked. There was a deep dent in the sphagnum moss. The pressure of a footfall had forced the water out of the moss and left a hole. She got up and walked to it.

"Moose," she said, standing over a five-inch track. The cloves were not spread as wide apart as those of a caribou, and they were sharper and more elongated. She found many more. They led in and out of the river bottomland. Julie raised her arms in joy. Caribou were wanderers who moved from northern to southern Alaska in a huge continuous circle, but moose were different. A moose rarely moved more than eight miles from its birthing spot.

"Moose," she repeated. "The wolves will live."

But moose live in the bottomlands along rivers, and somehow she had to get her pack over the invisible line and into river bottomland.

Something moved. Julie focused her eyes on the far side of the Colville. Above the ten-foot willow trees a wolf trotted, and Julie realized why her wolves would not go forward. On the other side of the river was another pack. Julie watched them motionlessly.

The silver wolf was joined by a gray wolf. It lifted its leg to scent mark, stating that it was a male. The pair sniffed the air. The wind was carrying Julie's scent to them. They turned their heads looking for her, but were unable to locate her with their eyes. The male sprayed again, then trotted down his invisible border. His line was above moose country too.

What is going on? Julie asked herself. There is a

pack over there and a pack over here and a great space in between that no one will enter. And it is full of moose. She recalled Kapugen telling her that certain Indian tribes set up corridors between their territories where no person could go without fear of death. Over the ages this no-man's-land became a game preserve. Overhunted animals would retreat to the safety corridor and in time recover their numbers. When there were too many deer or moose for the corridor to sustain, they were forced up into Indian land and were harvested again. When the white man changed the land laws, the Indians starved. The wolves, it seemed, had a similar arrangement.

"Now what do I do?" she asked Amy, who had fallen asleep in the sun.

Julie's mind raced. The young ground squirrels were abroad, chattering noisily. The baby birds were out of their nests, catching their own food. The lemmings had many litters, and the weasels, foxes, owls, hawks, and jaegers were feasting. Mobs of white-fronted geese and their young gabbled along the river's edge. July, called Iñukkukaivik, the month when the animals are raising their young, was coming to the Arctic.

Julie lay down by Amy and slept.

Many hours later the three wolves came home

looking well fed, their stomachs round. Amy ran to her mother and stuck her nose into the corner of her mouth, saying, "Food, give me food," and Aaka did. Julie smiled. She had almost starved to death last year, before she had learned how to ask the wolves for food. It was Kapu who had taught her that the parent wolves brought food home to the pups in their bellies and that all one needed to do was to touch the corner of an adult's mouth and the wolf would give it up freely.

The wolves stretched out in the somber sunlight. Julie was glad they had eaten, but she knew well that this meal was only a snack. A grown wolf needed six or seven pounds of food a day. Their ribs were beginning to show through their fur. Time was running out.

And her pack could not get to the moose.

The sun was skimming lower along the horizon each midnight to say darkness would return to the Arctic. It was also saying something else. The light around the sun was a muddy yellow. Julie knew this color well. A very heavy fog was rolling in from the coast. Soon she would not be able to see her feet. Apparently the wolves knew this too, for having eaten all they could find, they were now scratching out beds for a long sleep.

As Kapu circled to lie down, Julie wondered if he knew about the wolves on the other side of the river. She should have known better. With his ears, whiskers, nose, and tail he was constantly monitoring the other pack and reporting their activities to Zing and Aaka. He knew exactly what was going on, and finally told Julie. He stopped making his bed and stared across the river. His fur rose straight up on his head and neck, then on down to the tip of his tail. Julie looked where he was looking. The distant pair was edging over their invisible line. Since they were too far away to hear Kapu growl, he was warning them to go back with ears and neck fur. They saw his threat and backed off. The wolves on the other side of the river walked into the grasses and lay down.

Julie hugged her knees and pondered. A wall of fog now was visible on the horizon. It came silently toward them, a soupy billow that was erasing the landscape. It could last for days, even weeks. She had a new plan.

When her wolves were asleep, she arose. On tiptoes she crossed the invisible line and broke into a run. Kapu was instantly on his feet. He sped to his border but did not make a sound. The mood had changed with Kapu's hair-raising threat.

At the river's edge, Julie noted, the willows and

sedges were clipped by moose teeth; their huge hoofprints poked the soil everywhere. Lynx scats dotted the grasses, and some flat stones were the tidy latrines of the wolverine.

Still, her wolves would starve. Her .22 rifle could not fell a moose. It could only irritate it to charge. Suddenly she knew what she must do. She must drive a moose to the wolves. Even one would keep them fed for many days, giving her time to think of a plan to break the taboo and get Kapu and his pack into the rich no-wolf's-land.

Quietly she stalked. On both sides of the river wolves watched her. Suddenly Kapu howl-barked frantically and fiercely—a warning. Julie turned. A bull moose was running down upon her.

There was no place to hide. The willows were sparse here and not much higher than she. She was exposed on all sides. The charging bull held his huge rack high. His bell swung under his chin, and the whites of his eyes gleamed. Julie knew better than to turn and run. To all beasts a fleeing animal invites a chase. She must not incite attack.

She did the only thing left to her. She faced him, and when the huge bull was almost upon her, she jumped to one side. He thundered by, unable to turn quickly and strike her. Several hundred feet away he slowed down and turned around.

Then he lowered his rack, dug in his hoofs, and charged again. *Noise,* thought Julie, *make noise.* She threw back her head and howled. Kapu, Zing, and Aaka howled.

The moose halted, flared his nostrils, and looked up the slope. The wolves howled again. He turned and ran. Now Julie felt what all predators feel—the urge to chase the fleeing beast. Howling and shouting, she ran the huge animal out of the river bottomland, up through the willows and onto the foggy tundra. The wolves took up the pursuit.

Her plan had worked. Now she must figure out how to break the taboo. She could not stay in the river bottomland all winter chasing moose out of the no-wolf's-corridor for Kapu.

The only answer was to join the two packs into one.

She took off her boots and waded into the icy river, selecting the shallowest water. The fog bank was still far from the river. Julie judged she had plenty of time to woo the two wolves and find their den. She would make friends with another puppy and carry it into the corridor. Then she would go back and get Amy and bring her into the bottomland. The adults would have to come for them. There probably would be a terrible fight, but Kapu, she was certain, would win. That would make the two new wolves obedient to Kapu. The taboo would be broken. They would hunt the moose in the corridor and not come to Kangik for musk oxen.

She was pushing through the sedges and willows, making plans, when a wolf suddenly appeared before her.

"Silver," Julie said. "Silver, it's you."

Silver looked at Julie and twitched an eyebrow. She seemed to be saying that she was not surprised by her presence, that she had known about her arrival on the Colville for a long time. She wagged her tail once, turned, and trotted off. Julie pranced behind her on all fours. There was another wolf with Silver, and she did not want to threaten him by walking on two feet like a human hunter. A slight rotation of Silver's ears told Julie she was behaving correctly.

They walked among the sedges and dwarf willows, Silver moving like a meandering stream. Julie moved like an Eskimo dancer telling the story of the wolf person who lived before the raven turned the world from dark to light. She also reached in her pocket and rubbed her totem of Amaroq.

Silver stopped to sniff a wolverine print, trotted on a few yards, and sat down. Julie sat down and, whimpering her affection, held out her mitten. Kapu's scent was on the mitten, and Julie hoped it would tell Silver that he was nearby. Silver sniffed the mitten, glanced across the river, then back at the mitten. She was not at all excited by Kapu's scent. Julie understood she knew very well her son was there.

They sat quietly side by side. While Silver cleaned a paw with her tongue, Julie searched the stony riverbank for a den. She could find none, nor did she see any pups appear. Apparently Silver and her new mate had adjusted to the food shortage by not giving birth at all.

Suddenly Silver's mate stood up. Julie swallowed hard. He was no more than ten feet away. The dwarf willows he had been crouched in came only to his white belly. He was large and rangy, his body lean, and his face hard. However, he was smaller than Kapu. That was good. The head of a pack was always the biggest. Kapu would win the fight for leadership if she could get them together. Julie named the rangy wolf Raw Bones. She whimpered, begging his friendship. He ignored her by looking down the river at nothing.

Silver stood up and pushed her rear end toward Julie, lifted her head, and closed her eyes. Julie knew what she wanted. Carefully she reached out and scratched Silver's back just above the tail, where wolves and dogs love to be scratched. Silver growled in pleasure.

"I wish," said Julie wistfully as she dug her nails in and rubbed hard, "that you and Kapu would let each other hunt moose."

Raw Bones took a few steps and stared across the river. Julie followed his glance. Kapu and Zing were standing just back of the invisible border. Their ears and ruffs were up. Their eyes were pinned on Raw Bones. He glared back. Julie thought some great decision was in the making; then Raw Bones suddenly relaxed his gaze, rotated his ears, and stepped closer to Julie. He sniffed her scents as if reading some message she had carried from the other side of the river.

Julie wondered: Had Kapu not called her back because he had marked her with a scent message?

Raw Bones stared across the river and whined the whine of friendship.

Silver bounded forward.

Kapu and Zing leaped over their invisible border and rushed into the bottomland.

Raw Bones and Silver splashed into the river, sending water six feet in the air.

The four met, exchanged signals, and chased a

moose that Julie had not even seen. Back on the tundra stood Aaka and Amy.

The moose knew the call of death. He lifted his huge hoofs and ran effortlessly, rack and head back. The wolves leaped at his side. They circled out and loped back, keeping up with the prey without sound. Kapu signaled with his eyes. The wolves took positions for the kill.

Then Kapu stopped dead in his tracks and so did the others. He had called the hunt off. Panting, lips pulled back in smiles, the four watched the moose for a moment, then turned and trotted away. The moose slowed down, looked back, and as if nothing had happened, lowered his head. He browsed unafraid. The predator and prey, over the millennia, seemed to have worked out some understanding with life and death.

Having chased the moose, the four wolves ran down the gravel shore, ears up, tails flowing behind them. They sped along as if there were nothing more important in the universe than running. Julie was spellbound. They seemed to be performing a ritual of wolfdom. They had not killed the moose, just chased it together. Now they seemed to be running joyously, as if they were celebrating the first law of their kind—cooperation. An elder had put it to Julie another way: "We are all here for each other; the Eskimos, the mammals, the river, the ice, the sun, plants, birds, and fish. Let us celebrate cooperation." That, Julie felt, was just what they were doing.

Through some mysterious signals the wolves had told each other they would join forces and become one pack. And, it seemed to Julie, she had been the messenger. How it had all come to be she did not know.

Julie waded through the sparkling water, put on her boots, and on all fours climbed the embankment to the land that had once belonged only to Kapu and his pack. She looked across the flat landscape to locate the moose she had chased to her pack. It was nowhere to be seen. Apparently it had outrun the wolves, as a moose can do. She did not care. The taboo was broken and there was plenty of wolf food in the bottomland. She was ready to go.

Aaka and Amy did not look at her as she picked up her belongings. They stood perfectly still watching the pack of four agile hunters below them. Then, at some signal from Kapu, Aaka stepped forward and whimpered to Amy, and together they trotted down into the river bottomland.

Julie watched the six wolves sniff and lick each other, wag tails, and discuss wolf matters. That done, they began searching the air with their noses.

"Ceremonies or no ceremonies," Julie said, "they're hungry." She pulled Peter's whistle out of her parka and walked down the slope to a bare hummock where ground squirrels lived. She piped a chitty cry. A squirrel appeared. She blew again. Another rushed out of a burrow and looked around. Raw Bones dashed to the colony. Julie blew many notes. The ground popped with squirrels. Kapu joined Raw Bones. Zing followed Kapu, scaring one down a hole. But the wolves did not catch them. They played with them, chasing them back when Julie whistled them out. Julie laughed. The wolves seemed to be laughing too, as the pipe sounded and the ground squirrels came up. She wondered what note Peter had fashioned to bring the little squirrels out of the ground. Then she remembered how she had waggled her finger last summer on the tundra to imitate the tail signal of the little squirrels' "All's well—no enemies are around, come out." Peter, she realized, had created the ground squirrel's call that also says, "All's well. Come out."

Suddenly the fun was over. Raw Bones was too close to Aaka. Kapu growled at him. Raw Bones bared his teeth back to the molars. Kapu leaped and grabbed him by the scruff of the neck. He shook him and let go. The two snarled as they raised their hackles, showed their teeth, and circled each other. Suddenly Kapu threw Raw Bones to the ground and stood full stature over him, silently showing his canine teeth. Then he stepped back and Raw Bones slunk to his feet, his head lower than Kapu's, his tail almost to the ground. His ears were flattened against his head. The fight for leadership was over. Kapu was the head of the pack. The fog rolled down upon them.

All five adult wolves gathered in a circle and howled. Amy yipped. The song traveled across the river to be echoed back by the cliffs and hills. The song was full of the rightness of the earth. Julie felt the harmony and sang, too.

When a cold wind swept the fog away and revealed the midnight sun, Julie gathered her belongings to go home. A raven winged out of the sky and boldly alighted on her pack. He *quoink*ed, the call of his kind to assemble. Soundlessly, on great black wings, three more ravens appeared, then seven more.

"Wise birds," Julie said. She had not seen a raven since that first day on the tundra. "They know what is going to happen."

A red fox appeared. He had followed the ravens, knowing they could see food from on high. He would share what they found. "But there is no food yet," Julie said aloud, puzzled. Two moose had been chased, but no moose had been felled. The raven and fox knew something she did not. Perhaps, she said to herself, that chorus of wolf voices told the tundra life that there were now five, not just three, adult wolves and they were ready to hunt big game as wolves do.

Julie shouldered her pack and left the Colville. She was satisfied that her wolves had enough game to hold them for many months, perhaps even until the caribou returned. She looked down at her boots, and with a smile she pointed them homeward, toward—she was surprised to admit—Peter Sugluk.

PART III

MIYAX, THE YOUNG WOMAN

On her homeward walk Julie tracked herself and the wolves back across the tundra. The fog had cleared and she could see the groove in the grasses their caravan had made. In addition, tufts of wolf fur caught on poppy seed heads and grasses were like white flags marking the way.

She had not gone far before she heard the ravens dong the death knell. She stopped to listen. Above the raven anthem rose the voices of the wolves heralding the end of one life and the continuation of others. The moose had given himself to the wolves. She smiled. The musk oxen were safe. If the caribou returned this autumn, Kapugen's industry would go on thriving.

Happily she walked. When weariness overcame her, she lay down on her caribou skin and was quickly asleep. She slept through birdsong and weasel chitter, through wind change and the red-purple cloud

performance at the perigee of the midnight sun.

She was awakened by the wurping laughter of foxes. Four alert pups were dancing around her. Their eyes twinkled in the high-noon light as they pulled at her boots and mittens. She sat up. There were no parent foxes.

"Fox pups out of the den," she said out loud. "June is old. The baby is due the fifth of July—and I want to be there."

She shouldered her pack and strode off. The fox pups followed her until a ptarmigan flew up; then they turned and pursued it on their long swift legs.

A wolf howled. The voice came from in front of, not behind her. Alarmed, she stopped. Kapu was with her. He had gone ahead to scout the way. He must not do that. She dropped to all fours prepared to meet him eye to eye and forcibly send him back with a stare. Another howl. Julie got to her feet and she burst into laughter.

"Kapugen," she shouted, and broke into a run. "I'm here. I'm here." In the misty distance she could see the stubby outline of her father. He had CB on a leash and was leaning backward as he strained to hold in the dog.

They met with such happiness that CB felt the glee too. He greeted Julie first, jumping up and licking her cheek. She hugged him, then ran into Kapugen's arms.

"The oxen are safe," she said. "The wolves have moose to harvest."

"Moose; they found moose," he said with deep satisfaction. "That is good news, all right," He hugged her again. "Now I have good news for you." Julie waited.

"You have a brother." Kapugen's eyes were shining tenderly.

"A brother," Julie said. "That is good news, all right. What did you name him?"

"Amaroq."

Julie could not speak. She put her fingers to her lips and looked into her father's eyes.

"It is not strange," Kapugen said, seeing her bewilderment. "It is customary among the Eskimos to give the name of a deceased spirit to a baby. Then the baby becomes that one." She frowned, and he went on. "By giving my son the name of your great wolf leader, Amaroq, I have said that he will be like him. Little Amaroq will hunt for himself, he will hunt for his family, and he will defend his tribe against enemies. Like the wolf he will be integrated into the universe."

Julie knew well the Eskimo custom of atiQs, or

namesakes. Babies were often given the names of deceased people. Aunt Martha had been named for a friend who had died, and the friend's family had thought of Aunt Martha as that woman. "You are my grandmother," the family would say to the baby, and no one thought it odd. The spirit of the deceased Martha was present. She was the baby.

"Do you find it strange?" Kapugen asked after Julie had been quiet for many minutes.

"I understand naming a baby after a loved person or a splendid caribou, or strong polar bear," she answered. "But you named your baby after a wolf you did not like and killed. I do not understand that."

"I admired Amaroq," he said. "He died to save Kangik."

"The Minnesota law?" asked Julie softly.

"The Minnesota law."

Julie stood a long moment trying to reconcile the wolf Amaroq's death by repeating over and over to herself, "That is how it is," the Eskimo words that brought acceptance and peace. Finally she looked up at Kapugen.

"The baby will be outstanding," she said. "And"—she looked out across the tundra—"the baby will be my adopted father." She saw once more the magnificent black wolf. His head was lifted, and intelligence lit his eyes. He had just felled a caribou by her camp.

She smiled and thought of his namesake.

"Is the baby's hair red?" she asked curiously.

"Black as the wind cloud."

"And his eyes?"

"Blacker than the new moon."

"He is Amaroq, then," said Julie. "That is good."

"His skin is pale and rosy," Kapugen said. "I hope it does not crack and blister in the sun and cold."

"Ernest Adams's doesn't," Julie said. "His grandfather was a white whaler who came to the Arctic. He is pale, but he does not crack and blister."

Kapugen laughed.

"You are right, all right," he said, shaking his head. "I should not repeat those prejudices. Many Eskimos have white ancestors, and they do not crack and blister any more than the rest of us." He chuckled and leaned down to gather dry grass.

Kapugen cleared a small area on the ground and piled up the grass. Over it he built a tepee of dry sticks he had gathered from streamsides along the way; the kindling had washed down from the mountains, where stunted trees grew. He struck a match to the grass and a flame burst up, licked the driftwood, and set it afire. He opened a large can of store-bought stew, and when the coals were red, he placed it upon them.

"Does Ellen feel well?" Julie asked belatedly.

"She is very well and happy," Kapugen said.

"When was Amaroq born?" she asked.

"June the fifteenth," Kapugen said. "He was a bit early. He caught us by surprise, like the good hunter he is."

"Did you fly Ellen to the hospital?" Julie asked, now eager to learn all the details about the birth of her adopted father.

Kapugen shook his head. "The little wolf decided to be born the day the summer fog rolled in. I could not fly."

"What did you do?"

"I ran for Uma. She came over."

"Uma knows lots about babies," Julie said.

"She does, all right," Kapugen replied, stirring the stew with his hunting knife. "And she knows Eskimo wisdom. She rubbed Ellen's stomach with wolf fur. She said it would give Ellen the power of the female wolf. That is super power," he said, and smiled. "It makes the birth easy and her love for the baby strong."

"Is that what happened?" Julie asked hopefully.

"That is what happened. Six hours later the baby

was born and Ellen was holding him to her breast with fierce love."

"She would do that, all right," Julie said. She could picture Ellen and the little boy with hair as dark as the wind cloud.

"It was then I knew the child was Amaroq. He will be a fine person."

Julie put down her caribou skin and stretched out on her stomach. She watched the fire and thought about little Amaroq. His name bound them all together: herself, the baby, Ellen, Kapugen, the oxen, and the wolves she had led away. They were now one household.

"Aapa," Julie said slowly and cautiously, "what if the wolves come back and kill another musk ox? Now that we have Amaroq with us, will you still go by the Minnesota law? Will you kill them?"

"I must do that," he said.

"Even though we have the little wolf in our house? You would be killing his spirit brothers."

"Industry is under another law," he said. "We must protect it as the wolf protects the game, the plants, and his family."

"That is mixed up," Julie said, and frowned.

"That is how it is in our modern world," said Kapugen.

"Ah, Aapa," she said, looking back toward the mountains. "I hope the caribou return soon."

When the stew was eaten, Julie and Kapugen lay down on their sleeping skins and pulled their parka hoods over their eyes to make their own night. The sounds of July piped across the tundra, as baby birds sang bits of their parents' songs and ground squirrels scurried after berries.

Julie closed her eyes, but she did not sleep right away. She was thinking about baby Amaroq—and Peter.

She was awakened a few hours later by the whacking throb of a helicopter engine. She sat up. The air shook. The whirling wind from the airship's blades twisted her hair and stung her face with dust. She got to all fours and watched as the aircraft, its motor blattering and roaring, started to land not fifty feet away.

Kapugen was up and waving his hands to tell the pilot he and his daughter were present. The pilot saw him, nodded, lifted the craft and set it down two hundred yards away. Kapugen and Julie watched two men climb out of the cabin and walk toward them.

"Morning," the taller of the two said.

"Morning."

"I'm sure surprised to find you here. Sorry about

disturbing you." The man took off his helmet and dark glasses, and Julie saw he was a white man.

"I'm a biologist," he said. "The name's David Bradford. This is my pilot and assistant, Mark. I'm studying the moose. I put radio collars on them so I can track them and learn their numbers and distribution."

Kapugen nodded.

"There's a moose with a collar right around here," he said. "I'm getting a beep on my receiver." He chuckled. "But you two are hardly a moose."

"I am hardly a moose all right," said Kapugen, his eyes twinkling, "and my daughter, Julie, is not a moose either. Don't you know a moose when you see one?" Kapugen laughed out loud. "What a good joke. The biologist finds two Eskimos and thinks they are moose."

"I must admit I did," said David, laughing too. "We heard the beep and followed it. When it was very loud, I looked down and saw a big lump of fur. 'Moose,' I said to Mark.

"When you are eager to see a moose, you see one," he went on, and laughed again. "By any chance have you seen a radio collar? Sometimes they fall off and lie on the ground."

Julie went to her pack. "Are you looking for this?"

she asked, holding up the collar.

"By golly," David said, "this is great. Where did you find it?"

"I found it on a caribou calf," she said. "At least I thought it was a caribou. The animal was so long dead and battered, I could only guess." She looked at him mischievously. "When you are eager to see a caribou, you see a caribou."

David smiled and took the collar. "I put this on a calf only a month ago," he said. "I wonder how the little guy died? Wolves, I would guess."

"Where were you when you put it on him?" Julie asked.

"Along the Colville about twenty miles southwest of here in the river bottomland."

"Then he must have been killed by a grizzly."

"Wolves," David said authoritatively. "I've seen a pack in that area."

"Not the wolves," Julie said. "There is only one pack from Wainwright to the Colville, and I know them well. They would not have gone into the river bottomland. Taboo."

"I'm sure you know a lot about wolves, Julie," David said, smiling condescendingly.

"Julie does know wolves," interjected Kapugen, "like you will never know them. Believe her."

Still David smiled smugly.

"Dave," said Mark, "this man is Kapugen. He is a remarkable hunter and businessman. You can believe him and his daughter. It is said she was lost on the tundra and lived with the wolves and survived."

"Is that true?" David asked with more respect.

"It is true," said Kapugen.

Still skeptical, David took out his notebook, found the date he had tranquilized and collared the calf, and wrote down the date found. After taking a compass reading, he recorded their present location and took Julie's name. He did not fill in the last heading—HOW DIED.

"Do you think you could show me on this topographical map just where you found the radio?" he asked Julie.

"I could do that," she said. Kapugen had such a map on the wall in his bedroom.

"We are here," David said, pointing. "And this is where I collared the calf." He pointed to a spot on the Colville River. Hills rose on each side of it—the mountain beyond was extremely high. It was the area where Julie had led her wolves. Now to find the whelping den on the map. She followed the drainage lines with her finger.

"Here," she said, pointing. "The calf was about

thirty miles from the Colville."

"Grizzly," said David changing his mind. "Wolves carry food to their pups in their stomachs. They don't bring it to them."

"Do grizzlies carry food to their cubs?" asked Kapugen.

"To be honest," David said with some embarrassment, "I don't know. They probably don't. Wolf kill."

"It was not a wolf kill," Julie said. "I see by your notes that the day you put the radio collar on the moose calf, the wolves were in Kangik."

"How do you know such a thing?" David snapped.

"They killed a musk ox," answered Kapugen.

"And," Julie continued, "the wolves were far from the Colville when the calf was killed. A pup was born on the Avalik about that time."

"Why would a bear drag a carcass that far?" David mused.

"She probably didn't," Julie answered. "After killing it, she most likely dragged it inland to her cubs. They feasted and left it, intending to come back. A tender carcass is a treasure to many animals. A fox might have dragged it, an eagle carried it, but I would guess that the wolves found it and brought it back to their pup for a toy. They carry toys in their mouths. Forty miles is a jaunt for a wolf."

"And how did you find it?"

"With my nose," she answered with a grin, knowing she had told only part of the truth.

David wrote down "Death by grizzly" without any more questioning and thanked Julie. He was very pleased with the information she had given him.

"How about our flying you two home?" he asked.

Julie was tempted. She had never ridden in a helicopter.

"Can we, Aapa?" she asked.

"Do you have room for the dog?"

"If you hold him in your lap," Mark answered.

"I will do that, all right," Kapugen said.

David and Mark started toward the copter.

"Speaking of bears," said Kapugen, "there is your lady." He gestured.

Aklaq, the bear, and her two large cubs were on the other side of the helicopter. Mark slipped his rifle out of its scabbard.

The grizzly stood up on her hind legs. Her red tongue emphasized the whiteness of her huge teeth. David jumped into the helicopter. Mark turned to Julie.

"Get in," he said. "I'll scare her away."

The grizzly growled. Then she lowered herself to

the ground and ran straight toward the helicopter. CB barked and snarled. Kapugen picked him up and tossed him into the cabin. Mark went under the copter blades and shouldered his rifle.

Julie threw out her arms, signaling "human."

The rifle boomed.

Another shot followed. The bear roared and bluff charged, then again rose to her hind feet. Before Mark could get off a third shot, Julie was waving her arms at Aklaq and shouting. She walked toward the bear, head down, threatening the big grizzly. Surprised at her aggression, Aklaq dropped to all fours. Her eyesight was poor, but her nostrils were long-range sensors. She smelled gunpowder and Julie's message. Her deepest instincts took hold. She loped back to her cubs, then turned and stood up. She was ready to attack again.

Julie charged her. Aklaq lowered her big feet with the long gleaming claws and walked calmly away as if nothing had happened. Her cubs romped behind her.

"Good girl," Julie said, and walked backward to the helicopter so as not to inspire the bear to chase. She picked up her pack and climbed into the cabin beside Kapugen. CB licked her face.

"How did you know to do that?" Kapugen

proudly asked her. "I did not know you knew how to fend off a bear."

"The wolves taught me," she said. He nodded knowingly, his eyes crackling with pleasure.

The copter motor roared, the blades thrummed, and Julie was lifted up over the tundra.

As the helicopter clattered into the sky, Julie saw Aklaq and her cubs loping southward toward the Colville. A raven scout soared above them on the chance that the bears would scare up a lemming or catch some fish.

Kapugen, in a voice loud enough to be heard over the whack of the helicopter blades, asked David if he would mind flying down the Colville before going home. He wanted to see if there were any solitary caribou in the foothills that he and Malek might harvest. David nodded and told Mark to change course. He needed information on the caribou too.

The noisy machine tipped, hung still in the air like a tern, then sped toward the Brooks Mountains. Looking down, Julie could see the miles of mountain peaks. They were white and jagged like salmon teeth. How wonderful, she thought, to be an animal that could survive in such harsh beauty.

Mark swept the machine low as he followed tree

line on the mountains. After many miles without sighting even one caribou, Kapugen signaled Mark to go to Kangik, and he swung the craft north. David turned around to Kapugen in the rear seat.

"The caribou are over east beyond Prudhoe Bay," he yelled. "A few are starting south, but not toward Kangik."

"They must," Julie whispered to herself. "They must come to Kangik this fall."

"Worrisome spirits," Kapugen said to David. Turning to Julie, he said, "Let's go see the baby." She crinkled her eyes happily.

The helicopter clattered down onto the steel-mesh runway in front of the Quonset. David, who was now much impressed by Julie—particularly because of how she had handled herself with the bear—shook her hand and told her to come to Fairbanks with Kapugen someday. He would show her the radio receivers and the charts he had made for each moose he had collared. He would tell her a lot about moose habits. Then he added, "Or maybe you can tell me." Smiling, he waved good-bye and closed the copter door.

Impatiently Julie waved and waited until the metal insect had lifted off the ground and droned away; then she ran home. Kapugen strode along trying to keep up with her.

"Ellen," she called as she ran into the living room. "Amaroq. Where is he?"

"Sshh—he's sleeping," Ellen said, tiptoeing to a caribou-skin cradle hanging from the ceiling. The little boy's nose and forehead were all Julie could see beneath a soft white fox blanket.

"Amaroq," Julie whispered. "Amaroq." His smooth skin was more pink than white, but his hair was definitely black, very black. His dark eyelashes curled against his fat, round cheeks.

Julie stood quietly before him for a moment, then softly sang,

"You are my adopted father.
My feet dance because of you.
My eyes see because of you.
My mind thinks because of you.
And it thinks with your birth
The wolf and the Eskimo are one again."

Julie looked at little Amaroq a long time. Then she turned to Ellen.

"May I pick him up?"

"No, no," Ellen warned. "Never awaken a sleeping baby, my mother always said."

Julie did not see Kapugen until he was at her side. "Amaroq, Amaroq," he sang as he reached into the cradle and picked up the little boy.

"No, no, Kapugen," Ellen scolded. "Please, let him sleep. He'll be off his routine."

Kapugen rocked the baby in his arms, kissed his soft cheek, and handed him to Julie. She pressed him lovingly to her.

"Dear Ellen," Kapugen said, putting his arm around her shoulder, "there is no routine for babies and children except love and more love."

"Oh, Kapugen," said Ellen. "Our child must be disciplined or he will be like Uma's wild thing."

"Much wilder," said Julie, kissing the baby. "He is Amaroq, the wolf pup. He will pounce and wrestle, even bite. He will run where he pleases as fast as the wind." The baby opened his eyes. They were oval eyes blacker than the new moon and inquiring. He looked right at Julie as if he knew he was her adopted father.

Ellen reached out to rescue her baby. Seeing that she was upset, Julie put Amaroq in his cradle and swung him gently back to sleep.

"Ellen," Julie said softly, never taking her eyes off the baby, "little Amaroq will pounce and snarl and wrestle. He will romp out on the tundra like a caribou calf. You will think he is naughty, but he will be good. All you have to do is call like a mother wolf, and he will come right back. I have seen this."

"I have seen this, too, all right," Kapugen said, checking the thongs on the cradle he had made so that the baby could hang in the midst of the living activities.

Ellen looked at her child and then at Julie.

"Julie," she said, "I have the feeling you believe the spirit of your wolf is in my son."

"He is," Julie said unabashedly. "This is Amaroq." She patted his tiny head.

"Can't you feel his strength?" Kapugen said, taking Ellen's hand and holding it against the baby. "He is strong. He will submerge his personal needs for the good of the whole. That is what the wolf does. The wolf is the only animal that understands the universe. People do not understand it, only amaroq."

"At first," Ellen said, "I did not think you really believed Amaroq's spirit was in our baby." She pulled away from her husband. "Now I see that you do."

"It is so," said Kapugen.

He sat down on the caribou skins and gently drew Ellen beside him. Julie crossed her feet and gracefully sat down, too.

"Close your eyes, Aaka," Julie said. "Kapugen and I have a story to tell you." Ellen clung to Kapugen's hand and closed her eyes.

"See the polar ice cap?" Kapugen said, speaking slowly. "See the earth swell out around the top of the world?" Ellen nodded.

"You are above the North Pole looking down," Julie said slowly. "It is one country up here. Alaska, Canada, Siberia, Greenland, Lappland, all are the same. See it?"

"Yes," Ellen said. "It looks like one country when you look down on the globe instead of up as our maps show it."

"See the ice and wind and animals?" Julie asked. Ellen nodded, eyes still closed.

"Once," Kapugen went on, "two wolves ran and romped. There were no people at that time and no light. The earth was upside down in darkness. One day a raven came to the wolves and told them to hold tight. The raven flew, and as he flew he turned the earth over into the light. The wolves became Eskimos. That is why we are so much like them. We hunt in groups like the wolves. We have leaders like the wolves, and we love our children like they love their pups.

"Since that is so," Kapugen went on, sensing Ellen still could not fathom their words, "it is easy for the wolf to send his spirit into a baby when we give it his name. Child and the wolf spirit live happily."

"Amaroq is here," Julie said, patting the baby. She took the totem from her pocket and held it up for Ellen to see. "Look, he is gone from the totem." Ellen looked, then sighed, trying hard to understand.

"Now, dear Ellen," said Kapugen slowly and carefully, "be a wolf for a moment." She frowned as she tried. "Now, open your eyes. See, Amaroq is that little boy, all right."

Ellen's gray-blue eyes blinked, then widened. She looked from Julie to Kapugen's and then at her sleeping baby.

"I love you both so much," she said helplessly. "But some things are not meant for my understanding. You see what I cannot." Dewlike perspiration arose on her forehead and trickled down the curl by her ear. "I must try to be more like an Eskimo."

"No," Kapugen corrected her. "We must be more like you. To survive in our polar world today, we must join your businesses and learn your language."

Julie looked warily at her father. "Does that also mean we must also go by the Minnesota law?" she asked, her voice low and fearful.

"That too," said Kapugen, and Julie understood that for the good of the village he had adopted the Minnesota law and his heart had frozen solidly around it. She was distressed. When her wolves came back—and they would; this was their territory—Kapugen would shoot them. He was telling her that.

Little Amaroq awoke with a cry and the household went into motion. Kapugen held him while Ellen heated water for his bath and showed Julie how to lay out his paper diapers.

Peter came in the door. Since no one had heard his knock, he had taken it upon himself to enter. He stood quietly for quite a while.

"Julie," he finally said, stepping over to her and whispering into her ear. "Are the wolves safe? Did you lead them to game?" She turned in surprise, then laughed at herself for being so involved with the baby.

"Ee-lie, I did." she said, happy to see him. "Come here and meet Amaroq Kapugen. He has only an Eskimo name."

Shyly, Peter crossed the room and looked down at the little baby kicking and screaming on the table.

"He's a very small wolf leader," he said, and Julie and Kapugen laughed with great enjoyment.

"I give up," said Ellen. "He *must* be Amaroq. You say so too, Peter?"

"Of course," said Peter.

Peter picked up a silver rattle Ellen's mother had sent from Minnesota and shook it, beating out an

Eskimo drummer's rhythm. Kapugen began to sing, Julie hummed, and the baby gurgled softly as he listened to the sounds of the world into which he had been born.

When little Amaroq was washed, dressed, and nursing, Peter took Julie's hand and danced her into the qanitchaq. He closed the door and kissed her on her lips. Her heart raced and her cheeks grew warm. She stepped back. So this is what Ellen had meant when she had said she and Kapugen had fallen in love. She had not understood until now.

"Julie," Peter said in a low voice, "now that the wolves are far away, I can go on with my plans."

"What are they?" Julie asked.

"I am going to school in Fairbanks. I have been admitted to the University of Alaska." Julie felt a pang of disappointment, which Peter quickly saw in her eyes.

"It will be all right," he said, holding her face in his hands. "We'll be together. Ellen sent in your application to the high school in Fairbanks. She said you would be accepted."

"But I can't go," she said, coming to her senses.

"You must," he said.

"The caribou are far away at the Canadian border, Peter."

"What does that mean?"

"That they will not be coming to Kangik. The wolves will come back, and when they do, Kapugen will shoot them."

"It cannot be helped," Peter said. "You must go to school. You want to go to school. I can feel it."

"Yes," she answered. "I do." She opened the outer qanitchaq door and they strolled out into the sunshine. "I want to study to be a teacher and teach Yupik and Iñupiat to the Eskimo children so they will not lose their identity. They are forgetting the language, you know."

"Then you must come with me."

"Who will tend the musk oxen with Malek when you and I are gone?" she asked. "Kapugen is too busy."

"Malek has asked a young nephew to come to Kangik," said Peter.

"I must stay here," she said. Peter pondered as they walked toward the treeless riverbank.

"You could go to school in Barrow, Miyax," he said. "That is not far away by air. You could come home weekends and tend the oxen."

"Barrow?" Julie sat down abruptly on Kapugen's boat.

"What is the matter?" he asked, sitting beside

her. "You seem frightened. Please tell me."

Julie took a breath. "I once lived in Barrow. I was married," she said. "We were married according to the old Eskimo custom, an agreement between parents." She looked at him. "I was not happy. We were never partners."

Peter took her hand. "In Provideniya you would not be married. Two people must agree to make a marriage."

"We did not," Julie said forcefully. "That is why I went out on the tundra. We were too young and I was not ready to marry. I left Barrow to walk to Point Hope and take a boat to San Francisco.

"I would feel uncomfortable in Barrow," she said.

"A good reason to go to in school in Fairbanks," Peter said enthusiastically.

"Not yet."

"Is it because of the wolves?" Peter asked.

"That is a lot of the reason," she said. "But I can learn a lot from Ellen. She has lots of books and music." Both were silent for a long time.

"Come to Fairbanks, Miyax," Peter pleaded softly.

Julie got to her feet and smiled. "Peter," she said in a clear voice, "tell Malek I will take care of the musk oxen while you are gone."

"We are in love," he said, rising and pulling her gently to her feet. He put his arms around her, and she rested her head on his chest.

"I must stay in Kangik," she answered. Peter kissed her warmly, then lifted her chin until he was looking into her eyes. She looked back at him without blinking.

"You are right," he said, dropping his hands to his side. "I can see that you cannot go to school this year. I will miss you." He looked away as if seeing his future a little differently now. "I'll study hard; then I'll come back and marry you and we'll make our own industry. We are good cooperators."

Julie smiled and looked at the river. It ran black through the land.

"When do you leave, Peter?"

"I go next week. Kapugen is taking me. I will find a place to live and work until the end of August, when school begins. I will improve my English." He took her hands. She felt the pressure of his warm fingers; then a bright light shone in his eyes.

"We still have time to get married, lovely Miyax," he said.

"It is a strange thing, Peter," she said thoughtfully. "I find I have acquired a bit of white culture. I get angry with Kapugen for adopting the Minnesota law of the white men, but I find their custom of being older before marriage is a very good thing. That is a good plan the white families have."

Arms around each other, they walked to the river and watched the ciscos streak swiftly past in waves like northern lights. Peter scratched his head.

"Miyax," he said, "I still think you should come to school with me. Kapugen will not shoot Kapu, now that he is related to him through his own son, Amaroq. That would be a difficult thing for him to do."

"But he will," said Julie. "Because he believes the white men are right about wolves and the prey."

"That I do not understand," said Peter. "Kapugen knows we must live with nature, not control it."

Julie looked at this tall young man with the high cheekbones and bronze skin and knew she loved him very much. She also knew he would come back for her when she was ready.

Peter left Kangik. He kissed Julie good-bye, holding her so close she wondered if the old Eskimo ways weren't the best after all. It would be many years before she finished high school and college. The ways of the white people, she mused with a sigh, were not the ways of nature.

But nature still dominated in Kangik. The musk oxen had to be fed, and Ellen needed help with baby Amaroq. And the wolves—the wolves were still somewhere out there in the wind and grass, and if the caribou did not return in the October migration, they were a threat to the musk oxen and thereby themselves.

Almost every evening Julie walked far up the river and howled her I'm-Julie call. Then she waited, holding her breath and listening. When the pack did not answer, she breathed again. They had not come back that night.

In early September snow fell and stayed on the ground. It was the month when the caribou lose the velvet on their antlers. The river iced over and the freeze-up was upon the Arctic.

On a clear afternoon a voice on the CB reported "lots of aiviq in a cove north of Icy Cape." This was good news for Kangik. Walrus was not a favorite food, but it was nourishing and, fortunately for the villagers, not too far away.

Walrus ride the ice floes of the Arctic Ocean that circle endlessly clockwise around the Polar ice cap. When Kapugen heard of their arrival at Icy Cape, they were on their way from their summer feeding grounds in the Arctic Ocean to their overwintering waters in the Bering Sea. There they would dive for clams and loll along the coastal shores until the breakup circled them north again.

"Atik, good afternoon, Atik. Do you hear me?" Kapugen spoke into the CB. "Let us go get aiviq for Kangik."

"I hear you, Kapugen. That is a good plan, all right."

Kapugen harnessed the dogs to a sled loaded with hunting and camping gear, then hooked onto it the sled carrying his sealskin boat. Elated to be going on the last hunt of the year, he went inside to find Julie.

"Miyax," he said, "would you come with us? We could use your help with the camp and the dogs." She slid off the iglek, happy to be asked. Then she hesitated.

"Who will help Ellen?" she asked.

"Uma is coming over," Kapugen said. "She will also check the musk oxen while we are gone." Julie still hung back.

"Ee-lie, little Miyax," he said, his eyes bright. "I spoke to David Bradford. He said he saw the Kangik wolves yesterday."

"Where were they?"

"Down in the bottomland feasting on a moose kill." He smiled. "You made them happy wolves."

Hearing that, Julie quickly dressed in her warmest clothing, truly delighted to be going to the sea ice, the spiritual home of the Yupik Eskimos.

Little Amaroq fussed and she picked him up, patted his straight, sturdy back, and hummed to him. Ellen hurried out of the bedroom.

"Let him cry, please, dear," she said. "He must learn routine and discipline." Julie respected Ellen's wishes. She kissed him and put him back in his cradle, then hurried into the qanitchak to put on her boots. She could not bear to hear the little boy cry.

In the low light of late afternoon Julie, Kapugen, and Atik set out across the frozen tundra. They stopped that night at a well-used campsite of the Eskimo hunters. The next afternoon they arrived at the cove.

Julie helped Atik set up the sleeping tent while Kapugen crept on his belly to a mound above the beach. He wiggled back to say he had counted nine walruses on a floe close to shore.

"How many shall we take?" Atik asked him.

"Two," Kapugen replied. "That is all we need."

"But the ivory," Atik said. "Two sets of tusks will bring fourteen hundred dollars for the corporation. Six will bring forty-two hundred dollars."

"Two," said Kapugen, lifting his head high like a

wolf leader. Atik understood the matter was settled and said no more.

"Miyax," Kapugen said, turning to Julie, "I need your help, all right. There is a female walrus on the floe with a calf that's in trouble. It has fallen into a crevasse. When we shoot, the herd will dive into the sea and the calf will be stranded. We'll be too busy to rescue it. You must try."

"I will try," she said. "I do not know walrus talk, but they must know Yupik. They have been hearing it on all sides of the Arctic Ocean for ten thousand years." Kapugen smiled at her.

"Walruses go *mooo*," said Atik, and winked.

"Let us go," said Kapugen, getting down on his belly to keep out of sight of the walruses. Julie and Atik followed his lead. The light would linger for several more hours, although the sun had set. The afterglow at this time of year brightened the land until almost nine o'clock. The temperature was five above zero. They slithered up the embankment soundlessly.

Suddenly there was a loud hammering sound. Julie lifted her head. Kapugen pushed up on his hands. The dogs barked soft *woof*s to say they were not certain what was abroad in the twilight. There was a pained bellow.

"That's a cry of desperation, " Kapugen said, and

the three, using their elbows and toes to push, wiggled noiselessly up the shore mound. At the top they looked out on a thinly iced sea and nine adult walruses on a floe near shore. Eight were males; the other was the huge mother walrus, her neck and shoulders wreathed in rolls of fat. She was bellowing and cracking the ice floe. Her canine teeth, two enormous gleaming white tusks, were her axes. Chips as big as snow geese were flying in the air as she sought to rescue her calf from the crevasse. Her flexible hind flippers braced her as she worked. She was demolishing the ice before their eyes.

Near her lolled two huge bulls.

Kapugen looked at Atik. Atik looked at Kapugen. Kapugen's eyes said, "Shoot," and they did. It was all over quickly. Two bulls were dead. As Kapugen had predicted, the rest of the herd plunged off the floe and crashed through the slushy ice into a wave of purple water. All but the mother. She did not leave. Paying absolutely no attention to the shots or her dead companions, she kept splintering the ice to free her baby.

She worked on as Kapugen and Atik ran down to the water's edge with the skin boat. Nor did she stop her frantic efforts when Julie stepped into the boat with the hunters and paddled.

Kapugen leaped to the floe and roped his bull. Atik secured his bull. Julie crept forward to try to lasso the calf and pull it out of the cravasse. With that, the female became concerned. She roared at Julie and Kapugen, opening and closing her mouth rapidly and making the jackhammer sound again. Then she bluff charged.

Kapugen and Julie stood still. The walrus glared at them out of her mournful eyes, turned away, and frantically slashed the far side of the crevasse. In less time than it took Julie to wind her rope to toss, the great tusks had demolished the sea side of the ice floe. The calf was free. It slipped into the water. The mother plunged in after it, lifted it up on her back, and swam off.

"So much for my job," said Julie, watching the mother and calf. "She didn't need any help at all." She smiled in admiration.

Kapugen rested his hand on Julie's shoulder. She looked up and saw that his eyes were shadowy with dreams as he watched the fearless mother walrus swim away. Even after she had disappeared among the floes, Kapugen still did not take his eyes from the icy spot where she had vanished. Finally he spoke.

"Once the elders told me this," he said very slowly. "We are all related." He gestured toward the

caring mother. "They were right, all right."

"Yes," said Julie. "They were right, all right."

Something had happened to Kapugen, Julie realized. Here on the bleak and lonely shore the mother walrus had brought him back from the white man's land. She slipped her hand into his, and her shivering fingers warmed.

Suddenly they were in great danger. One half of the floe was gone, and the half on which they stood was tipping. The tethered bulls slid toward the sea. Kapugen eased one into the water with the rope, trying to stabilize the floe, but it was too late. It began to roll over. Atik leaped into the boat and pulled his walrus into the sea. Kapugen picked up Julie, threw her into the boat, and jumped in after her.

They paddled landward slowly, hindered by the one-ton walruses. Behind them the floe kept tipping until it was straight up like a breaching whale. Then it fell. Julie saw it was about to crash onto Atik's walrus and pull boat and hunters down into the sea. With a swift movement she severed the rope with her ulu. The floe thundered down upon the bull, and he disappeared from sight. Kapugen shot Julie a grateful glance.

They beached the boat. Kapugen and Atik jumped ashore and hauled the remaining walrus to safety. For a moment the three hunters stood quietly looking at the huge animal, each thinking his own thoughts.

After a respectful silence Kapugen took out his man's knife and slit open the belly. He reached into the warm body, found the heart, and carried it to the sea edge.

"Great Aiviq," he said. "I have borrowed your body. My flesh will be your flesh." He threw the heart into the waves. "I return your spirit to the sea. I give you birth again."

When the ceremony of respect was done, Kapugen and Atik got into the boat and paddled out to rescue the other walrus. It was a terrible thing to kill an animal and not use it. They paddled around the floe searching the water but could not find the dead walrus.

"I apologize, Aiviq," Kapugen said in his low, slowly paced voice. "I am sorry I wasted you. I shall walk around the house four times when I return to punish myself for losing you." Julie listened and felt peaceful. This was the father she remembered.

"I am very sorry, Aiviq," Atik said. "Your hide was to be a beautiful boat cover, your intestines to be rain gear, your flesh my flesh. I am sorry."

When they were on shore again, Kapugen and

Atik removed the two smooth white tusks, then butchered the huge animal into portions for Kangik.

"You can still make your boat cover," Kapugen said to his friend as they carried the hide to the sled. "This is for you." Atik smiled his thanks. The Eskimo languages have no words for "thank you." One does not give to be thanked. A person gives to please himself; that requires no thanks.

When the skin was on the sled and the meat packed, Atik picked up the intestines and packed them.

"Uma will make little Amaroq a raincoat of these intestines," he said. "She was going to do that if I brought an aiviq home."

In the pitch blackness Atik lit the Coleman stove and placed a large piece of walrus meat in a pot for a harvest dinner. Julie fed the dogs their portion. They ate happily, wagging their tails. The stars shone like huge silver lights as the hunting party feasted and the moon circled around the sky. Kapugen looked up in thoughtful silence.

The next morning the hunters packed their meat, ivory, tent, and gear and faced the dogs toward Kangik.

"Hut," Julie called, and barking and leaping, CB

in the lead, they took off for Kangik full of the energy of the walrus.

The days grew quickly shorter.

"Taggaqtugik," Julie said to Ellen on the first of November. "That means 'the month when the lakes are frozen and you can see your reflection on the ice.'"

"Very pretty," said Ellen, burping Amaroq on her shoulder.

"It is also the month," said Julie, "when all the whales are south in the Bering Sea, when the pregnant polar bears come inland to dig dens in the snow. It is the month when the seals swim under the sea ice and the only birds that remain with us are the snowy owls and the guillemots.

"Except for ice fishing," she said, "the time of food gathering is over."

The sun did not rise on November eighteenth, and everything turned blue—the snow, the footprints, the shadows. The Arctic night was a palette of blues.

Julie, Ellen, and little Amaroq went to school every weekday. Ellen put the baby on a warm polar-bear skin on the table, and lessons began.

With Amaroq to inspire the teacher, the ten children of all ages learned such English sentences as "The baby sees his toes" and "The baby needs diapering." From Julie they learned how to say the same thing in Iñupiat and Yupik. Julie also showed them how to add five baby fingers and five baby fingers to get ten. She followed this with a lesson on how to take away four baby toes from five. Ellen taught them to sing "The Far Northland."

An important lesson was devised by the North Slope Education Department. Each child was given ten dollars. With it they bought stock in the Kangik School Corporation. Then Marie came to the school to set up an Eskimo doughnut business. She paid for the flour and ingredients by writing out a corporation check, financed by the children's investment stock. She and the students mixed and cooked doughnuts. When they were done, the children ran through the village streets, following the lights through the blackness to homes, and sold the doughnuts to Kangik families. With the money they took in, they paid the corporation back for the ingredients. Then each child was paid a five-cent commission. The rest was profit. It went into the corporation. In this way they learned about the native corporations that had been supporting the Alaskan Eskimos and Indians since 1971.

A letter from Peter to the children of Kangik arrived at the school one December day, and Ellen asked Julie to read it aloud.

"Dear friends," the letter began. "I am in Fairbanks in a student room on the campus of the University of Alaska. We eat in a big dining room and go to classes. I am taking four courses—English, biology, mathematics, and sociology. Each one is in a different building.

"Miyax asked me to tell you about my Siberian village. You would feel at home there. It looks very much like Kangik. My father wears maklaks and parkas and hunts for polar bears and walrus. My mother wears traditional clothing and makes our food. In Russia we have to borrow guns from the government when we go hunting. We have to bring back the empty shells when we turn in the guns. For that reason my father uses traps and spears to hunt.

"I miss you all." Before Julie could stop, she read: "Tell Julie that I love her and that I am her forever-partner. Your friend, Peter."

She blushed and picked up little Amaroq to hide her embarrassment.

"Peter loves Julie," said Marie's adopted eight-year-old, Bessie, and the children giggled and broke into a chant. Ellen clapped her hands, and the school day was over. Hastily Julie dressed them in their warm overclothes to much teasing and laughter and sent them all home.

After the last child had zipped up his parka and stepped out into the cold wind and darkness, another school day began. Ellen taught Julie world history and mathematics, and Julie taught Ellen Yupik and Iñupiat.

Julie closed the Iñupiaq-and-English dictionary at the end of their study period and took Peter's letter out of her shirt. Smiling shyly, she looked at it.

"What do you think of Peter, Aaka?" she asked.

"I like him," Ellen said.

"Why does he keep saying he loves me?"

"I think he does."

"He has school to attend, and when the caribou return to Kangik, I have school to attend. We are not ready to make an iglu."

"Do you love him?"

"Not yet," Julie said. "Kapugen will not let me."

"Julie," Ellen said in shock, "why do you say that? You know Kapugen wants you to grow up and love and marry. You know that."

"He does, but he stops me." She put the dictionary on the desk. "I must stay here in Kangik so he doesn't kill the wolves. I cannot think about Peter or school as long as he is thinking about the Minnesota law."

"Oh, Julie," Ellen said, looking down at the gurgling Amaroq. "I am sorry to hear you say that."

Julie looked at her father's wife. This stepmother she loved so much did not know what every Eskimo knew from birth: that people and animals coexist for the welfare of both.

In early April a warm wind from the east brought rain that turned the snow to slush. The villagers took off their heavy parkas and visited in the community yard and along the river. They wondered if the early spring would bring the caribou to Kangik.

Then a blast of below-zero air hit like the sting of a scorpion's tail. Land, slush, and water froze in an hour. An icy rain put down a covering of ice. Kangik, its houses, boats, and sleds were under a sheath of glass. Doors were frozen shut. Walking was treacherous, and food caches were almost impossible to open. This was the worst possible weather in a land of impossible weather conditions.

The freeze dropped below minus thirty degrees and held for almost a month. Kapugen's plane could not fly at that temperature and food became a problem. Marie's store ran out of supplies. Atik, who still had frozen walrus meat on his sled, switched on his CB.

"Atik has walrus meat," he said. "Come to my sled at my house if you want walrus meat. Out." Not long after the announcement, qanitchak doors were kicked open and children with plastic bags and adults with pots skidded and skated to Atik's for a share of his harvest.

One night the electricity went out. Marie had to walk to Kapugen's house to tell him she was out of gasoline for the generator. The villagers lit candles for light and their camp stoves for cooking. They turned their coal-oil heaters low to conserve oil. The weather station reported no change in temperature.

Several of the hungry children became sick. When the temperature rose to minus twenty degrees, Kapugen lit the kerosene heaters in the Quonset and warmed up his airplane. The men from the village helped chip ice off the runway, and he and Malek took off for Barrow to purchase supplies. Ellen's last words, as he left the house, were "Pampers, please, bring Pampers."

In Barrow, Kapugen rented a Beaver, the workhorse plane of the north, and loaded it with gasoline, heating oil, alfalfa pellets for the musk oxen, and boxes of groceries. He paid for them with a corporation check. At the U.S. weather station in Barrow he was told that the forecast for the day was clear and would hold at minus twenty degrees.

"A good time for flying," Kapugen said. "We can go to the Brooks Range and see if the caribou herd is coming north."

With a catlike purr the big Beaver took off, and Kapugen headed it south to the Colville. He saw no caribou in the foothills or along the river.

On the way back to Kangik Kapugen spotted a gang of ravens and a lonesome wolverine. That was all. No moose, no caribou. Disappointed, he flew home, landing safely on the still-icy Kangik airstrip.

Kapugen and Malek were planning to call for help in unloading supplies, but did not have to. Everyone had heard the Beaver arrive, and men and women were streaming across the tundra, pulling their sleds, ready to help.

Kapugen did not go to his house until the generator was going again and the supplies were in the store. He then joined Ellen and Julie. Unable to tell them that the caribou would not come again this year, he picked up sleeping Amaroq and held him in his arms. The baby opened his eyes.

"I have a song for you," Kapugen said to his little son. "Listen to me.

"O caribou, where are you hiding?
I know where you walk.
In the darkness of the trees,
In the passes, in the tundra grass,
I know where you walk."

He held the baby against his shoulder and patted his firm body.

"O caribou, where are you hiding?
I cannot wait—my children are hungry.
I know where you walk.
In the darkness of the trees,
In the passes, in the tundra grass,
I know where you walk.
You will not come to Kangik,
Aya, ya, ya, you will not come to Kangik."

"Aya, ya, ya," sang Julie, in sadness and fear for the village's well-being. "You will not come to Kangik."

"Aya, ya, ya," sang a voice from the qanitchak. Kapugen handed little Amaroq to Julie and opened the inner door.

"David Bradford," he said to the Fish and Game man. "Do you bring us good news? Are the caribou coming to Kangik?"

"I've come to see how you all are faring in this

treacherous weather," he said, not answering the question. "But I can see you are okay."

"Come in," called Ellen. "I'll make tea. You must be cold."

Julie nodded to him and smiled.

"Hello, little bear lady," he said to her. Ignoring his greeting, she held up the red-cheeked Amaroq for him to admire.

"So this is your little brother, Julie," David said. "He looks as strong as a wolf's jaw."

"And he is," said Julie, laughing at the idea of a baby being compared to a wolf's jaw.

David sat down in the overstuffed chair and gratefully accepted a steaming cup of tea from Ellen. He warmed his hands on it.

"Terrible weather," he said. "I had to leave the copter running or I'll never get it started again, so I can't stay long.

"What I've come to say, Kapugen, is that those wolves you said killed your musk ox left the Colville and are headed this way."

Julie's heart thumped.

"I thought I'd warn you before they kill another."

"That is good to know," said Kapugen, slowly rising and picking up his gun. "I will intercept them before they get here."

"No, Aapa, no," Julie cried, running to her father. "You promised you would not kill them unless they killed another musk ox. They have not killed one." She hugged little Amaroq closer. "Let me take them away again. You promised."

Kapugen frowned.

"I did say that, all right," he said. "But I am like the wolf. I must defend my family from the enemy."

"The wolves are not our enemy, Aapa," Julie whispered. "You know that. They are part of us. We are part of them." She put her cheek against the soft, smooth head of the baby. He arched back and bawled.

"Even little Amaroq," she said, patting him to calm him down, "knows you should not shoot the wolf."

"Well, that is one interpretation," said Ellen from her seat at the table, where she was correcting school papers. "I would say little Amaroq is crying because his father woke him up."

"Ayaa, I woke him up," said Kapugen, smiling and putting down his gun. He gently took his son from Julie and placed his forehead against the small nose. "You do not mind, do you, little wolf pup?" Amaroq stopped crying and kicked his feet.

Julie scrambled up on the iglek. Her thoughts

were interrupted by the conversation between Kapugen and David. They were planning how best to intercept the wolves and shoot them. Ellen listened too.

"I've got to return the Beaver before I can do anything," said Kapugen.

"You have time," David said. "The pack was feeding on something in a watershed of the Avalik River. They ought to sleep a day or two."

David walked to the door. "I've got to get to Barrow," he said. "I have to examine a polar bear that killed a white man there." Kapugen's face did not show any expression.

"That is how it is," he said softly. "Where was the gussak?"

"Right near his house on the beach. He had gone out to start his car. A polar bear charged him, and he turned and ran. That was a mistake. Julie taught me not to run. He did not make it."

"Did they get the bear?" asked Kapugen.

"His neighbor shot the bear."

"Dangerous time of year," said Kapugen. "The polar bear mothers are rejecting their two-year-old cubs—and they are hungry."

"And so are the wolves," said David before putting on his face mask and dark glasses. He opened the door, and cold air from the qanitchaq ballooned into the room. Ellen shuddered.

"I don't think I'll ever get used to cold," she said, and laughed. "Or is it the forces moving in the wilderness that make me shiver?"

Julie did not speak.

"I'm ready," called Malek from outside. "Time to take the Beaver back." Kapugen turned to Ellen. "Malek and I are going to return the rented plane and bring back mine to Kangik."

"Hurry, before the wolves come," she said. Kapugen nodded his head once. His eyes did not shine. He put little Amaroq in his cradle and kissed his booted foot. Then he left.

When Julie and Ellen were alone, Julie came down from the iglek and sat beside her.

"Ellen," she said, "our next lesson is about how every beast and plant is dependent on every other beast and plant."

"I understand that," she said. "You have taught me well."

Julie despaired. She had been talking to Ellen since the sun had gone down about cycles and the rise of one animal and the fall of another. She had held up her hands and told her how the Eskimo knew they were related to all the animals because they all had the same bones in one shape or another. She had told her that wolves keep the environment healthy, and that when the environment is healthy, people are healthy.

And still Ellen had told her she would kill a wolf to save the oxen and Kapugen agreed with her.

Julie knew she must do something right now. "When things are not working, you are doing something wrong," she had said to herself on the tundra. "Change what you are doing." She looked long at Ellen and took a deep breath.

"Dear Ellen," she said. "I will stop lecturing and tell you a story.

"A young girl was lost on the tundra. She was starving. One day she found the summer nursery of a wolf pack and made friends with the wolves. A puppy taught her how to get food from the wolves' stomach baskets by touching the corner of a wolf's mouth. She did that, and a wolf generously gave up food for her, but the food was not enough. She ate moss and fungi.

"A fog rolled over the land and she could not see. The earth vibrated. The fog thinned and Kapu, her puppy friend, came into view. As alert as an eagle, he was sniffing the wind and wagging his tail as if reading some amusing wolf story. She sniffed, too, but for her the pages were blank." Julie looked into Ellen's eyes.

"Amaroq, the great leader of the wolf pack, howled. Nails, his best friend, bark-howled. Then Amaroq slid into a musical song and Silver, his mate, joined in. Their voices rose and fell as each harmonized with the other. The windy voice of Jello, the baby-sitter, crooned, and like the beat of drums, the five pups whooped and yipped. The girl rubbed her chin; something was different about this hunt song. It was eerie and restless. It spoke of things she did not understand, and she was frightened.

"The fog cleared again and she saw Amaroq, his hunters, and the pups running across the tundra. Even Jello was with them. Were they leaving her? Was this their day to take up the wandering life of the wolves? Was she now on her own? She crawled around her frost heave and frantically gathered the leafy plants that the caribou eat. She stuffed mushroomlike fungi into her pocket, and bits of reindeer moss. She could no longer pass up anything that might be edible.

"As she worked on her hands and knees, the vibrations in the earth grew stronger. The girl drew back. Out of the fog came a huge caribou running her way. At his neck, leaping with the power of an ocean wave, was Amaroq." Ellen glanced around the room. Her eyes fell on the spot where Kapugen had put down his gun. It was gone. Julie went on.

"Nails was diving in and out under the caribou. At his flank was Silver.

"Then Amaroq jumped, floated in the air for an instant, and sank his teeth into the shoulder of the beast.

"The fog closed in briefly, and when it thinned, the caribou was poised above Amaroq, his cleaverlike hoofs aimed at his head. There was a low grunt, a flash of hoofs, and the huge feet cut uselessly into the sod; for Amaroq had jumped again and sunk his teeth into the animal's back. Snarling, using the weight of his body as a tool, he rode the circling and stumbling beast. Silver leaped in front of the bull trying to trip him and slow him down. Nails had a grip on one hind leg. The caribou bucked, writhed, then dropped to his knees. His antlers pierced the ground. He bellowed and fell.

"Miyax, the girl, could not believe her good fortune—an entire caribou felled practically at her feet. This was enough food to last her a month, perhaps a year. She would smoke it to make it lighter to carry, pack it, and walk on to the coast. She would live.

"And I did."

Ellen sat very still. Presently she got up to look for Kapugen's gun in the qanitchaq. It was not there.

"Julie," she said, "I understand. I understand. Please go tell Kapugen I am wrong: The Minnesota law does not work here."

Julie put on her warm qivit pants and sweater. Over these she pulled her down pants and parka. Then she put on her wool cap, gloves, and mittens. She stuffed her pockets with jerky and went out into the glaring ice world. She walked to the sled she had loaded with alfalfa pellets last night, and rather than take the dogs over the treacherous ice, she picked up the rope and pulled the sled herself. She slipped a few times, then got her footing. After she fed the musk oxen, she was going to go out on the tundra to find Kapu and Aaka, Silver, Raw Bones, Zing, and Amy, and turn them away. She glanced at the Quonset and listened for the doors to open and for Kapugen to start up the Beaver. He would be able to shoot well from that plane.

At the corral she dumped the pellets in the feed trough, closed the gate, struggling for a moment with the icy bolt, then headed for the riverbank. She had not gone five paces before she stopped. Kapugen had been here. His boots, with the distinctive crimping on their soles, had broken through the ice layer and left their imprints in the snow. He was here with his gun. He was not taking the Beaver to Barrow. His footsteps were fresh and led off around the corral. He was stalking the wolves on foot.

A howl sounded in the distance. It was followed by an alert bark, and then, urgently, the voices of her wolves rose from the tundra wilderness. She ran toward them. The ice broke under her feet, slowing her down, but she plugged on, determined to save them somehow.

What can I do? How can I scare them? A gun would help. I have none. A dead wolf would work—my wolf-head mittens perhaps. They're at home. She noted that the wind was blowing her scent in the direction of Kapu and his pack. She hoped he would smell her and the fear odor she was exuding. That would turn them away. She struggled, looking back to see if Kapugen was following.

The earth shook, a crackling roar sounded. Julie turned around again, to see the musk oxen thundering out of the corral, bulls first, calves in the middle, cows bringing up the rear. Their skirts flowing in the wind, they rushed out onto the tundra and headed for a knoll above the river. They had escaped. They were free. For a moment Julie was thrilled; then she was frightened.

The industry was gone. Kapugen had failed. Little Amaroq would not have a future. She must drive the herd back to the corral. Running, stumbling, she tried to swing around them with flying arms and shouts. Snow burst up from their feet, obscuring them and the corral. She ran.

A shimmer appeared on the river ice. Julie dropped to all fours and focused as her wolf pack, Kapu in the lead, the others behind, trotted down the frozen river. They moved like flowing water. They left the riverbed and dashed into the ox herd. Weaving among them, pacing their own steps to the steps of the wing-footed bulls, Kapu and his pack sized up the herd.

The cloud of snow the oxen had stirred settled down. Julie rubbed her eyes. Kapugen was standing beside the corral. He had no gun. His hands were clasped behind his back, his head forward.

Julie looked from him to the wolves. They were loping along easily as they scattered the herd. She didn't understand why the oxen hadn't formed a defense ring. They were making themselves easy targets by scattering. She closed her eyes, not wanting to see what came next.

When she opened them, the wolves were walking. The musk oxen had stopped running. They cracked the ice with their huge hoofs and leaned down to browse serenely on the emerging tundra grass. The wolves, panting and wagging their tails, trotted off a short distance and lay down on their bellies.

For some unknown reason the hunt was over. There would be no kill. The predator knew something that was not for Julie's understanding.

Then she saw that the gate was open.

Had she left it ajar? she wondered frantically. Had she not locked it tight enough? No, she remembered the difficulty she had had in throwing the bolt in the cold. She had locked it well.

And then she knew.

Kapugen had set the musk oxen free.

She walked across the ice to him, pulling the sled behind her.

"There they are again," he said. "The wolf and the little oxen of the north."

For a long quiet hour Julie and her father watched the animals moving beneath a white sun that shone down on the top of the earth.

"The industry, Aapa," Julie whispered. "What will happen to the industry?"

"We now have a wild herd," he said. The look on his face was peaceful.

"The Eskimo wiped out the musk oxen of Alaska

when the white men gave us guns. Now the Eskimo has restored them. They will live and reproduce and become part of us again." He turned to her. "As for the industry, you and I will have to walk a lot farther, as our people used to do, to gather the qivit for the knitters. That is all."

He added slowly, "But I don't know what Ellen will say."

"I have just left her," Julie said. "She has said the Minnesota law is not the law of the Arctic. She thinks so, all right."

"Then I think so too, all right," said Kapugen, squinting out over the magnificent tundra, his home.

The wind buffeted them but they did not leave. Like the musk oxen and wolves, they, too, had been restored to order.

"When are you going to school?" Kapugen finally asked.

"When the caribou return," Julie said.

"They will, all right," said Kapugen. "The wolves have been talking." He pushed back his parka hood and cupped his hands behind his ears. "Listen," he said.

Kapu howled. He began on a low note and climbed to the highest pitch of the wind and held it there. Zing, Silver, Aaka, Raw Bones, and Amy joined in. The air quivered, the ice snapped, and the land crackled with life.

"They are saying," Kapugen said, "that the caribou are coming." Julie shaded her eyes and looked at the river and tundra.

A dark-gray mass quivered on the glare ice. It seemed to be a wind cloud moving toward them. Julie squinted. Above the darkness rode antlers, a sea of them.

"Aapa," she cried. "The caribou are here!"

Like the irresistible force of nature that it is, the female caribou herd surged toward them. The males were days behind. The females carried their heads high, these beasts of the icy past who, together with the wolves and musk oxen, had kept the tundra flourishing for an eon. The breath clouds behind them streamed out like white banners heralding their return. The herd was magnificent to see. Kapu howled one penetrating note and held it. The musk oxen snorted and stared at the tide of caribou without expression, and Kapugen and Julie threw their arms around each other.

"That is how it is," Kapugen said.

As Julie watched the life-bringing caribou caravan, she thought about high school, books, girls, boys, and teachers. Then she felt Peter's whistle

against her chest and she thought about him.

If I can think of school and teachers before I think of Peter, she reasoned, *I am not in love.* But images of little ground squirrels popping out of the earth and the vision of Peter dancing at the Nalukataq festival changed her mind.

"I will marry Peter," she said to herself, "when I am all grown up."

Kapugen picked up the sled rope, Julie took hold, and together they walked back to Kangik. They listened to the howl of the wolf mingling with the tatoo of an Eskimo drummer announcing the return of life.

A Note About the Eskimo Languages in *Julie*

The Inuit Eskimos of Barrow, Alaska, began writing down their language in the 1940s using the English alphabet and its phonetic sounds. They were able to use the English alphabet to write *nanook,* for polar bear, and *igloo,* for house. But something was lost. Many of the melodic sounds of Iñupiat and Yupick, two of many Eskimo languages, could not be produced using the English alphabet. Spellings such as *uminmak,* for musk oxen, leave out the *ing* sound that should be in the middle, for there is no letter in the English alphabet that represents that sound. I have used my best judgment in approximating the richness and subtleties of the Eskimo languages in *Julie* and hope that readers will understand that compromises always need to be made when one language is translated into another.

—J.C.G.

Twenty years after *Julie of the Wolves* was first published, **Jean Craighead George** decided it was time to write its sequel. Children all over North America had been asking her about what had happened to Julie after she left the wolves. Frequent visits to Alaska over the past two decades continued to provide a fresh picture of this natural world for Ms. George to draw on in her telling of the continuation of Julie's story.

Ms. George is the author of many beloved books for children, including the Thirteen Moons Series and three Ecological Mysteries: *Who Really Killed Cock Robin?*, *The Missing 'Gator of Gumbo Limbo*, and *The Fire Bug Connection*. She lives in Chappaqua, New York.

Wendell Minor is well known for his paintings featured on book jackets and in picture books. His work includes *Sierra, Heartland, Mojave,* all by Diane Siebert; *The Seashore Book* by Charlotte Zolotow; and *The Moon of the Owls* by Jean Craighead George. Mr. Minor lives in Washington, Connecticut, with his wife, Florence, and their two cats, Willie and Mouse.

JULIE'S WOLF PACK

ALSO BY JEAN CRAIGHEAD GEORGE

Acorn Pancakes, Dandelion Salad,
and 38 Other Wild Recipes

Animals Who Have Won Our Hearts

The Case of the Missing Cutthroats
An Ecological Mystery

The Cry of the Crow

Dear Rebecca, Winter Is Here

Everglades

The Fire Bug Connection
An Ecological Mystery

Going to the Sun

The Grizzly Bear with the Golden Ears

Julie

Julie of the Wolves

Look to the North
A Wolf Pup Diary

The Missing 'Gator of Gumbo Limbo
An Ecological Mystery

The Moon of the Alligators

The Moon of the Bears

The Moon of the Chickarees

The Moon of the Deer

The Moon of the Fox Pups

The Moon of the Gray Wolves

The Moon of the Moles

The Moon of the Monarch Butterflies

The Moon of the Mountain Lions

The Moon of the Owls

The Moon of the Salamanders

The Moon of the Wild Pigs

The Moon of the Winter Bird

One Day in the Alpine Tundra

One Day in the Desert

One Day in the Prairie

One Day in the Tropical Rain Forest

One Day in the Woods

Shark Beneath the Reef

The Summer of the Falcon

The Talking Earth

The Tarantula in My Purse

There's an Owl in the Shower

Water Sky

Who Really Killed Cock Robin?
An Ecological Mystery

The Wounded Wolf

HARPERCOLLINS*PUBLISHERS*

JEAN CRAIGHEAD GEORGE

JULIE'S WOLF PACK

ILLUSTRATED BY WENDELL MINOR

Julie's Wolf Pack
 For information address HarperCollins Children's Books, a division of HarperCollins Publishers, 10 East 53rd Street, New York, NY 10022.

Library of Congress Cataloging-in-Publication Data
George, Jean Craighead, date
Julie's wolf pack / Jean Craighead George ; illustrated by Wendell Minor.
p. cm.
Summary: Continues the story of Julie and her wolves in which Kapu must protect his pack from famine and disease while uniting it under his new leadership.
ISBN 0-06-027406-9. — ISBN 0-06-027407-7 (lib. bdg.)
1. Wolves—Juvenile fiction. [1. Wolves—Fiction. 2. Survival—Fiction. 3. Leadership—Fiction.] I. Minor, Wendell, ill. II. Title.
PZ10.3.G316Ju 1997 96-54858
[Fic]—dc21 CIP
AC

Typography by Wendell Minor and Al Cetta
01 02 HAD 15 14 13 12
❖
First Edition

To Luke and Sam,
my grandsons of Barrow, Alaska,
friends of the wolves, whales, foxes, owls,
and the Iñupiat Eskimos

WOLF PACK TERRITORIES
BARROW
WAINWRIGHT
Meade River
Ikpikpuk River
KANGIK
Avalik River
SUMMER DEN
WHELPING DEN
Kikiakrorak River
AVALIK RIVER PACK
Colville River
Nuka River
WHELPING DEN
POINT HOPE
NUKA RIVER PACK
BROOKS
UPPER COLVILL
RIVER PACK
MOUNTAIN PACK
KOTZEBUE

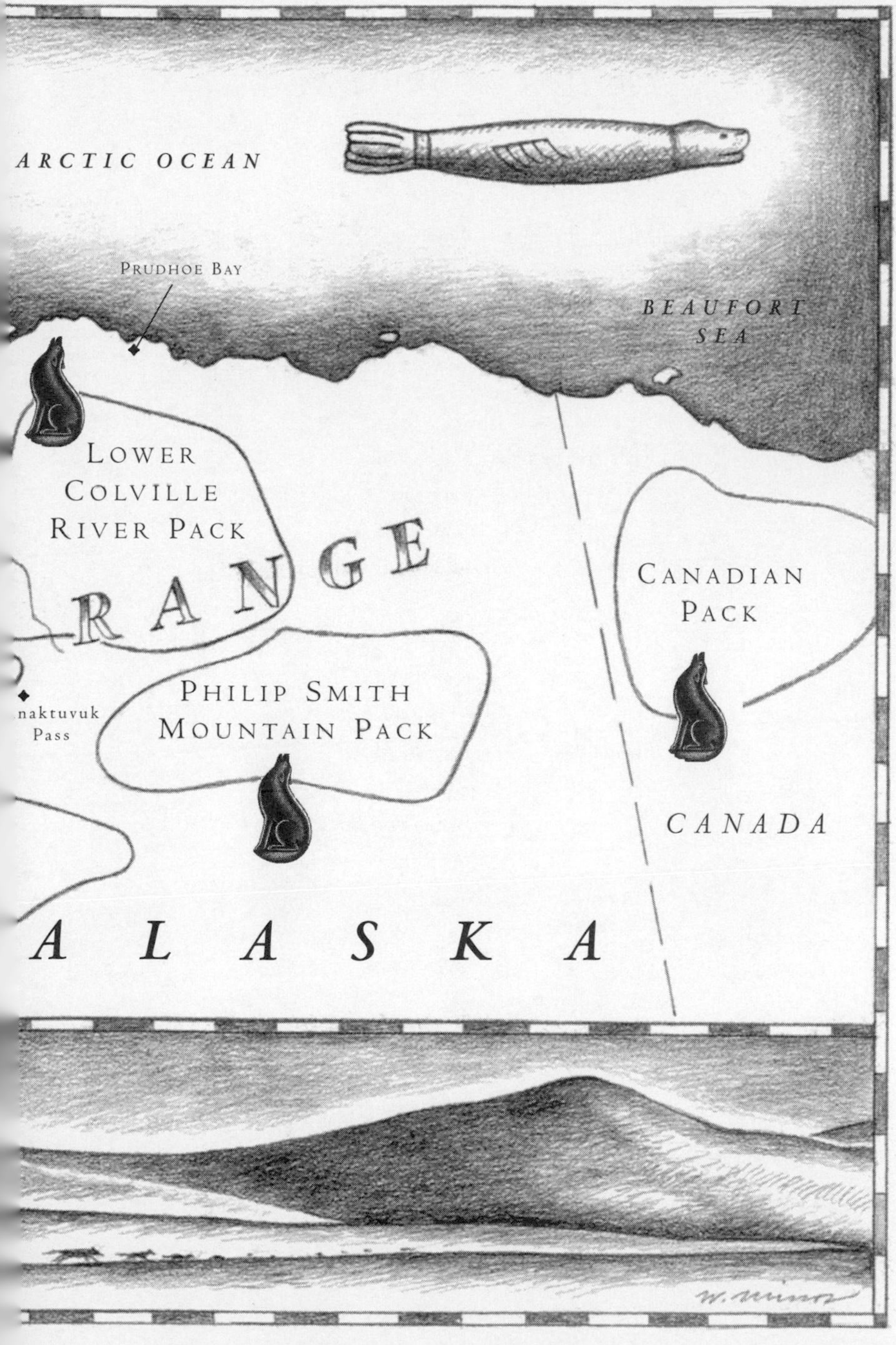
ARCTIC OCEAN
PRUDHOE BAY
BEAUFORT SEA
LOWER COLVILLE RIVER PACK
RANGE
CANADIAN PACK
PHILIP SMITH MOUNTAIN PACK
naktuvuk Pass
CANADA
ALASKA
W. Minor

Julie's Wolf Pack
YEAR BY YEAR

YEAR ONE	
Parents/Alpha Male and Female	Amaroq, Silver
Beta	Nails
Offspring	Kapu, Zing, Zit, Zat, Sister
Other	Jello
YEAR TWO	
Parents/Alpha Male and Female	Kapu, Aaka
Beta	Zing
Offspring	Sweet Fur Amy
Special Event	Julie's half brother, Amaroq, is born
YEAR THREE	
Parents	Raw Bones, Silver
Offspring	Nutik, Uqaq
Alpha Male and Female	Kapu, Aaka
Beta	Zing
Others	Sweet Fur Amy, Storm Call, Lichen, Ice Blink
YEAR FOUR	
Parents/Alpha Male and Female	Kapu, Aaka
Beta	Zing
Offspring	Cotton Grass, Long Face, Grappler, Smiler, White Toes, Black Lips, Nameless Moonlight
Others	Sweet Fur Amy, Raw Bones, Uqaq, Storm Call, Lichen, Wind Voice

YEAR FIVE	
Parents	Wind Voice, Uqaq
Offspring	Big Ears, Owl Feathers, Bird Egg
Others	Zing, Aaka, Raw Bones, Lichen, Storm Call, Sweet Fur Amy, Cotton Grass, Long Face

YEAR SIX	
Parents	Storm Call, Sweet Fur Amy
Offspring	Six (unnamed)
Others	Aaka, Zing, Lichen, Wind Voice, Uqaq, Big Ears, Owl Feathers, Bird Egg, Cotton Grass, Long Face

OTHER PACKS

LOWER COLVILLE RIVER PACK	
Alpha Male	Storm Alarm
Alpha Female	Star Gentian
Offspring	Aaka

NUKA RIVER PACK	
Alpha Male	Low Wind
Alpha Female	Moon Seeker

PHILIP SMITH MOUNTAIN PACK	
Alpha Male	Sedge Ears
Alpha Female	Alder Whisper

MOUNTAIN PACK	
Alpha Male	Snow Driver
Alpha Female	Cloud Berry

CONTENTS

PART I
KAPU, THE ALPHA
1

PART II
ICE BLINK, THE STRANGER
55

PART III
SWEET FUR AMY,
THE NEW ALPHA
153

Part I

Kapu, The Alpha

The wolves of the Avalik River ran in and out among the musk oxen. Their ruffs rippled like banners. Ice crystals danced up from their feet. The pack swirled like a twist of wind-blown snow. Their yellow eyes flashed and dimmed in the coming and going of the ice mist. Like the snow, they made no sound.

The musk oxen stopped and stared at the enemy. Then they lowered their shaggy heads and pawed down to the new grass growing under the snow. Their breath rose in steamy clouds and froze on their brows.

Kapu, the young leader of the wolf pack, reared on his hind legs, leaped to point the way, and led his clan to a turquoise-blue rise on the treeless Arctic tundra.

He carried himself proudly, with his chest forward and his head high. His black fur was brushed to a shine by the wind. His body was strongly muscled.

He was the leader of the wolf pack that had saved the life of the young Eskimo girl, Miyax—whose English name was Julie Edwards—when she was lost on the Arctic tundra. She, in turn, had saved them by leading them to a new food source during the great caribou famine. The Yupik and Iñupiat Eskimos of Kangik called them "Julie's wolf pack."

Kapu was keenly aware of Julie. She was not far away. He whisked his tail. She had read his message to the oxen, for she was no longer afraid that he would kill one. The villagers collected the wool from these sturdy animals to weave into light, warm clothing, and they zealously protected them.

"We are not hunting you," Kapu had said to the oxen with his body movements. "We chase you for the joy of it. We are wolves of the caribou."

Kapu and his followers were having fun. The shaggy herd deciphered this and returned to their grazing. Julie deciphered it and told her father, Kapugen. He chuckled and slipped his arm around her shoulders. The two walked quietly home.

Kapu wagged his tail. Chasing the oxen was a fine wolf joke. His rime-gray mate, Aaka, playfully spanked the ground with her forepaws, her rear end in the air. Zing—the beta, or second in command—enjoyed the joke even more than Kapu. His breathing came faster, and the pupils of his eyes enlarged ever so slightly. He smiled by lifting his lips from his glistening teeth. Pearly-white Silver, Kapu's mother, and her ill-tempered new mate, Raw Bones, also smiled. But Amy, Kapu's night-black daughter, did not get the joke. She was not old enough to know that her pack preferred caribou to musk oxen. Nor did she know that some packs harvest only deer and ignore moose, or harvest moose and caribou and ignore deer. Others take elk; a few take musk oxen. When the Avalik River Pack had a choice, they were wolves of the caribou. Wolves have their cultures.

The adolescent Amy studied the curled horns and bony brows of the musk oxen, then looked at her regal father. If he thought the chase was fun, then she did, too. She wagged her tail.

Amy could not possibly know that her pack were caribou wolves. She had been born in a caribou famine. These big Arctic deer had failed to come to Avalik territory for many years. The pack had taken what food they could find—a musk ox killed by a grizzly bear, rabbits, lemmings. Late in the fall they were able to add an occasional moose to their diet, but by March of her first year Amy's pack was starving again. The moose were gone. The wolves grew thin. They tired easily. When the breeding season arrived that month, her parents did not mate. Aaka, her mother, was undernourished. There had not been enough food for her to develop healthy puppies.

The rangy, self-important Raw Bones knew well that the pack had not had enough to eat for years. Nevertheless, he approached Silver to start their family. Kapu rushed to him. Hair rising on his back, ears erect and pointed forward, Kapu talked to him in the wolf language of posturing. Then he lifted his head above him and rumbled a dark authoritative growl that said plainly, "No pups." It is inherent in the leader of the wolf pack that he uses his judgment and makes such a decision. Raw Bones ignored him. He stepped closer to Silver.

Kapu bared his teeth and drew the corners of his mouth forward. His forehead wrinkled.

Raw Bones challenged this reprimand with a jaw snap. Kapu grabbed the back of his neck but did not clamp down with his bone-crushing jaws. He did not need to. He was saying, "I am the leader. No pups." Raw Bones drew his ears back and close to his head. He pulled his tail between his legs and lowered his body. This posture said, "You are the leader. I submit to you."

Obediently Raw Bones slunk off to the edge of the pack in the manner of a chastised wolf citizen.

But he did not mean it.

He glanced back to see if Kapu was looking at him. If not, he would sneak-attack him. Kapu was looking. He displayed one canine tooth. It shone lethal white against the black of his lips. "Don't dare," it said. Raw Bones lay down. Rumbling sounds of peevishness rolled in his chest. He did not like being dominated, especially by a younger male.

Kapu did not completely relax. Raw Bones was his rival. He wanted to be leader of the Avaliks, Kapu's pack. He had been alpha male wolf of the Upper Colville River Pack for many years. Then the famine struck. One by one the members of his pack starved to death until he was the only one left alive. When his new mate, Silver, joined him, they survived on rabbits and other small mammals and waited for the famine to end and the feasting to begin. Feast and famine are the natural rhythm of the Arctic tundra. The caribou eat themselves out of grasses and moss and move to greener lands. The wolves adjust. Many die. The alpha males and females have few or no pups. Then time heals. Without the caribou to crop them, the grasses and mosses spring up in abundance. The caribou return. The wolves feast and have pups again. This has been the rhythm of nature for the past 500,000 years.

Raw Bones and Silver waited for the cycle to end by sleeping long hours to conserve energy. They were curled tightly, saving body heat, when the Avaliks arrived at the border of their own property across the river. Between Kapu's and Raw Bones's territories was a broad corridor into which neither pack would go. It was the no-wolf zone, an area fenced off with howls and scent marks to keep wolf packs from fighting and killing each other.

Silver heard a wolf voice beyond the no-wolf zone. She lifted her head. Kapu, her son, was calling, "Come hunt with us," communicating in the wolf language of song.

She jumped up, eager to join him. Relatives can cross the no-wolf zone when invited. She trotted toward the river. Raw Bones held back. He had been trained all his life not to enter these corridors. Adolescents leaving home to look for a new pack, and lone wolves, can hide in them, but not leaders. Not Raw Bones.

Yet he had heard Kapu's invitation. Invitations are important in wolf protocol. He arose. A raging hunger and the scent knowledge that Kapu was Silver's son urged him slowly forward.

Silver took a deep draft of air. The perfume of Willow Pup Julie was on it. She wagged her tail. The human cub who had joined her family long ago was coming her way.

Willow Pup Julie appeared among the knobby alder trees. She carried Kapu's invitation in the odors on her clothes. Silver pranced a wolf dance of survival. By joining the Avaliks, she would live. She ran to the river. Raw Bones was reluctant but understood what he must do. Head down, he skirted Willow Pup and splashed into the river behind Silver. They crossed to the forbidden land.

The packs met. Stiff-legged, nervous, they greeted each other with mouth sniffs and brief tail whisks. All tails curved downward and cricked in suspicion, then each hung loose and relaxed to tell the other wolves they would cooperate and hunt together. Antlered animals with their sharp hoofs are violent prey. The more wolves, the better.

But it was not that simple. There can be but one alpha male and one alpha female leading a pack. Kapu and Raw Bones snapped at each other, testing to see which it would be. They were both leaders. The battle for rank began as they lifted their tails. Then each inhaled the other's scent and learned of his health, vigor, and dominance. Finally each growled his lowest note. Raw Bones was older. This gave him the advantage. He raised his head above

Kapu's to say he was boss. Kapu would not tolerate it. He threw Raw Bones to the ground. Raw Bones quickly got to his feet. Kapu lifted his head above Raw Bones's. Both wrinkled their brows and curled back their black lips to show gleaming white fangs. Growling, they threatened each other. Raw Bones tried to get his paw on Kapu's back, but Kapu kept his head and chest above him. He snarled deep and low. With that the battle was over. Not a drop of blood was spilled. Kapu had won.

This was an important victory for the young wolf leader. Upon the death of his father, Amaroq, he had taken over the leadership of the pack. The death of an alpha male wolf is a tragedy, like the death of a nation's president. For the wolves it takes many years to make a leader as strong and knowledgeable as Amaroq had been. Kapu did not have time to develop with Raw Bones in his pack. To survive, he had to be dominant now. He had the fearlessness and initiative of an alpha, but he was young. That is a disadvantage when confronted with an older wolf. By sheer bravado, by snarling and growling and keeping his head above Raw Bones's, Kapu had held on to his rank as alpha male wolf of the Avaliks.

Raw Bones did not like it. He would try again.

Leadership settled for the moment, the six wolves

worked together that early-autumn season hunting the moose that had been protected for years in the no-wolf zone. At first they fared well; then the moose became scarce. Grizzlies and human hunters were also harvesting them.

The famine went on. The caribou did not migrate south through Avalik land in the late fall. The wolves lost weight and vigor.

In March, the breeding month, Kapu made the decision for himself and Aaka as well as for Silver and Raw Bones not to have pups.

Many sleeps later, his sensitive ears picked up the sounds he had been waiting for: the snorts and bleats of the western Arctic caribou herd. The pregnant females had left the forest and were migrating by the tens of thousands to their calving grounds on the tundra. The bulls and adolescents would follow later.

As the murmur swelled into a drone, Kapu paced the riverbank. He mapped the course of the herd using his senses—smell, taste, sight, sound, and, through the pads of his feet, touch. He paced faster. The caribou were in the territory of the Mountain Pack. They were crossing creek beds eating willows, star gentians, and butterworts. Then they were trotting through Raw Bones's old territory and approaching the Colville River.

Would the herd go east, as it had for so many years, or come back to the grassy Avalik territory? The beta wolf, Zing, Kapu's faithful brother, trotted behind him waiting to be told what to do.

The sun set. The sky grew blue-purple, and the moon, a feeble glow by day, shone like a lamp.

Kapu tensed. He heard the musical click made by the tendons in the legs of the caribou snapping against bones as they walked—a sound only caribou make. He judged the herd to be in the Colville River valley. The river was deep in some places, shallow in others as it braided its way amid stunted alders and grass to the Arctic Ocean. Kapu waited.

The moon set. In the darkness the river gurgled and boiled. Two miles of caribou were throwing themselves into the deeper waters of the Colville and swimming. Others were splashing across the shallows.

Two hours later the moon came up. Like the Arctic sun, the Arctic moon has its long night or long day. In the deep of winter the moon does not set. The sun, on the other hand, does not rise from late November until late January—the long Arctic night. It does not set from early May until early August—the long Arctic day.

In the pale moonlight of March, Kapu—who, like all wolves, could see in the dark as well as in the day—saw a tide of movement. He stopped pacing. The smell of trodden grass and moss filled his nose—his grass, his moss. The western Arctic herd was on Avalik land.

He lowered his haunches, threw back his head, and howled. His canyon-deep voice climbed an octave and faded. He repeated this song of celebration. Aaka sang a note and slid up the musical scale to harmonize with Kapu. Zing glided up to a note lower than Aaka's. Raw Bones found a note below Aaka's. Silver harmonized with him. They howled a chord of harmonizing notes that rose and fell and rose again. Their music gave the wolverines pause. The Arctic foxes listened. Amy was quiet for the first half of the song; then she began howling low and soared up to take a silver note above Kapu's. The princess of the Avaliks had made her debut.

The song ended abruptly. The caribou thundered up the riverbank and out across the tundra. The Avaliks melted into them, gliding quietly like shadows. The caribou paid them no heed. They were bound for their ancestral calving grounds.

Kapu, with faithful Zing at his shoulder, sped into the mass of caribou and split off a small group. He chased along beside them, watching for an animal to stumble or dash off alone in terror.

The isolated group sensed the wolves and put on speed. All were too swift and healthy for the wolves to catch. Kapu did not mind. The caribou were back. With no pups to keep his pack members at the den, he could lead his pack north to the calving grounds and harvest the weak and sick caribou. The Avaliks would become stronger and stronger, and Kapu would grow in wisdom and experience until he was as grand as his father, and Raw Bones would forever be subdued.

The birth of wolf pups in late May and early June is well timed for both prey and predator. When the female caribou are dropping their calves, the wolves are at their dens raising pups. This gives the calves six weeks or more to grow and develop their running skills. As for the wolves, it is to their advantage not to prey on the calves. A herd could be wiped out by overharvesting the helpless young.

But this year Kapu had changed the biological plan. No pups. He and his wolves would travel right into the midst of the calving grounds and regain their strength and vigor during the summer. They would eat well. Next year, when they were healthy and strong, they would have super pups. Only super wolf pups can survive in the wilderness.

Yet Kapu loved pups. Pups aroused the most

tender emotions in him and all wolves. Those emotions were so strong, they could overflow to pups not their own. When Kapu was young, his parents, Amaroq and Silver, had nurtured a lost girl-pup. She had learned to speak wolf with whimpers and posturing and had endeared herself to them. She had shared Kapu's puppy food and romped with him when he spanked the ground inviting her to play.

As Kapu became friends with the girl-pup, a name for her formed in his mind. It was a scent name: Willow. She smelled of the tiny tundra willows she had crept through to join him and his brothers and sister at their den. She was a puppy herself, and so she became Willow Pup.

Many months later, when she went back to her people, he heard them call her "Julie" and added that sound to his scent, sound, and sight picture of her. She was Willow Pup Julie. The wolf names of the Avaliks were changed by their association with Julie. Kapu's wolf name had been Wind Caller for his lilting voice, Zing's Berry Brother, and Silver's Saxifrage, a scented plant she liked to roll in. But Willow Pup Julie had named them only with sound—Kapu, Zing, and Silver. The sounds were vivid, and they began to know each other by Julie's names for them.

Willow Pup Julie became more than a playmate to Kapu. She was a mother-sister. She had nursed him back to health after a hunter in a roaring metal bird had sent a bullet into his flesh and another had killed his father. Her care had inspired in him a deep loyalty. It was the love he felt for his parent alphas, and the love that dogs, the descendents of wolves, feel for their masters.

After Willow Pup Julie returned to her people pack, devoted Kapu checked on her often. He would stop out of sight of her home and call her back to her pack. She would answer with concern in her howl, and he would go away. She was afraid for him.

In the purple darkness of winter Kapu had found Aaka, the graceful rime-gray daughter of Storm Alarm and Star Gentian, leaders of the Lower Colville River Pack. They lived east of the Avaliks and were a powerful tribe of nine. Amaroq had respected the Lower Colville wolves. He had marked the border between their properties with stronger messages than on any other border.

When Aaka was two years old, she became tired of helping Storm Alarm and Star Gentian with their puppies. She wanted her own. On a sunny afternoon she stole into the no-wolf land between the Avaliks and the Lower Colvilles and hid in the scrubby alders. She listened and waited for Kapu to find her. She had liked him for a long time.

Aaka and her pack had read messages on the wind telling how young Kapu had struggled to hold the Avaliks together. Nails, his father's second in command, had fought Kapu for leadership and lost. Tail between his legs, he had run off, taking with him Kapu's siblings Sister and Zat, who became his beta wolf.

A few weeks later Zit, Kapu's third brother, was killed by a hunter, and the once-magnificent Avalik River Pack dwindled to three: Kapu, Silver, and Zing. The Lower Colvilles began moving into Avalik territory. With Zing as his backup and Silver as the experienced elder, Kapu had held his land against them with howls and scent marking.

So Aaka knew all about Kapu, and Kapu was keenly aware of Aaka. He liked her. Her voice was the only one in the Lower Colville chorus with a little tune to it. Sometimes he would hear her from miles away and wag his tail.

When she slipped into the no-wolf zone, she did not have to wait long for an invitation from Kapu. He saw her enter and gave two soft whimpers, and she romped over the border. The young monarch and his loyal partner, Zing, welcomed her.

Silver did not. She departed almost immediately to make room for the new female leader. She headed for the Upper Colville River Pack, where she knew Raw Bones lived alone and needed a mate. The alpha male and alpha female of a wolf pack are not related. Family members do not mate.

In March of that year Aaka became pregnant. Kapu was young for a wolf father, but leadership had matured him. One evening, at Aaka's urging, he, Zing, and Aaka went off to check the den where Aaka would give birth. They trotted many miles to the old den where Kapu and Zing had been born. Aaka did not like the site and ran off to take charge of the den hunting. After many days she found a steep embankment on the Avalik River. Halfway down was a bench formed by the river. On it grew tiny flowers. She stepped around them and began to dig into the permafrost. The work was slow and difficult, for the earth was frozen hard. Kapu and Zing helped her. After many hours the three wolves jogged off to hunt.

They returned to the site frequently for the next two months and finally managed to chip out a shallow den. The site pleased them all. For miles around poppies and cotton flowers colored the landscape white and yellow. Snow buntings tinkled their songs from grass tufts and moss cushions. Ground-nesting birds—redpolls, longspurs, and horned larks—flitted up from the flowers in explosions of wings. In early June in this delightful environment, Aaka crawled into the whelping den.

Only one pup was born, a little female. Aaka had not eaten well enough for more embryos to develop. All her strength went into making one big, strong pup. She licked and cleaned and loved her pup so much, she became known as Sweet Fur.

But the little family was in trouble. There were no caribou. They hunted ground squirrels and rabbits and even lemmings.

One day in summer, when Sweet Fur was cutting her molars, Willow Pup Julie walked up the river to the white beach near the den. Kapu greeted her cautiously, then with pleasure. Julie got down on all fours. He licked her cheek and released ambrosia around her from the gland on the top of his tail. The sweet scent fell on Julie and again turned her into an Avalik.

Willow Pup Julie camped on the beach. Aaka was afraid of the girl, but eventually came to love her as Kapu did. As a supreme gesture of her trust, she asked Willow Pup Julie to baby-sit Sweet Fur while she ran off to hunt with Kapu and Zing.

The girl called Sweet Fur "Amy," and before long the wolves knew her as Sweet Fur Amy.

After many days had passed, Willow Pup Julie put Sweet Fur Amy into her pack and walked toward the Colville River. Kapu, Aaka, and Zing followed their pup. They were not concerned that the girl would harm Sweet Fur; they simply wanted to be with her.

At the border of their property Kapu stopped. Wolf rules of territory prevented him from taking another step. Beyond lay a strange and dangerous land, the no-wolf zone.

After much indecision Kapu howled a low, wistful note of invitation to his mother, Silver, who was on the other side of the river. He knew she was there. She knew he was there.

Then Willow Pup Julie walked over the Avalik boundary and into the no-wolf zone. When she was not attacked, Kapu whisked his tail as he remembered: Willow Pup Julie was not a wolf but a person, and wolves did not attack people.

Willow Pup Julie, heavily weighted with scent messages, put Sweet Fur Amy on the ground, then crossed the grassy river bottom and splashed into the water. She entered Upper Colville Pack land.

From the embankment Kapu heard her call,

"Silver," her name for his mother. He wagged his tail. Sweet Fur Amy wagged her tail, too, but not for the same reason. Braided among the rich odors of the river, the fish, plants, and ermine, she had picked out a family scent. A wolf over there was her grandmother. She whimpered the grandmother call.

The grandmother answered.

Kapu looked at his daughter. She was pounding her front paws excitedly. He lifted his lips in a smile. The bold move to invite two packs to join forces would work. This wonderful little pup with her keen sense of smell would bond with her grandmother. There would be five loving wolves, as well as the ambitious Raw Bones.

The six made a skilled family of hunters, and they all lived through a harsh and relentless winter.

Now it was spring—a spring to favor the wolves. The caribou were back. With Kapu's good planning they would eat well and grow strong. No pups.

As the caribou moved north, the Avaliks moved north, stopping to feast on caribou that had died of natural causes, or on weak ones that they could isolate and fell. They put on weight. Their fur began to glisten again. They raced north slightly ahead of the great caribou herd, their heads high, their tails straight out behind them. Kapu grew in confidence,

and Raw Bones dropped farther behind the young alpha.

Near the Avalik River, Kapu smelled willow, a very special willow: Willow Pup Julie. With a bound he led his pack around and in front of the browsing caribou and came into Kangik head up, tail up. His pack followed like wind dancers. Their muscles rippled under flowing fur. They ran close together, friendly, loving.

Kapu stopped a distance from Willow Pup Julie. He sought her eyes to tell her he was pleased to see her. She understood and dropped to her knees. But she was afraid for him. She warned him away. Then he saw Kapugen, the hunter. He did not smell his gun or see any aggression in his stride, so he walked toward them.

The musk oxen caught his attention. They were outside the corral where Kapugen kept them to raise and harvest their wool. An amusing wolf thought struck him. Chase them.

Off he went, telling Willow Pup Julie through body language and attitude that this was a wolf joke. She read it and smiled.

The musk oxen, after a brief panic, read the wolf message, too. They did not form a circle with their bony heads out, as they usually did when attacked by wolves. They trotted lightly, spread out, and grazed.

The Avaliks romped in and out among the musk oxen until they had had enough fun and their tongues were hanging out from overheating. Then they ran off a short distance and watched Willow Pup Julie and her father disappear in the frozen mist. With his extraordinary wolf ears Kapu tracked them back to Kangik. Faintly he heard the door of their green house close.

A quick glance at his pack said, "Follow me," and the Avaliks jogged back toward the caribou now thundering into view. Julie's wolves heard their bleating voices and snorting noses, and they saw the antlers of the females ride above the mass of bodies like a forest of dead sticks.

Kapu had not gone far when he was startled by a faint message he had ignored since Raw Bones had led Silver off among the caribou last week.

Silver was pregnant. He stopped running.

Pups.

He was not angry. Pups under any conditions are thrilling. He announced the news with a soft, wavering howl. The pack responded as wolves do to the song of pups. They praised each other by licking chins and cheeks. They chased each other in circles. Then they gathered around Kapu—all but Raw Bones.

He snarled. He had challenged Kapu's leadership by siring puppies, and as the father he was demanding to be recognized as leader.

He snapped at young Kapu. Kapu did not snap back, and because he did not, Raw Bones could not fight. He needed a response in order to do battle. There was none.

Pups. Although these pups threatened his rank and leadership, Kapu ignored their father's challenge. He gathered the dancing pack around him. Pups!

Kapu's love of pups surged through him. He felt no rancor, no jealousy. Pups were coming. Pups were magic. Thin and winter weary as the Avaliks were, they lovingly rubbed against each other, sniffed noses, and licked cheeks. Pups were coming.

When the celebration was over, Raw Bones walked stiff-leggedly toward Kapu to fight. Kapu ignored him again. The young alpha took off. He would lead the pup-happy wolves to the whelping den where Sweet Fur Amy had been born. The flower-bedecked den above the white stony beach was the soul of the Avaliks—the birthing place.

Kapu and his pack flowed like water on the still, flat tundra. Raw Bones closed in behind Kapu. The rangy father-to-be shouldered him, trying to force him toward his ancestral den on the Upper Colville

River. It had been in Raw Bones's family for twenty-five years. Kapu would have none of it. He raised the fur on his neck and back until he appeared twice as big as he was. "I am leader," he was saying, and sprinted on ahead. Zing passed Raw Bones and took his place behind Kapu. Raw Bones dropped into third place.

Aaka ran beside Silver, sharing the affection that the coming of pups creates between females.

Kapu turned into the wind. The pack turned into the wind. Their ruffs and manes swept back. They squinted to protect their eyes until they could barely see where they were going. They did not need to see. They were on the snow-covered trail to their den. Their guides were the sounds of the stunted willows jangling to their right and the sigh of the reindeer moss beneath the wind-packed snow. And there was another guide: their innate sense of direction. They knew at all times exactly where they were.

A long-tailed jaeger flew over the wolves. The bird saw them running hard, which usually meant they were hunting. A wolf kill is a banquet for mammals and birds. The jaeger looked down on the ribbon of wolves and followed them. Then they took to the open tundra and traced graceful S's, not the V-shaped formation of a pack about to make a kill. The bird turned away toward the frozen Arctic Ocean.

The Avalik Pack reached their nursery den on the riverbank. Kapu got down on his side and clawed through the snow to the den entrance. He raked out grass and wind-blown debris.

Silver sniffed the den. It smelled of Aaka and Sweet Fur Amy. She backed away. She was not pleased. She would seek the den where Kapu and Zing had been born.

Raw Bones felt her discontent. "Come with me," he whimpered, and started off for his family den on the Colville River embankment. He loped into the ice mist and was gone. Silver did not follow him.

Kapu let him go.

Silver was not housecleaning but looking off to the north. Sweet Fur Amy sensed her grandmother's reluctance to den clean and scrambled through the entrance. She dug furiously, piling up icy stones. When she backed out, Zing went in. He kicked the stones and dirt out onto the playground as his contribution to the family.

It was the smell of the earth and the sight of everyone working that finally inspired Silver. She crawled into the tunnel and all the way back to the nursery. With her forepaws she dug the room wider, then scooped out a cozy bed for her pups and herself.

She was content with the Avalik den.

Raw Bones returned as Silver came out of the den. The low rumbles of protest in his chest were audible as he entered the group, but he stopped complaining when he looked at Silver. Her face had softened. She wore the gentle look of an expectant wolf mother who had found a place for her pups. She glanced at him. His pups, her eyes said, would be born here. Her digging the nursery had worked the magic.

Good news for the Avaliks. They wagged their tails and exchanged scents. Pups here at the family site.

This decided, Kapu looked north. The pack must now put on the muscle and fat needed to raise tough, energetic wolf puppies. Thanks to Raw Bones they did not have much time.

For the next month and a half they wandered their huge territory searching for the caribou. The female caribou had spread out seeking solitude and isolation to give birth. They were secretive and difficult to find.

One morning near the Colville River, Sweet Fur Amy pricked up her ears and took in short sniffs of air. Then she broke into a sprint.

Kapu followed. She was on the trail of a caribou.

Although he could not smell it himself, he trusted Amy. She could pick up scents five and six miles away and track them down. All wolves have incredible noses lined with hundreds of scent receptors, but Amy was extraordinary for even a wolf. He let her take the lead pointing their way into the wind.

They came upon a female caribou on the open flats. Everyone stopped, listened, looked, and sniffed. Eye messages from Kapu sent the wolves fanning out around the prey. Aaka, whose talent was herding, ran wide to bring the caribou toward the others. The hunters lowered their bodies and stalked slowly forward. The caribou sensed their intent and bolted.

She ran far ahead of the wolves. They slowed their pace, looking this way and that as if not at all interested in hunting. The cow stopped fleeing and browsed. When her head was down, the wolves stole closer. With two glances Kapu directed Silver to the right and Raw Bones to the left. Raw Bones saw an opportunity to cut off the leader and take his place, but he was not fast enough. Kapu saw what he was up to and put on a burst of speed, and he, Zing, and Amy charged the caribou. She lifted her head and ran nimbly away.

Ten times they tried to fell her. Ten times they failed. They gave up the chase. The life of a wolf is hard. Panting, their tongues hanging out of their mouths, they scanned the tundra for prey. The only movements were flowers and grasses dancing in the wind. Raw Bones sneaked up on the young leader and tried to ride up on him. A wolf statement of dominance. Kapu threw him off with a twist.

Suddenly a wolverine not far away startled a caribou to her feet. Infested with parasites, the cow had been resting on a last patch of snow. Her flashing departure set the wolves on a chase.

Within the half hour the hungry pack had their quarry. Raw Bones ran in to eat first as alpha males do. Kapu grabbed the scruff of his neck and pulled him away to let Silver eat first. Raw Bones snarled and grabbed Kapu by the throat, but the young alpha twisted him down. Snarling viciously above him, Kapu held him down on his belly with his regal posture until Silver and then Aaka had eaten. Then he let him up. Raw Bones must be kept in line. He was close to usurping the leadership by virtue of his age and his high rank as the father of Silver's pups. Winning a fight would do it. Kapu kept watch.

When each wolf belly bulged with the good food, Kapu led them to the top of a nearby frost heave, where he rode up on Raw Bones's back to say, "I am alpha." Raw Bones's forehead went perfectly smooth and his eyes became slitlike in submission. He got the message. The others licked Kapu's face and neck, and all tails hung free and loose in contentment. After a brief howl to their alpha, they made wolf beds by scratching out saucers and circling three or four times. Then they lay down and slept like wolves, deeply on one side of their brains, lightly on the other. They slept for almost twenty hours.

On the light side of his sleep Kapu listened to the ravens arriving at the carcass. He heard an Arctic fox yip to his mate to come eat. The low-slung, massive wolverine, who had scared up the prey in the first place, crunched bones in his powerful jaws.

To Kapu food was to be shared. He slept on.

Darkness enclosed the tundra around ten P.M. and lowered the air temperature below zero. A wind drifted the snow over the Avaliks, and they slept and listened—all except Raw Bones. He got up and returned quietly to the kill. Might is right in the wilderness. Knowingly, he ate.

When Raw Bones was sated, he awoke Silver. She opened her yellow wolf eyes that turned the night light into day. Mouthing her nose gently, he told her he was leader. Then he whimpered, "Come with me," and headed toward the den on the Colville.

Kapu heard the dwarf willows tinkle and lifted

his head to see Raw Bones leaving. Shaking snow from his eyebrows and ears, he checked his mother. She was curled so tightly, he knew she was not about to follow him.

Kapu did not call Raw Bones back.

Hardly had the young alpha settled his nose in his tail fur than the willows tinkled again and Raw Bones returned. Kapu sharpened his senses. He had enemies not only around his borders but within. Raw Bones would kill him if he was not alert.

The wolves feasted and slept, feasted and slept, eating five or six pounds a day. In between major meals Raw Bones went back for snacks. He must grow bigger than Kapu.

When only the calcium-rich antlers and a few bones remained, the wolves traveled on, leaving them for the lemmings and snowshoe rabbits. Pregnant caribou would also chew on them for the calcium.

With all his senses alert now, Kapu tuned in on yet another threat to his leadership of the Avaliks. On a wind rode an aggressive scent from the Nuka River Pack. They held the territory to the west and south. Their scent signal was followed by a howl. They had closed in on Avalik territory and were only a night's trot away. Kapu rotated his ears to fine-tune the sounds to the center of his eardrum, where he could hear best. The Nukas were nine strong.

The Avaliks were six.

When the Nukas howled again that night, they were closer. Kapu arose. The guard hairs stood erect on his back. He beat his tail, twisting it toward them like a saber, threw back his head, and howled. His pack howled, sliding up to their harmonizing notes, sliding down, and fading out. Then all was silent.

The Avaliks rubbed necks and chests over the scent glands on the tops of each other's tails and exchanged odors. Their individual aromas were joined into one scent. The mix said "Avalik." The air reeked with this invisible banner as they set off to meet the Nukas. Raw Bones wore the flag grudgingly, but he wore it.

The Nukas were on Avalik property, lying in one of the ravines cut by ages of snowmelt running to the Colville. The Avaliks stopped at the edge of the dip and barked, "Leave or die."

Low Wind and Moon Seeker, the alpha male and female of the Nukas, barked a snippy "no." With that, Kapu and the Avaliks charged into the ravine.

The Nukas fled. Although they outnumbered the Avaliks, the landowner is victor in the wild.

When the Nukas were out of scent and sight, Kapu lifted his leg and sprayed a grass tussock on his border. In the urine was a raging message. It said, "Stay back of this marker or face the fangs of a powerful wolf." He scratched open the ground with his hind feet to back up his scent message. It was an angry visual remark. Then he ran to the top of the highest swell on the flat land and, lifting his head, tail, and ears, calmly and serenely posed. He was saying, "I am the alpha of this land we have scent marked." Even Raw Bones felt his nobility and instinctively lowered his ears and tail in deference. He rumbled his jealousy.

Kapu scent marked again. He was followed by Zing. Although Zing was a male, he did not lift his leg to mark. Only the alpha male and alpha female can do that. He, Raw Bones, Silver, and Sweet Fur Amy must squat.

Raw Bones would not accept his low-ranking status. He lifted his leg in defiance. Kapu went stiff-legged and stared at him. Raw Bones squatted.

Aaka proudly lifted her leg and sprayed warnings to the Nukas.

When the southwestern border was thoroughly drenched, Kapu led his pack north. After a short lope, he turned around and went alone back to his border. He doused it once more. This very area had been a battle zone between the Nukas and the

Avaliks for generations. Amaroq, Kapu's father, had killed the Nuka alpha here, and so had his father before him. Kapu's last message would remind the Nukas of those battles. Scent marking evokes memory and brings peace.

Alert to his territorial duties, Kapu led his pack on a long circular trip scent marking borders. Theirs was a big land. It included much of the caribou calving grounds and Kangik. It stretched from west of the Avalik River south to the banks of the Upper and Lower Colville. On the north it ended far south of Barrow and Wainwright. That territory belonged to Iñupiat Eskimo hunters, a pack to be wary of.

The long legs of the Avaliks carried them as smoothly as shadows. They paced along almost continuously, stopping briefly to look over their herd, mark borders, and gypsy on in the manner of winter wolves.

When possible, Kapu put his scent over the faint but still discernible scent of his father. He let it be known that he, the new leader of the Avaliks, was gaining the power of the departed Amaroq. He must gain all the power and status he could before fatherhood put Raw Bones at the top of the hierarchy.

Raw Bones for his part was plotting the overthrow. At each scent-marking stop he lingered over the messages to learn more about Kapu. He did not like what he read. Kapu was fearless, the essential attribute of a leader. He was also calm, and of good humor and abundant health. But Kapu also revealed in his scent messages that he was young and inexperienced. Raw Bones was old and experienced. He could win.

On one of the trips to houseclean the den, Kapu went into the tunnel to dig and leave his mark on the family home. When he came out, Raw Bones was snarling above him. A wolf alarm rang inside Kapu. He was low, his head beneath Raw Bones's. He was in second position. Surprised at how easily Raw Bones had gained the alpha posture, he lingered as beta almost too long. Another few seconds in this humble stance and Raw Bones would dominate. But Kapu came out of the den with a high leap and landed on Raw Bones's neck snarling savagely. He was backed up by a growling Zing and Aaka. Raw Bones pasted back his ears and slunk away, but he was not done. He would wait until Kapu was alone before attacking again.

That opportunity came soon. One misty dawn the pack bedded down south of Kangik, and Kapu trotted off alone to the rise above Julie's house. Raw Bones watched, then sped down the riverbed out of Kapu's scent range. He waited for him below the rise.

Kapu appeared in the April fog. His fur was shining with silver icelets. He stopped and looked down on the green wooden house. Raw Bones bellied toward him, avoiding dwarf trees that would jangle.

But Kapu was attuned to the tundra. He sensed Raw Bones through his paws and threw himself downhill upon him. Raw Bones got a jaw hold on his shoulder. He pulled Kapu down the slope and twisted him onto his back. Kapu was belly up in the loser's position. This should have been his dethronement, but youth, not experience, counted here. Buckling his young body, Kapu pressed all four paws on Raw Bones's throat and cut off his air. The would-be usurper backed off, and Kapu jumped to his feet. Kapu rode up on Raw Bones before the older wolf could leap. Kapu's head was higher, his chest and his tail were higher, and he growled until Raw Bones lowered himself to the ground. Then he let him up.

Once more Raw Bones had lost. He slunk off, ears pressed back, tail down. Zing came over the rise. Raw Bones rushed him, but youthful Zing stared at him and displayed his white fangs. "I am the beta," he said.

Raw Bones disappeared in the early-morning ice mist.

Kapu turned his attention to the green house now

taking form as the air warmed and cleared. There near the river Peter Sugluk, the young hunter-dancer, and Willow Pup Julie were hitching the dogs to the sled. Kapu sensed their pleasure in each other's company. Peter was Julie's alpha male. He wagged his tail and howled to them, "Come home to us."

Willow Pup Julie snapped a dog into his traces and straightened up. She looked in his direction and called gently, "Someday, someday." Kapu howled again. This time he drew his tongue up and down in his pursed mouth, undulating his tone. Julie harmonized with him. Then they abruptly stopped and spoke no more.

Listening to the mysterious wild language, Peter said, "It would be good to live close to the wolves and nature as our elders did. There is much to learn about ourselves out there."

"Ee-lie," answered Willow Pup Julie, and called once more to Kapu. He did not answer. He was busy. The scent of an arthritic caribou had drenched the wind, and he had gone off to locate it.

Raw Bones returned to the pack in its camp south of Kangik and nosed Silver awake. He would take her back to his old territory, where he was king. She growled. She did not want to go. He lay down and his back fur bristled.

The border check went on for weeks. The more Kapu scent marked his territory, the stronger he felt and the more peaceful the pack became. Slowly Kapu was healing the devastating loss of the great Avalik alpha male wolf Amaroq. Social harmony was being restored as Kapu developed leadership skills. When he was truly in charge, Raw Bones would not be able to challenge him.

That glorious moment was not yet in sight. Raw Bones's disposition worsened. Unable to dethrone Kapu, he began to nip at Sweet Fur Amy. Her keen sense of smell had raised her to a rank above him. She had become a second beta, equal to Zing. As father of the pups-to-be Raw Bones deeply resented this. If he could not be alpha, he must certainly be beta. At every opportunity he bared his teeth and wrinkled his forehead to threaten her into battle. But Sweet Fur Amy would not fight back, and this rendered Raw Bones annoyingly helpless.

Sweet Fur Amy's talent developed. She learned to recognize sick animals not only by scent but by subtle limps, the tilt of a head, and the droop of eyes. She no longer wasted the pack's time on the healthy. When she picked out a feeble animal, she signaled the news to Kapu and he let her take the lead, much to Raw Bones's displeasure.

In daylight and shadow, whenever the opportunity arose, the resentful Raw Bones gave Sweet Fur Amy a painful smack with his rear end. She controlled her desire to fight. He was bigger and older. She could not possibly win.

But she did not like it. When the pack was resting, she strengthened her neck muscles by thrashing heavy caribou hides from side to side. She strengthened her leg muscles chasing the fleet-footed Zing. She ate often. Her black fur reflected blue lights, and her body grew hard and muscular. Raw Bones with all his nastiness was forcing her to become a more powerful wolf than he.

The sun stayed up longer and longer. From twelve hours above and twelve hours below the horizon at the March equinox, it was up all but a few hours in late April. During this time Sweet Fur Amy's ability to find weak and sick animals dramatically increased the Avaliks' hunting success. It rose from one try in ten to one in five. With abundant food they put on muscle and weight.

In the second week of May the sun stayed up night and day. Without trickle or sound most of the tundra snow vanished in vapor. The birds returned to their grassy nesting grounds by the tens of thousands. The Avaliks ran in constant sunlight. They split caribou herds into smaller groups by running through them. They checked each individual, noted the pregnant females and those with calves. They noted the healthy and pinpointed the sick and old for harvesting at some later date.

One foggy hour in early June, Silver spoke to her son, Kapu, with her eyes. "Pups." With a right about-face he led the pack to the den on the Avalik River embankment. The alpha male wolf leads the pack to the den when the mother-to-be gives the signal. Raw Bones snarled as he followed Kapu and Silver. The young alpha had taken over this ceremony that would have elevated him to that rank.

The next day the pups were born. The wolves wandered out on the tundra away from the den. They whined, flashed their tails, and howled in celebration. Far to the west the Nukas heard and pricked up their ears and hurried out to mark their eastern border. More Avaliks had been born.

Ten days after the birth of the pups, Silver came out of the den. Tails wagged, feet pranced, tongues licked cheeks and faces. Now pack members would know how many pups had been born. Kapu let Raw Bones listen first; then he and Aaka listened. Sweet Fur Amy and Zing listened. Each wolf cocked its ears until the tiny voices were counted: two—that was all.

The famine had taken its toll on Silver's body, but the vigorous swishing of tails spoke of the pack's pride.

Two or ten, it mattered not. The Avaliks had pups. Kapu dashed to the top of the embankment, sat down, lifted his head, and sang. He was joined by all but Silver, who had gone back into the den. The others whimpered, squeaked intimately and softly to each other, then howled as if a big litter of fat puppies had been born. The pup serenade done, Kapu, Sweet Fur Amy, and Zing sped off to hunt for food for the mother. Raw Bones ran last until he saw that Sweet Fur Amy was only a few paces in front of him. He bolted past her.

They had not gone far before Kapu stopped. He lifted his head and tasted the wind coming off the Avalik River. With a glance at his pack to say, "Stay where you are," he ran back toward the river. Raw Bones took this opportunity to strike Sweet Fur Amy with another hard whack. Again she did not react. She cricked her tail to express her annoyance, but she would not fight.

Serenely she opened her nostrils and breathed in the scent image of Willow Pup Julie. She was not far away. Kapu had gone back to greet her. Sweet Fur Amy sat down. Zing and Raw Bones sat down.

Willow Pup Julie was sitting on the white stone beach where she had met Kapu last summer. She was calling the ground squirrels out of their burrows with the little whistle she wore around her neck. She was dressed in a flowered summer parka and blue jeans. Her thick black hair fell to her shoulders. Her beautiful face was serene. Kapu whimpered. She looked up.

"Ee-lie, Kapu." She got to her knees. She did not move, giving Kapu time to adjust to her. Presently he spanked the ground in wolf pleasure and greeted her with the family whimper of affection. She whimpered back and he ran toward her, whisking his tail.

"I came to see the pups," she said, looking eagerly toward the den.

Kapu did not understand her words, but he understood why she had come. Much wolf talk goes on through the eyes, and Willow Pup was looking at the nursery.

"You have puppies, all right," she said. "But they are still young. They're not out of the den. I don't see them. I'll come back another day." But instead of leaving, she sat down.

She patted the stones at her side. "May I see them?" she asked. He stood perfectly still. "Come here," she said. Kapu did not accept the invitation, nor did he look into her eyes.

"Ee-lie," she laughed. "You are a leader, all right. No one can tell you what to do." Kapu looked away, then back, and walked closer.

"You are lean," she said, noting how the black fur parted over his shoulders and clung to his ribs. "You are hunting long hours. The pups and their mother need lots of food, all right."

Kapu dropped to his belly. Slowly he turned his head and stared at her. His large yellow eyes with their black pupils pulled her unblinkingly into his world. She willingly came along and was part of his family again.

With that Willow Pup Julie began to talk.

"Kapu," she said, "my little brother, Amaroq, your father's namesake, is running. He's not quite a year old. That's very unusual. He must have your spirit in him."

She went on. "The boy-pup keeps me busy chasing him. He runs to the umiaq. I try to catch him. He runs to the river. I try to catch him. He is very fast." Kapu did not understand these messages, but he did understand other scents that she carried on her person. She was living with her father and stepmother and someone else, a baby. Peter Sugluk had not been around lately.

After Willow Pup Julie stopped speaking, she

and Kapu sat in silence, enjoying each other's company. They watched the fish swim upstream and the redpolls sing from tiny three-inch-high willows. Their eyes followed a snowy owl swooping down on a lemming and watched two ravens eating birds' eggs.

The sun dipped to the horizon, hung there for a while, then started up the sky again. Kapu and Willow Pup Julie arose simultaneously. As if they had talked it over, each went home. Julie walked down the river shore; Kapu climbed the embankment.

He found Silver stretched out in the vermilion sunlight, taking a rest from the puppies. Raw Bones was on his belly looking into the den. He tilted his head from side to side, picking up subtle odors that informed him one pup was a male and one was a female. Raw Bones wagged his tail once and withdrew. Aaka listened.

The pups' whimpers were weak. Aaka wrinkled her brow and let Sweet Fur Amy take her turn. She too was disturbed by the weak whimpers. Slowly she pulled back, but before she could get to her feet, Raw Bones jumped on her.

Amy reared and hit him with her back, then vaulted away. Raw Bones stalked her, snarling for a fight. Again Sweet Fur Amy refused. This sweet-tempered wolf was growing very tired of Raw Bones's heckling her. When he growled again, she suddenly knew what to do. Lifting her head, she sniffed the air. Her ears went up and her eyes sharpened with excitement to say, "I smell a very sick caribou." The pack arose. Sweet Fur Amy glanced at Kapu and sent him a different message.

He answered by starting the hunt. The Avaliks followed. No sooner were they on their way than Kapu fell back with Aaka and Zing, and Sweet Fur Amy took the lead.

Raw Bones put on speed, passed Zing and Kapu, snarled past Aaka, and took second position. No wolf objected. Aaka, the herder, moved to her position at the side of the pack and loped along gracefully. Occasionally she stopped to investigate the bearberry plants now sweet with tiny flowers.

The tundra rolled out in all directions, spreading wide and gold-green. The wind blew gently. The warm sun coaxed cushions of starwort flowers into bloom.

The Avaliks ran several miles before Raw Bones caught the scent of Sweet Fur Amy's prey. When he was certain he had the trail, he knocked her out of first place and took the lead. She did not object.

Holding a steady pace Raw Bones led the Avaliks down the river valley, up onto the tundra, and into a ravine carved by snowmelt. He was leader of the pack. He thrust his head high. He lifted his tail into alpha position. The pack came on. Running full out, he came upon a huge bull caribou. His new antlers of the year were dark with velvet.

Raw Bones gave orders to the pack and rushed him. The bull did not run. He reared. His cleaver-sharp hoofs slashed toward Raw Bones and hit the ground with the power of a falling meteor, missing their mark by inches. The bull reared to strike again.

Raw Bones drew back. Sick animals do not charge. He signaled Aaka to close in. She was nowhere around. He glanced behind him. The pack sat in a wide semicircle looking at him. The bull saw them, turned, and jogged off. His tendons snapped like bongo drums. Snowmelt splashed up from his footsteps.

Raw Bones dashed after him. With little effort the bull left him far behind. He disappeared in the dim light of the midnight sun.

Raw Bones slowed and stopped, tongue hanging out from overheating. Feeling peculiar, he glanced back at his pack. They were looking at him and smiling at Sweet Fur Amy's wolf joke. He growled for a full five minutes.

On the way home Sweet Fur scented an old cow

with torturous botfly infestations. She glanced at Kapu. Her eyes said, "This is no joke"—and they were off. Within two hours the pack had eaten well. Kapu encouraged Raw Bones to carry a hindquarter back to Silver.

And the wholeness of the pack was restored.

In June the sun rose to its highest point in the Arctic sky. Life responded. The tundra flittered with young mammals and fledgling birds learning to pounce, fly, and play—all but the Avalik pups. Tiny Whimper and No Growl—this was how the wolves now thought of them—did not leave the den. They were long overdue to come out and romp on the playground.

Something was wrong. Silver went into the nursery and picked up Tiny Whimper by the scruff of the neck. She carried her outside and gently put her down. The little pup could not walk. Her baby-blue eyes looked from Kapu to Silver. She whimpered a thin squeak. Silver went back for No Growl and placed him beside his sister.

The Avaliks paced anxiously around the pups, nosing and licking them. They cricked their tails in uncertainty and puzzled over them. Then they lay down and put their heads on their paws. The pups were doomed to death. Silver had not recovered from the winters of famine. She could not give them enough milk.

Kapu watched in distress. The pups were in trouble. He blinked and cocked his head to one side and then the other.

Aaka lay down beside them. She licked Tiny Whimper first and then No Growl, trying to get their blood flowing and to stimulate them to walk. They were too weak.

Kapu suddenly pricked up his ears and looked toward the Avalik River. With a swing of his tail he bounded down the embankment and trotted along the shore to meet Willow Pup Julie.

"Kapu," she called. "Kapu, I'm back." He knew why she had come. He did not take time to adjust to her presence but let her scramble up the embankment to the playground.

"Ee-lie." She dropped to her knees. "The little pups are sick."

She picked up listless Tiny Whimper. Silver and Aaka watched intently. Willow Pup Julie whimpered wolf pup talk and stroked the little head. She held one limp paw between her fingers.

"Kapu," she said, "I must take the pups home, all right. I will feed them rich milk from bottles. When they are strong, I will return them to you." Kapu stared into her eyes. He understood her intent by the mothering tone in her voice. He did not take the pup back, nor did Silver come for them. Julie tucked fragile Tiny Whimper into her parka and glanced at Aaka and Sweet Fur Amy to see if they objected. They did not reach for the puppy. Their alpha had not, so they would not. Kapu was beginning to direct the behavior of the pack. The pups would go with Willow Pup Julie. Although they responded to Kapu's wish, each individual quickly expressed its feelings. Aaka walked to Kapu's side and nuzzled his chin. Sweet Fur Amy took a deep breath of Julie in through her nostrils and relaxed her tail and face. The pups were in loving hands. Silver lay wearily on her side, and Raw Bones slunk off to the top of the embankment, put his head on his paws, and rumbled a protest from deep in his chest. Zing, the loyal beta, kept his eye on the disgruntled Raw Bones, whose rank was about to sink to an all-time low without the pups.

Kapu was close to achieving the highest form of wolf government—leadership that holds strong individuals together but allows for personalities and feelings. Kapu was close to greatness. He lifted his head high.

Feeling the pack was with her, Willow Pup Julie

put No Growl into her parka with Tiny Whimper and pressed them close to her body.

"They'll be all right," she said, locking her gaze on Silver's golden eyes. The mother looked away. After a moment she turned and looked unblinkingly into Julie's eyes. "Trust" was the message. With a soft whimper of affection, Willow Pup Julie walked down the embankment to the river's edge and strode off along it. Released from ice by the sun, the water chortled and leaped beside her, accompanying her happy song—"Pups, little pups, little pups."

When she was out of scent range, the Avaliks milled in a small knot, passing scent, passing mood, passing love, reaching a decision. Then they trod lightly down the embankment. They walked behind Willow Pup Julie and their pups until they came to their favorite resting site on the outskirts of Kangik. There they listened quietly as their Willow Pup opened the door of the green house and went inside. Gusts from within smelled of Kapugen; his wife, Ellen; and their son, Amaroq. The wolves inhaled deeply, sat down on their haunches, and waited for their pups to come out.

Julie's wolves stayed on the knoll for many sleeps. When it became apparent that the pups were not going to come out, Kapu went down the path and tasted the air that surrounded the house with tongue and nose. There was no scent of Tiny Whimper or No Growl, just the odors of rich milk, the sweet scent of a human baby, and people. He returned to the pack, whimpered a message, then threw back his head and howled in misery. The Avaliks sang a song of the lost and missing.

When their chorus had diminished down the scale and into silence, Raw Bones and Silver curled up to sleep. Zing, Kapu, and Aaka jogged off to hunt in the orange light of the ever-circling summer sun that was now climbing toward three o'clock in the morning.

Sweet Fur Amy had her own mission. She walked closer to Julie's home. She had smelled the pups in the heavy mix of scents that surrounded the house. She was kin and baby-sitter to these pups. She could not leave.

Part II

Ice Blink, The Stranger

Four hundred miles away a rangy white wolf ran desperately across the border of her territory in the Canadian Arctic. Her eyes were mustard yellow, her muzzle long and regally sharp. She took a bearing on the sun that did not set and, sensing the magnetic forces of the Earth, jogged west into Alaska. A chilling fear had driven her from her beloved home.

The white wolf came to the foothills of the Philip Smith Mountains, where icy snow lingered in the higher elevations. As she crossed a swatch of ice, the sunlight was reflected up onto her white belly for the length of an eye blink.

Sedge Ears, the male leader of the Smith Mountain Pack, saw the flash, and the white wolf became Ice Blink. He watched the stranger.

Ice Blink was in the no-wolf zone that ran along his border. She zigged and zagged, nose to the ground. A scent in a clump of spike moss told her a ptarmigan had been there. A sniff down an Arctic fox den flashed an image of pups. From rock to moss to animal trails she went. Finally she came upon the scented border of the Smith Mountain wolves. She sniffed the information in their urine. The pack consisted of four healthy adults: the alpha male, Sedge Ears; the alpha female, Alder Whisper; the second in command, a wolf with a nameless odor; and a yearling baby-sitter. Her faint scent told Ice Blink she had not been out border marking recently. She must be with the new pups of the year. Pups there were. Alder Whisper's scent was rich with milk.

Ice Blink scent read deeper into the layers of messages. Sedge Ears feared the humans in the valley. Alder Whisper had a stomachache. She had eaten grass to cure it. Over the normal wolf odorous chitchat rose a stronger message—the Smith Mountain Pack had recently killed a strange wolf in their territory.

Ice Blink adjusted her route to avoid them. Keeping their scent on her left and the distant odor of the Shublik Mountain Pack on her right, she continued northwest in the no-wolf zone.

Curious about her, Sedge Ears shook moss bits from his fur and climbed a fungus-freckled slope. The Smith Mountain Pack lived among the caribou bulls that hung out together at this time of year.

They were powerful animals and difficult to fell. Sedge Ears's pack could use another adult, but only a strong and perfect one. He rolled in caribou droppings to disguise himself and stole to the edge of the no-wolf zone. For almost an hour he walked parallel to Ice Blink. Her footfall told him she was a large wolf, well fed, and four years old—in her prime. He liked that, but other things about her made him wary. She was too old to be seeking a new pack and too young to retire alone, as old wolves do. Her scent disturbed him, and he sniffed her air again and again. She bore a strange odor, sickly sweet. It warned him not to invite her into his pack.

Ice Blink knew she had been turned down. She took to a river valley and jogged along shores that frequently smelled of oil. Airplanes had landed in these places and set men free to hunt wolves, moose, and caribou. She knew about airplanes and men. Hastily she trotted out of the river valley and up Salisbury Mountain. The winds blew with such force here that only lichen gardens could live. In this frozen desert water was scant. The ice and snow rarely melted. To survive, the lichens would dry up and wait years for the sun to melt a few drops of water. Then almost instantly they would become a lovely green-gray and grow ever so slightly. The gardens were thousands of years old.

On a slope of these plants, Ice Blink tasted the air for the caribou that savored them. She had just caught the faint scent of several bulls browsing uphill and started after them when a Cessna 185 airplane droned out of the clouds. It circled above her. Ice Blink pulled her tail between her legs and dropped to her belly. Her white fur blended with an ice field. The plane circled three times and then flew off. Ice Blink licked her paw and wiped it over her ears to relieve her nervousness.

The airplane had brought back feelings of distress. Her pack had met with a great misfortune she connected with them. Last autumn such a plane had come out of the sky and landed not far from her pack. A human had stolen to a knoll and shot at her with a dart gun. He had missed, but the gun blast and the man were imprinted on her mind by fear.

About a week later her adolescent sons behaved strangely. They snarled and chased her. Their mouths drooped open, their tongues swelled and drooled saliva. They were hot with fever. She bolted into the dwarf trees to watch them in safety. One son stumbled, fell, and lay still. Almost immediately the other fell. When, after a long time, they did not move, her mother love brought her hesitatingly to their sides.

The alpha son was unable to move. His eyes were open and staring. She smelled his noxious breath and whimpered to him. He did not get up. She turned to her other son and called to him. When he did not respond, she withdrew to the edge of the dwarf trees.

Ice Blink watched as foaming saliva bubbled out of their mouths. She saw them pant heavily. First one and then the other panted no more. They were dead.

Safe in the trees, Ice Blink put her head on her paws and stared into space. Nine members of her pack of eleven had died this way. Only she and her mate, Bear Scratcher, were alive. Her wolf mind flicked quickly from death to life. She needed to be with her breathing, lively mate. Getting to her feet, she sought out Bear Scratcher on a favorite bluff above the river. She lay down beside him. The next morning another plane landed, and an Eskimo and a white man stole toward them. Again they shot darts from guns, and again they missed. Ice Blink and her mate sped away.

"We've got to inoculate them before they spread the rabies to dogs and people," said the Inuttut Eskimo Qignak.

"We'll never do it now," the white man said. "We scared them good." He paused, then added, "Maybe the epidemic won't be too bad. The scientists say very few wolves die of rabies. They're much more likely to die of mange."

"I know these wolves," said Qignak. "They have been dying of rabies—first one, then two, then eight. My family hunts this river valley."

"I understand that," said the white man, "and we're trying to inoculate them, but we may have to give up." He put another tranquilizing dart into his gun and scanned the dwarf trees that grew in the river bottomland. There was not a wolf to be seen.

"The wolves are our brothers," Qignak said in his deep, soft voice.

After the sun rose in January, and before the March breeding season of the wolves, Bear Scratcher awoke beside Ice Blink and moaned in pain. He was hot and feverish. Saliva dripped from his open mouth.

Two days later he attacked her. Terrified, she sped into the no-wolf zone. He would not dare enter the forbidden land.

But he did. Snarling and drooling, her disease-maddened mate bore down on her. Then he, too, fell and lay stiff, unable to move.

Ice Blink crept toward her lifelong companion. He growled through bubbling foam. She came nearer. She licked his saliva-wet cheek, and with that the virus entered her bloodstream through a small wound in her mouth.

Bear Scratcher bit the air, and the stench of the rabies virus filled her nostrils. It smelled of the death that had taken her sons and all the other members of her pack. Ice Blink drew her tail between her legs and crept away.

She came back once. He was dead. Whining softly to herself, she returned to the no-wolf zone and began walking. She would find a new pack far from the disease that had been passed from one family member to another in bites and saliva. Some had died a few days after being bitten; others had carried the virus a month before falling ill. Her mate had carried it for a year.

When the Cessna 185 was out of hearing, Ice Blink trotted across a wind-blasted territory where no wolves lived. She ran steadily like a leaf on a rushing stream.

She covered three hundred miles before she stopped. Ice Blink was in the no-wolf zone that bordered the Lower Colville River Pack, Aaka's original family. Odors in the urine revealed that the pack had no beta. They could use her. She was an experienced adult. Ice Blink hid in the dense grasses that grew in the river valley and waited for an invitation to join them.

Storm Alarm and Star Gentian were aware of her almost as soon as she entered the valley. They scented, listened, and peered through the ground brush at her. Like Sedge Ears, they learned she was capable and that she was looking for a new family. They had room for her, but like Sedge Ears they were wary of her scent messages. Storm Alarm watched her through the leafy bushes, one bright discerning eye sizing her up. Presently the eye vanished. Storm Alarm and Star Gentian walked deeper into their territory.

Ice Blink saw the eye shine in the bushes and snap off. There was no invitation. She lifted her head and ruff and trotted on.

Keeping to the no-wolf zone, the white wolf circled the northern border of the Lower Colville Pack's territory and arrived at the border of the Avalik Pack. They had not been in this part of their territory since pup time and would not be until the pups could run with the pack. That time was not far away. The August sun was setting for an hour or so to mark the night.

Boldly she walked onto their land, exploring every scent and sound, watching every twisting grass blade and fluttering bird. A mile inland she slipped into a forest of two-foot-high aspen trees growing in a drainage and came upon the body of a wolf. It was frozen in packed snow at the bottom of the ravine. Ice Blink could not know that this wolf had been named Nails by Julie. But she did know by the shape of his wounds that he had been killed by a knifelike moose hoof. Ice Blink sniffed for more information. The faded odor of the Avalik Pack was on the mosses around him. They had come to investigate the fallen wolf. She rubbed herself in the Avalik scent and trotted on.

Coming around a frost heave, she saw ravens circling above the horizon, marking a kill.

She broke into a smooth low run and came upon a dead young musk ox. Holes and rips in the carcass were drenched with grizzly bear scent. Ice Blink tasted the air. The bear was not far away, eating blueberries and guarding her kill.

Ice Blink was not concerned about the closeness of this powerful female of the tundra. Wolves and bears often share food. Furthermore, Ice Blink could easily outrun her. She could even turn around in the middle of a sprint and chase the bear.

Ice Blink scared off the ravens and three Arctic foxes, then set upon the food. She was eating with great satisfaction when the bear returned and charged.

The white wolf glided away, her shoulder fur pulsing softly as she ran. Miles along, she settled down in a garden of tundra grass and fell asleep. She was deep in Avalik country.

On the western side of Avalik territory Sweet Fur Amy was leading the pack toward Kangik on the trail of something the others could not yet smell. Knowing her gifts, they simply jogged trustingly behind her, their noses, eyes, and ears scanning the flat, gold-green landscape for game. They saw only a darkening sky.

Sweet Fur Amy came to a halt below the knoll where she often stood to view the green house. Silver, who was far behind, was glad for the rest. She had not recovered her vigor since the pups had been born. Curling up with her head on her tail, she snuggled her nose into her warm fur and shivered. Aaka saw her tremble and lay close beside her to share her own warmth. Kapu watched Silver with concern. Raw Bones ignored her. He was watching Sweet Fur Amy, who on the far knoll was sniffing the prey he ought to be smelling. The threads of air coming to him carried no odor but the cold of an icy wind. Remembering her wolf jokes, he eventually lay down.

Kapu did not. He saw the alertness in Sweet Fur Amy's pose and, nosing Silver gently, walked off to join his daughter. Zing followed him. The two males breathed in deeply but did not smell anything unusual. They glanced at Sweet Fur Amy. Her focused posture was saying, "Put all your senses to work. Excitement is here." Kapu and Zing twisted their ears and expanded their nostrils, but nothing was revealed to them.

The three wolves waited in silence. Behind them the late-August sun turned red-orange. Just before the sun disappeared, the atmosphere flattened it into an oval, and in a blink it was gone. Four hours later it arose. The wolves were still watching the village of Kangik. The wind parted their shiny ruffs as if it were a comb.

Suddenly Kapu and Zing scented the news that Amy already knew. Their pups had not died. They were in the house with Willow Pup Julie.

Kapu whimpered a high, thin call to his pack, a call so high it was out of the range of all ears but theirs. The Avaliks got to their feet and stole softly to the ridge in time to see Kapugen walk out of the house. With him was a fat wolf pup.

"Come, Nutik," Kapugen said to No Growl, who was no longer dying but was a big healthy pup with a new name. "Nutik" means jumper in Iñupiaq. He ran to the man and was rewarded with a fish treat and a hug. "Good, Nutik, good, good."

Kapugen placed him between his legs and slipped a harness over his head and chest, then hitched him to a cart with wheels. Nutik jumped up and down in excitement. Then Willow Pup Julie appeared, carrying Tiny Whimper under one arm.

"Ho, Uqaq, little talking girl," Julie said putting her down.

"WoooOOO, OOOOooo," Tiny Whimper replied, justifying her Iñupiaq name, Uqaq, "to talk." The boy Amaroq and his mother came out of the house and joined the Green House Pack, which consisted of an alpha male and female, Kapugen and Ellen; a beta, Julie; and three pups, Amaroq, Nutik, and Uqaq. They milled and vocalized in the blue light.

Julie picked up her half-brother, Amaroq, and put him in the cart. Uqaq ran in circles. "WoooOOO. WOOOooooo, oooo." She had been named well. The Avaliks patiently waited for the opportunity to walk down the embankment and take back their pups.

"Hut," Kapugen called to Nutik, and he lunged joyfully forward, pressing his big feet to the earth and heading toward the village. Kapugen, Willow Pup, and Uqaq ran beside them. The little boy's mother did not. She smiled, waved, and walked to the school, where she taught in the winter.

Uqaq kept close to Julie's heels. Her need to run in a pack was developing. She kept a small space between herself and Willow Pup's boots, just as she would have done with pups on the tundra.

"Gee," Kapugen shouted to Nutik, who obediently pulled the cart to the right. They went up the rise to the Quonset hut that housed the airplane Kapugen owned and operated. His sled dogs were tied to their kennels at the back of the big structure. They barked at Nutik, then suddenly stopped, sniffed, and burst into a volley of wild barks. The scent of the Avalik pack had reached their noses.

"Wolf, wolf, wolf," they exclaimed furiously.

Kapu heard them tell of their whereabouts and led his pack into the shelter of a thin cloud of mist. He did not wait to see if Kapugen, the hunter, knew what his dogs had said. He ran until he was on the other side of the low cloud. He would wait here until he could get the pups. The pack gathered around him, licking his face and chin excitedly to say the pups were alive and fat.

The days grew dramatically shorter, telling Kapu it was time for the wolves to wander afar. Nevertheless he and his pack stayed near Kangik, keeping out of sight of the town and the dogs. The Avaliks were ready to rescue the pups at the first opportunity.

One morning a large flock of male eider ducks flew in from the nesting grounds along the Arctic coast. By the hundreds they landed on the inland ponds. Hiding in the sedges, they shed all their wing feathers and were unable to fly. In silence they sneaked around the dwarf reeds and water crowfoot waiting for their flight feathers to grow back in.

Kapu watched them arrive with detachment. But when they flew south, lifting off the water by twos, sixes, and hundreds, it was time to change wolf activities. The inner clocks of the caribou were sending them south.

Kapu glanced in the direction of the Brooks Mountain Range. He must lead the Avaliks toward the forests where the caribou wintered. He looked at Aaka. Her rime-gray fur gleamed. She was well fed and strong. She was ready for the rigors of the long, bitter winter of the Arctic. Zing, Raw Bones, and Sweet Fur Amy were also well honed for Arctic wolf life. Silver was not.

This was a problem. A pack is the sum of all its individuals. Kapu would have to slow the pack to Silver's pace.

He was torn. To accomodate his mother, Silver, he must leave now for the forest. On the other hand, the health of the pack depended on waiting for the vigorous pups in the green house in Kangik.

He needed to go. He needed to stay.

Indecision in an alpha male wolf is weakness. Raw Bones saw his chance. But his eyes flickered, telling Kapu he was about to attack. Kapu leaped up and dropped his entire weight on Raw Bones. Raw Bones went down. Kapu snarled, teeth shining in his blue-black face. He held the usurper down by standing stiff-legged across his prone body. Raw Bones shivered.

Kapu opened his mouth wide and barked his annoyance in a deep, guttural voice. He was saying it was taking too much energy to keep Raw Bones in line. He would find a way to end this constant conflict. Snarling viciously above him for almost a minute, he asserted his dominance. The only obstacle to Kapu's becoming as magnificent a leader as his father was this ill-tempered male. And yet he could not kill him. He was his mother's mate. He was a member of the pack.

Suddenly above his threat barks he heard a wolf chorus. He cocked his ears. It was led by Low Wind, the Nuka male leader. He and his pack were on Avalik land. Low Wind had taken advantage of Kapu's plight—a sick mother and pups that held him near Kangik. He had moved into Kapu's territory.

Kapu snarled authoritatively and let Raw Bones up. He swished his tail in the direction of the enemy, and the Avaliks were off to meet the Nukas.

Silver did not join them. She curled into a tight ball and dug her nose into the fur of her tail. Kapu noted her absence and set a swifter pace.

The Avaliks and Nukas met where Avalik borders faded away at a National Petroleum Reserve outpost. The activities of humans had wiped out the wolf borders. Oil and machinery held this territory within the Avalik home range.

They came toward each other with fur rising on their bodies, making them enormous warriors. Kapu eyed Low Wind. Low Wind eyed Kapu. Kapu scratched his signature on the ground with hard strokes of his claws. Low Wind placed his signature on an oily piece of ground, where it could be plainly seen and dreaded. Kapu lifted his leg and scent marked the top of a tundra grass blade. "Come no farther," he said.

Now that Kapu's attention was totally focused on Low Wind, Raw Bones saw his opportunity. With a quick movement he knocked Kapu toward the enemy. Startled, Low Wind attacked Kapu, and so did Raw Bones. Instantly, loyal Zing was upon Raw Bones. Head and chest above him, he bossed him to the ground and pinned him there. Zing had had enough of this wolf too.

The alpha fight began. Kapu and Low Wind mouthed each other's shoulders and rose on hind feet, each trying to lift his head higher than the other's. The growling and snarling was terrifying. Both wolf packs watched in silence. In the midst of the fight Sweet Fur Amy signaled Aaka, and the two sped into the middle of the Nukas. They encircled two adolescents and herded them behind the Avalik lines.

Low Wind, momentarily distracted by the departure of his young adults, turned his head, and in that second Kapu rolled him to the ground. The battle was over. Kapu let Low Wind get back to his feet; then he scratched the ground. Stiff-legged, he walked to a battered oil barrel and shot his scent higher than ever before. Low Wind responded to this statement of victory by pressing his ears against his head and lowering his tail. His face was smooth and expressionless. Kapu's eyes were wide, his tail high, his fur and ears erect. He was magnificent to see. The two leaders looked at each other; then Low Wind signaled his adolescents to return and walked away.

The young Nukas did not move. Kapu, the victor, had told them to stay. Low Wind stepped forward to get them. Kapu lifted the fur on his back and, scratching the ground, drew a new border. He gave Low Wind the oily territory he was on, then turned and walked off with the two strong Nukas. With them in the pack Raw Bones would not be needed.

The rival packs trotted apart. Not far from the battleground Kapu whimpered his joy, sat down, and threw back his head. He howled. His pack howled. The Nukas howled. The wolf music continued until each individual in each pack felt that the business of the day had been concluded satisfactorily.

Then, rising from his haunches, Kapu took time to look at the young Nukas. Storm Call was a male Sweet Fur Amy's age. His back and head were gray as old sea ice, and his dense ruff was tinged with a reddish hue. The other adolescent—his sister, Lichen—was darker and more slender and agile. When Kapu turned his attention to her, she walked right up and licked his cheek to tell him he was her leader and a very good one. Kapu looked from Storm Call to Lichen and invited them into the Avalik Pack. They mixed scents and, pleased with their new family, jogged in silence, following Kapu back to the wolf pups at Kangik.

Along the way Amy picked up the scent of a young caribou and invited Storm Call and the swift-footed Zing to join her. Storm Call hesitated, but when he got Kapu's approval, the three ran wide around the animal. They chased it back to Kapu, Aaka, Raw Bones, and Lichen. It was felled with ceremony and pride. The two new Avaliks were good teammates.

Several hours later, when the wolves were sleeping off their feast, Aaka arose, selected a tasty slice of meat for Silver, and carried it toward Kangik. Wolves care for their weak and unfortunate.

To the north a lone raven flying over the tundra circled Ice Blink. She had come to a road. Snow machines in winter and four-wheel drives in summer had laid it down. Their runners and wheels had broken the plant skin of the tundra, and the sun had poured in and melted the permafrost beneath. The road was now two long lakes of water that would freeze in winter, thaw again, and grow bigger. Human scent all along the road made it a no-wolf zone that needed no scent marking. Wise wolves stayed away.

Ice Blink zigzagged back and forth across it, ignoring the humans and seeking wolf messages. She found none. Her fur swinging, her big white feet lifting and falling rhythmically, she trotted down the road deeper into Avalik country.

Eventually the watery path brought her to the headwaters of the Meade River. Finding no fresh sign of wolf, Ice Blink went on.

On the bank of the Avalik River she picked up a whiff of wolf ambrosia—the perfume of the pack that had visited the dead wolf. The scent was buried under other odors. Carefully she sorted out Avaliks from snowy owl, wolverine, and ground squirrel. Then, using it like a string, she followed the Avalik scent to the whelping den.

The flowers above the entrance had gone to seed, and the nearby redpoll nests were empty and frayed by the wind. The den's commanding view of the vast tundra was a wolf's dream, and Ice Blink lay down to rest.

The wind shifted and a leathery scent, mixed with smoke and whale blubber, drifted up from the riverbed. Ice Blink knew it well. A human was nearby—in fact, two humans. She slipped into the den and hid.

"Sometimes," said one of the two men, who were around the river bend sitting on a shoal, "sometimes the wolves come back to their dens at this time of year just to check them out. They like their dens, all right."

Ice Blink listened to the meaningless words.

"We've been here many sleeps," said the second man. "Do we really have to see a live wolf?"

"Yes, Steven Itta," said Peter Sugluk to his friend from Barrow. "We are The Wolf Dancers; we must have the spirit of the wolf in our feet. If we want to win the dance prize, we must watch the wolves to capture their spirit." He was silent as he thought. "We do want to win the Kivgiq dance award, don't we?"

"You want to," Steven Itta said, "so you can be a hero in Julie's eyes, and you and she can get married."

"I wish that was so, all right," replied Peter.

Then he was silent. Marriage wasn't a simple matter. Gone were the days when the Eskimos could live off the land without the help of modern technology—radios and refrigerators and electric light bulbs. To get those things, one needed a job that paid money, and these jobs were in the gussak's—the white man's—world. To get gussak jobs, one needed a gussak education, and that cost money.

Steven Itta also had been thinking during the silence. "It is too bad," he finally said, "that the Kivgiq does not give money for prizes. How are you going to go to college if you have only dancing feet?"

"I am not only a dancer; I am a very fast runner, Steven. The Fourth of July Foot Race pays lots of money. I have signed up for it already. I will win gussak money and do what I must in this new Arctic world. But I will keep on dancing. Dancing is our culture. I want to keep our traditions alive. Do I want too much, all right?"

The two young men sat quietly. Like their families and friends, they thought a long time before answering questions.

"The Arctic has gotten very complicated, all right," said Steven. "We cannot live as our ancestors did even if we want to."

"And I do," answered Peter Sugluk longingly. "With Julie I have watched the brotherhood of the wolves, and we have wished we were one with them again."

"That world is gone," said Steven Itta.

"Ee-lie," whispered Peter. "Get down on all fours. I smell wolf."

"All fours?"

"They don't know what you are when you're on all fours. When they see you standing on two legs, they know you're a human and they run away. But on all fours they don't know. Sometimes they come right up to find out."

They knelt with their hands on the ground for almost an hour. When Ice Blink did not appear, they began to talk again in their low, musical voices.

"Since we've been watching Julie's wolf pups for many circles of the sun," Steven Itta said, "we should be good enough wolf dancers by now. We saw how they wrestle with bones and hides and how they chase their tails. That is their spirit, all right."

"We are not pups," Peter answered. "We are adult wolves. We are regal, elegant, full of the sense of the Earth and our work upon it. A pup dance won't do."

Peter, silent now, pointed with his eyes to the top of the embankment.

As if struck into being, a white wolf stared at them. Her eyes were mustard yellow. She tilted her head curiously from right to left, trying to make sense of the strange animals lumped by the river. Although she smelled humans, these four-legged beasts were not humans in her mind. She reared onto her hind feet to see them better. Then, like a gyrfalcon's shadow, she came down the slope sniffing and rotating her ears to learn more about them. She hesitated, crouched low, still uncertain of what they were, and trotted to within fifteen feet of them. She stared quietly; then Steven sneezed and his human face became clear to her. She leaped, turned in midair, and sped away.

"I've got it," said Peter when she had disappeared in the tundra mist. Rising, he stamped out the rhythm of the Eskimo man dancer. He spread his feet, bent his knees, and with hands and body told the story of a wolf approaching a strange object that became a human. He even leaped and turned in midair, eyes round with fear.

"Teach me, teach me," said Steven Itta.

On the lonely beach beyond the bleak bend in the Arctic river, with the ice mist playing around their feet and bright-blue skies above, two young men danced the dance of "White Wolf Running from Two Men."

By the time they were satisfied with their art, Ice Blink was far down the scented Avalik highway that led to Kangik. The ambrosia of the wolf pack grew continuously stronger as she ran. She threaded along it, then suddenly came upon Silver. The rime-gray female was curled in a tight knot on the lichens below the crest of a rise. Ice Blink drew back. She had not been invited to trespass on this wolf's property. She whimpered her apology. The wolf did not move. After a long wait Ice Blink took one step toward her, then another. The wolf smelled cold. Ice Blink touched her with her nose. There was no life in the body.

She backed away and lay down a short distance from Silver, her nose on her paws, her eyes on the dead female. After a while she dozed.

Suddenly she was awake. The Avaliks were standing in a circle around her. Ice Blink lowered her ears in humility, at the same time making wolf judgments as she rolled her eyes from wolf to wolf. One female carried food in her mouth—a kind wolf, Aaka. Her daughter was constantly sniffing—a sensitive wolf, Sweet Fur Amy. One was disgruntled, Raw Bones. Then Ice Blink saw the alpha. He was larger than the others, and his fur stood up on his back and head like a regal cape. He was wolf nobility. She groveled toward him, her belly almost on the ground. She turned her eyes away from his to say he was leader. Then, in humility, she looked at him and begged for admission into the pack.

Kapu read her application. She was older than he, far from home, and alone. She was strong and well fed—a good hunter. One odor worried him. It was a sickly odor. That was enough to cast doubt. He turned his head away and refused her admission.

The Avaliks milled restlessly as they watched her retreat. Then Aaka dropped the food she was carrying and barked an alarm. She had found Silver's lifeless body.

Kapu howled. Sweet Fur Amy howled, Zing howled, Aaka howled, and Raw Bones moaned. The

Nuka adolescents lay down and put their heads on their paws. In silence they listened to the windlike voices of the Avaliks slide up the musical scale and glide down to silence. The life of Silver had fled.

When their mourning was over, Kapu led his wolves away. Silver was now part of the wilderness. She would enter the lives of the ravens and foxes, the lemmings and wolverines.

That rosy midnight, subdued by the loss of the old alpha female, the Avaliks gathered together on a desolate frost heave. Some stretched out on their sides and closed their eyes. Some watched the birds. Kapu watched the caribou on the horizon. The animals were behaving oddly. They were pressed tightly against each other. They were not spaced apart as usual. Then Kapu heard a high-pitched whine. Billions of mosquitoes and botflies were darkening the sky. They sought out the caribou. With no tails to whisk off the pests, the caribou were using the mass of their bodies as a fort. This was a problem for the wolves. It was going to be hard for them to isolate one or two.

Kapu was pondering a strategy when, over the sound of the pitiful bleats and snorts of the caribou, Sweet Fur Amy passed a message to him: "Time to go for the pups." Kapu arose, and the two trekked off through a massive cloud of insects. They swished them away with their tails and snapped at them. A few mosquitoes lit on the furless parts of their eyelids and noses, but they wiped them away with their paws. The dense underfur of the wolves protected their bodies.

They were just out of sight of the Avaliks when Raw Bones suddenly jumped out of the blueberries and landed on Kapu's back. Kapu reacted quickly. He clenched Raw Bones's shoulder in his jaws and twisted him to the ground. Once again Raw Bones bowed to Kapu's might and cringed before him. Head high, Kapu felt his own confidence rise. Raw Bones, in spite of himself, was making Kapu more and more powerful.

When Ice Blink, who had been watching them from some distance away, saw Raw Bones go down, she sensed it was time to take up her cause again. Silver was dead. Raw Bones was an annoyance to the leader. She caught up with Kapu and Sweet Fur Amy and followed them at a respectful distance. Kapu was immediately aware of her. Before he reached Kangik, he turned and waited, his back bristling. She walked into his personal tolerance zone and stopped. He stared at her. Silver was dead. The caribou were a formidable mass. He needed another wolf. With a soft whine and an unblinking look he invited Ice Blink—a biological time bomb—into the Avalik Pack.

A brief sense of uneasiness swept through him; then Sweet Fur Amy whimpered to remind him of their mission, and the three trotted on. They climbed to the knoll and looked down on the scene Amy had smelled and responded to. Willow Pup Julie and the little boy, Amaroq, were outside on the riverbank. The boy was laughing and romping with the wolf pups.

Signaling Ice Blink to stay and Sweet Fur Amy to follow, Kapu swept down on Uqaq. He picked her up by the scruff of her neck. She instinctively curled her body into the pup-carrying position, with her hind feet curled up to her head. She was almost too big to be carried. Her rump bumped the ground. Kapu lifted his head higher and trotted off with her.

Sweet Fur Amy picked up Nutik. He was even bigger and heavier than Uqaq, and she could not carry him. She dragged him along.

"Amy," Julie said when she saw what was happening. "Not yet. Don't take Nutik. Don't take Uqaq. Not yet. They need shots. Qignak from Canada has tracked a rabid wolf to our tundra. It carries a deadly disease." Sweet Fur Amy tugged, slowly moving toward Ice Blink, who was coming to help her.

"Wolves must not die," Julie whispered as she came toward Amy. "You manage the tundra, the caribou, the berries, the birds, the plants—all the wild things we need." She dropped to her knees and reached out for Nutik. Ice Blink leaped away. Amy pulled harder.

"Amy, stay. Stay. The veterinarian is coming to Kangik to give the dogs and your pups rabies shots. I will bring them to you after that, all right. Do not take the pups."

Amaroq, seeing Julie on all fours, thought she was playing wolf and climbed on her back. He tumbled her to her side, and she could not reach Nutik.

"Drop, Amy. Drop," she called, and barked an alarm. Sweet Fur Amy stopped.

"Drop," Julie said, and reached out to gently hold Sweet Fur Amy's nose in her hand. She shook it in the manner of the alpha male wolf saying he is boss. Sweet Fur Amy dropped Nutik. The big fuzzy pup looked from Sweet Fur Amy to Julie, then ran to Julie, the only mother he remembered.

Sweet Fur Amy barked at him, demanding he come with her. He ignored her.

"Not now, Amy," Willow Pup Julie said. "I will soon return him to you, all right." She gathered Nutik up in her arms. He licked her cheek.

Peter Sugluk came around the far side of the house, his leather pants swishing softly, the weasel tails on his boots swinging with the rhythm of his stride. His dark, lean face was serious as he sat down on the ground beside Julie.

"I heard you talking to Amy," he said. "I know you want to give the pups rabies shots, but somehow wolves know how to control the disease. Not many die of it."

"That is true," she answered. "The wolves know, all right. But we don't know how they do it, and we cannot take a chance. Dr. Flossie Oomittuk says there are too many people and dogs hunting on the tundra. She asked me to give the pups shots."

Sweet Fur Amy stopped to listen to Peter's and Willow Pup Julie's voices and to the boy who was playing pounce with Nutik. Nutik snarled.

"No, no," Amaroq said. "Don't get mad." The snarls stopped.

"Good, Nutik. Good pup," Willow Pup Julie said, and she and Peter took Nutik and the little boy into the house.

Sweet Fur Amy had seen that Nutik had a human alpha, a little boy with a kind voice. But she would not give up. She lay down in a patch of dwarf peas to wait until the pup came out to play.

Kapugen's voice reached her from inside the house.

"Uqaq is gone?" he said. "That is too bad, all right. She was a lovely pup."

"We must return Nutik soon," Julie said.

"Return him? I do not agree. I need him. He is a strong leader and he is friendly. The greatest dogs come from such a wolf."

"But I promised the wolves I would bring him back," she said.

"Ee-lie, Miyax," Kapugen said, calling Julie by her Yupik Eskimo name. "Think, my little panIk, my daughter. The village will have a new industry—sled dogs with the friendliness and endurance of the wolf. That means money for the things we need."

"The caribou need Nutik," Julie said softly. "The grasses and lichens need Nutik. The birds and mammals need Nutik. And we need them all."

The father and daughter stopped talking. When they disagreed, they turned inward to think. Finally Kapugen broke the silence.

"I want my son to learn the strength and wisdom of the wolf from young Nutik," he said.

Willow Pup Julie did not answer.

Sweet Fur Amy waited for the pup she was responsible for to come out of the house. Presently the villagers came outside, and she trotted the several miles upriver to the pack.

They were standing around Uqaq looking at her with curiosity. The pup held her tail between her legs, her ears back, her eyes cast down. Although Uqaq knew she was among her kind, she was waiting for her human mother to tell her what to do. She did not know Raw Bones was her father, nor did he feel very parental. She was too big, the size of an independent pup.

On the other hand, Sweet Fur Amy's baby-sitting instincts sharpened. The pup was frightened and helpless. She licked the pup's cheeks and ears. Uqaq relaxed in this tenderness and sank to her belly. Sweet Fur Amy lay beside her and licked her so hard, the pup fell onto her side. Sweet Fur Amy went on licking. When she had removed the people scent, she rubbed her own Avalik scent on her. Then she got up and woofed. Uqaq followed her baby-sitter to the Avaliks' last kill.

Sweet Fur Amy's world was in order at last. She had a pup to tend. Slowly Uqaq would shift her love for her human mother to her baby-sitter.

When the sun dipped toward the horizon, then started up again, Uqaq and Sweet Fur Amy were curled side by side near the pack.

Hardly had they closed their eyes than Storm Call lay down beside Sweet Fur Amy. He liked her. In fact, he had liked her from the moment she had herded him into the pack. She wagged her tail once.

Raw Bones stayed away from the Avaliks until Ice Blink settled down; then he curled up beside her. She snarled, got up, and lay down near Aaka. Aaka snarled and went to Kapu's side. Lichen whimpered because her brother had left her for Sweet Fur Amy. Zing heard her protest and took sides with her. He rumbled at Storm Call.

Kapu listened to the restless whimpers and shifting arrangements. This was not the first time he had noticed that his pack was breaking up into cliques. Sweet Fur Amy had isolated herself with Uqaq and Storm Call. Zing and Lichen barked at them, and all of them stayed away from Ice Blink. Raw Bones rumbled alone.

Kapu got to his feet. This was not good. A pack must cooperate. The time had come for him to lead them on another long trip around their territory. A pack's land—the herds, the plants, the weather, and the winding rivers—binds wolves together. Trips across and around their land fill each individual with a sense of his importance to the pack and the pack to him. It was time to fuse the Avaliks into a more friendly nation. He would lead them off as soon as the night was long enough for them to travel great distances in the dark, which they preferred to the light.

That day came in September after the first snow fell. Kapu was dozing when, with his head on his tail, he heard the subtle call to winter travel. A wooly bear caterpillar was walking down the tines of the moss beneath him. The fuzzy brown-and-black larva was so cold, he could no longer eat. He was going to the warmest layer on the frigid tundra—the inch or two of atmosphere right against the ground. Here the caterpillar would freeze for the winter but not die. Next summer he would thaw and eat until the cold stopped him again. Fourteen years of freezing and thawing would pass before the caterpillar would become an adult tiger moth. It takes only three weeks in the lower forty-eight states. Kapu heard the caterpillar stop creeping. It was time to go.

He stood up, shook sparklets of rime from his fur, and howled the Avalik song of travel. The wolves awoke and got to their feet. Aaka howled, Zing harmonized with her, then Storm Call came from his rendezvous and joined in. Eager to please her new alpha, Lichen howled half tones that quivered the air. Kapu wagged his tail and stepped closer to Aaka.

The spirit of the gypsy howl touched Ice Blink. She howled. Raw Bones took his own note and bellowed authoritatively. The wolves sang, sending their glorious music out over the land—all but Sweet Fur Amy and Uqaq. They were not going to travel. They listened to the song and dug their noses deeper into their tails.

The howl ended when Kapu's deepest note faded away. The Avaliks touched noses, cheeks, shoulders and milled in joyful anticipation of the long run.

Kapu burst free. The pack followed, feet flying, tails loose and out, fur sweeping back and rippling.

When Raw Bones realized they were not going to the Colville River, he broke off from the pack. Ice Blink followed him. Kapu glanced at them as they headed south. For deep reasons of survival he did not understand, he was relieved to see Ice Blink go.

Rid of them both, he led on with renewed inspiration. The Avaliks covered almost ten miles in less than an hour. Near a frost heave they picked up the trail of a grizzly bear, sped off to find him, and chased him for the fun of it. Then they circled back to their own trail and ran on.

The chase gave Raw Bones time to change his mind and catch up with them. Ice Blink trotted beside him. Kapu saw the two return, and his spirits darkened. He increased his pace. Zing sensed trouble. He left Lichen's side and ran behind Kapu, putting his feet precisely in his footsteps. Storm Call ran third to support his alpha.

Suddenly Raw Bones passed him and caught up with Zing. Unruffled, Zing put on speed and kept ahead of Raw Bones. Then Aaka passed all three and took her honored place with the alpha male. Ice Blink took up the rear. This pack was not at ease with her. She would keep her distance. It had been seven months since her mate had died and she had licked saliva from his face. She had no knowledge of the death bomb she was carrying, but she did know she needed this pack to survive.

Although she was not fond of Raw Bones, the troublemaker, he was necessary to her. Without him and his friends she would not survive. The winters were long and hard, and the caribou and moose dangerous. Ice Blink caught up with Raw Bones and ran by his side. He glanced at her, raised the base of his tail, and let his handsome bush hang loose in the friendly position. To Ice Blink this was acceptance. They were a team.

Before dawn Kapu brought the pack to a resting site and took Zing off to study a bull caribou. The animal was covered with infections where the botflies and mosquitoes had bitten. He limped. Kapu and Zing looked at each other and nonchalantly walked to within a few hundred yards of the bull. The bull kept a wary eye on them. The pack lay on their bellies and watched. After a long while the bull decided the two wolves were not hunting him and leaned down to browse. Kapu signaled Zing to attack. The bull saw the signal and trotted off. Raw Bones and Ice Blink ran in to help. Lichen and Storm Call closed in behind, and Aaka circled out to herd the animal. She would head the bull toward them. Wolves stay clear of the kicking rear feet.

Illness and strategy notwithstanding, the buck thundered away behind a screen of frozen mist. But the wolves did not stop running. Without losing a step, they used their noses and ears to follow the prey. Shoulders pumping up and down, tails flowing, they saw him again, rushed at him, but could not catch up. The Avaliks sorely missed Sweet Fur Amy. They trotted on.

Two days later the food was finally won. They ate their fill and retired to the top of a small rise, where they could look in all directions night and day. By night they saw with the aid of the light-gathering rods in their eyes. The cones gave them daytime vision. Night and day were of no concern to the wolves.

A helicopter clattered into the morning sunshine. Kapu feared machines whether they came by land or air. He aroused the pack with one woof-bark and raced to the top of a cliff above the Lower Colville River valley. There Aaka took the lead. She had grown up in this area and knew all the overhangs and gullies. The helicopter followed her. She turned abruptly and vanished. The pack zigged, zagged, and joined her beneath an overhang on a creek embankment.

"Lost them," said Dr. Flossie Oomittuk, the North Slope Borough veterinarian, who was seated by the pilot of the helicopter.

"Want to land and find them?" asked Jeremy Smith as he steered the copter toward the river. "They're around here somewhere."

"The pack's too big for the two of us to tranquilize them all. Let's go back for help. They'll stick around. Some of the caribou haven't gone south yet."

The pilot nodded and swung the clattering machine in an arc. Flossie Oomittuk spoke again.

"Who told you a big white female ran west after her whole pack died of rabies?"

"Qignak," the pilot answered.

"Qignak. He should know. He's the Inuttut Eskimo who first reported the rabid pack."

"He knew them well," said the pilot. "He's lived in their territory all his life. He said the big white female with the long pointed nose survived. He tracked her over the Canadian border into Alaska. He has seen her from time to time. He flies over this country when he's counting caribou to help our Fish and Game Department. Think she's carrying the disease?"

"She's certainly a candidate," said Dr. Oomittuk. "But so far no rabies has turned up on the North Slope, and it's been almost four months since she entered. Of course, the incubation period can be as long as a year."

"What's the point of inoculating wolves against rabies?" the pilot asked. "The less wolves, the more caribou."

"The reason is people," the veterinarian said. "Rabies is deadly. We can inoculate a few people against it—vets, wildlife researchers, and people who work with dogs and wild animals—but it's not practical to inoculate whole human populations. It's more practical to inoculate dogs, cats, foxes, and wolves when we can."

"Come to think of it," Jeremy said, "I did see a large white wolf in that pack we just lost."

"I noticed one too," said Flossie Oomittuk.

"Are you sure they'll stay around here until we get back?"

"I think so," the veterinarian said. "That's a fresh kill at the headwaters of the creek. Fly back over it. Let's get its location on the Global Positioning System and come back."

The copter flew over the kill, circled several times, and went on.

When it was no longer audible to even the keen-eared wolves, who could hear a caribou tendon click a half mile away, Raw Bones got up and started out for the kill. Kapu intercepted him, ears straight up and forward, brow wrinkled. "No." Raw Bones stopped and Kapu bounced on his hind feet, took a long leap, and ran southwest. Raw Bones looked in the direction of the kill, hesitated, and joined the run. Kapu was headed toward his territory.

But Kapu did not go to the Upper Colville. He led the pack day and night, checking borders, harvesting food, howling to distant packs. He ran until the sun no longer rose and the air and the land were shades of blue and white and the northern lights made the snowy world almost as bright as daytime.

One night he lost Ice Blink. The older wolf could not keep up with the swift pace of the young alpha. Kapu put on more speed. He had an urgent need to lose Ice Blink, but not for any clear reason. She did her part, she stayed the omega, the helpless, so he could not drive her off or kill her. But he sensed he had to lose her. Then, fortunately, when she could no longer keep up, Raw Bones dropped back to be with her.

By the twilight of noon the next day Kapu and the Avaliks were racing free of anxiety. They were kicking up snow with their heels, playing wolf jokes on little herds of musk oxen.

When they had traveled almost two hundred miles, Kapu brought the pack to the den on the Avalik River. They wagged their tails, rubbed bodies, and licked each other. Fellowship reigned. The Avaliks howled their anthem proudly and carried their banner of scent.

From across the freezing landscape Sweet Fur Amy answered, then Uqaq. Kapu bounced up and down and called back. They talked over the long distance, letting each other know where they were, but neither moving. Sweet Fur Amy was not coming home.

She and Uqaq were watching the village. The people of Kangik were outdoors in the bright moonlight getting their sleds and snow machines ready for moose hunts under the new sun in January. Kapu called to her again. This time she did not answer.

Amaroq and Nutik were alone on the riverbank.

Sweet Fur Amy sent a high call note to Nutik: "Come here." It was so high the boy could not hear it. Nutik heard it, but it meant nothing to him. The boy and his family were his pack, and he heard only their commands. The toddler ran toward the ice-filled river. Nutik pulled him back by his big, warm parka. Amaroq laughed. The two woofed and whimpered the wolf sounds of best friends.

Nutik did not answer Sweet Fur Amy, but Kapu did. He called her to come back and hunt with them. The bulk of the herd had migrated to the forest to breed and renew life. Kapu needed her keen nose to locate the scattered winter herds. He called her again.

She did not answer. The northern lights were illuminating the green house. Its door was opening. Willow Pup Julie walked out. She cupped her hands around her mouth and howled to Amy, as she had every day during these long dark months. "I am here. I am here," she had always said, and Sweet Fur Amy had always answered, "Here am I waiting for the pup." Today Willow Pup Julie's wolf call was different. It was low with sadness. Sweet Fur Amy came closer.

"Amy," Willow Pup Julie said when she could

make out her shadow, "I cannot return Nutik. I have kept him too long. He is a member of our pack. He cannot and will not leave."

Amy listened.

"I am sorry," Julie went on. "We will love Nutik and learn from him." Amy did not understand the words, but her wolf eyes saw well by the green and yellow lights of the aurora. The girl's body was speaking. She was saying in gesture and pose, "I am sorry, the pup is not yours anymore."

Sweet Fur Amy threw back her head and sang about a wolf pup lost to humans. It was not a sad cry. It was a thoughtful song inspired by the distant past. Long before there were domestic dogs, people raised friendly wolf pups. The people and wolves had much in common. They were both social animals who hunted big game. They both lived in family groups. Both groups had leaders and shared a deep love for these alphas. When humans saw what good hunters the wolves were, they took the most friendly pups into their families, and the wolf pups came to love the human alphas as they loved their own. Over the eons friendly wolf pups were bred to other friendly wolf pups, and the dog evolved in its various shapes and sizes. Even today a wolf pup who is taken from its parents very early in life will substitute the human

alphas for its own. And that is what Julie was telling Sweet Fur Amy.

Sweet Fur Amy understood. She went back to Uqaq and led her to a distant sleeping spot. They lay with their heads on their paws listening to the sighs of blowing snow and the boom of river ice freezing deeper as the temperature dropped to forty below zero.

The northern lights faded, and the stars shone down on the icy snowflakes and lit up the tundra. Sweet Fur Amy heard Aklaq, the grizzly bear, and she tucked her paws against her belly fur. The bear was sighing. Sweet Fur Amy lifted her head. In the starlight she saw Aklaq sitting upright on an embankment of drifted snow. A wolf hunter had landed his noisy plane on the river ice. Aklaq awakened. Although she was in her winter sleep, she could arouse herself if she must. She struggled sleepily from her den and ran.

A hunter got out of his plane and walked across the creaking cold snow. A dart gun was slung across his shoulder. He circled the Avalik den, saw no bear sign, and went back to his plane. He took off.

Aklaq went back to her den. She sat down. Her big shoulders were slumped, her head drooped. Her cubs of four years were on their own. In a warmer climate where food is more abundant, grizzly cubs leave their mothers when they are two years old, but in the food-scarce Arctic it takes more years to learn the resources. Cubless in August, Aklaq had mated with a boar grizzly of the Lower Colville River. She would give birth in January.

Now she was sensing the three atmospheric signals that were telling her she would be safe if she went back into her den. The air pressure was dropping. That was one signal for Aklaq. The cold intensified. That was a second signal. The stars went out and storm clouds blackened the land. Aklaq got to her feet. She lumbered past a weasel who was plugging his den with moss against the coming blizzard. She passed a wolverine digging into a burrow near a sleeping ground squirrel colony. She smelled the ptarmigan who were hunkered down in the grass waiting to be buried under a blanket of snow that would keep them warm. They all felt the storm coming.

The wolves felt it too, but reacted differently. The Nuka River Pack howled in celebration of a storm that would pile snow high and slow down the caribou. The Avaliks sang to the wind that would pack the snow as hard as cement and set them free to run on top of it. The Lower Colville River Pack ran out in the storm to hunt moose, who could not run in this weather, and the Mountain Pack trotted into the forest to locate the young caribou who would not have the strength to run in deep snow. They all howled to welcome the blizzard.

At midnight the storm hit. That was the third signal. As Aklaq went into her den, the blowing snow wiped out her footsteps so no human hunter would know where she slept.

The weasel was inspired. He began digging a tunnel under the snow to a lemming nest. The ptarmigan grew warm.

Sweet Fur Amy and Uqaq dove in and out of the snow, rolling in it, biting it. They barked the delight woof of the wolf.

Suddenly on the wind came a delight answer. Sweet Fur Amy peered through the swirling whiteness. Storm Call was coming through the blizzard carrying a polished caribou tine in his mouth. He dropped it in the snow at Sweet Fur Amy's feet. She wagged her tail and picked it up. She tossed it. Storm Call caught it. Sweet Fur Amy chased him, took the tine in her mouth, and pulled hard. Growling and swishing their tails, they played tug-of-war in the whirling snow while Uqaq tumbled and watched.

The storm raged for three days before it blew south to the Brooks Mountain Range. When it passed, the stars burned brightly, and by their light the Sweet Fur Clique ran until they came to the land between the Meade and Ikpikpuk rivers. There they bedded down near a small herd of resident caribou spending the winter on the North Slope.

The Sweet Fur Clique worked well together. Amy found the weak animals, and Uqaq annoyed them with her ooing and woofing until they turned to charge her. Then Storm Call would give the signal to attack. Sometimes he did not. He had good judgment. He knew when to call off a chase and when to drive on. He knew when to rest and when to run. They lived well in the land between the rivers.

The joy of being with Storm Call and Uqaq, hunting and diving in the snow, helped Sweet Fur Amy forget about the lost Nutik. When the sun came above the horizon in January, the Sweet Fur Clique was fat and spirited. They wandered, chased each other in circles, and rolled in the snow.

Near the Colville early one morning, Sweet Fur Amy stopped and sniffed. Storm Call and Uqaq stopped. On the air was the scent of Willow Pup Julie. She was nearby. Sweet Fur threw back her head and called to her. Julie called back. Silence, then a creak of sled runners, and over a rise came Nutik pulling Amaroq in the one-dog sled and Julie running beside them.

Uqaq ran to her brother.

"Stop," barked Sweet Fur Amy, but Uqaq could not. She was too excited. She leaped on Nutik. He twisted her off, pulling the harness and overturning the sled with Amaroq. The little boy rolled into the snow, his laughter muffled in a pile of cold crystals. Nutik dug around him, yip-barking for the fun of it all.

Amaroq stood up. Nutik pranced. "Stop," the boy barked, and Nutik stopped. Uqaq whimpered, begging him to play, but Nutik did not move. His leader had spoken. Uqaq sat down and cocked her head from right to left.

Willow Pup Julie straightened out the tangled traces and put Amaroq back in the sled. Then she came toward Sweet Fur Amy whimpering wolf niceties. There was love and authority in Julie's voice. Sweet Fur Amy got down on her belly. Uqaq got down. Suddenly, with a move as swift as a falcon's strike, Julie jabbed a hypodermic needle into Amy's thigh and then quickly into Uqaq's. There was no pain, but the wolves were so startled by Julie's jumping at them that they ran quite a distance before they stopped and looked at her.

"Forgive me, Amy," Willow Pup Julie said. "I have no way of telling you this, but there is a rabid wolf on the tundra. I have given you a vaccine so you will not get sick and die." Then she saw Storm Call standing on the snow pile. She crept toward him. "Come," she whimpered in wolf talk. "I want to be your friend." He had seen Sweet Fur and Uqaq run away from Julie, so he was cautious.

"Bring me your friend, Amy," Julie said softly. "I must give him a shot too." The three wolves stood motionless, staring at her.

Then Storm Call barked danger and ran off. Sweet Fur Amy and Uqaq ran after him. Julie pushed a glossy strand of her black hair under her parka hood.

"Amy," she called, "where is Kapu?" The trio kept running, and Julie returned to the sled.

"Hut," Amaroq said to Nutik, and they moved on.

Kapu was several miles away, loping toward the Upper Colville River with his pack. He was in a fine mood. Raw Bones and Ice Blink were gone. Sweet Fur Amy and Storm Call were on their own with Uqaq, and the Avaliks had stopped feuding. Good feeling prevailed. It had come through their feet as they ran. It had come through their eyes and noses as they learned where each fox and rabbit lived and each group of overwintering caribou. It had come through their bodies as they pierced the snowstorms with the ease of a salmon swimming upstream. Kapu jogged along, head high, spirits elevated. He was, at last, a great alpha.

The Avaliks threaded their way across the snowy wilderness in perfect harmony. They moved as one, vanishing into snow clouds and reappearing in spotlights of yellow sunshine.

As they approached the Upper Colville River, Raw Bones suddenly sprang out of a clump of dwarf willows and dashed to the head of the pack. Kapu ignored him. Feeling the power of being in first place, Raw Bones snarled and growled gloriously. Kapu did not return the challenge.

When he was tired of Raw Bones's nonsense, he simply expanded his chest and sped past him. Raw Bones bared his teeth. Kapu turned and faced him. "I am the alpha," he said, posturing regally. Raw Bones pulled his ears back and down, and not only lowered himself but rolled over on his back. He flashed the wolf flag of surrender—the white belly fur. Kapu cocked an eye at him. Never before had Raw Bones taken this pose of complete defeat. Was he at last subdued? It seemed so. He let him up. Raw Bones slunk away with his tail between his legs.

Kapu turned to Aaka, licked her cheek, and took a long high leap, and the two ran toward the river. Beside them ran Zing and Lichen.

Near the frozen Colville Kapu stopped. Sensing something was not right, he looked back. Raw Bones had returned to the pack and brought Ice Blink with him.

A searing bolt of fear ran through Kapu. All his instincts told him to drive off the white wolf. Then Aaka called him. A moose was in the valley. Devotion to his mate won over fear, and he joined her. Raw Bones and Ice Blink followed well behind, but part of the pack.

Ice Blink stumbled. She stopped, wiped a watering eye against her foreleg, then caught up with Raw Bones. She whimpered in pain. Whatever had bothered Kapu now bothered Raw Bones. He dashed away to catch up with the pack.

They raced over their old border and into what had once had been the no-wolf zone between Kapu's and Raw Bones's territories. They ran through the dwarf alders and grasses to the other side of the river and into Raw Bones's empty territory.

An odor struck Kapu like a sharp fang, and he jerked to a stop. The fur rose on his back. Eyes wide, he gave a silent signal and turned his pack around.

Not Raw Bones. He wanted to be king again. He walked through the stunted brush and up an incline to his old whelping den. He would return to his beloved land and regain his self-confidence. He lay down and put his head on his paws. As he sighed a peaceful sigh, Ice Blink appeared. Her eye had stopped watering. She drooped her head wearily, then lay down to rest.

It was March. The wolf mating season was beginning, the season that marked a new year for the wolves. Although wolf pairs stay close together all year—in fact, all their lives—they mate only once a year. This year, with Aaka in good health, Kapu could expect lots of fat pups.

Ice Blink as well as Aaka was coming into estrus. She was not ready to mate quite yet, but she was willing to be courted. One night she ran to Raw Bones and spanked her front feet on the snow, asking him to play. He bounced to her. She wagged her tail and ran. Raw Bones ran. As they came around a cluster of stunted spruce trees, he was suddenly struck a powerful blow on his rear. He was spun completely around.

Snow Driver, the alpha male of the Mountain Pack, had hit him with a rump blow, and before Raw Bones could recover, he had him by the scruff of his neck. Cloud Berry, the alpha female, rolled Ice Blink to her back. Seven other handsome gray wolves surrounded them.

The powerful Mountain Pack had taken over Raw Bones's old territory. The riverside was his home no more. He cowered before Snow Driver, waiting for the Avaliks to come to his rescue.

They did not. A deep draft of moist air had told Kapu what Raw Bones had discovered the hard way—that Snow Driver and his pack now owned this land. Kapu had smelled the news, crossed the river, and returned to his own territory. He scent marked the border, once again setting up the no-wolf zone.

On the south side of the river in view of the Mountain Pack, Ice Blink suddenly went stiff. Her eyes rolled, foam bubbled from her mouth. She snarled.

Cloud Berry looked at her. A defeated wolf did not growl at the conqueror. Ice Blink had threatened her with a growl. The white wolf staggered to her feet and, lunging, sank her aching teeth in Cloud Berry's front leg. Snow Driver rushed in to defend Cloud Berry. He postured like an alpha, but Ice Blink did not roll onto her back. It was as if she had not seen him. Something was wrong. With a tail command he sent Cloud Berry up the mountain into the taiga, ice-dwarfed spruce trees. Then he turned back to the business of dominating Ice Blink. As she snarled toward him, mouth open, he smelled the sickness, turned, and followed Cloud Berry.

When he was gone, Raw Bones slowly got to his feet. He glanced at Ice Blink. She was on the ground stiff with paralysis. Fear gripped him again and he ran. Crossing the Colville, he slithered up to the top of the embankment, where he lay down with his tail between his legs.

Within a few hours Ice Blink went into convulsions and died the horrible death of the rabid animal, wracked with pain, wanting but unable to swallow water, and blinded by headache and fever. She had carried the disease for more than a year before it had taken over. And she had contaminated the Mountain Pack before she died.

On their side of the river the Avaliks urinated and howled to tell the Mountain Pack where their border lay. The Mountain Pack howled back from the taiga. Storm Driver acknowledged the rights of Kapu, leader of the Avaliks, and Kapu acknowledged Storm Driver as leader of the Mountain Pack. With howls and scratches on the snow they defined the no-wolf corridor.

That night the Avaliks started back toward Kangik. In the quiet of the blue twilight after the sun went down, Kapu and Aaka mated.

Pups! And they would be the alphas' pups.

Pups! Far away, Sweet Fur Amy heard the news and led Storm Call and Uqaq across the tundra back to the Avaliks. Before she reached them, she picked up the scent of a caribou weakened by infection, and the three easily and swiftly felled it. Their quick harmonious howls announced the kill. Sweet Fur Amy ate first.

Kapu, Aaka, Zing, Lichen, and Raw Bones heard the news and joined the feast. Kapu let Aaka eat before him, making sure she would give birth to many healthy Avalik pups. When Aaka could swallow no more, Kapu ate and generously permitted the others to eat with him. Their bellies round with food, they milled and mixed scents and celebrated their good fortune. Then they made sleeping beds.

Sweet Fur Amy, Storm Call, and Uqaq made their beds with them. The alphas' pups were coming. They would stay with the pack and help. Uqaq found a bone toy and took it to bed with her.

As old as she was, almost a year, Uqaq was still a puppy. The many mothers in her life—Silver, Julie, and Sweet Fur Amy—had kept her from growing up. She was stuck in puppyhood, a sweet playful pack member who could not contribute much to the survival of the group. She was Sweet Fur Amy's and Storm Call's welfare case. With their return to the Avaliks she was everyone's welfare case. Uqaq needed a kindly pack to keep her alive.

A March blizzard covered the sleeping wolves that morning, and from time to time Kapu awoke, shook off the snow, and listened to the sounds of the tundra. A human voice traveled to him.

"Peter," said Willow Pup Julie. Kapu lifted his head. "There are the wolves. See the ears above the snow? They are sleeping. Kapu is awake."

"He's a prince," Peter whispered softly. Shifting on his caribou skin, he lifted his binoculars to his eyes.

"Be very quiet," Willow Pup Julie murmured.

The hours passed. The wolves knew Julie and Peter were there but they were not concerned. Too full to move, they went on sleeping off their huge meal. Later they got up, exchanged scents, mingled and licked cheeks. With the Sweet Fur Clique back among them, their society was nicely balanced—four adults, three young adults, one yearling, and pups on the way. The Avaliks were peaceful.

Voices floated to them from the caribou skins.

"He's all nobility," Peter breathed softly. "I shall become him. I will dance as I have never danced before."

"But you have already won the Kivgiq," Julie whispered.

"I need to win next year, too," Peter whispered back. "Then I can tour the state and earn money. Living in Barrow and going to college is very expensive—especially when you can't hunt and fish."

The clatter of a helicopter sounded in the distance. Inside it people were talking.

"Ravens," said Jeremy Smith, the pilot. "There must be a wolf kill over there."

"Get in touch with Kapugen's party," said Flossie Oomittuk, the veterinarian. "He's on a moose hunt somewhere along the Upper Colville River. He should be ready to help us." She turned to two men in the back of the copter, Agiaq and Uvigaq, the best hunters in Barrow. "Check the tranquilizing drugs and the guns," she said.

After a few screeches and static on the radio Jeremy got Kapugen's CB.

"Have you seen Julie's wolves?" he asked.

"Julie and Peter are near them now," Kapugen said. "They are not far from that kill where the ravens are circling. Julie has a CB; you can talk to her."

"How long has she been there?" he asked.

"Hours."

"How many wolves?"

"Eight. Two have been given shots. The smaller of the two black wolves and a gray adolescent pup."

"Did Julie and Peter see the white wolf?"

"She is dead," replied Kapugen. "I found her on the other side of the river."

"That is good, all right," said Flossie Oomittuk.

"Do you still want to inoculate the others?" Kapugen asked.

"Yes," the vet answered. "We don't know how many she infected before she went down. They all need inoculations. Join Julie and Peter. We'll need all three of you to help. I am numbering the wolves and will assign each of them to one of us so we don't all shoot at the same wolf."

The copter circled far away from the wolves to give Kapugen time to cover the distance to Julie and Peter. He decided to ski to save time.

"While we've got them knocked out," Jeremy said to Flossie, "we could get the alpha male wolf for Dr. Hardy."

"What's he want an alpha for?" Flossie asked.

"He wants to observe the heart rates of a leader and a subordinate to see if the roles they play make any difference in stress on the heart."

"That's important research," said the vet.

"Why?" asked Agiaq, one of the dart-gun men.

"Animal studies tell us a lot about humans," Flossie answered. "It's pretty hard to put a president in a room with a subordinate and put monitors on their hearts, but wolves can give us insight. They have a society very much like our own. They have presidents and vice presidents, talented ones with rank and ne'er-do-wells with no rank—like we do."

"Seems like a leader sure wouldn't be nervous with an underling," said Agiaq.

"It does, but you don't know for sure until you run a scientific experiment," said the vet.

Jeremy looked down at the tundra. "It would be nice to get Dr. Hardy an alpha," he repeated. "He's a good man, and he's been trying to capture one for years. I'd like to help him."

"But the wolf is our brother," Agiaq said with controlled disapproval in his voice. "We hunt them, but we don't torment them."

"Julie," said Flossie Oomittuk, "do you hear me?"

"I hear you, Flossie. Kapugen is here with me and Peter. We are ready."

"We are going to land behind the wolves and shoot them with the tranquilizing drugs. They should run toward you. We will follow them in the copter and note where they fall. You find them and give them the shots.

"Are you ready? Out."

"We are ready. Out."

Jeremy came in low and set the craft gently down.

Each person in the copter took aim at a different wolf, and they pulled the triggers almost simultaneously.

Kapu felt the needle hit him, leaped to his feet, and ran full out in Julie's direction. The others ran when they were shot. Finally they slowed down and fell as the tranquilizing drug took effect. They slumped onto the snow in quiet sleep. The copter rose and came down near three of them.

"Julie," said Kapugen, "inoculate Kapu and the steel-gray one."

"That's Zing," she said.

"Peter, take the rime-gray and smaller black one."

"Aaka and Amy," said Julie. "Amy has had shots."

"Okay, Peter, take the rangy gray wolf, and the one next to him," said Kapugen.

"Raw Bones," Julie said. "The other is Uqaq—she's had her shots too."

Julie and Peter skied quickly to their wolves and inoculated them. Then they skied away, glancing back to see Flossie climb out of the copter and inoculate the last two wolves.

"That's all of them," Julie said. "My beautiful wolves will live."

"That's good, all right," said Peter, picking up the caribou skin and their packs. She and Peter skied back to Kapugen's moose-hunting camp.

"Someday," said Julie when she had closed the tent flaps and tied them, "I would like to find out how the wolves keep rabies from spreading. Flossie says it perplexes her. Whole populations of white foxes are wiped out, but not wolves."

"Maybe they tell each other to stay away from a rabid member of the pack," said Peter. "They are very intelligent."

"They are intelligent," said Julie softly. "I hope Kapu knows I am trying to help him. It is not very pleasant to be darted."

"He knows, all right," said Peter. "Wolves hear other voices."

On the tundra Kapu came out of a deep sleep. He staggered to his feet, lost his balance, and regained it. He blinked. Far away a helicopter clattered into the ether. He seemed to be alone. He scanned the landscape and waited. Presently Aaka stood up and stumbled to him. He licked her face and eyes and cheeks. Zing walked over a rise, shaking his head. One by one the Avaliks awoke and found their way to Kapu.

They sensed something had happened but had no memory of what it was.

Nervously they rubbed their scents on each other to regain their confidence and unity. Then Kapu pranced and wagged his tail, and they all played a game of chase.

"Wooooooo." From the far distance Willow Pup Julie's voice sang the "all's well" song of the wolf. Kapu stopped and let the message sink in. "All's well." Some danger was over. He pressed his big feet on the snow, and with tail relaxed, head high, he led his wolf pack toward the Avalik River.

A cloud dropped snow so dense they could not see. This did not slow their speed. They traveled on by sound and internal compasses. As they jogged along, the tranquilizing drugs wore off and were forgotten.

Pups were coming. Kapu's own pups. Tails swished as the wolf pack came down the embankment to the bench where the whelping den was dug.

Kapu watched a group of caribou in the distance; they moved north as they grazed on moss. The natural flow of the migration had been restored. Once more the females had come out of the mountain passes and crossed the Colville into Avalik land. The pups would be big and fat.

Aaka dug the snow from the den entrance and clawed her way into the chamber. Kapu watched her, his tail wagging. The others made wolf beds on the top of the embankment and looked out across the snowdrifts that were slowly melting in the longer hours of sunlight.

Three sleeps later they were on the move again, noting the thin and disabled herd members, checking the mosses and grasses where the herd would be likely to feed. From time to time they harvested a caribou, then ran again. Occasionally they circled past Kangik and stopped to watch Nutik lead Kapugen's sled dogs. He ran with his head up to say he was proud to be leader. He worked with enthusiasm.

On the first of June Aaka nudged Kapu. He jumped to his feet. Pups! He glanced at the pack and with his eyes signaled them to follow. They were wide awake, waiting to go. Kapu and Aaka took off for the den, tails wagging, mouths open in excitement. Pups!

In the rosy light cast by the midnight sun Aaka gave birth. The firstborn was a male, black and aggressive: Grappler.

Kapu stood at the den entrance until the seventh pup was born—seven fine, healthy pups! When Aaka was resting quietly, he signaled Sweet Fur Amy,

Storm Call, and Zing. They howled the pup-arrival song and raced off to hunt for Aaka.

A few miles beyond the den Kapu felt the ground shake. He knew the rhythm—caribou were stampeding. Quietly, keeping low to the ground, he and his wolves stole within view of the panicking herd. A charging grizzly bear was chasing them.

Kapu saw his opportunity. The bear had the caribou's full attention. Kapu glanced at Sweet Fur Amy and sent a message to Zing and Storm Call, and all broke into a run. They sped into the herd, split off a group, and separated a calf from its mother. The bear saw the frightened calf, changed direction, and rushed it—only to find Sweet Fur Amy rushing him. He turned and ran. She chased him a long distance before she returned to Kapu.

"Bear fun," her whisking tail said. Kapu wagged his tail. Chasing a grizzly bear away from his prey was the height of wolf sport.

The fun over, Kapu got serious. He picked out an animal, and they all pursued it until they were successful.

Before he ate, Kapu left the three wolf hunters at the kill and carried food back to Aaka. She had not eaten the day before the birth. Now she would be hungry. He pushed the food into the den with his nose, and Aaka snatched it into the darkness.

Putting his head on his paws, holding his ears erect, he heard Aaka eat. Then he stretched out on his side and listened to the pups suckling. Every so often his tail wagged furiously.

Suddenly he sat up. A helicopter was hovering out on the tundra. He listened to it circle what he knew was the kill and his hunters. He waited, fearful it would swing over the den, but it did not. It rose high, circled the den area, then headed back toward the ocean.

It was midnight when Kapu returned to the kill finally to eat.

In ten days the puppies' eyes opened and they saw light at the end of the den tunnel. A few days later their ears opened and let in the sounds of their mother and their squirming siblings. No sooner could they see and hear than they began to growl, jump on each other, and fight.

On the day of the summer solstice, when the sun was as high as it would climb at noon and as high as it would be at midnight, the Avalik pups tumbled out of the den onto their Arctic playground. Seven fine pups bounced and growled.

The pack gathered to look them over. They noted Grappler's large body and head—a potential leader. They noted Smiler's friendliness. They approved of Black Lips's alert movements and of Long Face's steadiness, and they liked the two smallest ones, White Toes and Cotton Grass. They were sweet-tempered. They saw no outstanding features on the seventh pup, so she got neither a visual nor a scent name. She would have to go about her life and earn a name for herself.

When the adult wolves had sniffed, measured, and approved of each pup, Aaka led them back into the den—all but Grappler. He stayed outside to dig a hole. Sweet Fur Amy did not approve of this. Pups must obey the alpha female. She picked him up by the scruff of the neck and put him down in the den entrance. Aaka disciplined him with a growl-bark and herded him underground.

This was the debut of the wolf pups, their coming-out party. Each adult wolf had looked them over and noted their personalities. Some were strong, some were pleasant, some were quiet, but all were wonderful.

The debut was also the signal that the pups were being weaned. Solid food was needed.

Ceremony over, Kapu broke into the hunt howl, then ran off toward the Upper Colville River. He and his pack had culled out the weak and sick caribou near the den, and the ones that remained were too swift to catch. It was time to hunt farther afield in accordance with the plan of the wolf and the caribou.

Zing, Sweet Fur Amy, and Storm Call followed their alpha. They left the coming-out party and sped across green grass and blue moss. Lichen and Raw Bones trailed behind.

Uqaq did not go. Aaka had signaled her to stay with the pups. When she was nicely settled with them, Aaka took off. She leaped up the embankment to the tundra and ran like a winged creature until she was out of sight of the den. She was free. The pups no longer needed her every minute, day and night. Ears up, nose taking in the wonderful scents of blueberries and rabbit trails, Aaka exercised her leg and back muscles. She stretched her neck, shook her fur, and ran ten miles before turning back to Uqaq and her puppies.

The hunters did not turn back. They trotted at a constant, steady pace for one sunny day and one sunny night. This brought them to their Upper Colville River border. Kapu howled to tell the Mountain Pack they had arrived. Two strange wolves answered. Kapu howled again, then cocked his head to listen for Snow Driver and Cloud Berry. They did not answer. Nor did Ice Blink.

Kapu sniffed the air, whimpered his worried note, and scent marked the border. He walked away, came back, and scent marked again. Zing observed the crick of concern in Kapu's tail and stuck out his tongue to taste the scents on the air. A disturbing odor alerted him. Ice Blink had carried it, and Kapu had once kept her from joining the pack because of it. Worried, Zing too cricked his tail and marked the border.

Nervous about the change of power across the river, the Avaliks spread out and jogged along their border, marking it generously.

At midnight Kapu was about to go north when he heard snarling in the no-wolf zone. Up the embankment, out of the little willow forest, and over the Avalik border came a wild-eyed wolf drooling and panting.

Kapu waited for the Avalik border to stop him. It did not. The wolf came on. Kapu growled, "Stay where you are." The mad wolf did not. Kapu rose to his full height and roared out an avalanche of exploding growls. He flashed the white fangs under his black lips, stating his great power. He postured, "I am the alpha—obey."

The disease was driving the Mountain Pack wolf to do the unforgivable—attack an alpha. But the wolf who loomed before him was the most powerful wolf he had ever seen. His voice was deeper than the rumble of a glacial avalanche. He appeared to be as big as a grizzly bear. Thousands of years of wolf law held the mad wolf back. He cringed in agony before this thunderous alpha.

Kapu relaxed when he saw the wolf lower himself. That was a mistake. The wolf lunged. Kapu postured more strenuously. His fur rose higher, his teeth glistened more threateningly, his eyes narrowed, and once more he kept the rabid animal from biting him. Moments passed, then many minutes. Kapu trembled from exhaustion but held his advantage.

Suddenly a seizure shook the Mountain Pack wolf, and tortured for water he needed but could not drink, he charged once more. Kapu reared and the grasses trembled as he rumbled, "Stay."

Paralysis struck the rabid wolf to the ground; he yelped but could not move at all.

Kapu held his posture until life drained from the Mountain Pack wolf, then walked quickly away. Wolf society had defeated the disease. A strong leader was mightier than the virus.

Kapu returned to his pack but did not rest. A caribou was swimming frantically to his side of the river, headed right for the Avaliks. He puzzled over this for no more than an instant. A helicopter was circling the far side of the Colville, and Kapu recognized it. Its engine sound matched exactly the one he had heard before the dart had hit him. He started off for the den. Already his pack members were ahead, running as fast as they could toward home. They too recognized the copter.

The copter came on, then swerved, speeded up, and followed the Avaliks.

"There he is—that big black one. He's the alpha male."

"I'll run him down."

Kapu saw the copter coming toward him. He ran, ears back, tail down. The machine came on. He zigged. The copter zigged. He was being pursued. With the details of his territory vividly in mind, he turned completely around. He ran. It took the copter several minutes to maneuver a turn. Kapu noted that. When the thunder beater was almost overhead, he turned again. While the copter swung in a wide arc, Kapu headed for the fog rising off a sun-warmed pond. He trotted into the mist.

"Did you see where he went?"

"No. Lost him when we turned. He was running north when I last saw him, probably headed for the den."

"Where is it?"

"I don't know. I tried to get it out of Julie, but she wouldn't talk."

"Of course not."

The copter circled the rugged foothills, with their swales and threads of mist, then disappeared to the north.

Hours later Kapu caught up with his pack, who were milling in confusion during his absence. He tossed his head, and they quickly organized themselves and ran on.

Not far from the Avalik River, the wolves came upon a grizzly kill and shared his bounty in accordance with the laws of the wilderness. The bear would share their kills. The Avaliks were not bashful—each swallowed a huge amount of the food. There were seven pups to be fed.

As the wolves came to the top of the embankment, the pups saw, smelled, and heard the family. They pranced up to greet the adults and bounced, jumped up and down, and ran in circles. They followed the pack to the playground, running in and out between their legs.

The pup Long Face kept sniffing the air. Wonderful, mouthwatering food was somewhere in the midst of the adults, but where? Although he had never eaten meat before, he had seen his mother gobble it. He followed a meat trail to Kapu's mouth. He whimpered. Kapu turned his head away. Long Face stuck his nose in the corner of the mouth, where the food smelled strongest, and with that he signaled Kapu to feed him. Kapu regurgitated the food and put it on the ground. Long Face did not dally. He took a chunk in his mouth and swallowed it whole. Two other pups saw what was happening and stuck their noses in other adults' mouths. They, too, were rewarded.

When Aaka and Uqaq saw the pups eating whole food, they ran to the bear kill and returned with belly treats. Aaka fed the pups willingly, but Uqaq was reluctant. She wanted the food for her puppy self and held her jaws tightly closed. Then Grappler poked the corner of her mouth very hard, and the button went off. Up came the food.

By the end of June the pups were running in a pack. A tight little knot of legs, ears, and tails went down the embankment, along the beach, and back up to the den. Occasionally Smiler bumped into Grappler and the big pup growled. Smiler gave him a little space but not too much. The need for space had to be balanced with the need to move together. In mere days the pups achieved a perfectly coordinated puppy ballet—no one hitting another, all dashing, turning, and leaping to some inherited cue.

And then a strange thing happened. Despite Grappler's size and energy, the puppy pack began to follow Long Face. He was a pleasant pup who took up for the weaker ones. He defended little White Toes and Cotton Grass against the mob, and pushed Grappler away to let Black Lips eat. Leadership, the pups had discovered, is more than size and fearlessness. Compassion is what separates out the true leader, and so the pups followed caring Long Face.

The pups returned home one morning after digging a big hole. They collapsed on the playground, panting to cool off. Kapu was stretched out on his bed on the embankment top. He opened one eye and thumped his tail to greet them. Then a sound reached his ears and he was wide awake. He stood up. Quietly he walked down the embankment to the water's edge.

Willow Pup Julie came around the bend. She smiled and sat down on the beach some distance away. He lay down on his belly. They looked at each other. Finally she spoke.

"I've come to see your puppies, Kapu," she said. "It is that time of year." She put her chin in her hands, her elbows on her knees, and waited.

Kapu looked away. He knew why she was there, but he was not ready to honor her request. Right now

he did not want Willow Pup Julie to lay eyes on the most precious part of himself. Julie knew this. She picked up a stone and studied it.

"Peter Sugluk's group," she said in her soft voice, "won another dance prize. This one was Alaska's state prize, and he was the best of all the dancers."

Kapu heard the affection in her voice and relaxed. She talked on. "He won because he was you. He was magnificent just like you, and I missed you."

Kapu inched toward her. She sighed.

"Peter Sugluk and I still cannot get married." She tossed the stone. "He is going to school, and school is expensive." Kapu listened to the wistful longing in her voice.

"I will go to school, too. We need lots of money to live as husband and wife. I will study to be an animal biologist." She picked up another stone.

"Because of you I want to learn mammalogy. Dr. Hardy will teach me after school while I'm in high school. He is the science professor of the Iñupiat College in Barrow. So will Dr. Flossie Oomittuk, the veterinarian. They know a lot about animals, all right.

"I will live in Barrow with a schoolteacher friend of Ellen's, but I will come back to visit Amaroq and Nutik often. And I will look for you and call you." She was quiet while she thought for a minute.

"It seems strange to study animals in books—and in a town far away from them." Julie looked from the stone to Kapu's clear yellow orbs. He was looking directly at her. She noticed his rich black fur and how smoothly it lay on his muscular body. She noted his size and posture. He was half again bigger than she remembered. Alpha male wolves grow even after other members of their pack stop, and Kapu was no exception. Well aware of his stature, he held himself like the king he was.

"You have become a great leader like your father," she whispered. They both looked away and watched a leaf twisting in the wind.

After a while Kapu got to his feet. Julie got to her feet and walked quietly toward him. He waited for her. He was ready to take her to his pups. They climbed the embankment to the flower-edged playground.

"Kapu," she whispered, "they're wonderful. Ee-lie, Kapu, they're so cute." She dropped to all fours. The pups looked at her, then quickly at Kapu and Aaka. Their parents were not frightened. They looked at Uqaq, who was making a big fuss over Julie, her human mother. She even picked up a bone and gave Willow Pup Julie a toy.

"Good, Uqaq," Julie said and, pulling hard on the bone, played tug-of-war with her friend.

The pups looked from Uqaq to the other adults. They sent out no fear signals. Smiler sniffed Julie and edged closer. The seventh pup, now known as Nameless Moonlight, twisted her head to see better, and Grappler sat down. Long Face walked right up to her.

Julie bent over and sniffed him a wolf greeting. He sniffed her nose right back. One by one the others came up and greeted her. And each smelled the faint scent of Avalik about her. She was all right. Then Long Face wagged his tail and brought her a bone as a gift. She tucked it into her parka.

"Where's Amy?" she asked. Hearing her name, Sweet Fur Amy came to the top of the embankment with Storm Call.

"He's a fine one," Julie said, looking at the white puffs above the eyes of Storm Call and the dark-gray line down his nose. His cheeks and chest were like snow, his paws enormous.

"Where is Zing?" He too heard his name and stood up.

"And Silver? I don't see Silver." She did not appear. The wolves stared at Julie as if she should know.

For his part, Raw Bones hid in a blueberry patch.

Presently Julie got to her feet and walked down the embankment to the river shore. There she stopped and looked back.

Kapu was watching her from the top of the embankment. Raw Bones, feeling safe now that she was leaving, slunk to Kapu's side. Lichen squeezed in between the two and stared at Julie.

"Kapu," she said, "Aaka, Zing, Amy, Amy's friend, Uqaq, Raw Bones, his friend, and seven pups. My pack." She threw them a kiss and backed away.

"Silver is gone," she said to herself. "I am sad. Silver and I shared sorrow. We mourned together for Amaroq when he was killed. We nursed Kapu back to health when he was shot. I miss my beautiful friend."

She sang,

"Silver, Silver, you are out on the tundra,
Fly to the grasses,
Fly to the lemmings,
Fly to the foxes and owls,
Fly to the grizzly,
Fly to the caribou,
And then you'll come back to your grandpups.
That is how it is.
Fly to your beautiful grandpups."

The wolves listened until a shifting wind carried her voice toward the ocean and she was out of sight.

With that they went back to their wolf work.

July is a busy time on the tundra. Baby birds flew, flowers bloomed, and young mammals bounced about. Butterflies flew to flowers and sipped their nectar. They held their wings at a tilt to catch the direct rays of the slanting Arctic sun and keep warm.

The pups were almost half grown. The time had come for wolf pup graduation.

On a bright day when the fuzzy fledglings of the water pipits were testing their wings, and the puppies were spilling out of the den to sleep in the doorway and on the playground, Aaka gave Kapu the signal: "It's time to go." By the rosy light of the midnight sun the Avalik pups graduated from the whelping den. They followed their pack northeastward.

Eventually they came to the summer rendezvous, an open tunnel on the top of a bluff above the Ikpikpuk River not far from the ocean. Down the slope lived an Arctic fox couple and their six bluish pups. A wolverine family denned in a swale nearby, and below the cliff on the gravel bars were nesting plovers, gulls, arctic terns, and jaegers. Multitudes of geese and ducks nested in the grasses at the edge of the river. Life had exploded in the sunny Arctic summer. The wolf pups watched everything that moved, played wolf pup jokes on unsuspecting tundra citizens, and stalked each other. They got into yipping and yowling fights, which Aaka and Kapu settled with sharp barks and nips.

One morning a helicopter flew overhead and the summer community disappeared from view. Jeremy Smith and Dr. Flossie Oomittuk were flying to Anaktuvuk Pass to inoculate the villagers' dogs against rabies. Jeremy spoke.

"Dr. Hardy still wants an alpha male wolf."

"I thought he had given that up," Dr. Flossie Oomittuk said, as if she hoped he had. Her tone ended the conversation. They looked down on the river and tundra. No wildlife was to be seen.

"I wish copters weren't so noisy," said the vet.

"Yeah, we miss a lot in this bus," said Jeremy. "But we also pick up a lot. We can pursue. I once wore down a wolf chasing him with this thing, and before he could catch his breath I darted him."

Flossie Oomittuk did not reply.

Nothing moved on the river clifftop until the helicopter had passed out of sight and sound. First a few birds went back to their young, then many. The foxes tiptoed out of hiding, and Long Face emerged from the open-ended tunnel. Not knowing about copters, he immediately led the pups on a tundra run. The nursemaid, Uqaq, cricked her tail and barked,

"Stay!" but the pups had no intention of obeying her. The day was bright, and wild things were flying and hopping everywhere. Uqaq barked again and again, but to no avail. When, at last, the pups disappeared into a swale, she picked up a bone in frustration and ran in circles with it.

Curiosity was driving the pups. No sooner had they chased a young weasel into its den than Long Face saw a gyrfalcon alight on the clifftop. He led an expedition to investigate it.

The stunning white falcon saw seven pups coming toward her and flew to her barely feathered nestlings. They sat on a ledge almost halfway down the high, steep cliff. Long Face looked down and saw them. He pursued, carefully manipulating the incline, his siblings behind. The falcon flew, climbed high above the pups, and folded her wings. She dove headfirst at the pack, strafing them with her talons and wings. Black Lips yelped and stumbled against Nameless Moonlight. Both lost their footing and plunged out of sight. The falcon struck again and Long Face took a blow on the shoulder. Instantly he came to his senses. He led a fast retreat.

When the pups had thundered back to the summer rendezvous, Black Lips and Nameless Moonlight were not with them. Aaka and Kapu immediately tracked the expedition back to the steep cliff. Far below on the rocks jaegers were screaming and feasting. The scent from their meal told of the tragedy. The parents howled in grief.

Kapu did not go back to the summer rendezvous. He signaled the pack and trotted inland. The clifftop was not healthy for pups who were not perfectly coordinated.

He stopped at a site that satisfied his wolf need to be the surveyor of the land. It was the top of a frost heave with a view in all directions. Aaka dug a pup bed behind a line of tundra grass tussocks. She did not dig a hideout tunnel, since the pups soon would be running with the pack.

The sun set in August, and the hours of darkness, though brief, chilled the air. A change set in. The caribou became restless. Birds took directional readings on the sun and pointed their beaks south. The Avalik pups were wiser but still impetuous.

Aaka kept a sharp eye on them. One evening she stared out across the tundra. The pups followed her gaze. There walked a grizzly bear. The pups were thrilled. Aaka read on. The bear's body language told her she had a cub. The pups could not read such tundra messages yet, and they tore off to see her. Aaka gave the alarm bark. Cotton Grass stopped.

Long Face, Grappler, Smiler, and White Toes did not. They ignored her warning and enthusiastically raced to the bear.

As they neared, a cub came out of a berry patch and bounced to his mother, who was glaring at the wolf pups. She let them come rollicking up, yipping and sniffing. When they were very close, she swung her huge paw. Smiler went flying into the air, then White Toes. She missed Grappler with the next blow and charged.

Suddenly fangs were set into her leg as Kapu took hold. At her armpit was Aaka. Zing and Storm Call danced before her while Raw Bones and Sweet Fur Amy dashed between her and the pups herding them back to safety.

Enraged by the pain, the half-ton grizzly rose to her hind feet. She swung her huge paws. The wolves let go, hit the ground, and dashed at her. She backed up, saying, "I surrender."

The bear snarled, her mouth wide open. The wolves flashed their teeth and breathed nasal threats, and the conflict ended. The grizzly turned and ran off with her cub.

The Avaliks whimpered and circled their dead pups, howling so long and pitifully that it seemed their hearts would break. But life went on. Kapu and

Aaka gently led Long Face, Grappler, and Cotton Grass back to the rendezvous.

Kapu lay down and crossed his forepaws. The wilderness was testing his pups. Four had lost the battle for wolf survival. "That is how it is," the Eskimos say, and in his way, so did Kapu. He lifted his eyes and focused on the living. Geese were flocking, and the ducks were back from the inland ponds with their new wing feathers. Ice crystals tickled his nose. He arose, and howling his deep minor note, he slid up an octave and held it there. The pack harmonized with him. It was time to take up the wandering life of the wolf.

The Avaliks jogged west looking over the caribou herds that were slowly moving south. Their rutting season was nearing and the bulls were collecting harems as they moved toward the forests. They held their big antlers high to display their power. In October they would not even eat, so intense would be their battles for mates. Now they were chasing each other in short spurts. Kapu took advantage of their preoccupation.

He split up a milling herd and isolated an old bull, who had a deep head wound from a rival's antler. He isolated a female with infected legs. He chased several calves and noted their good health. Three of his pups were alive and needed to be fed.

Kapu busied himself and the pack taking inventory of their herd. Winter was coming. The wolves took off.

As they ran, Kapu memorized the whereabouts of the ground squirrels, lemmings, hares, grizzly bears, moose, mice, and weasels. He noted the mosses and grasses that would soon be covered with snow. To these the caribou would come in winter. He noted the storm clouds and winds. All this knowledge became part of him.

Kapu and his pack were the stewards of their part of the Arctic tundra and as good stewards checked on its productivity.

In wind and ice storms and aching cold they traveled. Behind Kapu ran Zing, then Aaka and Lichen. Sweet Fur Amy trotted a little to Kapu's side, tasting the air for distant scents. Storm Call jogged in her shadow, followed by Uqaq. Tagging behind, listening and learning, came Long Face and Grappler. Raw Bones and Cotton Grass trod off to one side as the pack worked its way to the Nuka border.

Kapu stopped them at the no-wolf zone. He listened. A wolf had called to him. By his voice he knew he was not a Nuka. He was a traveler from the mountains. The lone wolf called again, his voice as melodic as a winter storm. To Kapu he was Wind Voice, a two-year-old. His birth pack was beyond the Mountain

Pack. He had traveled three hundred miles looking for a home. He was big, alert, and calm. Kapu read all this and invited him across the border for pack approval. Such a fine specimen should not be left for the Nukas. The Avaliks invited him into the pack. Wind Voice rubbed his scent into their ambrosia and proudly galloped off with his new family.

Twelve spirited Avaliks arrived outside Kangik on a cold September day. Men were packing sleds for the hunting season; their dogs were barking. A wet snow was being driven before a wind that was breaking the new ice on the Avalik River into chunky froth. The pack rubbed cheeks and bodies, exchanged scents, and howled.

Sweet Fur Amy broke away and loped to her viewing knoll. Her nose separated the multitude of scents. She identified dogs, whale meat, fish, people, oil, but not Nutik. She moved closer to the green house. A careful scenting told her Nutik was not there, nor were Julie, Kapugen, Ellen, or Amaroq.

She returned to the pack and through her lack of enthusiasm relayed the news. The green house was empty. Kapu led them away.

Running effortlessly through the snow, the Avaliks traversed their territory. They ran over frozen ponds and stopped to investigate snow machine tracks and snowshoe hare burrows. Eventually they wound up at their western border again.

Kapu had not tallied the Nukas when he was last here. He initiated a howl. The Avalik music had grown from an ensemble to an orchestra. Kapu's voice had deepened with his strengthening role, and Amy's clear voice had brightened. Aaka's howl was warmer and more melodious. Wind Voice added a rising portamento to the chorus. Everyone sang out in rich tones that spoke of the contentment and security of this well-ruled pack.

The Nukas answered. The alpha female, Moon Seeker, harmonized with a new mate. Low Wind was missing. Only five wolves answered, not nine.

Storm Call asked his relatives for the roster again.

Moon Seeker led off. By the end of the howl, Storm Call recognized only his mother and one brother. The others were wolves who had been invited into the pack. There was no shortage of food. Some tragedy had befallen the Nukas. Had the curse of Ice Blink traveled to this pack?

Kapu briefly scent marked the borders, scratched messages of no-trespass on the ground, and headed out for the Upper Colville River, where they howled to the Mountain Pack.

Their message went unanswered. The only sounds

were the distant bellows and roars of the caribou in the taiga. The rut was in full swing.

The Avaliks would not be challenged if they went over the border, but Kapu did not cross. He stopped at the no-wolf zone and rested his pack in the snow. Each groomed his or her fur with tongue and paws, and freshened ruffs with a roll in the snow.

Raw Bones grew restless. His home was a jog away. He yearned to return to it. As he started off, Kapu stopped him with a growl. The mad wolf was still in his mind. He led his pack away from the river.

The Avaliks wandered on, camping in old sleeping sites established by Silver and Amaroq and Amaroq's parents before them. At one site Uqaq found a bone toy and teased Cotton Grass with it until she broke down and played tug-of-war with her. Uqaq still loved being a puppy.

An early blizzard screamed in from the Arctic Ocean. Well fed and lazy, the Avaliks curled up near the Upper Colville. Noses buried in their tails, they watched the land and sky turn white.

Raw Bones got up, shook, and called to the Mountain Pack. The others listened for an answer, their eyebrows twitching under piles of snow. There was no reply.

After the storm ended, and hearing no voices in Raw Bones's old territory, Kapu decided to take it over. He led the Avaliks across their border, through the no-wolf zone, into the land of the Mountain Pack that had once belonged to Raw Bones. Each Avalik checked for wolves.

Raw Bones sped off to his den. Only a wolverine was there. Kapu went up the mountain. No wolves. Zing and Lichen checked along the river. They found only moose. Aaka, Amy, and Uqaq trotted over the low hills, and Storm Call and Wind Voice investigated the alders on the shore. Long Face took Cotton Grass and Grappler on a circular sniffing expedition. No wolves. The Avaliks were puzzled but eagerly enlarged their territory. Only Kapu and Sweet Fur Amy knew what had happened to the Mountain Pack. A faint stench of the rabies virus clung to the ground around their summer rendezvous.

Finding no alpha wolf to fight, Raw Bones ran his old trails. As he raced along the river and into the forest, his sense of power returned. He came down from his den that night and charged Kapu. Thoroughly bored by the ever-striving Raw Bones, Kapu simply stood up and loomed above him. He was once again bigger than Raw Bones. Obediently the would-be usurper gave up.

They traveled foothills, climbed mountains, and crossed creeks that drained out of the Brooks Mountains and never met another wolf.

When the Arctic night came to northern Alaska, the Avalik Pack were keepers of an enormous territory and Kapu was their wise and benevolent leader. He cared for them, watched over them, and led them to wholeness.

In late January Kapu walked to a knoll and looked down on the Ikpikpuk River. He was back on his father's original land. The breeding season was approaching—new pups—new enthusiasms. He lifted his head to sing when a helicopter clattered into the soundscape. He listened, ready to run, but the copter did not seek him out. It flew up the river and landed on the frozen Ikpikpuk, and he heard it no more.

The sky grew brighter. A glowing arc of yellow burned the eastern sky. Throwing back his head, Kapu called his pack to assemble. As they gathered around him, an orange fireball rose over the horizon. The sun was up again. A new year was beginning. The Avaliks pointed their noses to the sun and sang. They sang for many minutes, flooding the tundra with the most beautiful of all wilderness music—the call of the wolf to the new sun. Kapu sang a last note: "Let's run." Springing off his back feet, he vaulted down the knoll.

Fur rippling, the pack spent the next several hours running old family trails and sprinting after swift young caribou. When the caribou were out of sight, they trotted westward and looked at the musk oxen. In good spirits they circled back to the Ikpikpuk on their frozen river trail.

Suddenly Kapu buckled in the air and fell. He made no sound.

His foot was caught in a trap. He looked at the iron lock on his paw, got up, ran, and flipped in the air at the end of the chain. He lay still. The pack gathered around him staring at their helpless leader. They sniffed the trap, the chain, and the human scent that lay on the overturned snow. Aaka whimpered. Sweet Fur Amy bit the chain. Raw Bones dug at the base of the stake to which the chain was fastened. Storm Call and Wind Voice watched for the enemy. The loving wolves were in numb distress.

A snow machine roared in the distance, grew closer, and suddenly shot around the bend in the river. The wolves vanished into the low brush on the riverside. With a sled in tow two men climbed out of the machine and stopped short of the growling Kapu.

"What luck," said the Eskimo trapper, Benjamin

Ooglik. "He's in fine shape. Only been in the trap a few minutes. Pure black, too. He will make a fine parka ruff."

"No ruff out of this one," said Jeremy Smith forcibly. "He's the alpha male wolf of the Avalik Pack. My good friend Dr. Hardy wants him alive."

"Alive? Why is that?"

"For a medical study," answered Jeremy. Stepping back from Kapu, he shot a tranquilizing dart into his thigh. Kapu twitched but did not utter a sound. He clawed the snow until the drug took effect and he slumped into sleep. Jeremy opened the trap and examined the huge paw.

"Good trap. He's not even bruised."

"I told you so," said Ooglik. "Foam padding is good, all right."

They wrapped Kapu in a cargo net, tied him to the sled, and drove back to the copter near Benjamin Ooglik's house.

As soundless as falling snow, the wolves floated out of the brush and stood above the empty trap site.

The Avaliks had lost their great leader. Tragedy had called their name.

Part III

Sweet Fur Amy, The New Alpha

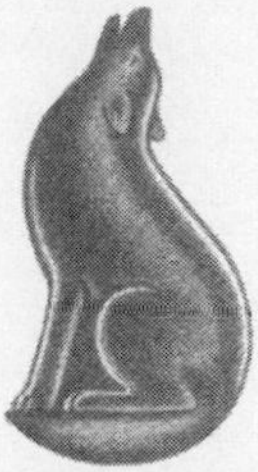

The sun stayed up less than an hour that first day of its return—the day that Kapu vanished. When it set, the afterglow colored the white snowscape rose, violet, and then sea blue. The wolves milled shadowless around the cold spot where their leader had been.

They waited. He was not dead. There was no blood scent to say he had been killed. There were no tracks to say he had run away. He would be back. They called to him and waited for an answer. None came. They howled once more.

An Eskimo and his son, snowshoeing home after checking their trap line, heard the heartbreaking lost-alpha call of the wolves. Not knowing its meaning, they smiled.

"Good sound," said Akvik, the father. "The wolves are like us. They hunt in families. We are cousins." The Avaliks howled again.

"The tundra is all right," said his son, Nagiak. "The wolves are here. They take the sick and leave us the well." They hauled on their trapping sled and strode into the darkness.

The Avaliks called, off and on, until the sun came up at noon the next day; then they were silent. Each looked at the others waiting for someone to do something. They knew they must move on, but no wolf had the power to lead them. Kapu was gone. The pack was totally disabled.

It was Zing who finally acted. He went out on the frozen river to find Kapu. Lichen, Aaka, and Grappler followed.

That sparked Sweet Fur Amy to search up the mountainside with Storm Call and Uqaq. Raw Bones, seeing the pack break up, headed out for the Colville River. Eventually they all returned to the vanishing spot, even Raw Bones. There they waited. When a wolf leader is lost, the pack is lost. They broke up into smaller teams and hunted the moose and caribou that were bogged down in the snow.

After three weeks, Aaka felt a need to return to her den. Zing, Lichen, and Long Face followed the female alpha of the Avaliks. Sweet Fur Amy, Storm Call, Wind Voice, and Uqaq went up the river. Raw Bones, Grappler, and Cotton Grass took off for the foothills. The pack splintered into small pieces without their leader.

Before the Raw Bones team left the valley, another trap snapped and Grappler was caught. Cotton Grass lay down on her belly near her brother while Raw Bones stood back barking, ordering her to follow him. When she did not obey, he walked slowly back to join her and the struggling Grappler.

A snow machine buzzed in the distance. Raw Bones turned and sped away in terror. Cotton Grass caught his fear fever and ran after him. Far away from Grappler and the machine they slowed down and looked at each other. Even young Cotton Grass knew what the trap meant. Another Avalik was dead. Raw Bones whimpered. The pack that had been supporting him had fallen apart. Its leader was gone. Raw Bones didn't want to be on his own another moment. He lifted his nose and howled, "I'm here, where are you?" Cotton Grass joined him. From far away Aaka, Lichen, Long Face, and Zing answered. From another direction Sweet Fur Amy, Storm Call, Uqaq, and Wind Voice howled, "Here, here, here." The three groups called back and forth, trotted toward each other, howling until they met.

Ten Avaliks licked cheeks on a wind-packed land rise between the den and Kangik. They wagged tails and whimpered. Cotton Grass's pained cry told them another pup had failed the hard test of a wolf's first year of life. They sang for Grappler, milled around, ran off in their splinter groups, and came back together.

Without Kapu they were lost. Raw Bones at last saw his opportunity to become alpha.

Sweet Fur Amy smelled prey and signaled her group to follow her. She jogged off on the scent of a lone caribou. Raw Bones eagerly joined her. Cotton Grass, Aaka, and Zing came along.

Three miles along, when the prey was in sight, Sweet Fur Amy sent her hunters to the right and left of it. The animal was in a wind-cleared area where a caribou could run well. She and Kapu usually drove prey toward deep snow to slow it down. She signaled Raw Bones to her side. He ignored her. He would lead. He ran full out for the caribou. It turned back to the hard-packed meadow, quickly got up speed, and outran Raw Bones and the pack.

Sweet Fur Amy trotted on. When she scented an old cow, she took the lead again. Aaka and Zing came with her. Snarling Raw Bones ran into first place. To Raw Bones females were the alphas of the pups and of social interactions and, in Sweet Fur's case, of finding the game—but she was not and would never be the alpha of the kill. He ran ahead of her. She swept ahead of him. He nudged her off the trail. She snapped at him. Zing, trotting in second place, watched passively. He was content with his role as vice president. He had held this position for so many years, he could not change. Wind Voice ran with Zing.

When Raw Bones passed Sweet Fur Amy again, the caribou saw him and fled. Amy, by raising her head and tail above his, sent Raw Bones to the rear. Head down, tail lowered, he stayed there.

Two hours later they felled an arthritic bull, and Sweet Fur Amy ate first. She was not hesitant. She had been chosen by her father to lead the hunts, and now that he was gone, she was the leader of the Avaliks.

For six weeks they followed her, but loosely. The pack was made up of strong individuals, and they were still disorganized as they tried to make their own packs. But obedience to the leader was in their genes, and Sweet Fur Amy slowly brought the pack into harmony.

The month of March came, the only time of year that female wolves can breed. Sweet Fur Amy refused Storm Call's invitation. Pups would confine her to the den for two weeks, and her leadership was not secure enough for that. Without her the pack would fight and break apart. She needed every member.

Raw Bones, knowing pups were strength and ignoring wolf custom, approached submissive Uqaq. It is, however, the female who decides whose traits will be passed on to her pups. Uqaq snapped at Raw Bones and ran off with the handsome Wind Voice.

Pups!

Sixty-three days later the pups were due. Raw Bones took over. He wanted pups, any pups, to be born on his own territory. In a fierce battle he fought off youthful Wind Voice and, with coaxing and sweet whimpers, led Uqaq to the Colville River den. Sweet Fur Amy could not make Uqaq obey her and stay at the Avalik den. Raised in captivity, Uqaq had never learned the birthing laws of the wolves, and she followed her father. Wind Voice took his place behind them.

Sweet Fur Amy took the rest of her pack to the shabby den on the Upper Colville River. Her nieces and nephews must have a society to grow up in.

Raw Bones cleaned and reconstructed the battered den while Wind Voice watched in confusion, not understanding the strange rules of his new pack.

The next night nine pups were born. Excitement ran high. Pups! The Avaliks mingled, rubbed scents, licked cheeks. Pups! Their summer work was cut out for them.

Hearing them suckle inspired Sweet Fur Amy, and she organized her allies, Aaka, Zing, Lichen, and Storm Call, into a cooperative hunting team. She took them out each evening to harvest injured calves and ill cows and bring the food many miles to Uqaq. Wind Voice stayed at the den to protect his fatherhood rights from Raw Bones. They fought often.

When the pups were two weeks old, Uqaq became impatient with them. They nursed relentlessly. They fought each other. She could not keep them clean. She did not know how to discipline them. All she wanted to do was get away from them. When she could not take the yelping and suckling another minute, she ran out of the den and down to the river.

She stood with her tail between her legs. She did not know how to be a mother. Her puppyhood had been in human arms, her sustenance a bottle. She had no memory of Silver and how she had cleaned and nursed her. She had been too weak to do anything but whimper and sleep.

Wind Voice barked, telling her to return, but she had never truly bonded with him. She had no knowledge of a father's importance either. She looked at the other side of the river and waded in.

Aaka and Sweet Fur Amy rushed to her. She walked deeper and, catching sight of Raw Bones on the other side of the river, she swam across to him, whimpering and woofing. Even Raw Bones did not know what to do with a mother who deserted her pups. He had not counted on that. He turned and ran. Then Uqaq ran.

Sweet Fur Amy and Aaka watched the strange behavior, then walked through the alders and back to the den. They had a job to do.

The hungry pups waddled out of the nursery whimpering and crying piteously, searching for their mother and milk. They leaped up at Sweet Fur Amy's belly to nurse. They knocked Aaka down and crawled over her. Feeling puppy feet and suckling mouths, her maternal instincts surged through her. She lay as still as she had with her own pups. They suckled her voraciously. Had they nursed her empty teats long enough—several days—she would have produced milk. But Uqaq returned, and the pups abandoned milkless Aaka and swarmed over their mother. Uqaq rolled her eyes, let them nurse a few minutes, then broke away. She swam across the river again.

The pups followed her, sniffed the river, got water up their noses, and yelped in pain. Sweet Fur Amy and Aaka picked them up by the scruffs of their necks and carried them to the den entrance.

Aaka did not have time to let the pups stimulate her mammary glands, and when they had fallen asleep from exhaustion, she and Sweet Fur Amy signaled Storm Call. Messages went from wolf to wolf. Long Face trotted off to find Uqaq; Aaka and Cotton Grass stayed with the pups. Raw Bones sat on a knoll defending his property, and Sweet Fur Amy, Lichen, Storm Call, and Zing went north. Wind Voice kept his eye on Raw Bones.

Sweet Fur Amy and her group traveled in constant sunlight and did not stop until they were on the rise above the green house. Leaving Storm Call and Lichen behind, Amy ran down the incline to Julie's door. Julie was not there. Amy trotted on through the town, passing people who were packing sleds for fish camp. Quick sniffs told her Willow Pup was not among them. She ran up the slope to the Quonset hut. The dogs were gone. Nutik had been tied there, she noted, but he, too, was missing. The sled was gone.

The schoolhouse door was ajar. Sweet Fur Amy looked in and focused her yellow eyes. Amaroq and Ellen were inside. She called to the boy, "I'm your friend," and he stopped scribbling on the blackboard and ran to the front step.

"Come here," he howl-barked happily to Sweet

Fur Amy. She stepped forward, and Amaroq wolf-whimpered a pleasant greeting. Sweet Fur Amy lowered her tail in disappointment. The scent of Willow Pup Julie was faint on the boy. She had not been here for a long time. With a woof-bark she greeted him, then sped like a jaeger's shadow over the tundra to Storm Call and Lichen. Her body language said, "Back to the Colville."

Sweet Fur Amy was on her own. Willow Pup Julie could not help these pups as she had their mother, Uqaq, and Uqaq's brother, Nutik.

Along the route home the wolves stopped at an old frozen kill and packed their stomachs with good food.

They crossed the river, threaded through the dwarf alders, and approached the den.

Growling ferociously, Raw Bones rushed at Sweet Fur Amy. She ignored him—an insult that dropped him to his belly. He groveled to her. Every wolf saw his shame.

Sweet Fur Amy walked to the pups, who were now too weak to suckle. She stood above them waiting to be asked for food with a poke in the corner of her mouth. They were not able to give this signal. They knew only how to nurse. Their pitiful voices weakened.

Sweet Fur Amy leaned down to the pup Big Ears and opened her mouth to let the scent of food pour out. He sniffed and tried to suckle her lips. That misplaced touch did it. Sweet Fur Amy delivered food.

Big Ears licked it, then gulped chunks whole. Owl Feathers, named for the white tufts of puppy fur behind her ears, caught on and touched Storm Call's mouth. Bird Egg, with the rounded head, begged from Lichen. The others were too weak to learn. They whimpered and fell asleep. The three wolves trotted back for more food. This time Wind Voice went with them. Raw Bones was still humbled by Sweet Fur's insult.

Three pups survived: Big Ears, Owl Feathers, and Bird Egg.

One misty day Sweet Fur Amy was coming home through the dwarf alders with pup food when Raw Bones jumped out and grabbed her throat. She angrily twisted him over her back. He let go.

Sweet Fur Amy had had enough of Raw Bones. She fought with her teeth, a rare event among wolves, and he went down for a last time.

Totally humiliated, Raw Bones slunk away. Even his fur clumped in gobs, reflecting his mood. Sweet Fur Amy watched him cross the Colville carrying his tail not only between his legs but up against his belly. He would not be back.

Uqaq, who was still hiding out on the other side of the river, ran to him and begged him to let her join him. He ignored her. He was too low in spirits even to give her an invitation. He had been defeated before, but never on his own territory. To be subdued at his den site was more than defeat. It was living death. No spurt of energy, no fire of purpose could change it.

Uqaq sensed all this and turned back. Raw Bones could not help her.

In late July Sweet Fur Amy moved the pack and the three pups to the Avalik summer rendezvous. Along the way they came upon Raw Bones feeding at one of their old kills. His fur was rumpled and unkempt. His tail was pressed up under his belly. The pack did not run him off the food. Although he was defeated, he was part of the tundra community—the lone wolf surviving on old carcasses and the small mammals the wolves so carefully cultivated. Sweet Fur Amy nosed Owl Feathers, Bird Egg, and Big Ears on down the trail to the bluff above the Ikpikpuk River. The eight older wolves followed them.

One day the copter flew overhead carrying the vet and the pilot to the Eskimo villages to inoculate dogs. The Avaliks lowered their tails and lay down.

"There's Julie's wolf pack," Jeremy Smith said. "You know, I finally got the alpha for Dr. Hardy."

"I know," she said coolly.

"He's finished his research," pilot Smith went on. "The alpha heart rate is normal and steady when he's with a low-ranking member of his society. The omega's heart raced like a jackhammer in the presence of the alpha." Flossie Oomittuk did not comment.

"When he returned them to the captive pack," Jeremy went on, "it worked the other way. The alpha's heart rate went up with the pressure of all his responsibilities, the omega's down. We are learning the effects of leadership on social animals like us."

Flossie listened and stared at the river below.

"What are they going to do with the black alpha now that the experiment is over?" she asked.

"Send him to a zoo."

The helicopter clattered on toward Anaktuvuk Pass.

On the ground Sweet Fur Amy waited until the earshattering sound of the copter had faded, then checked her family. They were all there. No traps had gone off. She sat down and watched the terns and gulls circle over the river.

The days shortened. The permafrost, which had

thawed about eighteen inches during the summer, froze solid again. Sweet Fur Amy felt the messages from the sun and the ground and led her pack off the bluff and out onto the tundra. Owl Feathers, Bird Egg, and Big Ears could have benefited from more pouncing and stalking lessons, but they were wiry and strong like Wind Voice, their father. It was time to teach them how to hunt and to help them learn to avoid the perils of winter. They were full grown but not hunters. They knew nothing about the death blows of caribou and moose; they did not know how to attack or to work with an organized hunting group. It would take all winter to teach them.

That night the Avaliks loped along through falling snow, mouths slightly open in wolf smiles as they melted ice crystals on their tongues. The time of the gypsy wolf was here, and their spirits were high. They moved gracefully, occasionally bounding like dancers and stretching their long legs as far as they could. The land lay flat and silver-gray before them. Winter clouds with their blue-black bottoms scurried above them. Julie's wolves were free and running behind a trim and warmhearted female alpha.

Sweet Fur Amy rested the pups at daylight and urged them on at sundown.

When they reached the banks of the Meade River, Sweet Fur Amy made a longer stop at a sleeping site where Kapu liked to rendezvous. It was close to an overwintering caribou herd and only a night's trot from Kangik. They rescratched old beds, howled a song of wandering and winter, then lay down. The pups flopped without making beds and were instantly asleep. Their underfur had grown so dense with the shortening days that they were now wrapped in warm, thick blankets.

As the moon rose above a low bank of black clouds, the earth began to shake. Sweet Fur Amy awoke. She got to her feet. An enormous herd of caribou was clicking and snorting just over the horizon. Something was wrong. They were moving north when they should be moving south. She strained all her senses.

The hordes were boxing themselves into a land corner. Caribou are leaderless herds, not thinking packs. They had cropped the grasses and lichens in front of them eating their way north. Near the ocean they turned around but could not go south. There was no food in that direction. They had eaten and trampled it all. The trapped caribou were starving.

Hearing the distress in their bleats, Sweet Fur

Amy jumped on her hind feet and signaled the pack—even the pups—to come see what was happening. They raced north to the horizon, stopped, and looked. Sweet Fur Amy picked out a hungry cow and, with Storm Call's cooperation, split her off from the edge of the enormous herd. Using her own style, not Kapu's, she signaled Zing to the left.

Accustomed to Kapu, he misunderstood her and ran straight at the cow. Storm Call, who did understand Sweet Fur, tried to compensate for Zing's mistake. He came in from the left, cutting off Aaka. Confused, Aaka stopped. The cow sprinted away and was lost to scent and sight.

They selected another.

Two days later they still had not eaten. Aaka felt the need to try her skills. After rolling in the snow to clean her fur, then stretching and yawning, she howled the hunt song and sped toward the bleating herd. Zing followed her, happy to be beta to Kapu's female alpha. Long Face followed Zing. Uncle Zing was his role model. He imitated his movements, followed him everywhere, and now joyfully jogged behind him. Cotton Grass trotted behind her brother. To her Long Face was still the alpha pup to follow. He was a regal wolf with his rime-gray fur and dark facial mask, and she adored him. Long Face saw her tracking him and whisked his tail to tell her where to go. Alphaness was growing in him.

Sweet Fur Amy watched Aaka's group depart but did not join them. Her instincts told her she must go back to her first talent—finding the scent of a sick caribou and tracking it down. That was what her pack respected her for, and that was what would bring Aaka back to her. She rounded up Storm Call, Wind Voice, Uqaq, and Lichen and took off. She did not like the feel of having two groups, her mother's and hers. It was not good wolfdom.

On the edge of the big herd she picked up the odor of a young caribou with an advanced leg infection, and she and her hunters easily claimed her. Feeling like an alpha, Sweet Fur Amy howled to announce the feast to her whole pack. They were not long in joining her. Her mother's group stayed somewhat apart. After eating, they slept on separate frost heaves.

Sweet Fur Amy knew what must be done.

A few days later, when the food was eaten, she danced and threw up her head to get their attention, then led them on a run. She was going to circle their territory as her father had done when members were not cooperating. After two weeks they came back to the campsite licking cheeks and mixing scents. They scratched their beds close together. Once more the land had bonded them.

By December the boxed-in caribou were dying. They snorted and bleated in the darkness. When the sun came up in January, thousands were strewn across the tundra. The Avaliks inspected the disaster, but moved away when humans arrived in the area. In planes and helicopters, on snow machines and sleds, they came to study the phenomenon and to figure out what the wolves already knew. Sweet Fur Amy led her pack back to the Avalik River.

In March, when the vernal equinox divided the day into twelve hours of sun and twelve hours of no sun, Storm Call was Sweet Fur Amy's shoulder-to-shoulder companion. He did not just run beside her, he ran close, touching her cheeks, her ears, and her nose. She was coming into estrus, and he would be her mate. Cotton Grass was also coming into estrus. She too wanted this fine gray wolf. She flirted with him, whimpered love notes, and begged him to romp with her. Storm Call ignored her. He and Sweet Fur Amy had been loving friends since the day he had come over the Nuka border. That day they had chosen each other and could not be separated.

They mated when the herds of caribou that had

migrated to the forest in October were on their thundering march north.

Pups! The message shot through the Avaliks' scent system, inspiring whimpers, tail wags, and cheek licks. It also sparked a trip to houseclean the den above the Avalik River.

Sweet Fur Amy enthusiastically cleared out the debris of winter and dug the ancestral nursery doorway wider. The years of excavation had expanded the length of the passageway to almost four feet. After looking over the home, she took it upon herself to enlarge the whelping room. She stopped when she could lie on her side with her feet outstretched. The den was as cold as the permafrost, about eighteen degrees Fahrenheit, but Sweet Fur Amy did not feel the chill through her dense winter underfur, nor would the pups. She would snuggle them into her belly fur. Pups. At last, her own pups.

Sweet Fur crept out of the den, breathed a deep draft of air, and walked to the top of the embankment. The icy world sparkled in all directions around her, and as if to make it prettier, the wind lifted snow and carried it like a scarf over the river. Sweet Fur Amy was at peace. Pups. Storm Call came to her side. She licked his chin and cheek. He was the alpha male and would take her place for about ten days when she disappeared into the nursery to give birth and tend helpless infants.

Suddenly she cocked her head. The wind had changed. On it was information she had not picked up before. She licked far around her nose and muzzle to gather scents and confirm the news.

Without a sound she crossed the snowy tundra and trotted up a slight rise. A white-walled Eskimo hunting tent sat in a swale out of the wind. Heat radiated from it, and as she already knew, Willow Pup Julie and Peter Sugluk were inside. They were talking softly to a third Eskimo, the dancer Steven Itta. He had joined his friends to help them set up camp.

Peter put his arm around Julie. "How can this wonderful thing be happening to us?" he said.

"Ee-lie," she answered softly. "To think the college is paying us to live on the tundra."

"How did this come about?" asked Steven. "I haven't heard the whole story."

"It's a good story, all right," said Julie.

"It began," said Peter, "when Flossie Oomittuk learned Dr. Hardy was going to send Kapu to a zoo.

"She went right to his office and told him that science would be better served if Kapu was released on his territory.

"Then she said, 'You know what an alpha wolf's

heart rate does, but you don't know what happens when an alpha who has been long removed returns to his pack.'"

"'They'll kill him,' said Dr. Hardy.

"'We don't know that,' said Flossie Oomittuk, 'but I do know who could find out.'

"'Who?' he asked.

"'Julie Edwards, your afternoon student,' Dr. Oomittuk said. 'Her father is the famous elder Kapugen. He tells me she lived seven months with the wolves of the Avalik. Your black wolf is their alpha. She calls him Kapu. I took her to see him, and she cried. Then she talked to him in wolf talk. Kapu became very calm when she spoke.'

"'So?' Dr. Hardy asked her. 'What are you suggesting?' And Dr. Oomittuk reminded him that Jane Goodall had lived with wild chimpanzees in the African game preserve of Gombe. She learned all about them. She learned chimpanzees are quite like people—they are jealous, respectful, playful; they love and mourn—and much, much more.

"Then Flossie said, 'We have our own Jane Goodall. She is Julie Edwards. Her Eskimo name is Miyax. She is well known as Julie of the Wolves. She could live on the tundra as she has before and study the wolves.' He was quiet, so she went on talking.

"'We need to know more about wolf society. Wolves are very important. They are our brothers.'

"'You're right,' Dr. Hardy finally said. 'Bring her to my office and we can talk about it.'"

Julie listened to Peter as she pulled off her warm sealskin parka. Her thoughts went back to the day she had gone with Flossie Oomittuk to Dr. Hardy's office. She recalled how he looked out the window at the vast tundra and said, "Flossie wants you to have this job, but I would not go out there by myself. How can I be responsible for sending you?"

Without a moment's hesitation she had said, "Peter Sugluk and I wish to marry. The tundra is our home. Two are safer than one and two can do a better job than one." The professor's face had become thoughtful. Peter Sugluk was well known. He had won the Kivgiq Award. He had herded musk oxen for Kapugen, and he had come from Siberia, where he had lived with his family in the manner of his Eskimo ancestors.

Julie recalled Dr. Hardy folding his hands on his desk and telling her that under those conditions, she had the job. She could still feel her face glow and her heart beat hard as she realized she and Peter could get married and be paid to live as they wanted to live.

With a happy smile she stirred the caribou stew bubbling on the kerosene stove. Steven Itta was packing his sled bag to leave.

"One more question," he said. "My mother will want to know where you were married."

"In my father's house," said Julie. "In Kangik." Her words brought back memories of that day. She recalled the minister from Barrow in his black suit and white collar as he stood in front of the stack of furs. Peter was dressed in a reindeer shirt with an ermine ruff. She was wearing a white Eskimo dress trimmed with rich embroidery from Japan. Ellen and Kapugen wore their dress clothes. Their boots were elaborately decorated with black-and-white calfskin and laced with caribou hide. Amaroq wore the cowboy suit his Minnesota grandmother had sent him, and Nutik sported a beaded collar. A few close friends stood beside Kapugen and Ellen.

Outside, the villagers were waiting until the ceremony was over and Julie and Peter came out to greet them. Then tundra drums throbbed, voices rose in song, and Peter swept Julie up in his arms and kissed her lovingly. As she hugged him back, the villagers began to dance and cheer. Drums beat. He put her down, and breathlessly she slipped her arm around him. Together they greeted the wedding guests. Then the maktak and whale stew were served. The party lasted far into the night, she was told, for she and Peter slipped away early and went out to their tent on the tundra.

"I hope Kapu returns in good spirits," Steven said as he finished a bowl of stew before departing.

Sweet Fur Amy walked restlessly back to her pack.

She had heard the name Kapu.

Snow began falling.

The Avaliks, sparked into play by the swirling flakes, ran out onto the tundra. They pranced and rolled in the clean snow. Storm Call put his cheek and shoulder in it and pushed until he rolled on his back. When he was sweet-clean, he stood up. His tail whisked once, then twice. He could hear the *click-click* of the caribou coming north to their calving grounds. He howled. The pack howled; then, pushing off with a flying leap, their fur blowing and swinging, they trotted out to meet them.

The herd was miles long and miles wide. The Avaliks ran among them, judging them and herding them into little groups. Spring was upon the Arctic tundra.

When her pack had eaten, Sweet Fur Amy led

them off to check out the Nukas. At their border they howled. The Nukas answered. Sweet Fur absorbed their information: eight adults and three adolescents—and they were on Avalik land. They had slunk over the agreed border at the National Petroleum Reserve outpost. Sweet Fur Amy was too pregnant to lead a territorial fight, so she resorted to other wolf weapons. She scratched the ground and lifted her leg to border mark. Then she howled and started a voice contest. The two packs howled back and forth until Sweet Fur Amy conceded them the stolen land. She did not need it. Much of the western calving grounds were hers, as well as Raw Bones's old territory. The Nukas were pleased with the treaty. They howled friendly quips to their relatives Storm Call and Lichen.

Coming home, Sweet Fur Amy made a side trip to the rise that looked down on the green house. Voices murmured.

Ellen was reading aloud to Amaroq. Nutik was curled on the front step with his ears straight up listening to the tundra and the village.

Sweet Fur Amy called to him. He called back but did not move.

The CB crackled.

"Aapa, Daddy," said Julie.

"I hear you, Miyax. Over."

"Amy is very pregnant. The den is ready. The pups will soon be born. It is time to release Kapu. Over."

"Good. I shall get Dr. Hardy on the lab radio. Is Amy there now? Over."

"No, I heard her call from somewhere near you. She likes to talk to Nutik. Take him inside, and she will go home.

"Let me know when Dr. Hardy gets the cage out of Barrow onto the tundra and opens the door. Over."

"Roger. Over and out."

When the Willow Pup Julie voice stopped, Kapugen opened the house door. Amaroq ran out, put his arms around big, handsome Nutik, and led him inside. Sweet Fur Amy waited a short while. Finally she woof-barked and trotted back to the pack. They were waiting for her not far from Kangik.

Then in scent and sound she said, "Pups," and hurried to the den. They followed, kicking up little storms of snow in excitement. The entire pack ran right past Julie and Peter, who were stretched out on caribou skins not far from the den. They were mere residents of the tundra, like the wolverines and grizzly bears.

"Here they come," Julie whispered into a recorder. "Right to the den." Peter watched through binoculars.

"Amy's ears are back," Peter said. "She looks serious."

Julie recorded his words on tape as well as this: "Amy's mate is scanning the tundra. His hackles are up. He looks like he will take on the world to protect his pups."

"Zing is here with his pretty mate," Peter whispered, and pointed down the river.

"Here comes my dear friend Aaka," said Julie. "She is crossing the thawing river. Three pups are with her. They are well-trained adolescents and friendly. They wag their tails a lot and lick Aaka's cheeks.

"Now the handsome stranger we named Strong has joined Aaka and the pups. He is watching them anxiously as they cross the water and ice. They stick close to him and lick his cheeks. He must be their father.

"Alpha Pup, his sister, and now Uqaq are here. They all know that Amy's hour has come."

The tundra was quiet. Sweet Fur Amy paced the playground, avoiding stepping on the tiny sweetpeas that were blooming there. The others lay down, got up, dug beds, and watched her. Soft human voices reached their ears. They paid them no heed, even though the humans were walking upright. Peter went to work to kill time; Julie went into the tent.

"Aapa," Julie said into the CB, "has Kapu been released? Over."

"Well, funny thing, all right," he answered. "We're here inside Avalik territory, and the cage door is wide open, the humans are gone, but he won't leave. He hangs at the very back of the cage. Even food on the ground does not lure him out. Dr. Hardy is watching from a distance. Over."

"That's interesting, all right," said Julie. "I must think about that. Over. Out."

Julie did think about it while Peter Sugluk checked the caribou carcass that he had hung on a rack. He looked at the wolves, decided nothing was happening, and picked up his axe. He climbed down a ladder into the refrigerator he was digging. He worked for a while, then sought Julie.

"We've got to get our food underground," he said. "It's beginning to thaw."

"I don't have much to do until Kapu runs free," said Julie. "I will help you."

The morning passed. Peter Sugluk and Julie worked at the refrigerator. Then at noon Peter carried smoked meat from the tent to a five-by-ten-by-five-foot wooden box on a sled. It stood behind the tent. Inside the box were skins, a kerosene stove, and food containers. Two months from now, when it was cold, he and Julie would hitch this warm home to the snow machine and follow the wolves in winter.

Julie walked out on the embankment thinking about Kapu and watching Sweet Fur Amy.

She went into the tent in the early evening.

"Kapugen, do you hear me? Over."

"I hear you, Miyax," he answered. "Pups? Over."

"Pups soon. Amy is in the den. She has not come out. What about Kapu?"

"Kapu won't leave the cage. Over."

"I have thought of something. Over."

"What is it? Over."

"Remember how Nutik had his own little comfort space behind the water barrel? He would go there when strangers came into the house, and he would feel safe. Over."

"But he eventually came out," Kapugen said. "Kapu has not. Three days have passed. He needs food. Over."

"Cut a hole in the rear of the cage," Julie said. "Humans came in through the front door of the cage to feed him. The front is filled with bad dreams. Open his comfort space to the tundra. Over."

"All right," said Kapugen. "That is good wolf thinking. I'll tell Dr. Hardy. Over. Out."

Julie glanced at the wolf den. Storm Call was snoozing with his head on his crossed paws. Nothing was happening.

She climbed down into the refrigerator with Peter and chipped at the rocklike permafrost with her ulo. Together they made a little progress.

"How do the wolves dig in this?" Peter Sugluk asked, and climbed to the surface to dump a small bucket of the earth and gravel he had chipped away. Suddenly he backed down. "Miyax," he whispered. "The wolves are up. They are restless."

Julie climbed out of the refrigerator and crept toward the den on all fours.

Storm Call was standing at the entrance staring into the darkness. Owl Feathers and Bird Egg stood beside Aaka and Zing on the far side of the playground.

Julie lay still. Snowbirds were sitting on their eggs. Water pipits were circling their nests. Snowy owls were hunting lemmings. At three A.M. Julie spoke into the tape recorder.

"A pup has been born. The father is on his elbows

looking into the den. He is smiling and wagging his tail."

By eight o'clock in the morning six explosive wags of Storm Call's tail had announced six pups.

Pups! Sweet Fur Amy's pups. Owl Feathers lay close to the den entrance, ready to be a baby-sitter. Zing and Lichen ran in circles. Uqaq, Long Face, and Cotton Grass romped to the top of the embankment and chased each other, scratching up the last patches of snow.

The crackling CB brought Julie back to the tent.

"Miyax, do you read me?" Kapugen asked. "I'm back at the Arctic Research Lab in Barrow. Over."

"I hear you, all right, Aapa," Julie said, then quickly added, "Six pups have been born. Over."

"That is good news, all right," said Kapugen. "And I have good news. Your thoughts were right. Dr. Hardy and I cut off the back of the cage. Before we reached the truck, Kapu walked out of the cage and devoured the food we had left for him. Over."

"That is very good. I am so very happy. Kapu is free. Over."

"He was calm," said Kapugen. "He ate the whole meal, then looked about. He seemed to know where he was. Then he walked away. Over."

"He was calm, you say? Over."

"It was as if nearly a year in a laboratory had never happened. He walked, then trotted. His radio collar says he is going right straight for the Avalik River den. He's yours now. Over. Out."

"Kapu," Julie whispered. "Kapu's coming home." Her eyes glistened with unspilled tears.

She sat on her caribou skin, feet out straight.

"Now what will happen?" she asked herself, and watched a silvery fog roll in.

Out of scent range of the men, Kapu rolled in the snow, cleaned his fur, and groomed his tail with his teeth. The fog rolled over him. He closed his yellow eyes, sniffed deeply, and read the information held in the moist fog droplets.

The caribou were far south. Arctic foxes were scarce. Lemmings were scarce. Plant life was scarce, eaten and trampled by the caribou mistake. He lifted his head high. His yellow eyes brightened. A more important message was in the droplets. The Nukas were on Avalik territory. The fur rose on his back. He took off for the border, where he discovered from the scent marking that a new border had been established by the Avaliks and Nukas on Avalik property. He was irked until he came upon the truly important message: Sweet Fur Amy was the alpha of his pack—

and pregnant. Pups! He lifted his leg high and scent marked.

Avoiding Kangik, he set off for the den on the Avalik River. Around ten o'clock the fog burned away, revealing a tundra flashing with wildflowers and small birds on wing. He stopped and took in the scene before him. Under blue-gray clouds in bright sunlight lay an endless tundra with its cycling future. It erased the memory of men poking him, and voices, radios, and other annoying equipment that had been attached to his body. Before him caribou were giving birth, wolf packs were cuddled around puppy-filled dens, and he could run forever.

He shook his head and was reminded of the radio collar around his neck. It rested comfortably. He ignored it, breathed deeply, and walked on.

Then he heard Storm Call leading a hunt.

He did not go to the den. The Avaliks were stable under Sweet Fur Amy's leadership and Storm Call's intelligence. He turned around and went back to the Nuka border.

With great gulps he dined on one of their recent kills, then trotted into their territory and lifted his leg high, higher than ever before. He sprayed again and again as he pushed his western border back into Nuka land.

He whisked his tail at them and walked slowly back to the kill. He had played a wolf joke on the Nukas. His scent marks had put the kill on his side of the border. The Nukas would not be able to reach their food. He howled to them, but they did not answer. They had withdrawn to their den.

Kapu was back.

He trotted on south into the foothills and to the edge of the Colville River valley. The embankment where he had so often established borders was not marked. The no-wolf zone was gone. Kapu went down the slope, wound among the alders, and surprised a moose and her calf. She charged him. He turned and chased her, separating the two. She did not run far but stopped, turned around, and stood belly deep in the little trees ready to kill for her calf.

Kapu sent her the "not interested" message, jogged to the river, and crossed it. He wandered the empty home of the Mountain Pack for several days. He took down an old arthritic caribou bull and dined. Well stuffed, he visited the den Raw Bones had so persistently coveted. Uqaq had given birth here, he read.

He trotted back to the Colville River and plunged into it. He swam to a deep pool and paddled in circles until he had washed off the disinfectants, shots, and other human odors embedded in his thick underfur.

"Dr. Hardy to Julie. Do you hear me? Over."

"I hear you, Dr. Hardy. Over."

"We've lost Kapu. His radio has stopped emitting signals. We are dispatching a helicopter to the location on the Colville where he vanished. Over. Out."

Julie tried to contact Dr. Hardy several times, but he was gone.

She slipped an arm around Peter and tucked her head against his shoulder. She was giggling.

"I think we have a wolf joke out on the Colville," she said. "And I can't reach Dr. Hardy to tell him to stay where he is."

"What's up?" asked Peter.

"They tracked Kapu to the river and lost him. Wolves swim, and radios don't work underwater."

"Will it work when he comes out of the water?"

"I don't know," she said. "But we do know he is not coming straight home. I wonder why he's at the Colville."

Half an hour later the copter hung in the air above the location on the river where the radio had gone dead. Seeing no sign of wolf or collar, Kapugen landed the craft on one of the beaches, and he and

Dr. Hardy climbed out to look for wolf sign. Not far from the spot where the radio had gone dead were huge wolf prints. Trodden into the silt along the beach, the prints left the shore and went up a low embankment and out of the river valley.

"He's on his way to the Avalik den," said Kapugen. "Julie will record the meeting."

"What do you think will happen when they meet?" Dr. Hardy asked.

"Who knows?" Kapugen answered softly. "Wolves are unpredictable. What do you think?"

"I think either he will kill the new alpha or the new alpha will kill him," replied Dr. Hardy. "Alphas do not like alphas."

Kapugen chuckled. "That is true, all right," he said.

Two days later Kapu caught the scent of Willow Pup Julie and Peter Sugluk on a wind from the Avalik River. He stopped and howled his wolf name.

After a startled pause, Willow Pup Julie howled back. Kapu was not far away. She walked in his direction; he walked toward her.

They saw each other and stopped. Kapu did not come forward, so Julie made the first move. Taking slow, friendly steps, her body telling him she loved him, she came toward her friend. He hesitated. Julie dropped to her knees. He came closer, with his head turned away in mistrust. She whimpered. Slowly, slowly he brought his eyes to meet hers. His golden eyes looked steadfastly into her beautiful black eyes. He whimpered his affection for her and let her put her arms around his neck and hug him. She was family again.

Julie felt the radio collar and unsnapped it.

"You won't need this anymore," she said. Kapu shook his shoulders and head. The last of the human annoyances was gone. He spanked his front paws on the ground, his rump in the air, then got up and ran free. He was headed for the den.

Julie and Peter Sugluk could not keep up with him.

"We won't see what happens," Julie lamented as she came over a grassy rise. She stopped. Kapu stood on the highest point of land. Posed like the king he was, chest out, head up, fur glistening, he pointed his nose to the sky and howled.

"Peter," said Julie, dropping to all fours, "that's his love call to Aaka.

"Drop down, Peter. We are about to see what happens when our alpha returns to his pack."

The sun dipped toward midnight. Red and orange streaks of clouds hung across it. Julie could barely make out the silhouette of Kapu on the hill. Suddenly there were two wolves.

"Peter," Julie whispered, "it's Aaka."

The graceful pair rushed together, tails whisking, feet vaulting them into the air, bodies coming together and apart. They danced.

"No one can tell me," Peter Sugluk whispered into Julie's ear, "that wolves don't love just as we do." He kissed her cheek.

Julie straightened up. Kapu and Aaka began running—not toward the Avalik den, but toward the Upper Colville River and the empty territory there.

Rising slowly to their feet, Peter Sugluk and Julie watched Kapu and Aaka until they merged with the midnight haze and disappeared.

A wind stirred. It shook seeds from their stalks. Some seeds ballooned on the wind. Some slid down snowfields to new land, and still others dropped to earth under parent plants. For their part, Kapu and Aaka traveled on silent feet to the mountains where they in their wisdom knew they were needed.

Author's Note

Currently the name *Eskimo* is being replaced by *Inuit* to identify the circumpolar Eskimo people living in North America, Greenland, and Siberia. The Inuit language is a continuum of many dialects that extend across Alaska, Siberia, the Canadian Arctic, and Greenland.

There is some confusion in that it is assumed that the word *Eskimo* is a derisive word. This is not so. The native people of Alaska's North Slope call themselves Eskimos or Iñupiat Eskimos. *Iñupiaq* is an Inuit dialect and *Eskimo* is a longstanding name given to the Arctic natives by the Algonquins. It comes from "assime w," meaning "she laces a snow shoe." (The ending *t* on the word *Iñupiat* signifies the people; *q* signifies the language.)

On the west coast of Alaska the native people call themselves Yupik or Upik Eskimos, whereas in the Canadian Arctic the native people apparently prefer to be called Inuits.

Since I wrote *Julie of the Wolves* in 1972, the Iñupiat Language Commission, North Slope Borough, Barrow, Alaska, has compiled the *Iñupiaq and English Dictionary* and devised a written language. This changed the spellings of the English versions of words to reflect the true sounds of this unique dialect. In *Julie* and *Julie's Wolf Pack* I have used spellings to comply with the dictionary. I use the words *Eskimo* and *Iñupiat Eskimo* as my native friends in Barrow do to refer to themselves. *Iñupiat Eskimo* tells who you are—where you live and your cultural attributes.

Jean Craighead George